SANIBEL
SCRIBBLES

Books by
CHRISTINE LEMMON

Sanibel Scribbles

Portion of the Sea

Sand in My Eyes

Whisper from the Ocean

SANIBEL
SCRIBBLES

A young woman's journey of
facing mortality and embracing life

CHRISTINE LEMMON

Penmark Publishing
Ft. Myers, Florida

ISBN-10: 0-9712874-3-0
EAN: 978-0-9712874-3-3

Penmark Publishing, LLC
www.penmarkpublishing.com

First Trade Printing: July 2010

Cover by Julie Metz. Book design by Carla Rozman.
Editorial production by Jeffrey Davis, Center to Page.

Printed in Canada

10	9	8	7	6
5	4	3	2	1

In Loving Memory of
My friend, Laura Fleming
My grandmother, Betty Jann

———————————————————

And for Mom, Dad, Laura, and Katie

Show me, O Lord, my life's end and the number of my days;
let me know how fleeting is my life. You have made my days a
mere handbreadth; the span of my years is as nothing before you.
Each man's life is but a breath. Man is a mere phantom as
he goes to and from. He bustles about, but only in vain;
he heaps up wealth, not knowing who will get it.

—PSALM 39:4

The butterfly counts not months but moments,
and has time enough.

—TAGORE

AUTHOR'S NOTE

THERE IS A HISTORY to *Sanibel Scribbles*. I wrote it at a young age with the intention of passing it around my family. I then dabbled with it at various older ages, changing it here and there. I would print a few copies at a time to hand out to friends and family as gifts. Its title at this time was *Tablecloth Scribbles*.

Word of mouth spread, and others requested copies. Local stores carried it, and one merchant suggested I change its title to *Sanibel Scribbles* due to its setting. The book at this time had not truly been professionally edited, as we did not expect for it to sell as it did.

But soon we took the advice of others and self-published it with a new cover and new title. We sold through the first, then second print run and stopped there. I never felt proud seeing it on shelves, as I knew there were editorial issues with the book. We received numerous letters from readers who enjoyed it and from others who pointed out its editorial problems. Once we sold out of copies, we decided not to reprint. I was quite content letting it go out of print.

To my surprise, we have been inundated with requests for *Sanibel Scribbles*. People have been trying to find it online, and stores have asked us if we would reprint it for their customers who are looking for it.

For this reason, we are bringing *Sanibel Scribbles* back. We have had it reedited and redesigned, new cover and all, for the sake of my readers. I would like to thank those who have requested its return.

To me, *Sanibel Scribbles* is what it is. It has always been and will forever be an innocent, whimsical, coming-of-age attempt at making sense of things that were happening in my life at a young age. This is not at all to say it is a true story. It is not. It is, however, a first novel, inspired by real-life experiences. Despite rounds of edits and years gone by, the story will forever be confined and bound to the inspirations that went into it at the age in which I originally wrote it.

Sincerely,
Christine Lemmon

CHAPTER ONE

VICKI BRIGHTMAN SAT STARING at the row of red tulips framing College Avenue. She had sat there many evenings before and had always noticed the tulips lining the sidewalk beside her chair.

"I'm going to miss them," she thought. "The tulips and this town." But she wasn't going to miss the stressful semester she had at school. She shifted in her seat and turned her attention to the six tables, aglow in candlelight that surrounded her. They decorated the sidewalk in front of Till Midnight, a café in Holland, Michigan. The street, quiet except for the soft chatter of students and other outdoor diners, was a welcome relief from the typical hangouts. She glanced at her watch. Where was Rebecca? They had a lot to talk about.

While waiting for her friend, Vicki became absorbed in other people's conversations at nearby tables. Some discussed ancient philosophy; others debated the difference between religion and spirituality. Men at the table next to her brainstormed scenes for their screenplay, and women behind her talked about their upcoming modern dance performance. The nature of their discussions drew her eyes back to the red tulips. They were incredibly gorgeous, but now she only had one night left to pay them attention. Come morning, she would say good-bye to everything she loved in life, including the tulips.

And so she stared at one with the sort of covetousness she had only heard about in church on Sunday, and for the first time she understood what it felt like to want something she couldn't have. This particular tulip, standing proud and high above the rest on its tall, slender green stem didn't belong to her, but she suddenly craved it more than a caffè mocha, and more than a piece of French silk pie.

"You are gorgeous," she whispered to its petals. "Incredibly gorgeous."

"You're not bad yourself," said the waiter, who had snuck up on her. "What can I get you tonight?"

"A caffè mocha and a piece of French silk pie," she replied, then diverted her thoughts back to the item not on the menu, the item she really wanted to pick, the red-hot dessert she knew might cost a fortune in fines if she picked it. She knew all kinds of things about tulips because she had sold them at school. She liked the parrot tulip the best for its petals, which were wrinkled at the edges. That is not to say she didn't love the Darwin tulip with its deep-colored blossoms.

She looked around at the people sitting at nearby tables, resenting the fact that they were probably sticking around town for the approaching Tulip Time Festival, while she would be leaving Michigan come morning. How long might a tulip survive in her purse? She could flatten it between her psychology text pages and preserve it for eternity. Surely that was more than the soil could offer. She unfolded the cloth napkin and placed it on her lap and planned her capture, having only a fleeting moment to grab, then toss the tulip into her lap before concealing the goods. She started to reach for it when the waiter returned with her drink.

He walked away, and she knew she had to act quickly. When you see something you want in life, you have no time to pause. Pausing only leads to thinking, and that only leads to fear, which then leads to failure, well, unless you overcome it, so, isn't it simpler not to develop fear in the first place? Her mouth watered, not from the chocolate shavings resting atop the whipped cream in her mocha, but because she wanted the tulip like nothing else. She glanced around. No one paid her any attention. They were too involved in their own dramas, dreams, and discussions, so she made the decision to go after exactly what she wanted.

She reached down and pulled on the long green stem. It barely budged. She used more force, but nothing happened. She yanked, and still it wouldn't come. She had no idea a tall, slender stem could be so grounded. She couldn't stop now, halfway into the crime, so she quickly sat up again, making sure no one noticed, then grabbed her dessert knife and went for the kill.

"Busted," said a voice from above. "You know the fine for picking a tulip."

She jumped, sliding the knife up the stem and accidentally popping the tulip's head off. It looked full of life as it went flying through the air with its petals flapping in the breeze, but then it crashed onto the ground near the men who were discussing the screenplay, completely limp.

"I'll tell you what," said Rebecca Vanderhill as she sat down across from Vicki. "You treat tonight, and I won't tell anyone what you just did."

"And hello to you too. You're late," said Vicki as she bent down to collect the object of her obsession before anyone noticed.

"Were you your usual early self tonight?" asked Rebecca.

"Of course, and you were late. I've been waiting," answered Vicki, cupping the flower in her hands as if she had caught a butterfly and didn't want to let it go. "I'm going to the ladies' room where I can discreetly flatten this between two menus," she said. "I might as well preserve what's left of it."

"That's ridiculous," said Rebecca. "Put it in the dirt and leave it there."

Vicki hesitated and then laid the tulip to rest in the soil.

"Well, we survived," said Rebecca, pulling her navy sweater off over her head and hanging it on the back of her chair. "We survived our hectic semester. All I want to do now is breathe. Inhale, exhale, sip my coffee for starters," she said.

"There's no time for inhaling and exhaling. I'm leaving for Florida in the morning."

Rebecca took a deep breath, then let it out slowly. "You're always busy, productive, organized. Don't you ever want to hang out, relax, do absolutely nothing?"

Vicki rolled her eyes. "I've got too many things on my mind," she said. "Things I want to accomplish in life, things I want from life. There's so much to do."

"Like what?"

"Like finish school, launch a career, make money to survive, and hopefully afford my own apartment." Vicki rubbed her forehead and sighed. "I look around at all these other students, and they're eager as I am to figure out who they want to be in life and what they can do to make a mark in this world." She dipped her silver knife into the melting butter ball and painted her roll. "So, Rebecca, who has time to relax?"

"There is a time for everything, Vicki. Remember that."

"Okay, if you say so, if there truly is a time for everything, then I've got an idea. Right now, it's time for planning our futures."

"All I know about the future is that you are spending the summer in Florida, and I'm spending it here. So let's enjoy the moment."

"I can't," Vicki said with a laugh. "I told you, I have too much on my mind. Let's set some goals, and I mean, really set them, so specifically we can see, taste, and smell them."

The waiter delivered Rebecca's drink, and Vicki used her white cloth napkin to push bread crumbs off the table. Then she stacked their tiny plates on top of each other and neatly set everything in the empty breadbasket. "We're going to scribble something special on our tablecloth tonight."

"You mean something other than naked male stick figures?" asked Rebecca.

"Yes. Tonight we're going to write down all our dreams and goals. I heard it's the only way they come true. Something about writing one's dreams turns those dreams sacred. It sets them in stone. And I promise you, Rebecca, this is going to change the courses of our lives."

Vicki picked up a purple crayon that was lying on the center of the table and let the white, yellow, and red crayons remain napping between the crystal salt and pepper shakers. Those colors weren't noble enough for her purpose.

"It's a bit odd scribbling our dreams on a tablecloth," said Rebecca, taking a long silver spoon and searching the bottom of her mocha for the sunken espresso bean, determined to find it before the melted chocolate slid off. "But we may as well celebrate the fact that we're twenty-first-century modern American women and we can do anything we want in life."

"That's right. Now you're catching on to the significance of this activity. Everything that goes down in crayon tonight must be accomplished. Okay?"

"Okay, Madam Type A. You start."

"I will." In purple crayon, Vicki neatly wrote the words "Semester in Spain" on the white tablecloth, then clamped her mouth shut as an ambulance roared down College Avenue, reminding the outdoor candlelit diners that life speeds, slows, turns, and detours as it likes, without warning. "I know Spain is coming true. In fact, it's four months away, you and me, American women studying in the country of romance. You may as well write it down too."

"Write it for me, over here. Good. Thank you," said Rebecca.

"There. We've both got one goal down. You go now," Vicki insisted. "Okay. While studying in Spain, I'm going to fall madly in love with a mysterious, intelligent, sophisticated Spaniard." Rebecca wrote "Spanish hombre" and laughed.

"Do you honestly believe that loving a Spanish man might be any different than loving an American man? I'm sure they both leave their dirty clothes all over the floor and probably chew with their mouths open."

"But a Spanish man sips red wine and chews olives and calamari while an American man guzzles beer and chews greasy buffalo wings."

"And what does that have to do with loving him?"

"There's something to be said about no beer belly. But more importantly, poetry," said Rebecca. "Picture a man sucking an olive and whispering poetry in your ear. Now picture a guy tearing off a bite of buffalo wing and dipping it in blue cheese dressing, grease rolling down his arm. I don't think the poetry would sound as romantic."

"Why do you think a Spanish man is going to recite poetry to you while he eats?" asked Vicki.

"I don't know, but I'll find out. I've written it down as a goal of mine, so ask me again in six months. I'll share all the juicy details with you then. Your turn."

"Five to ten pounds, nothing more. Lose it and maintain it for life."

Vicki wrote "Lose weight." She closed her eyes and could see the skinnier her wearing a skimpy red bikini, jumping up from her beach towel and jogging toward the water. "I know I'll be a slightly happier person once I lose ten pounds. I also want to start lifting weights and tone up."

"My turn, and no mocking me for this one." Rebecca scribbled, "Noah." "It's odd, but I know I'll name my first son Noah. I've told you that before."

"You don't have a boyfriend, let alone a husband, and you're already naming your firstborn son. What about your career? You better launch that first before thinking about any baby, let alone man in your life."

"These are my dreams. I can write whatever I want, and I want a baby by age thirty-one. I can hopefully launch my career, save up money, find a man and get married, then sit outside on the porch of my dream home somewhere in the mountains."

"I was told that when you write down goals, you must also visualize them. Can you see that baby standing up in his crib at two o'clock in the morning? Can you hear him crying for mommy while you're in the bookstore trying to read?"

All at once, as the waiter tried pouring water and ice through the mouth of a silver pitcher, the rectangular cubes took off like logs over a waterfall tumbling down onto Rebecca's last goal. "I hope that's not an omen, Noah getting flooded out of my future," she said.

Vicki laughed, displaying the tiny space between her two front teeth. "My turn."

She moved her coffee cup over to make space for her growing list, and then wrote "Grow nails." "If I don't stop biting them, I'm going to see a hypnotist, or maybe, once I start practicing psychology, I'll just treat myself to self-therapy. It's really dysfunctional the way I bite them. I've tried manicures, lotions, stress balls, prayer. I still bite. You go."

"Family time," wrote Rebecca. "This will be easy. I've got all summer with my family."

"Travel the world," wrote Vicki. Then she closed her eyes and saw herself taking a train through Europe, backpacking past the Leaning Tower of Pisa in Italy, then the Eiffel Tower in Paris, and . . .

"Climb a mountain," interrupted Rebecca, scribbling quickly, and then closing her eyes. "I'm on the top of Mount Everest, and savoring the moment, viewing my life from an entirely new perspective," she mumbled in a hypnotized tone. "Oh, but now I have to survive the descent, which is where most people die, you know."

"Acquire the world's largest collection of shoes," wrote Vicki. "Shoes are what walk us toward our goals. There is nothing as important as wearing the right pair of shoes. They set the mood. When my toes are warm, I'm warm and friendly. If my toes are cold, well, don't mess with me. If they're cramped, like when I wear my thin little black pointy pair, I almost always feel socially uncomfortable."

"That's absolutely crazy. You're crazy," said Rebecca.

"A little insane, maybe. But the shoe thing is a fetish passed on from generation to generation in my family. My grandmother claimed her shoes could talk."

"What are you talking about?"

"Talking shoes. It's true. She heard them calling her from the closet."

"And what did they say?" asked Rebecca.

"Well, she had this pair of red high heels, and they used to whisper out to her in a sexy, raspy voice, 'Seduce grandpa, take him out for jazz music at the local club and show him a super sexy time.' "

"You're totally making this up," laughed Rebecca.

"I'm not. And when she was younger, she had these stocky moon boots that used to yell at her every time it snowed. If she didn't put them on, look out! They were the meanest moon boots . . ."

"You know what I think?" asked Rebecca. "I think your brain needs a rest."

"No, seriously, she had these sturdy black high heels, and when Grandma got mad, they always sided with her. She could take them off and throw them against the wall, and usually they loved it, but one time they landed on the floor quite hard and you know what they said to her?"

"What?"

"These shoes are made for talking, and talking is what they'll do."

The women laughed and wiped their tears away and nearby tables gawked, not at them, but at the two pieces of French silk pie passing by. The waiter apologized for having to set the dessert plates right over the women's scribbled lists. "No problem," they assured him, and drew arrows to continue the lists along the round edges of the table.

"Another tall, low-fat this time, decaf caffè mocha, please," said Rebecca.

"And a short, nonfat, decaf latté for me, please," said Vicki.

"Vicki, if you could only speak Spanish as well as you speak coffee language, you'll do fine in Spain."

"What are you saying? My Spanish isn't that good?"

Rebecca laughed. "Your Dutch accent gets stronger when you speak Spanish. I've never heard anything like it!"

"But I'm not Dutch." Secretly, Vicki felt thrilled, honored that after all these years she naturally sounded like the majority of the city, the city she had grown to love, the city she made her home.

"I know. I'm one hundred percent Dutch, yet you've got a stronger accent than I have. You say things like 'goooood' and 'youuuuu', and you sound friendly when you're mad. Then again, you did grow up here. What do you expect?"

"Well, I can't survive in Spain without you. I'm counting on you to be my personal walking, talking Spanish dictionary."

"You might not need me, Don't you own a sexy Spanish speaking pair of shoes? *Hola*, Vicki!" She twirled and gestured with open arms embracing her audience. "I'd like red wine, *por favor. Sí!* Why don't you walk me over there, to that park bench where you could sit down and together, with me, a sexy pair of shoes and you, a sexy blond from America, we could . . ."

"You've lost it. Now let's get on with our list," said Vicki. Rebecca wrote next. "Land a job as a Spanish professor."

"Never allow a man to get in the way of my dreams," scribbled Vicki.

"What if he's the man *of* your dreams?"

"No. There are dreams, and there are men. No relation between the two."

"Are you telling me that, if you fall madly in love before you accomplish your goals, you'll toss him aside?"

Vicki closed her eyes and saw the blurred heads of ex-boyfriends bobbing up and down in dark waves. "Absolutely," she said. "I'll toss him overboard into the Sea of Forgetfulness. I've done it a dozen times. No big deal. I'm not going to mention names. They're forgotten."

"You're harsh."

"No, determined. Your turn."

"Wake early," wrote Rebecca. And "do more with each day." "Practice psychology," Vicki scribbled.

Rebecca picked up the red crayon and added one more thing. "Enjoy the present." She pressed so hard and passionately that the crayon broke in half.

"You certainly set that one in stone," laughed Vicki.

"It's the best goal of all, and easy to accomplish. All I have to do is sip my wonderful mocha, listen to your beautiful words, my dearest friend, and try not to glance at that decapitated tulip stem behind you. Yes, enjoy the present." She spoke passionately and her voice sounded nice, easygoing.

Once they had licked every last morsel of chocolate from their plates, they left their scribbles behind, said a few hellos to class acquaintances dining at the other small outdoor tables, and started on the half-mile journey back to their campus apartment.

"Would you slow down?" Rebecca asked. "Why do you always walk fast?"

"It's my nature," said Vicki as they passed the park. "I'm always in a hurry." And it was true. It was as if somehow she had read the word "allegro" on the way out of her mother's womb, a labor and delivery lasting only two hours.

"Do you ever slow down?"

"No," said Vicki. "It's why I get so much done."

"A person like you," said Rebecca, out of breath. "I know all of your dreams will come true."

Rebecca's encouragement meant a lot. There was a kind of validity in it, maybe because Rebecca listened when people spoke. Like a journal, she was always ready to listen, and she always remained locked. No one could ever steal a secret from her, yet sometimes, when Vicki would throw an idea at her, Rebecca would listen and then toss it back with a refreshing perspective, just as a journal entry looks foreign yet familiar when a woman reads it over again at a later date. Vicki was about to tell Rebecca that her dreams would come true as well, but the *chang chang* of the city clock in the distance interrupted her. It was midnight.

"Well, now that we've written down our futures, you might not like what I'm going to say," declared Rebecca, stopping to take a seat on an antique rocking chair for sale outside a boutique. "We've got to stop counting down for everything."

"Oh, stop with the wisdom, will ya?" Vicki rolled her eyes. "Why can't we count down?"

"Well, before we know it," said Rebecca, out of breath, "even Spain will be a memory. And someday our tight skin will be wrinkled. Our colorful hair white. We'll be rocking in our chairs looking through photo albums and soaking dainty white handkerchiefs. Soon our tears will stop, not because we stop reminiscing but because at that age our tear ducts will have dried up for having spent our lives crying about every not-so-rosy incident that came our way . . ."

"Enough! Time for you to get out of that rocking chair." Vicki took her friend's hands and pulled her up. "Don't you think for a single moment I'm going to allow my hair to turn gray when I age. I'll turn it purple like my grandma did before I go gray."

"Purple? Your grandmother had purple hair?"

"Yeah. She used the same coloring kit every month and claimed she could never read the small-print instructions properly. But I know her eyes worked fine. She spent nights reading romance novels. If she could do this, she could read the instructions on a box of hair coloring. Oh well. We all accepted her with purple hair."

"There was no warning before she died?"

Vicki shook her head. "Nope. A heart attack in her sleep. Can you imagine?"

As ducks flew south for the winter, so did Grandma, and as they returned to Lake Michigan in the spring, so did Grandma. She would nest in her tiny apartment behind the family business, and the seventy- some-thing-year-old and the young woman spent summer nights together, vis-iting. They'd burn sandlewood incense, dance to Elvis Presley tapes, and reminisce about Grandma's past. To Vicki, the world without her grand-mother would never look as beautiful again. The seasons would come and go, the ducks would be here and gone, but their arrival would no longer mark the coming of her grandmother.

"Not to change the subject, but do you have any antacid tablets? This heartburn of mine feels like someone is dumping hot lava down my throat." Rebecca pushed her chest muscles with her fingertips.

"I think so, but only two this time. You're overdosing yourself with these, Rebecca. You're becoming a real antacid addict, and I'm worried."

Vicki laughed, rummaging through her purse. "Did you see the cam-pus doctor about the severity and recurrence of your heartburn?"

"No, not yet," said Rebecca. "She'd probably tell me no more cart-wheels after coffee, or worse, no more coffee at night."

"Or no more chocolate pie," added Vicki.

"No more this, no more that. No more, no more, no more," said Rebec-ca. "Why is it that the words 'no more' only make us want that much more?"

"We're women."

Back in their apartment, Vicki felt a wicked breeze entering the window and tickling the nerves in her stomach. "It's May. How could it be so cold?"

"El Niño."

"No, he came and went."

"Where did he go?"

"Back to Mexico, I think."

"Then where is that breeze coming from?"

"La Niña."

"Oh. Is she his wife or sister?"

"Wife, I think."

"I thought she left, too."

"Yeah, but I think she's back."

"Don't they ever travel together?"

"No, he snores too loudly, and she cries too much."

"Oh, well, it's cold in here, and my heart is pounding," said Rebecca. "I'll never be able to fall asleep."

"Then don't. It's our last night together."

"I've got to get sleep. What time do I need to get you to the airport?"

"Oh, I don't know. I should check my list of things to do. I feel bad you have to drive me all the way to Chicago, but you know I appreciate it. My flight was much cheaper leaving from there."

"My pleasure."

Rebecca walked over to the stereo, one of the few items not yet packed in the small one-room apartment. Gloria Gaynor's CD always occupied holder number four, and Rebecca knew just how to click it in the dark to their favorite song, "I Will Survive."

Rebecca sang and danced, utilizing all the space in the bedroom. "I've spent oh so many nights just feeling sorry for myself."

Vicki tossed her to-do list aside when she heard the music. "I've got all my life to live! I've got all my love to give," she sang, jumping up to join her friend. This song had moved the women many times. It eased stress the night before exams. It cured insomnia. It made them laugh. It made them cry the night of the Valentine's Day dance when Rebecca's date stood her up, and Vicki's blind date stood a good two feet shorter than her. Neither woman had danced at the disastrous event. Well, they danced to "I Will Survive" back in their apartment at midnight.

"Why do we love this song so much? It's old, and way before our times," shouted Rebecca over the music.

"Don't ask me. You're the one always playing it."

"Listen to the words. It's not like we can relate. I mean, neither of us have been dumped."

"It's got attitude. And who knows, maybe someday we will be dumped, and we'll know what to say to the men who dump us." Vicki stared a moment into the tiny flame of Rebecca's candle, which had vibrantly danced along, then blew it out.

"Well, I'm glad we did that. I can sleep now," said Rebecca, out of breath and climbing into her bed. "Oh, I almost forgot."

"Forgot what?"

"You're the one taking off to Florida this summer," Rebecca's voice said from across the room. "So I've said a prayer for you."

"For me? You did?"

"Yeah," said Rebecca. "I asked God to lend you my guardian angel for the summer."

"Oh come on," said Vicki. "Can you do that? Can you lend out angels like that?"

"It's not our job to employ angels. They work for God, so God willing, they're yours, but only for the summer."

"You are generous," said Vicki.

"Thank you."

"You're welcome. Just promise me you'll slow down a bit so my flock can keep up with you."

"What kind of shoes do they wear?"

"Angels don't wear shoes, Vicki. I think they go barefoot."

"If they want to keep up, they'll need shoes."

"They've got wings."

"True."

"Look, I don't care whether they wear flip-flops or high heels. Just bring my angels with you when we meet on September ninth! That's all I ask."

"LaGuardia Airport, New York, September ninth! We will depart for Spain together."

"Yes, meet me at the terminal that day, and don't board that plane without me! I know how you're always early," Rebecca said, reaching out of bed to turn the light off.

"Then don't you dare be late."

"I won't."

"Hey, did you know it's only fourteen weeks away?" asked Vicki. " I can't wait."

"There you go again, counting down. Enjoy your summer in Florida first. Enjoy the present."

"I don't want to go to Florida. It's going to feel weird going there without seeing my grandmother. The state means nothing to me anymore," said Vicki, entering her typical bedtime monologue. "I really want to stay here, but here isn't the same now that my parents sold the house and the businesses. Gosh, I still can't believe they moved. I guess here is still better than there because you're here, and well, at least there are the tulips and, soon, the festival."

Rebecca sighed. "The present may be cloudy, but clouds don't last forever. Live the present."

"Why are you always so profound?"

"Why don't you ever stop talking?"

"Okay, *buenas noches*. I'll get to sleep now. But hey, let's make our tablecloth scribbles come true. Let's do it."

Normally, Vicki felt cozy with her stuffed tiger, the male that had shared her bed for years, next to her and her friend in the bed across from her. Tonight she felt a strange coldness enter through the window. She didn't try shutting it. Rebecca liked it open. She liked to listen to the crickets and said they were performing like an orchestra for all insomniacs. Vicki listened and could only hear their noise. This was how she and her friend often differed. Rebecca would hear and see something more beautiful than she did. Maybe her eyes and ears had some kind of audio- visual devices that made everything look and sound crispier, happier, and better. The crickets paused at the honk of a car. Rebecca would hear it as part of the performance, the drums or something.

Good. She could hear Rebecca breathing slowly and loudly in the bed across the room. Something about the sound of it, like waves coming in and out with the Lake Michigan tide, always told Vicki that she too could fall asleep, and tonight she felt ready, exhausted from the busy semester. She closed her eyes and tried to match her own breaths with Rebecca's. This synchronized breathing took no practice. It happened naturally. Joining the chorus of a sleeping person's breathing might prove to be more relaxing than yoga. Neither taught nor contemplated, a sleeping person knew how to inhale and exhale perfectly. Vicki held her own breath to listen more closely, to listen to her friend's breath that suddenly sounded different, choppy, like a vessel struggling through rough waters.

"Rebecca. *Rebecca!* Are you okay?"

She listened more, then sat up. "You're sleeping, aren't you?"

No answer. Then again, no one answers that question when they're sleeping. "Our friendship means the world to me. I've wanted to tell you that," she said, self-conscious that her friend would wake, upset by her bedtime chatter.

She stopped talking. She listened. She no longer heard the crickets, nor cars, nor thoughts in her head. She only heard Rebecca's breathing and felt the hair on her arms stand up in response to the cold wind. She knew well the sound that Lake Michigan waves made as they arrived on shore in the month of May, but suddenly it sounded as if those waves had taken a couple of steps back to winter when they arrived out of sync, and some, frozen, never arrived at all. She felt dizzy, as if her mattress were in the middle of an ocean of rough water, and she couldn't see. She didn't want to get out of bed, to step on the icy tile floor, but the sounds coming from her friend didn't sound familiar.

"Rebecca. *Wake up, Rebecca!*"

Her friend began wheezing horribly, each heave for air desperately snagging on something stuck in her throat and ending in a pitiful gurgle. Vicki's body took over as she ran across the frozen ice to the light, sliding and stubbing her baby toe en route. It took a couple of seconds to focus on her friend, struggling in bed, eyes closed but gasping for air that she couldn't take in. Vicki placed her hands on her friend's shoulders, tense and jerking. She placed her hands on her face, but Rebecca did not respond. Her eyes stayed shut.

"Oh please, Rebecca. Don't scare me. It's not funny. *Rebecca!*"

Vicki nearly tore the door off the hinges as she opened it and screamed down the apartment hallway, "Someone, *anyone*! Help, *help*! She can't breathe! *Rebecca can't breathe!*"

A moment of sanity returned. *Help. I have to get help!* She grabbed the phone and dialed 911, then followed orders and performed CPR on her friend. She panicked, but the voice on the phone directed her. She started to count. Others entered their room now. Someone took over the CPR.

She felt an arm around her, a life jacket that held her up. The cold breeze hit her in the face like an iceberg, and someone was shutting the window after Rebecca's plant tipped over, crashing to the floor. Rebecca loved that plant. *Aphrodisiac,* she had named it. It grew faster than the others. Rebecca talked to it all the time.

Blue and white lights were flickering outside the window. Men in blue were working on her friend, for what felt like an eternity. One asked her what her friend's name was.

"Rebecca," Vicki said numbly. "Her name is Rebecca."

"Come on, come on, Rebecca. You can do it," chanted one of the men as he leaned over her, watching and listening for signs of breath. "I know you can do it. Come on back, come on back to us, Rebecca."

Next, after what felt like a frozen moment of time in which everything stopped and nothing could be heard, another man lifted Rebecca onto a stretcher. *Good,* thought Vicki. *They're going to rush her to the hospital where they can take better care of her.*

"Can, can, can I go with her? She'd want, she'd want me with her," Vicki asked a man in blue through lips that suddenly felt anesthetized, making the words almost impossible to form.

"I'm sorry. We did all we could."

Her legs shook from hypothermia setting in. "Well, I'll go with her. I've got to be by her side. She'd want me to."

The man in blue held her arm tightly as the stretcher left the room. "Look me in the eyes, please."

He slowly waved his forefinger in the air, catching her attention. "I'm so sorry to tell you this. Your friend suffered a heart attack. She did not make it."

"No, no. It can't be."

"I'm so sorry."

"No. This isn't her time."

"I'm sorry."

"She's got too many dreams, goals."

"I'm sure she must."

"I don't believe it."

"I know, I know."

"No! You don't."

"Is there anything else we can do?"

"Bring my friend back."

"There is no more we can do."

"No more? Don't you dare say *no more*. I don't want to hear it. Bring her back. I *want* Rebecca back." She started to pound his chest. "*Please* bring Rebecca back.," Vicki wailed through tears that choked her.

After the ice storm came a Lake Michigan fog. People she didn't know. Faces she recognized from classes and the apartment, but never spoke to, now drifted into her apartment all through the hours of the night. She sat anchored on a box, Rebecca's box of winter sweaters. She answered questions over and over to all kinds of people. Then came the woman who kept talking about her baby, of all things, at a time like this. She said she had craved lemonade and peanut butter in the middle of every night, and anxiously waited nine months for her first baby girl to be born, this woman who had gone through an uncontrollable nesting phase and scrubbed the walls, the floors and the windows days before the birth. This woman said she massaged her baby, then rocked her daughter night after night, long after the baby slept, just to hold her, and dream about her life ahead: of preschool and art projects on the refrigerator and temper tantrums and walking down the aisle with her father. This woman now held her hands out in a cradling position, crying that her darling baby no longer safely slept in her arms.

Vicki couldn't look Rebecca's mother in the eyes, fearful that she might drown forever in tears. She couldn't imagine this woman's depth of despair. Vicki felt the pain of loving and losing a friend. She didn't know the pain of loving and losing a daughter. She stared through the window, at Michigan's dark sky. How dare winter arrive in the season of spring? How dare it show up cruelly, catching everyone off guard? How dare a tulip wither before its time? And worse, how dare she pick one? Its life didn't belong to her. She resented the weather and regretted picking the flower as she stared at the sky with disgust, watching as it turned a hue of orange, then finally blue. The fog lifted a little.

CHAPTER TWO

THERE ARE FOUR PARTS to a symphony. There is silence between each of the parts. How dare anyone clap during a moment meant for silence? Vicki felt caught in this moment, not caring about making phone calls or pondering the night before, or crying or talking further with people who might have been in the room when the waves came crashing in, people who may have needed more details. She chose to be alone, solitary, refusing the comfort offered by others. She felt numb, a person trapped under a sheet of ice and nearly dead. She feared that any sort of emotional expression might cause her mind to become disconnected from where she was and where she was going. Then again, she wanted to forget what had happened the night before, and something about the silence between the four movements of the symphony only made her remember exactly what had just happened.

Nothing prepared her for this. Perhaps she had misunderstood. She had never heard the men in blue, nor any of the voices from the night before, mention the word "dead." Maybe Rebecca wasn't dead? What were the words they used? "Passed away," "gone," "didn't make it," but no one actually said "dead." Vicki closed her apartment door, not bothering to lock it. No one would steal Rebecca's boxes. No one would dare, not now. Her friend was gone, permanently.

She had much to do. She reached in her purse and pulled out a neatly folded list, aware of the fact that she lived life from dot to dot on her never-ending list of things to do, and whatever didn't make the list, well, those were the things she had no time for. She glanced over and over the list and couldn't find perhaps the most important item of all. Hadn't she written it down? Well, if it wasn't written down, she wouldn't do it. She couldn't do it now. She couldn't tell Rebecca how much she loved her as a friend and that she believed *her* dreams would come true as well.

Typically, when she missed an errand, she would simply add it to the next day's list. Impossible. She would never have a second chance with this one. She walked to the bank instead and cashed out her money and closed her account for the summer, then stood in line at the post office, and after placing stamps on five envelopes, she dropped her pile of credit card bills in the mail. She ran into the coffee shop for a tall mocha, not that she wanted to sip it in leisure at a time like this, but if she didn't consume the exact amount of caffeine on a daily basis, she would soon experience a pounding headache, worse than what she was already feeling. In fact, she wanted to order a plain black cup of coffee but wasn't sure if it had enough caffeine. The woman behind the counter had never made a caffè mocha before, and it was only her second day of work. Vicki waited as the woman harvested the berries, then dried them and removed the flesh from the hard stones inside. Her head began to pound as the woman treated the beans, then roasted and brewed them.

Finally, with her hot mocha in hand, Vicki passed the dry cleaners, re-membering she had a blouse to pick up, but first, her hot drink was scald-ing her hand, so she stopped in another coffee shop and grabbed a protective sleeve before going any further. Then she remembered she des-perately needed toothpaste and had forgotten to borrow someone's, so she stopped at the drugstore for mints.

Once each errand was crossed off her list, she rushed back to her apart-ment, grabbed her suitcases, and started to walk the block to the Grey-hound bus station. She scolded herself for packing too much and blamed it on her wooden shoes. Why bother to bring them to Florida, where it would be too hot to wear eight pairs of socks and wood on her feet? She started opening the suitcase to dump the shoes, just as a friend driving by spotted her.

"Vicki, we all offered to drive you to the bus station. And Jamie said she'd take you all the way to the airport."

She felt like a dog hit by a car, shocked and running down the road, away from everyone trying to help. "I know, I know. I need to be alone right now. Thanks so much. I'm fine," she said in the tone of someone under quarantine. She didn't want to be with anyone. She had declared herself legally isolated, not wanting to spread her shock, anger, denial, pain, and guilt to anyone else.

"Are you sure you don't want to cancel your flight and stick around? I'll help you with the arrangements."

"I can't. I'm fine. Thanks." She was glad when the car turned the corner, and she could no longer see the woman full of common sense and legitimate offers.

She sat down on a bench near the bus station and across the street from where she had sipped her last coffee with Rebecca the night before. She sat at a distance, staring at the same row of red tulips. Now, with a few minutes left in Holland, Michigan, the tulips reminded her of the green costume with white lace she had sold two weeks before. Dutch-blooded or not, it had never mattered. Every spring she had danced down the streets in the tulip festival anyway.

The tourists never knew her secret. She didn't come from Holland at all. She came from Chicago. They photographed someone they assumed was Dutch, but she was Irish, English, and Czechoslovakian. They left Holland by the hundreds on tour buses, taking photographs of the Dutch dancers with them.

As for the residents of Holland, well, many she knew never left. Why would they leave their hometown? Why would anyone? Leaving a hometown is like burning the fingerprints right off one's hand. Arriving in a new town, someone else's hometown, is like asking to borrow someone else's prints. Vicki had started school in Holland at age nine. Back then she had felt like an outsider stepping into someone else's hometown. Even the tulips belonged to the ethnic background of her friends—her friends who participated in family devotions after every dinner and went to church twice on Sundays. As a child, she lied about her family working on Sundays and refrained from saying things like "holy cow!" at slumber parties. She wanted to make the strange new place her home and, gradually, living there became so comfortable that she stayed through high school, and now college. She had felt safe in Holland then, and she felt safe there now. She didn't feel like leaving this comfort zone and that was why she stole the tulip. She wanted to grab onto something comfortable.

She glanced down the same street she used to dance down in wooden shoes. She stepped and swept that street with pride, a trait she borrowed from Dutch ancestors who were not her own. Looking at the tulips, she marveled how they always opened just in time for the annual Tulip Time Festival, as if the little bulbs could hear the Dutch dancers clomping down the street in practice before they started. Now they stood tall and proud, not wanting to disappoint anyone. They lined up obediently, not a single flower out of line, and their God-given costumes came in all colors, yet not a single alteration, washing, or ironing was ever needed. The red stood with the red and the purple with the purple and the yellow with the yellow, and they did this well. Now they only had to remain standing long enough for their performance, their season. Somehow she knew their sturdy stems would allow them to do so.

Then, even from a distance, she noticed the one and only stem not wearing its uniform. It stood out like a child on stage for a school performance, the only one not properly dressed and someone else was to blame. Yes, the festival would go on without that flower, just as it would go on without Rebecca this year, without noticing she had died. That's what festivals did – carried on.

She stood up and started walking to the bus, ready to say good-bye to more things she loved.

As the bus slowly passed the campus, Vicki wanted to ask the driver to accelerate. The flowers outside her window streamed endlessly along, rows upon rows, and as the bus moved on their colors blurred into a masterpiece fit for a museum. She braced herself for a bus ride through the Art Coast of Michigan.

Just south of Holland, the bus headed into Saugatuck, a harbor village thriving among towering sand dunes, framed by the winding Kalamazoo River. It passed by the public restroom, famous for its walls painted with post-impressionist Georges Seurat's "A Sunday on La Grande Jatte." With this sort of charm, some said the village belonged in a Thomas Kincaid painting, while others called it the Martha's Vineyard of the Midwest. Vicki called it home. As the bus passed the park overlooking the harbor, Vicki laughed as she spotted a young girl in a red velvet dress standing in the gazebo, answering questions into a microphone. She couldn't hear the answers. No, she couldn't *remember* the answers, her own answers that long ago won her Princess of Saugatuck, a title she had held for one year.

As the bus made a couple of turns and headed down Butler Street, lined with art galleries, boutiques, restaurants, and bed-and-breakfasts, Vicki stared at the nineteenth-century architecture, realizing the charm of the city would never die.

The bus stopped, and Vicki knew she only had about twenty minutes, so she got out and ran past everyone who might stop her to talk - past Tweetie sitting on the bench in front of the corner drugstore, and Old Dave rounding the corner with a cane in one hand and the morning paper in the other, and Greg biking down the hill with books in his basket, always ready to talk to anyone who felt like listening. Yes, she knew this place, and she loved its people.

Vicki rounded the corner of the one-hundred-year-old pink building, once her family's ice cream shop, and went inside. She knew by heart where all the fifty flavors stood displayed in the glass freezers, and she made sure the new owners hadn't changed them around. Mint Chip, her older sister Ann's favorite, belonged next to Chocolate Turtles, her mother's favorite. Dad, a John Wayne sort of man, liked to have the rugged, nutty, chocolate ones down near the windows. Vicki's favorites were two from each cooler. She could never decide on one, so she always insisted on scooping a cone with at least five flavors packed together.

Now, on the customer side of the counter, she knew how to order so as not to aggravate the person scooping. After all, the shop got so busy at times that, if customers didn't specify plain, sugar, or waffle cone . . . single or double . . . French Silk Chocolate . . . Chocolate Turtles . . . *or* plain old chocolate, things got held up.

She didn't feel hungry. Food might sicken her. Instead, she craved comfort, and ice cream brought her to a familiar place, a cozy state of mind.

She caught a glimpse of herself in the large mirror that covered the wall behind the counter, and then ordered in the tone of voice reserved for someone requesting a tissue to dry her eyes.

"I'll have a double dip sugar cone with Chocolate Rocky Road on the bottom and Chocolate Turtles on top, please."

She chose these two flavors because Grandma had loved the first one, and her mother loved the second, and she missed both right now. Since her family had sold the business, she knew that, for the rest of her life, licking ice cream could never simply be an innocent, mindless act. Each flavor generated a memory.

The teenage boy holding the scoop did not smile. He did not say a thing.

"Give me that scoop, please. I'll do it myself," insisted Vicki. "My parents used to own this place. We sold it a couple of months ago. You've got to let me dip my last cone."

"Sure. Whatever. I need a break anyway." He dunked the silver scoop in the water well, shook it off and handed it to her.

She ran around to the other side of the counter. "Thank you."

She dug hard and deep inside the box, making sure to rub her arm against the side. She had to get coated with ice cream one more time. Closing her eyes, she smelled the freezer, the ice. That ice she had scraped down once a week every summer for years. At the short age of nine she could barely reach inside, so her mother had her stand on a bucket. Now she recognized the work that had to be done: the box needed scraping and that boy shouldn't have been taking a break. She wanted the job. She longed to scrape with such intensity and passion that her father would reap more profits because she could gather more ice cream off the cardboard. Instead, she had a bus to catch. No, more than that, her family no longer owned the shop, the bed-and-breakfast upstairs, or the luncheon parlor next door. Someone else now wore the apron for the job she once had and loved.

She scooped the bottom dip bigger than the top so it wouldn't be top-heavy. Her dips never fell off. She knew how to dip ice cream the right way. She glanced at the old-fashioned pink radiator set against the window, and, for a moment, she could see her grandmother's frail little body dressed in purple, sitting there as she always did. Osteoporosis hadn't allowed Grandma to dip, but she always stuck around the family as they worked the business together.

Vicki shut the freezer lid and plunged the silver scoop into the well, splashing herself. She laughed, then nearly cried thinking of all the times her father used to shake water at her as they worked side by side. She looked around. No one was watching. She pulled two thumbtacks off the board behind her and stuffed the label that read "peppermint" under her shirt. Her mother had once painted each of the flavor labels by hand. She peeked under the wooden counter holding the cash register. Good, her family's scribbles still marked the wood. One night they had written silly little notes on the counter, as if marking their territory. Scribbling down dreams was a family tradition. The scrawl in blue magic marker she immediately recognized was her own ten-year-old handwriting: *Scoop Ice Cream Forever!* She shook her head, realizing how much her goals at ten had changed to become her current goals. She couldn't dip anymore. Her life there was no more.

Pulling napkins out of the silver holder, she felt sticky fingerprints all over it. Vicki had never let that thing get dirty. No, the napkin holders in her parent's shop never stayed sticky for long, not when she worked there. Just then, she glanced out the window and spotted a shapely pair of female mannequin legs hanging from a second-story window of the boutique across the street, and she laughed at the ploy to lure shoppers. Only in Saugatuck!

Then the bus slowly turning the corner caught her eye. It couldn't go without her. In a panic, she darted out the door, never leaving a dime behind for her cone and ran toward the bus, screaming, "Wait for me!"

The bus stopped, and when she caught up to it she clambered up its entry steps. The bus driver grinned at her, but she was too out of breath from running to reproach him. She reclaimed her seat by the window as the bus rolled forward again, and glanced back at the ice cream parlor falling behind, suddenly remembering she hadn't paid for her cone. Somehow guilt evaded her. In her mind, she had done the boy's job for him. She had earned it. Melancholy seized her. She had worked there for years. Where would she work now? How could she possibly work anywhere else for the summer? Just about every summer of her life she had spent scooping in that pink shop.

The bus continued past the area where she grew up, and she could picture her home, standing right next to the Red Barn Playhouse. Every morning she would wake to the sound of actors singing and rehearsing for plays such as *The King and I*, or *Camelot*. The house was so perfectly and acoustically situated next to the theater that she didn't need a stereo. There was always music in the summer when the windows were open. It was a happy house, but now she pictured it weeping. Yes, she decided, houses could weep. She imagined yellow and green paint running down the shutters as the new owners desperately painted over it with the ugly white they chose. The house hated the face-lift. This she knew. She wanted to break into the warehouse where everything her family owned was stored away temporarily and tear open the boxes. She worried about the geographic scattering of the American family and the evaporation of hometowns. If only she could become a hermit crab, carrying her home with her, switching shells only as she grew and needed to switch shells.

Eyeing ducks flying north through her window, she became caught up in the irony. Who heads south in the spring? Her trip south seemed like a defiance of nature, of everything seasonal. She closed her eyes. Her head slumped forward until it rested against the cold, misty-morning glass of the window. With each bump, her forehead banged against the pane. She liked the bumps. The repetitive thumping seemed to replace the pain of leaving everything comfortable behind.

Gazing out the bus window, she didn't want to leave. She felt like a potted plant turned upside down and getting hit. She wasn't ready to be repotted. There was still room to grow right here. She'd rather sit outside the local bakery on Butler Street early in the morning and read the paper with the other locals. Then again, with the businesses sold and her parents gone, she could no longer classify herself as a local.

She watched Saugatuck, with its mammoth, rolling dunes to the west and the rich hues of the orchard country to the east grow smaller. She noticed her memories growing larger as she left behind the place where she grew up, the place she called home. Just a half a mile south, the bus entered the village of Douglas, and she caught a glimpse of the S.S. *Keewatin*, a passenger steamship that once sailed the Great Lakes, before it became a floating maritime museum. She longed to stay anchored there with the Keewatin.

She didn't want to leave the Great Lake State, the eleventh largest in the country. She loved Michigan. The Great Lakes formed most of its boundaries to the east, while Ohio and Indiana bordered the south and Wisconsin bound the west. She didn't want to leave her hometown. It was like a mitten on the map. The mitten felt cozy and comfortable to her now. She didn't feel like taking it off.

Should she have stayed? Should she have talked longer with Rebecca's mother? Would there be a funeral? Of course there would be, and she would miss it. She had no choice, like a dislodged plant. She had a flight to catch in Chicago. If she could have hopped into the ice cream freezer and numbed herself for a few hours, she would have.

As she boarded the plane, she imagined the way her good-bye with Rebecca was supposed to have happened.

"Hey, I want you to do something," Rebecca would have said, standing in the gate area. "I want you to give me that good-bye wave sort of thing you said your grandmother always did."

"Oh, I don't know. It was the last thing I saw her do before she died."

"Please, *por favor*. Give me your grandmother's good-bye."

"Okay. Here it goes."

Vicki would turn her back to her friend, kiss her forefingers, extend her arm backward and wiggle her fingers. Just like Grandma, she would never look back, since that would break the rules of the backward good-bye wave. Her tears dripped shamelessly like drops of melting ice cream as she walked down the long hallway, not looking back, as if doing so might turn her into stone.

On the flight to Florida, she pulled her credit card out of her purse and picked up the phone attached to the seat in front of her. She would call Till Midnight to see if someone had saved the tablecloth with the scribbles on it. How ridiculous! She chided herself, especially with all the chocolate stains. No doubt the waiter had dumped it. She put the phone back.

She opened her purse and pulled out an envelope addressed to a woman living on Sanibel Island in Florida. Vicki had kept this particular letter in her purse for months now and didn't know what else to do with it, so she flipped the long letter over and started writing on the back.

Dear Grandma,

You once told me that the letters I wrote kept you up late at night, more so than any of the books in your paperback collection. You said my lengthy, embellished letters added spice to your life and that they kept you going. Well, I wish you had been more patient because my last letter simply got lost in the mail without a stamp. You should have waited a couple more days, and it would have arrived.

I promise to keep you going. That's why I'm writing, to keep both you and me going.

You won't believe this story! A twenty-one year old and a seventy-four year old, both full of life, both now dead from attacks in their sleep just a couple of months apart. My mind watches reruns over and over again–episodes of the younger one, and of the older one. In my imagination, I talk to them both as if they're still alive, and they talk to me.

I can hear the one named Rebecca warning me that we spend half of life counting down to a long-awaited event, and the other half looking back, remembering. I hear the feisty grandmother reminding me not to worry about things I cannot control. I got so upset that time I visited you on Sanibel, and it rained every day. Now I'd give anything for a rain-spent day inside with you, Grandma. No, we cannot control rain or death. I guess this all means there will be no more summer nights of eating Heavenly Hash ice cream with you, Grandma, and, now, no sipping espresso in Spain with Rebecca. And Grandma, just before you died, you told me you had discovered the recipe to instant gratification and that you were going to send it to me. Now I may never know what you were talking about.

P.S. They say you're not "dead." You've simply "crossed over," I know it's true, but it doesn't make it any easier for me.

She folded the letter, then opened it again. She had to write about the time Grandma walked the streets of Saugatuck in her pink, fuzzy robe and slippers. She had to write it down because someday, when she would be rocking back and forth with a box of tissues, freckled arms and purple hair, she'd at least have her letters to Grandma to comfort her. They would describe the details her mind might forget, and they would keep Grandma alive forever.

Dear Grandma,

Remember the time city cousin Michelle from Chicago spent the entire summer scooping ice cream in the shop? We were short employees and needed the help, and besides, Michelle loved you and wanted to spend time with you. The three of us night owls teased each other. Michelle and I used to call you "sexy woman," and you'd blush, saying, "Now, now girls." One night Michelle and I worked until midnight in the shop. The tourists kept coming, and I stayed open an hour later because it was the family business, and because I felt we could rake in extra cash.

One of the bars at Coral Gables had closed, and crowds were migrating from that bar to the Sand Bar. Luckily, our shop was situated right between the two. We were nice when we scooped ice cream, and that night we got so many tips that, when we finally did close down, we decided to hang out for late-night, thin-crust pizza across the street at Marro's.

It was then that we heard loud pounding on the window near our booth. We looked out, as did everyone else in the restaurant, and to our shock, there you stood, Grams, with your pink robe and pink slippers. You were waving your forefinger at us, and pointing to your wristwatch. We should have told you we were going for pizza that night. You were up and waiting for us in your little apartment behind the shop. We should have told you. You probably would have liked a pizza and beer yourself. I know you only drink beer with pizza and would not eat pizza without a beer.

Oh, Grandma, your refrigerator stored nothing but Kit-Kat bars, Swiss cheese, ham, butter, and thinly sliced rye bread. As for Rebecca, I haven't meant to ignore her in this letter- well, she kept our apartment meticulous. She alphabetized her books and fed her plants a weekly dose of Advil. They were gorgeous plants, growing out of control. Rebecca spoke Spanish to them.

P.S. And to think, Rebecca is now speaking with God. I wished she were here speaking with me instead.

Vicki folded the letter, then closed her eyes. She felt butterflies flapping about in the pit of her stomach, their wings—normally used for courtship, regulating body temperature and avoiding predators—now entangled and crumbling apart. They had danced about so many times through her life that she knew their choreography by heart. At times, they made her nervous for no good reason at all. She often feared they might be bats, but how ridiculous!

CHAPTER THREE

VICKY HAD ARRIVED AT Fort Myers International Airport many times during her life, always to visit her grandparents, who spent their winters living on Sanibel Island. After Grandpa died, she visited even more. She didn't know how she would like Florida now that one of its most treasured seashells, her grandmother, would no longer be found on its beaches.

"Well, she should stop searching for seashells on the Sanibel seashore," he slurred silently as she stepped off the plane. She was in no mood to recite silly little tongue twisters, but two little girls seated in the row in front of her had been tongue twisting for nearly the entire second hour of the flight, and as hard as she tried not to become infected, everything was more contagious on a plane.

"She should instead safely start the summertime stingray shuffle near the Sanibel seashore," she said slowly as she stumbled over someone's small suitcase in the gateway and stopped. She said it again, faster. "She should safely start summer's stingray shuffle near the Sanibel seashore.

Sea should shave . . . she should safely shart . . . shit . . . stop saying such silly stuff," she said. "So shut up."

There is nothing worse than a perfectionist tongue twisting, she thought as she spotted her parents standing in a crowd, everyone's faces bronzed and looking quite relaxed as if the entire crowd had just finished a great game of golf. "Great game of golf on gorgeous green grass . . . great game of golf on gorgeous green grass . . . gate game of goof . . . get off it!"

she scolded herself. "You can practice later."

"Practice what?" asked her mother as she threw her arms around her.

"Golf," she rapidly replied, noticing how much younger her parents looked, since relocating to Florida several months ago.

"We've been playing every morning, and we'd love for you to join us," said her father, joining the hug.

"Did I say 'golf?' I meant 'goof.' What a 'goof ' I feel like with my ears popped. I must be shouting right now," she said, and then forced a wide yawn, hoping that might help.

Could Florida, or golfing, actually take years off a person's life? Maybe, she thought, as she hugged both her mom and dad together, noticing a fresh glow to their skins and natural highlights in her mother's hair.

As she and her mother waited on the curb for her father to pull the car up, Vicki noticed a group of women standing around them, looking as if they were linen hung to dry in the scorching sun a bit too long. And, as quick and fleeting as a hummingbird's presence, a moment of déjà vu fluttered through her mind. Suddenly she could predict exactly what her grandmother would be about to say at this exact given moment were she still alive and picking her up at the airport for her annual visit.

"Sunscreen is the Fountain of Youth," Grandma would say before pulling a brand-new bottle of lotion from a drugstore bag stuffed in her large straw purse. "I'm only going to warn you once on this trip. You don't want alligator skin."

"Thank you, Grandma, but wrinkles are not something I need to worry about now. I don't care what I look like when I'm older. I only care about now."

But now, like never before, she did care about wrinkles, aging and even death. She reached into her bag and pulled out sunscreen she had bought at her layover. She rubbed it into her arms, legs and face, then, fearing that SPF 60 might not be strong enough to protect her from the sun's deadly rays, she reapplied a second, and then a third coat.

In the backseat of her parent's tiny white car, with the air-conditioning not working properly, Vicki felt as if she were sitting in a sauna, ready to exit, but unable to do so. The door was stuck. She felt a kind of panic she had never felt before, and suddenly she couldn't breathe. She closed her eyes and tried to inhale deeply, but there didn't seem to be anything for her lungs to inhale. She tried convincing herself that a few more minutes of socializing in the sauna would be nice. She and her parents had much to catch up on as they drove west on Daniels Parkway, then made a left onto Summerlin Road and followed the signs toward Sanibel Island. Like private cramps deep within her gut, Rebecca's death agonized her, yet she didn't want to make it public news just yet. She chose to suffer alone, like someone choking silently, dying unnoticed during a wonderful dinner with family. Several minutes later, they passed billboards that teased travelers with painted glimpses of paradise ahead. She still couldn't properly catch her breath, but like the man standing knee-deep in the water out her left window, she wouldn't give up. She had to catch it just as he had to catch his fish.

"Oh, thank God. The bridge is going up," said her father. "That means we're forced to stop and wait."

"There's no place I'd rather be stuck then here on this bridge," added her mother.

"I'm getting sick. I've got to get out of this."

Vicki waited as long as she could, then, as soon as the car stopped, she opened the door like a person escaping a burning house and rushed over to the side rail of the bridge, as if she might throw up, but then she couldn't help but notice the water below her, looking so clear. She glanced up and saw giant brown pelicans gliding overhead like creatures one might see in *The Wizard of Oz*. One lunged downward and caught a fish, and carried it toward land. She couldn't arrive on Sanibel carrying the heavy news of her friend's death alone. It would sink the island. Laughing gulls swirled around her as well, but she couldn't hear them.

As she watched a sailboat to her left with two—no, three, no, four— bottlenose dolphins riding its front wave slowly approaching the bridge, she noticed her parents getting out of the car to join her, and she knew she needed to share the weight that was pulling her down. She had finished telling them how Rebecca died by the time the sailboat finally showed up under full sail on the other side of the bridge. Grateful for their comfort, she stood embracing her parents and watching the pod of smiling dolphins now leaping through the air, weightless and exposing their pink stomachs behind the boat.

She took a deep breath and got back into the car, looking ahead toward Sanibel and Captiva Islands, the most amazing islands in Southwest Florida, surrounded by the Gulf of Mexico.

At the first stop sign on the island, they headed east down Periwinkle Way and drove another couple of minutes to the condominium where Grandma and Grandpa used to spend their winters, two birds of paradise—the Great Egret and the Snowy Egret—as they used to call themselves.

"Mom and I say it every day, honey. We still can't believe the timing of it all," her father said as he opened the door of the condo. "We sold the businesses and the house, and planned on moving here to be closer to Grandma."

"And now, the loss of your friend," added her mother. "There's so much in life we can't control."

"They both left at horrible times," said Vicki. "I just can't believe it." That evening Vicki wanted a break from the morbid thoughts that raced through her mind. She wanted to forget that her friend had died, to toss the incident into her Sea of Forgetfulness. Her parents suggested they stay in for dinner, but she insisted they go out so they went for all you-can-eat shrimp-and-crab platters. Vicki's parents tried urging her to return to Michigan for the funeral or to make phone calls to friends or send flowers. She appreciated their concern and their support, but still, as she spoke of it all, she felt like a dolphin tossed into a lake. Come morning she would be back in the ocean again, where everything made sense.

She could only talk so much about it all and, instead, wanted to enjoy the feelings that came from being reunited and sharing a dinner with her parents. They were a close family after years of mopping floors, cleaning toilets, waiting tables and horseback riding together through the woods at her father's ranch, the last of his entrepreneurial endeavors. Since the sale of the businesses and the southward migration a couple of months ago, they had only spoken on the phone and they had much to catch up on.

After dinner, they returned to the condo, and Vicki went for a quick swim in the pool. It felt good, hiding from the humidity that had clung to her ever since she stepped foot off the plane, but she felt guilty, as if she should be around people who knew Rebecca and were mourning her death. She should be walking up to the open casket at a funeral, not splashing around in a solar-heated pool! She didn't dare to smile because she should be wiping her eyes with a white handkerchief, not drying herself off with a beach towel. Instead of wearing a pastel-colored bikini, she should be wearing something dark, solid, and solemn. She didn't want to cry because that would only rub in a fact she couldn't accept: her closest friend had actually left this life without finishing anything she wanted to accomplish.

Oh, why didn't she just skip her flight and attend the funeral? How could she have made such a rash decision? She blamed it on shock. It had to be shock, because it all happened so fast that she didn't know she had any options. Then again, she had to leave. Her hometown would always stay where it lay on the map, between Lake Michigan and Lake Huron, but everything comforting about it had changed. She felt a chill and missed the cozy mitten.

That night in bed, minutes, perhaps hours, had passed when Vicki saw a woman sitting at the end of her bed. It took a moment for her eyes to focus and, like an Etch-A-Sketch filling itself out in midair, she gradually saw more detail: Rebecca's long dark hair, tinseled in silver, then her royal blue eyes.

"*Hola*, Vicki. I've got a Heavenly secret to share with you. Dreams not fulfilled on earth can still be fulfilled," echoed her friend, and then, in an instant, as if someone shook the Etch-A-Sketch, she vanished.

Vicki sat up in bed, staring at the foot of her bed like a magician staring confidently at her magic hat, awaiting the reappearance of a rabbit. "Rebecca," she called out. "Please come back. Don't go. I heard what you said, but tell me more. I need to hear more. I'm scared. My grandma died, and now you. Does death really strike in threes? Who next? Could it be me?"

She waited and listened, realizing no magic word would make Rebecca reappear. As much as she did or didn't believe in what she had just seen, she still felt thrilled to have had the perceived, and perhaps real, experience of seeing her friend moving and talking once more. She felt honored and wanted to memorize everything she had heard and seen. How could it be? Had Rebecca really visited her there in the room? Had she crossed the life-death barrier just to deliver that message?

She soon wanted to fall asleep so she tried talking to her arms and legs, urging them to relax, but there is nothing more boring than talking to a body part, which is probably why the activity puts a person to sleep in the first place. After a horribly dull conversation with her toes, she gave up. There is a time for everything, or there should be, so Vicki declared night her time to mourn.

Her mourning began the next night. As she lay in bed at eleven forty-five, she envisioned herself and Rebecca finishing up their list of goals on the paper tablecloth at Till Midnight. Still awake at mid- night, she analyzed age, and how so many things had gone unfinished in Rebecca's life. At one o'clock, she resented heart attacks for sneaking in and robbing her friend and her grandmother of life, while they slept. She felt angry at death, the disgruntled gunman randomly opening fire.

No, death chose Rebecca, and it chose Grandma. They must have been carefully selected for some holy reason. What is it the very devout say? *It must have been their time.* And just as there is a time to be born and a time to die, Vicki decided there was a time to climb out of bed, and to forget about falling asleep.

At two o'clock, the irony of life haunted Vicki. Half of life is spent looking forward, counting down to holidays, vacations, and weekends, while the other half is spent pondering backward. But if she didn't let herself reminisce, things she once loved would die. At three o'clock, she promised herself that from this day forward she would start living for the moment. At four o'clock, she cried for Rebecca's family and their lost time together.

She tried counting sheep but instead turned to counting the number of antacid tablets she had given Rebecca. It must have amounted to a full bottle within a one-month span. She felt psychic as she watched each or- ange-glowing second tick by. *I knew it would turn 4:46 at that exact second,*

I knew it! I knew it would turn 4:47 when it did!

After getting a tension headache, she covered the clock with a shirt. She envied others on the island for sleeping soundly. Why couldn't she, too, fall asleep? Why wouldn't she? She felt alone, lonesome in a world of sleeping people. She focused on her breathing, and then suddenly it changed. Perhaps it changed because she now thought about her every breath. She skipped a breath and her breaths sped up. She tried to slow them down again, and felt in need of an extra breath but couldn't catch one. As the hours passed, Vicki was becoming preoccupied with her own breathing and her own death. She felt a lack of air, as she had in the car on the way home from the airport. She didn't know why she couldn't catch her breath, or why she was now hyperventilating.

She quietly got out of bed and, still wearing her nightgown, walked out the front door of the condominium. She walked the five minutes to Lighthouse Beach, at the east end of Periwinkle Way. She wanted to thank both the rising sun, for providing her its natural light, and the historical cylindrical steel lighthouse, for giving her a destination to walk toward. She liked having a destination just as much as she liked having something to look forward to on her calendar. Every spring, Vicki and her sister had gone to Sanibel to see Grandma, and they went to Lighthouse Beach to walk. Before each trip, they'd count down days. When the annual trip to Florida rolled around, they savored those days, and when it passed, they remembered them.

Just as one might crave chicken noodle soup when feeling down, she craved a walk on the beach. Something about walking a beach always made her feel as if she could forget what happened yesterday or what might happen tomorrow.

She sat down where the water met the talcum-powder sand and stared out at the Gulf of Mexico. She sat with the shells and felt sorry for them, cast ashore by storms, tides, and wave action. She loved the shells, the sand, and anything related to a beach. She could never live in a land-locked world.

Carefully scanning the sand around her to see if she might be sitting alongside a Chinese Alphabet, her grandmother's favorite shell, she spotted a mound about two feet down. It looked like a sand castle. She got up and ran toward the mound with destruction in mind. She jumped and landed on the fortress and stomped it down to nothing more than silken sand. She felt good, yet wicked, and grateful that no one else walked the beach early on this particular morning to witness her anger-filled act. She picked up a Lightning Whelk that had decorated the top of the castle and tossed it as hard as she could into the water. She heard it land. She didn't know what to do now that the castle was destroyed. She felt energy, fierce as a Calusa Indian. Her surging power fascinated her, but she knew these first inhabitants of the island wouldn't waste their energy destroying a sand castle. Instead, they probably used it productively, for things like carving canoes and making masks for religious events.

She bent down to pick up a stick. Before long, she tossed it down, then fell to her knees on the damp ground, praying for Rebecca. After her torrent of words was spent, she rested her head and stared at the stick.

Without thinking, she took it and began scribbling in the sand. She wrote what she could remember of Rebecca's goals. She scribbled with so much intensity and enthusiasm that she was probably acting like the kid who built the castle she had just destroyed. The stick broke in two, but she continued, and now she no longer kneeled. Instead, her scribbles grew larger and larger along the shore, enough so that someone in a plane overhead might be able to read them. Suddenly, without warning, the water gently rolled further up the beach than before and made its way over the markings. As quickly as the water came, it also went, carrying Rebecca's goals and dreams with it into the Gulf of Mexico.

She felt sorry that nothing survived forever. The island Indians were eventually wiped out, not by an incoming tide, but by invaders with firearms and foreign diseases, things they couldn't compete with. She had stomped on the sand castle, and now her markings were washed away as well. Maybe it was a good thing. Something about the sacred goals being tossed in a trash can back at the café didn't settle well with Vicki. Despite the fact that her scribbles in the sand would never be seen again, Vicki's soul felt refreshed because now Rebecca's dreams were blended into nature.

As she glanced down at the sand, she noticed piles of different types of miniature shells, known to the islanders as "coffee grounds," and decided she could use a good, strong coffee drink herself, so she left.

When she arrived back at the condo, she decided it was too early for coffee, so she settled down in the recliner chair in the living room, attempting to fall asleep for a few minutes at least, but the hyperventilating returned. Why couldn't she breathe? Several times she dozed off, and it felt good and natural. Once there was a thud on her window, and she assumed it was a bird hitting the glass. She dozed again.

No! Wake up! an inner voice cried out. *Do not fall asleep! You might die!* The inner voice, her mind, tortured her exhausted body. This attack of hair-pulling insomnia returned night after dragging night.

CHAPTER FOUR

VICKI WISHED GOD HAD never created night. But nights of sitting up alone in the living room recliner attempting to catch her breath did pass, and day arrived to greet her rudely. Sure, day rescued her from night, but having had no sleep, day felt like unusual punishment.

During the days that followed, she took shelter under her dark sunglasses, which barely hid her red, bloodshot eyes and the bags that drooped as low as her cheekbones. No one fully understood the extent of her insomnia, or what to make of it, but she knew she needed one good night of sleep in order to survive—physically and mentally. She did her time and now wanted to declare this time of mourning over, complete. She wanted to enter a new time, perhaps a time for dancing, or one of the other joyful times that fall under the category of "everything."

Naps on the raft in the sunlit pool hardly competed with a dream-spent night in bed. She wanted badly to become a member of the rapid-eye movement, but she couldn't get in and didn't know why. She granted herself permission to enter sleep, but it stood miles away, a fortress up on a mountain, hidden behind brick walls and moats filled with dark water and knights prancing around on horses. She wanted more than anything to enter the kingdom of sleep but didn't have the strength to break down the walls, swim through the dark water and kill the men in armor guarding its doors. She could hardly catch her own breath and had no idea where it had gone. Despite her feelings of sleep deprivation, she rejoiced with more gladness than ever when the days that the Lord hath made kept coming. But nights came too, part of the package. She couldn't have day without night, she knew that, but still resented night — a punishment, solitary detention or abyss — that kept creeping up.

"When you have your shortness of breath tonight, just breathe into the bag." Her mother placed a brown paper lunch bag next to the recliner, her newfound bed. "Try relaxing your thoughts when it happens."

"But it's not my thoughts. It's kind of strange that my thoughts would do this to me. I know I'm not crazy!"

In truth, she knew her thoughts of death made their way through her mind like objects on a factory conveyor belt. She couldn't bring herself to yank the bad thoughts off, and just let them go by.

"It has nothing to do with being crazy," added her father as he turned the television off. "Have you been drinking caffeine past three o'clock?"

She pushed the lever on the chair and shot upward. She didn't want to recline. "No. I'm down to half a cup in the morning. No more." In truth, she knew that if anyone asked her blood type, she'd have to reply, "hazelnut coffee."

"I was thinking that it's asthma," she said. "Or who knows, my scoliosis might be constricting my lung cavity. I haven't had my scoliosis checked in years."

"Are you worried about anything?" Her mother turned off the lights in the living room.

"Wait, keep that small light on, please. No, I'm not worried about a thing. Just falling asleep, that's all." She sat in the recliner, ready to confront another night as a coward, as if death might come like a thief in the night.

"Why don't you have a gin and tonic with us?" asked her mother. "We can sit out on the porch and talk."

"I'd love to, but I'm exhausted," she said. Secretly, she believed her own hypochondriac thoughts. *It might be mitral valve prolapse, or some irregularity with my heart, or angina, or an undetected aneurysm ready to burst.*

"Try to get some sleep tonight. If it doesn't go away, we'll get you checked."

As they left the room, her mind began to tick along with the clock. So did her fingers, tapping the arm of the cold vinyl recliner. An hour later she could hear the distant snoring of her father, like the growls of a dragon from within the fortress of the world of sleep. She tried focusing on the present moment and the remote control in her hand. She felt frustrated with the new digital manner in which she had to flip through over a hundred different stations. This must be why Grandma had never watched television. Perhaps she would specialize her future psychology practice on patients who couldn't adapt to modern technology.

She clicked the remote, and then got stuck on a channel of static. The stubborn device wouldn't work as she desperately pointed and clicked, over and over again. She tried to enjoy the flickering static show in the dark living room, like fireworks on a smaller scale. The *stststststtstststststst* sound got to her, and she knew she'd have to quietly exit the vinyl, walk over to the television and turn it off.

Hours passed. She started to slip into sleep, the existence she longed for, but then someone kept tossing her out. *No, wake up, do not lose control or you might slip into the dungeon of death by mistake. Do not fall asleep!* She manned the graveyard shift, while the rest of the world slept. The living room in the condo looked ready for battle. A gaudy copper helmet posed on top of the TV, a medieval sword hung on the wall over it, and two black-and-gold shields were nailed next to it. Touched by sun, the decorations weren't bad, but at night, in the dark living room, they were eerie. She watched the walls, decorated by her grandparents who had traveled the world after retirement collecting cheap souvenirs. Nothing moved but a spider on a cross-country journey from the corner above the television to the corner above her recliner.

Day arrived and night followed, over and over again. Who said it was all very good? She disagreed with the Creator on this one.

Sitting at the kitchen table in her pajamas, she stared at the cereal boxes erected like buildings that formed a city around her bowl of milk. She could feel her hair, tangled by her night of tossing and turning, and she traced the skin on her face for pillow crevices. They remained, along with the head rush that should have disappeared a minute after first standing. She chose Life, Quaker Oats' Life. She chose it because she liked its name. Perhaps eating it might make her live forever. She read the nutrition facts on the side panel and the ingredients below. She placed her health in the hands of whole oat flour (with oat bran), sugar, corn flour, whole-wheat flour, rice flour, high-starch oat flour, salt, calcium carbonate, sodium phosphate (a phosphorus source and dough conditioner), reduced iron, and many more ingredients. Yes, this combination created the cereal she now ate, the cereal called Life.

Her lazy adrenal glands screamed out to her, so she poured herself a cup of coffee, added milk, then squeezed in chocolate syrup and stirred it all together.

"You know, Dad, I've never had a summer unemployment problem before. I always worked for you in the shop or in my internships in Chicago."

"I wish I had a job to offer you this summer, honey. I don't anymore."

"I know. I try not to look back, but this time last year, I'd be ringing the silver bell, alerting the town that the ice cream had arrived; that the season had started."

Her father set his paper down and stared out the window at a palm tree. "I'd be outside in front, painting a fresh coat of pink on those wooden benches."

"I'd be slicing strawberries for the guests' breakfast," added her mother, "and Ann would be sneaking testers here and there when I wasn't looking."

"And old Granny would be sitting in the window on the pink radiator," added her father.

"I feel horrible. I planned on making enough money this summer to at least reimburse you for my own airline ticket to Spain." Vicki sipped her chocolate coffee and burned the tip of her tongue, which ruined the experience of drinking the rest of her cup of coffee. "Is there a yellow highlighter anywhere? I've got to search the classifieds."

"You might not need to," her father said.

"What do you mean?"

"We got a phone call this morning. There are some legal matters Mom and I need to attend to concerning the sale of the businesses. We're leaving for Michigan in two days. We'd love for you to come with us; spend the summer there." He took a sip of his black coffee. "You could at least live back in Holland near your friends, and wait tables with them. That way you'd have some spending money for Spain."

"No, I can't go back to Michigan. I can't, not now." She poured herself more coffee, this time without adding chocolate. She felt as if she had done nothing to pursue her goal of finding a summer job. She felt like a crab walking sideways.

"We had no idea this would come up. We don't want to leave you here alone. You need to be around people, especially after the loss of Rebecca. It might be good for you to return."

"I can't return. I won't. In fact, I vow right now to find a job within two days. Maybe I needed a deadline to work against, and now I've got one. *Two days.*"

She gulped the muddy drink as if injecting herself with some ancient formula. With each gulp she could feel her creativity awakening, her ambitions screaming out, and her confidence building. "Someone will hire me, I know it. Just put me in front of an interviewer, and I will get the job."

"Whoa, Nellie. What kind of job do you think you will look for?" He often spoke as he would speak to his horses back in Michigan. His favorite horse was named Kid. He loved them all.

"When I drink coffee, I can do anything!" She laughed and poured herself the last inch from the pot. "This liquid bean stuff turns me into a wonder woman of some sort. Coffee inspires me. Don't worry. I'll go out and interview today, and I'll come home with a job!"

"Hey, hold the reins! Before you go, good luck, and we know you'll do great. Don't you forget that, you hear? Mom and I say it all the time - anyone who hires you is going to be the luckiest employer alive."

"Oh, Dad, I wish I could still work for you."

"Get out of here. Hit the pasture!" he said.

"Okay, but I've been meaning to ask you both something. Just before she died, Grandma told me she had discovered a recipe for instant gratification. She was going to send it to me. Do you know what she might have been talking about?"

"No. I have no idea."

"I wish I knew."

In one full day, she attended a brief seminar at Edison Mall on how to become a purified-water saleswoman, interviewed with Lee County to become a toll collector on the bridge linking Sanibel Island and the City of Palms, and phoned the Thomas A. Edison and Henry Ford Museums in Fort Myers, begging to get hired for anything. When the man there asked her why she wanted a job at the museums, she had desperately replied, "Because I'm sick of fearing death." She knew it made no sense to a complete stranger, but the man, once his surprise had passed, told her that when Thomas Edison was in a coma and close to death he awoke for a moment, looked up, and said, "It is very beautiful over there." The man didn't offer her the job, but at least he gave her a glimpse of hope.

By noon, the coffee high wore off, but she kept going. She filled out an application to be a manager of forty Spanish-speaking maids at a four-star resort. But after she and the person doing the hiring had a conversation together in Spanish, Vicki knew she'd never be called back. She left and attempted to apply for the Fort Myers Beach trolley driver position. They told her she needed a special license to drive a trolley. A woman interviewed her for a cash register position at a boutique where Grandma used to send friends and family to shop for books on shelling, for shells they couldn't find on the shore, and for souvenirs. She wanted the job, but then a senior with a case of serious "Sanibel stoop" interviewed for the position immediately after her, and Vicki knew the woman's charm alone would win her the job. Looking as if she had spent years stooping for shells didn't hurt her chances either. In sum, no one offered her a job. She felt defeated, overqualified and under-qualified, and completely unmarketable.

On the second day she did more of the same and returned home feeling rejected. Under the dock behind her grandmother's condo, a manatee, about ten feet long, with a small, wrinkled head and straight- whiskered snout, snuffed its nose slowly above the surface of the warm water before disappearing into the shallow canal with a pump of its tail. Glancing up from the classifieds, already highlighted from her morning perusal, Vicki watched the rippling current of the canal. *Where are the currents going? Where are they coming from?* Four hundred miles of canals running behind homes made Southwest Florida one place in the world with more canals than any city in Italy.

About three minutes later, the gray-black creature surfaced again, and this time brought with him one, two, three more manatees, each with cleft upper lips and bristly hairs. She couldn't tell if they were grazing for food on the canal's surface or simply spying on her. She waved to be friendly. She blew kisses. She felt the urge to grab the corpulent body of one of the slow-moving manatees and swim away with it and its family into the Caloosahatchee River, maybe the Gulf of Mexico. She knew the canals led *somewhere* exciting, and the manatees were surely living a more adventurous life than she was. But they had fears too: of boats speeding down the canal and killing them, of crushing or drowning in floodgates, of eating a fishhook by accident, of getting entangled in crab-trap lines, of pollution and animal haters with rocks in their hands, or of red tide and cold water. She felt depressed. Of course they did. They and all the other great creatures of the canal, and of the world all feared something. And if they didn't, well, they should.

She felt desperate. "Oh, dear Lord," she prayed aloud, "please guide me to a job. Charter me wherever you like, oh, please. There are so many things I want to do in life and so many options that I feel overwhelmed at times. I'm afraid that I might not be able to accomplish my tablecloth scribbles. I can't seem to even find a simple summer job. I shouldn't feel so lost. Please help!"

She then tossed the paper onto the dock, glancing one last time at the ads that left her no optimism. But there it was, hit by the first drop of Florida's daily summer downpour. She read it once to herself, then out loud: *Waitress with a lust for life needed for island restaurant. Interviews start daily at 8:00 a.m., Island Marina. Call first.*

Early the next morning, she set off like a mouse in a maze, trying to find the Island Marina.

There were many routes she could have taken, just as a person has end-less routes they can take in life. Some choose the major highways, while others take the side roads, or even back alleys. One might discover that a bumper-to-bumper ride works fine one day, but the next day a road with less traffic better fits the mood. Some days, it might take an hour to get to the marina. Other days, one might catch every red light and, therefore, it might take a couple of hours. There's the scenic route, and there's the speedy route. "It's a decision you must constantly make," said the man's voice coming from her cell phone.

"I don't get it. I'm just asking for simple directions to the island."

"Oh, but the island is symbolic for so much more, dear. I will give you practical directions to this magnificent island, and for this particular in-terview, but I also want to inspire you to discover more islands in life and more routes to those islands, that's all."

More or less, she followed the directions the man on the phone gave.

She drove over the causeway to Fort Myers, then over another bridge and continued to Cape Coral's far north end, and turned onto Pine Island Road. After a few miles, it changed into a narrow two-lane road with smelly swamp water on both sides. She laughed, recalling the man on the phone's vivid directions, "Once you enter a town called Matlacha, you'll see marsh water all around you. It's magnificent."

After a wooden bridge, she could smell morning coffee as she drove through the quaint fishing town with its waterside fish houses and casual-looking seafood restaurants—more designated landmarks. Between buildings, she caught glimpses of the picturesque water, unsure whether it was the Gulf of Mexico or an intra-coastal waterway, and it was turning a shimmering orange from the dawn's emerging sun. She felt renewed, re-stored in some way, as if *she* were rising with the sun. She felt competitive, ahead of the day, and all the late-morning sleepers of the world. They were still in bed, missing out on the sun's skyward ascent. She had never noticed morning and all its traits before. Now that morning no longer meant rushing off to class, she was observing things that never caught her attention before. Maybe she had stopped noticing life's details because she passed by those same details day after day, year after year, without ever leaving her comfort zone, or maybe because her schedule only allowed her time to notice things that needed to get done.

Despite a few old hotels and boat rental shops on the side of the road, Matlacha didn't *look* like a tourist town. It looked more like a lifestyle that had remained as such for centuries. Perhaps the local fishermen intended to keep their site a secret. Or maybe fishermen preserved it as a no-fuss, non-glamorous escape. She could smell raw fish, sushi. No, it was not sushi; just plain old raw fish, stripped of its scales, nothing glamorous, and certainly nothing edible in her mind. Then she passed by art galleries and a bookstore and knew there was more to the place.

North of Matlacha, she drove over a bridged creek and entered Salt Water Key, an island of its own. Continuing on her treasure hunt, she laughed when she spotted rows of banana trees—they meant "turn right." She did so and lost sight of the water.

Wow, she thought, turning a confident left at an orchard of mango trees. *Michigan has things like blueberries and apples, but nothing from the passion- and citrus-fruit families.*

She unrolled her window, smelling a sharp citrus fragrance magnified by the crisp morning breeze. It satisfied her more than a glass of grapefruit juice. She daydreamed.

Me? Commissioned the job for naming a new lipstick shade? I'm honored to accept such a glamorous position. You can pay me my million bucks later. First, I just need a little brainstorming session. Moon-lit Mango, Sunlit Papaya, Papaya Wine. No, no such thing . . . Mermaid Gloss, oh, stupid . . . Banana Peel, get off the rhyme, Vicki . . . Salt Water Drench, Whipped Banana . . . Ashe . . . Ashes to Ash . . . Dust to . . . Death Black . . . Heartbeat Red . . . Coffin brown . . .

A dead end diverted her thoughts as she made a sharp right and headed about two miles down a curvy road with old wooden stilt homes on one side and nothing but the wide open gulf on the other. Breathtaking, she thought, and turned at the sign that read, "Island Marina."

She took a seat under a bamboo hut and watched a white pelican balance itself on a narrow wooden dock post as she waited for the boat to arrive. When she called for directions, the man on the phone had told her it arrived every morning at around eight o'clock. She knew nothing about the restaurant and didn't ask. She just knew that a boat would take her out to the island for an interview. On the island stood a restaurant that needed a waitress. She planned to be that waitress. She felt foolish and irresponsible for not asking more questions, but she impatiently wanted a job, and a boat trip sounded nice, regardless. After all, her deadline to find a job expired today. So take it and stay in Florida or leave it and head back to Michigan, a place no longer comfortable.

What if there is no restaurant? No Tarpon Key Island? What if it's a big hoax? What if it's the type of place where the waitresses dance naked? Or worse? Why do they have to take me out to the island for the interview? Why can't they interview me here at the marina? Perhaps it is a joke, and I'm waiting for nothing, because there is no boat.

She opened her purse and turned the mace that hung on her key chain to ready position. She couldn't breathe and the pains she had felt in her chest at night returned. She didn't know why her shortness of breath always brought chest pains. They were only slight *pokes*, not stabs. The blade of the knife moved under *her* control. She wouldn't let it stab, *not* right now. She closed her eyes, focused on each breath—pushing her abdomen in and out, not up and down. She imagined mental gargoyles perching upon her thoughts and fighting off negative worries. This helped somewhat. Then, a few minutes later, she picked up a cracked coconut, closed her eyes again, and felt its rough, splintery skin. She concentrated hard on the coconut in her hands, anything to prevent her imaginative mind from wandering to the "what if " thoughts.

CHAPTER FIVE

A SURE THING! THANK GOD, she thought as she heard the motor of a small powerboat and opened her eyes. As it pulled up to the dock, she forced herself to yawn, stealing extra air.

"You here for the interview?" asked a man with leathery skin as he tied the rope. He wore all white but for dockside shoes with no socks, and the lines on his face belonged like the crevices on a seashell.

"Yes, I am. I probably should have asked a bit more about the job and the island." Vicki reached onto the boat to shake his hand. "So tell me, what type of island is it?"

"Ah, how does one describe Tarpon Key? Well, dear, let me tell you. It's a *magnificent* place to eat. Simply *magnificent*!"

He spoke with the passion of an auditioning actor. "You need to *visit* Tarpon Key to understand it, and I'll take you there if you're ready." He extended his hand and Vicki accepted, stepping onto the boat.

"My name is Simon. I'm the Tarpon Key dockmaster. I just need to load up a few things, and we'll be on our way, dear." He walked over to some boxes that were piled on crates under a Sabal palmetto palm tree and started loading them one by one onto the boat. Suspiciously, Vicki peeked inside the boxes each time he'd leave for more. Bulk amounts of ketchup bottles, cleaning detergents, and cleaning rags—typical restaurant items.

Within ten minutes, Simon started the boat, and they slowly pulled away from the dock. The smell of boat gasoline tickled her nerves as she watched the marina slip further and further away. She felt carefree and irresponsible at the same time, a dandelion blowing far from home but having fun along the way. The gasoline smell reminded her of Saugatuck and the yuppie boaters who would sail from Chicago to buy ice cream in their shop. But now as the wind hit her in the face, she knew that leaving that comfort zone behind might not be so bad after all. Looking at the water ahead of her reminded her that this present situation—no friends, no job, no money, and no idea where the boat would take her—forced her to pay attention.

"Tarpon Key is a privately owned intra-coastal island where time is measured in moments, not minutes." Simon stood behind the wheel still smiling, and in doing so, deepened the engravings on his skin. "There's not much on the island, just the restaurant and bar, a few log-cabin cottages, and an old lighthouse tower. But the place is simply *magnificent*, dear. *Magnificent*, I tell you!"

Vicki smiled too, aware of the crow's-feet forming around her eyes.

"Dear, you'll want to take a seat now and hold on. It's bumpy ahead."

She could feel the force of the boat's increasing speed sliding her and the cushion she sat on back toward the stern of the boat. She tucked her hair into the collar of her shirt so she could see and grabbed onto the side of the boat. Her lungs filled with the heavy sea air, as if someone had sprinkled a saltshaker over the boat.

A mile or two passed, and she saw a few distant islands and boats anchored everywhere, fishermen mostly. The eight o'clock morning sun provided a fresh perspective, vivifying everything - color, temperature, and sounds. The water looked like luminous turquoise-stained glass. *Any chapel would pay big money for such windows*, she noted. The air raised goose bumps up and down her arms. The birds of the air chirped clearly, loudly, as if through a microphone echoing across the currents. *Any chapel would pay big money for such a choir.* She closed her eyes and prayed under her breath, "Our Father who art in Heaven, hallowed be Your name."

Even if she *didn't* get a job, Vicki decided the boat trip alone made the early morning effort well worth it. Just feeling awake, alive, and on a boat before the official daytime actually began, rejuvenated her in a way that made her think of how an early-morning poacher who never got caught might feel. Being alive under the incandescent, dawning sun made her realize that her late-morning dreams didn't compare to what real life offered. She scolded herself for sleeping late into the morning. *There are things to see in this world, things that look different early in the morning.*

She no longer had to hold onto the side of the boat as it approached a large island capped with about a hundred extravagant old Florida-style, pastel-colored homes, clapboard-sided, and tin-roofed.

She bent down to scratch her ankle and to secretly catch her breath. She kept her sentences short, as always, when she sensed a breathing frenzy approaching. *Ouch, my heart. Darn, I'm a hooked fish,* she thought.

"Is that Tarpon Key?"

"No, dear. That's *Useppa* Island. *Some* consider it *Fantasy Island.*"

"Is Tarpon Key *that* gorgeous?"

"*Absolutely*, but Tarpon Key is more of ,let's see, it's more of a remote, rustic sort of place."

"Well, I'm no shipwrecked woman washing ashore. Once I see the place, I'll decide whether or not I choose to stay." She would think about that later. For now, she couldn't take her eyes off the island they were passing. She would certainly feel safe docking there.

"There's no bridge, no road, and it's so far from the mainland, but the homes look new!"

"Not as new as you think. President Theodore Roosevelt and his tarpon-loving friends used to fish here at the turn of the century. And the building that is today an inn on the island was built in 1896 by a streetcar magnate from Chicago."

The island looked luxuriant, and Vicki felt she'd be comfortable docking there. Maybe it was the pastel-colored homes that reminded her of her family's ice-cream shop, she decided. But, as the boat passed the ritzy residences, panic suddenly gripped her, and so did the same chest pains. She felt a knife stab her chest and knew what a fish felt like being filleted alive. *Maybe it's a hoax. Maybe there's no Tarpon Key, no restaurant. What's the worst thing that could happen?* she asked herself. *I might die in some wretched way.* She didn't like her answer.

They passed several small mangroves as well as a channel marker topped with an osprey nest, then passed Cayo Costa State Park, part of the chain of barrier islands, with the Charlotte Harbor on one side and the Gulf of Mexico on the other. The ten-mile limestone-based island stood completely undeveloped with a thick forest of pines and oak and palm hammocks in its interior and mangrove swamps on the bay side, one of Florida's most primitive state parks, according to Simon.

A few minutes later, Simon pointed. "*There's* Tarpon Key!"

"It *is remote!*" She had never seen anything like it, except on television or in the movies. A mound of shredded greenery appeared, a small, round island of about one hundred acres of lush green palm trees, lavish vegetation and tropical flowering plants. It looked like a floating head of broccoli. And thankfully, unlike an island on which someone is shipwrecked and washed ashore to fend for their life, this island had sailboats and several small boats bobbing in their berths. There was also what looked like a lighthouse of a faded red color looming before them.

"Wow, what do they use on their lawns? Monosodium glutamate? I've never seen anything so green and beautiful," Vicki asked, taking off her sunglasses to get a flawless view.

"No, no preservatives needed. It's *all* natural." He shook his head and chuckled. "Monosodium glutamate—that's the first I've heard that one, dear, and I've taken a lot of people out here, from all over."

As the boat drew closer, a rustic building, slate blue in color, with a white wraparound porch and wooden swing chairs grew larger and larger, as did the tower of natural red brick.

"That's the restaurant and bar. Once we tie up, follow the sandy pathway up to the front doors and go on in, young lady."

Simon easily maneuvered the boat into a slip. "Long before it was a restaurant, it was the lighthouse keeper's quarters. The tower stands exactly in the middle of the island."

"So, that is a lighthouse?" she asked.

"Maybe I shouldn't have called him a lighthouse keeper. Some call him crazy. John Bark and his wife bought Tarpon Key in the mid 1800s for a couple hundred dollars and later spent around fifty grand to build their dream – a lighthouse. No one supported this personal project, or obsession. It wasn't needed. The Sanibel lighthouse was being constructed at the same time, completed in 1884. Its light could be seen over fifteen miles away, so no other light was needed, but John Bark was driven by his obsessive goal of becoming a lighthouse keeper. They say he laid the bricks himself, one by one. The story goes that he also enslaved his wife, and she carried bricks day after day, year after year."

"That's a pretty big tower for two people to build by hand without any outside help," she said.

"He cheated. He built it on a natural hill so it looks taller than it is," laughed Simon. "He was territorial and wouldn't allow people on the island to help. Like I said, some call him mad. The Barks lived lives of solitude and privacy on the island until their deaths. They died shortly after finishing the tower, but before ever installing the light. No one knows much about them, but on occasion, guests swear they have seen a transparent man wandering through the restaurant carrying a lantern and a woman carrying bricks around the island."

"I don't believe in ghosts," said Vicki as she stepped onto the dock near the tiny red brick boathouse. There were a few sets of oars hanging on one of its walls, and rowboats and canoes were napping on the sandy ground beside it. A rusty pay phone stood out as noticeably as a polished silver fork in a bag of plastic picnic utensils, and a red Coca-Cola machine caught her attention like a glowing UFO landing on Earth.

As she walked up the coconut-palm-tree-dotted path, she didn't want to run into any woman carrying bricks, so she tried not to look too hard. Instead, she looked only at the natural beauty of the land and declared the tropical jungle her Utopia. No pavement, no light posts, no tourist signs, and no preservatives. It stood completely void of commercialization. Birds chirped, and waves rippled slowly on the shore. Some slapped against the wooden docks.

By the time she'd walked up the hill to the front doors of the slate blue clapboarded restaurant with its white wraparound porch, she felt like she had gone through a facial, a back massage, and an aromatherapy treatment – completely revived.

Inside the shady Florida bungalow stood a variety of different antique wooden tables, some painted pale yellow, others white or faded green. Each had white, straight-back chairs. Shaded by thickly shadowing palm trees that looked like monsters with long, slender bodies and wild, crazy green hair, the inside rooms were dark and cold, and there were ashes in the fireplace. Maritime murals decorated the walls, and in one of the restaurant rooms farthest from the front door, Vicki noticed wallpaper peeling off the walls.

"Go ahead. Give yourself a look around," said a woman. "I'll be right with you. Those things you see falling off are post cards of lighthouses. Go, look up close." She left the room.

The floorboards squeaked as Vicki walked around the dining rooms that encircled the bar. Jimmy Buffet music was playing. It was music she and her friends had played as they huddled in the fraternity houses on winter weekends, drinking and dancing to keep warm. She gave herself permission to sing the words "pencil-thin mustache" out loud as she hurried around the corner and into the bar. She looked around. Pictures and postcards of lighthouses from all over the world, secured with masking tape, covered the walls. Outside the large screened windows, she saw a jungle of Indian banyan trees with ovate, heart-shaped leaves and remarkable aerial roots that grew down from branches to form secondary trunks. Overshadowed by the banyan and fanlike leaves of palm trees framing the window, the rustic bar felt more like a tree house to Vicki, a place where, as Simon said, moments mattered more than minutes.

"I'm Ruth," said the woman, returning to the room. "I'm the head waitress and manager. It's going to be a busy day. Every day here is busy, so we may as well get right to the point. Why should I hire you? Why would you be good waiting tables?"

"Well, I have a strong work ethic."

"A strong work ethic? Explain."

"I went to school in a small Dutch town where they believe in doing everything to the best of their ability, whether scooping ice cream, waiting tables, or leading a country."

"I see," she said.

"And I grew up working our family businesses."

"Well then, I would love to talk more, but it's going to get busy quickly around here. Part of the interview includes busing tables. You can show me your work ethic in action. The boat leaves again at three-thirty. Maybe you can work until then?"

"Of course," said Vicki. "Thank you." After years of adding exactly one tablespoon of malt powder to make the world's best vanilla malts, it felt strange having to prove her workmanship to someone else, and it made her sad. She missed her family and the businesses. She wanted to kick herself for looking back, but just as a dragonfly has four powerful wings that move independently, allowing both forward and backward flight, so too do humans have the capacity to reminisce at the same moment they're moving forward in life.

"If you take the job," Ruth said, "you'll have to live here on the island for about twelve days in a row at first, then the boat will take you back for two days off every week. Two days in a row that is."

"Live here on the island? Where?"

"We have two houses for the cooks and waiting staff. Later, once things slow down, you can go and check out the living quarters. We also provide staff meals here in the restaurant before lunch and dinner serving hours."

"Does the waiting staff make good money?"

"They average about five hundred dollars a week in tips during the summer months."

"You've got to be kidding me. You can only get here by boat. That many people really make it out here?"

"Oh yes, just wait. You'll see for yourself soon enough."

"I don't know about this—about living out here. I can't give you an answer right now."

She looked around at the others who were working, and searched for a grandmother, one who wore purples and reds and added much color, even to an ice-cream shop. She didn't find one.

"Then think about it while you're working today. If it goes well, I'd like you to start within a week or two. I always lose waitresses before summer starts. I'd love for you to move out here tomorrow, but I understand if you have some things in your life you might need to settle before up and leaving for a remote island. Anyway, I'll show you where the rags are kept and how to set tables. We're going to be getting busy soon, so we better get started."

"Okay, so the fork goes on this rim of the place mat here?" Vicki asked Ruth in a conscientious tone.

"Over this way a little more, and make sure the napkin doesn't cover up any wording on the place mat."

Ruth looked to be in her sixties, and she was as small and powerful as a breath mint. Her voice was quiet, but her words were concise, focused, and seemed to have impact. She spoke matter-of-factly, displaying an overabundance of natural common sense about everything.

"Are you okay? You seem a bit out of breath," she asked Vicki.

"I'm fine. This is a better workout than kick-boxing," Vicki lied, dropping a rag as an excuse to bend down and gasp for breath. She didn't know why she couldn't breathe. No danger lurked and, with the sun directly overhead, night stood hours away yet.

As Ruth explained the busing procedures, both women recognized that they shared common work ethics. They both set up tables with intensity, carefully aligning the silverware with pride. As Vicki folded a napkin neatly, she could almost hear teachers from her past challenging her do everything with pride and to the best of her ability.

While busing her second dirty table, Vicki glanced out at the dock. She was amazed to see boats of varying caliber—big boats, small boats, sail boats, fishing boats and yachts—pulling up to the dock. Within half an hour, voices of every accent, language, and pitch imaginable rang through the three-room restaurant. Sun-tanned people in flip-flops started lining up outside the door and down the walkway. They spoke English, French, and German. A few minutes earlier, Vicki could never have imagined people from all over the world arriving on boats for lunch.

She sprinted from table to table, wishing she had more time to talk to Ruth about island life and the job. What would she decide come three-thirty when she'd have to catch the boat back? As dirty tables piled up, she had no time to talk to anyone, only to bus. Her family used to run around together like this every summer. She felt lonely without them working by her side, and it felt uncomfortably professional to call a boss by first name instead of Mom or Dad.

"Okay, you can stop now. The boat's waiting for you down at the dock."

Ruth walked up to the dirty table she was cleaning.

"It's three-thirty already? It can't be." For the first time all afternoon, she lost her breath again.

"Well, you were busy. And you did a fine job. If you're interested, you can be back on the boat any morning with your suitcases, if that works out for you."

"You're offering me the job?"

"That's right. I'd love for you to return tomorrow, but I understand if you need more time. I'll give you up to a week to think about it, but remember, you must stay out here and work twelve days in a row."

"I'll admit," said Vicki. "When I took the boat out here, I didn't realize I had to actually live on the island."

"Did Denver show you the staff house? I asked him to take you there."

"I'm not concerned about that," she lied. No one by the name of Denver offered her a tour of the staff house, but she didn't care. She couldn't possibly live on an island with no bridge, and no recliner chair to sit up in; not at this point in her life anyway. "I don't know about all of this. I've got a lot of things to get done this summer."

"Don't we all?" Ruth picked up a ripe grapefruit left on a plate and began to peel it, dropping the peelings on Vicki's tray before pulling the juicy sections apart. "Want some?"

Vicki took one piece. The juice burst inside her mouth, a sweet, tart taste. She'd never eaten grapefruit like this in Michigan.

"Opportunity's like this ripe grapefruit," Ruth pointed out. "It's up to you if you're going to pick it before it falls from the tree."

Walking down the path to catch the boat, she could hear a drunken voice singing an old, familiar song. " . . . with Gilligan, the skipper too, the millionaire and his wife . . . the movie star, professor and Marianne . . . here on Gilligan's Isle."

Wearing cut-off jeans, the barefooted singer had a beer in one hand and a rope in the other. Next to his tiny, inexpensive, rusty old boat, a seventy-foot luxury yacht and a few cabin cruisers docked side by side, and his boat fit in as well as a grapefruit on an apple tree. As she rounded the path that led to the boathouse, she caught a glimpse of a hammock hanging between two palm trees and craved sleep. She could hardly control the urge and began walking toward the bed that was slowly swaying in the breeze.

"All aboard, and I mean you, dear! I'll take you back now," the dock master called out to her, leading her to alter her steps.

"Do you make two boat trips to the island every day, Simon?" Vicki stepped onto the boat, determined to fully understand all island transportation options, including escape routes.

"Yes. I pick up inventory or guests staying in the rooms or couples on their honeymoons, writers looking for inspiration—all sorts who want to escape the busyness in their lives. There's also employees coming and going from their days off."

He stared at her and spoke again. "Dear, everyone comes out here for a reason. They don't always know the reason until many years later, hindsight. The currents of life bring individuals to Tarpon Key. The canals we go down might not make sense as we're cruising along, but there's a reason why our motors run out of fuel, get caught up in a mangrove or run aground from time to time. Everyone needs to discover an island where they can stop and think: to think magnificent thoughts they have never had time to ponder before and to notice magnificent details they've never noticed before. You've got a decision to make, but if you turn it down, you might be pushing yourself against the direction of the wind."

"You say everyone needs to find an island. What about people living in landlocked cities?"

He laughed. "For them, discovering an island might be more of a challenge, but if they take the time, I'm sure they will find one." He turned the key in the boat's ignition, and they were off.

She put on her sunglasses, which once were rose-tinted, but recently had gotten scratched, and noticed a blue heron quietly stalking prey at the edge of the mangrove. She glanced back at the island, then bent down to fidget with her shoelace and to catch her breath.

CHAPTER SIX

SHE HAD SPENT AN interesting day on her island interview. When she returned to the condo, her parents were gone. They had caught an earlier flight back to Michigan and weren't sure how long they would be gone. The details concerning the recent sale of the businesses might take the better part of the summer to work out.

She spent the evening grocery shopping on the island, at the same store where Grandma used to take her. "Now don't be shy, you've got to eat, and I don't have much food in my refrigerator. Pick out whatever you want to eat," Grandma would say in a very loud voice as the two would slowly make their way down each aisle. "Now why are you putting *that* in the cart? Don't you want something nutritious?"

After putting the groceries away and cleaning the kitchen, ten o'clock at night crept up quickly. As she watched television, she tried catching her stubborn breath while fighting nausea and a watering mouth. She felt like a woman facing her fear of public speaking, only she feared night or death or falling asleep and dying in her sleep. She took a long shower, then she threw a towel around herself and rushed to the kitchen where she guzzled 7UP. She then devoured Saltines in hopes of stopping the nausea. Little ants were crawling inside her left arm as it fell asleep. She took hold of her arm—the heavy object connected to her shoulder—and shook it frantically. Her fingers stayed numb as she ran to the comfort of the living room. Brief, repetitious, sharp pains struck where she guessed her heart was, like the blade of a windmill breaking off in a tornado and hitting her in the chest. She self-diagnosed a heart attack and silently waited for it to happen, wondering if Rebecca had suffered, if she had tried calling out for help that night, but without a voice. She couldn't feel sorry for Rebecca, now in the arms of God. She instead felt sorry for herself, not in the arms of God.

She knew it was time to prepare for bed. In the bathroom, she examined her pupils in the mirror. Her eyes looked browner than ever, and her black pupils were too tiny in proportion to the brown. Her knees shook.

"I'm having a weird pain in my heart area," she mumbled as she climbed into bed, choosing that instead of the recliner tonight. "I don't understand what's happening to me. I used to love sleeping."

As she began taking her own pulse, Vicki noticed a spastic dark blue aura around her arm. She'd noticed things like this around everyone lately, even dogs. It meant nothing to her. She wasn't psychic, didn't read auras. Her brown eyes were teasing her. They were mad, grouchy, resentfully tired. She knew it. She promised she'd stop applying mascara. They were feeling weak, and makeup only weighed them down. Rebellious, they entered the dream world without her. At first they'd fixate on something for so long that a blink felt like an eight-hour sleep. Soon, they'd spastically begin to blink, enjoying rapid eye movement though Vicki was awake.

Lying on her back again, her heart pounded. She placed two fingers on her neck—*b'dum, b'dum, b'dum, b'dum.* Two fingers on her stomach—*b'dum, b'dum, b'dum, b'dum, b . . . b'dum.* It skipped a beat. *B'dm, b'dm, b'dm . . .* it sped up!

Was this what Rebecca felt before dying in her sleep? Imaginary ants crawling from her left arm into her feet? *Where's my paper bag?* Turning over to her left side to reach for it on the floor, she suddenly felt a powerful wave of energy shoot up from her toes and spasm in her chest, like being slapped by an octopus all over her body.

Fearful that she might die unnoticed in her bed, she bolted up from her prone position, clutching her chest, and heaved back a silent scream. Her throat felt dry, yet she couldn't stop heaving. As if escaping the dark, the bed, and the room, Vicki sprinted into the dining room and turned on the overhead light, just as someone nearly reaches the end of the haunted house and sprints past the final creature and makes it through the door.

"A heart attack. I'm sure of it. I'm sure I just had a heart attack," she cried out loud in the car, just after running a red light on her way to the hospital. "Honk at me all you like, idiot. If only you knew why I'm driving like this." She crossed intersections as if she had sirens and emergency lights on her car, and her only comfort came from knowing that shortly she'd be in the company of medical professionals, who were awake and alert, as she was, at one o'clock in the morning.

"I've got a heart attack victim on her way," she shouted into her cell phone. "She's only twenty-one years old. I've given her aspirins. We'll be right there. Have everything ready." The phone went dead.

Running into the hospital's emergency room, Vicki accepted a nurse's offer and sat down in a wheel chair.

"Are you the one who called us?"

"Yes. I am."

"You look so young and healthy," said the skeptical nurse. "Have you been taking any drugs that might induce a heart attack?"

"Drugs?"

"Yes, cocaine."

"Of course not. I can't believe you're questioning me over this. I'm possibly dying, and you're asking me if I'm on drugs."

"The doctor will take a look at you in a minute." And the nurse walked away.

"A minute? I don't think I've got a minute. This is the emergency room!" yelled Vicki. She turned around to look at an older woman pacing back and forth. "I've just had a heart attack!"

"So did my husband," she said. At that moment, nurses wheeled a man wrapped in white sheets past them, his face nearly green. "Oh honey, I'm here, I'm here." The woman ran alongside him. "You're going to live, they tell me. You're going to be fine, sweetie. I'm with you."

As Vicki lay on the table, the doctor hooked her up to an electrocardiograph.

"This records the electrical activity of your heart. We're going to look for irregularities in the muscle, blood supply, or neural control."

Vicki looked up at the doctor as he placed sticky things all over her chest. Inwardly she felt guilty because she liked the wheelchair better than the recliner tonight.

"Describe your symptoms to me, Vicki."

"A viselike squeezing sensation beneath my breastbone, pain radiating from the front of my chest."

She did feel that way, but in truth the vivid description came right from the pages of her grandmother's medical encyclopedia that she had carefully studied the night before. She figured she'd get further by communicating with the doctor in his own terms.

"You are describing a heart attack. But no, rest assured, it is not a heart attack. Have you been under any kind of stress lately, Vicki?" the doctor asked. "Because it might be that you're experiencing extreme anxiety, which is routinely mistaken for cardiac or respiratory disorders."

"Anxiety? No. I'm a pretty stable person. Extremely in control of my life, Doc."

"Have you been under any kind of unusual stress lately, like a traumatic event or something?"

"No, none. Well, just finals at school." She wanted badly to tell the doctor, this stranger, that her friend died of a heart attack in her sleep, and that she had skipped the funeral. She longed to share with someone that her grandmother had also died recently of a heart attack in her sleep. She craved attention from someone who might listen, someone who would put his arms around her and cry along with her. Maybe the doctor would have time for coffee. Maybe he would want to listen.

"I want to assure you that you are not dying of a heart attack. You'll be fine, although your blood pressure has literally skyrocketed. You just went through serious progressive stages of hyperventilation, and the next step, after the wave, would have been to pass out."

"So my heart itself is okay?" she asked.

"I'd say so, yes!"

"Can you prescribe something for me?"

"There are options, but the problem with some of the medications is that once you go off them, the attacks may start again," he explained. "You could talk to a psychiatrist about that. My suggestion is that if it starts to happen again, Vicki, and it probably will, you should try talking yourself out of it. Convince yourself that you're not going to die from this, and just relax when you start feeling the shortness of breath. Hopefully you can stop it from getting to this point again, but it'll take some strong convincing on your part."

"Am I going crazy, Doc?"

"Absolutely not! Anxiety disorders are the most common mental disorders in the United States."

"Mental disorder?" How dare he diagnose her with a mental condition! She was the one studying psychology. She was the one wanting to help *others* with mental conditions.

"I'm not saying you have a serious mental or anxiety disorder. Just that you let your thoughts affect your body. If you let it get out of control, you may need treatment. This might mean drugs, psychotherapy, behavior modification, or relaxation training. Alone or in any combination."

"What triggers this sort of thing?"

"Well, some learning theorists say anxiety is learned when innate fears occur together with previously neutral objects or events. I don't know. You need to figure out what your fear is."

"What my fear is?"

"Yes, what do you fear most in life?"

"I have no idea."

"Well, figure it out, then face it in whatever way you like. It might require time. I hope you're ready to embark on a journey because facing one's fears is no simple trip."

Back in bed again that night, the spastic wave returned. It was not nearly as bad as being slapped by an octopus. It felt more like the sharp tingles from picking up a jellyfish.

She eventually fell into a light sleep, but frequently she'd wake and breathe into the paper lunch bag that slept next to her.

"I'm going to sit up all night, because every time I lie down, my toes get numb again," she moaned quietly to herself. "And someday, I'm going to invent quieter lunch bags!"

Her shortness of breath lasted for hours, and she dreaded the darkness called night. Sitting up in bed, as the doctor had ordered, she told herself she wasn't going to die and that her shortness of breath originated from her own mind. Throughout the rest of the night, she'd drift hesitantly into a shallow sleep, then her inner voice would wake her. Her neck felt tender from resting against the wooden bed board, but she'd rather feel a stiff neck than all the other crazy things, she decided. Her eyes, shrinking into puffiness, watched through the blinds, and at four-thirty the moon slowly disappeared behind a pattern of passing clouds. At five o'clock, the bedroom walls flickered with the headlights of passing cars. At five-thirty, birds began chirping—probably year-round Florida birds that didn't bother flying north for the summer. Or maybe they were mockingbirds, Florida's state bird. But if they were, she should hear them mimicking the sounds of other animals. But no, they were just normal *chirp chirps*, the happy, stress-free kind.

Looking at the birds of the air, she felt disappointed with herself. If they weren't worried, why should she be? As if worrying might actually add a single hour to life. She listened to the birds as if hearing their chirps for the first time.

She got out of bed and made a note to schedule an appointment with a psychologist, one specializing in anxiety. She got back into bed. If she took the job on the island, it would be difficult to make routine therapy appointments. She climbed out of bed and crossed it off her list. She climbed back into bed. She knew she was making excuses, so she started talking immediately to someone who required no appointment at all. She started talking to the Wonderful Counselor there in her bed.

She prayed to Almighty God, and then the sun rose and the show outside her window ended. Daylight, and the sun, that was all very good, she thought. She felt like a hypocrite. How dare a believer in God fear death? She had hardly discussed death, ever. During coffee, conversation and crayon time at the café, it had never crept up. Perhaps no one allowed it to.

In college, she took classes on everything from world religions to ancient philosophy to chemistry to biology, but everything focused on life. Not death. So how dare a believer in God fear death? Well, it was a great question because she did. She continued praying to the Wonderful Counselor even after getting out of bed.

The next morning she drove to a local island coffee shop, desperate for caffeine, but more than ever she wished she had Grandma's recipe for instant gratification, whatever it might be. She could surely use some instant gratification right now.

As she walked up the steps to the shop, her feet felt heavy. Amused at herself, she looked down to see if she was wearing her wooden shoes by mistake, instead of her sandals.

"I'll have a large, nonfat caffè mocha. No, make that a latté," she requested, then caught a glimpse of her tangled hair in the reflection in the window, and it reminded her of the restless night before. "I'll be right back."

"What's your name?" asked the woman behind the counter.

For a moment, Vicki went blank.

"I need a name, so I can call you when your drink is made." She actually paused another three seconds before answering, "Vicki."

"Is that your final answer?" The woman laughed.

"I think so. It's the simple questions in life that catch me off guard." She walked into the bathroom, known for its colorful magic marker scribbles on the walls. Anyone desiring to leave a footprint or a piece of their soul behind, for a chance at immortality, can pick up a marker and scribble something, anything, on the bathroom walls of the coffee shop.

As she shut and then locked the door behind her, she heard voices in her head. She saw scribbles. Together the voices and the scribbles screamed to be heard. As if tossed into a windmill on a wildly windy day, they whirled around madly, yelling out the one- or two-worded goals scribbled in crayon on the white paper tablecloth. She heard her dreams, like psychotic little voices in her head, crying out louder and louder. "Semester in Spain, semester in Spain, semester in Spain," the voices screamed. They screamed so quickly that they turned into a tongue twister, and then switched to, "summer on island, summer on island, summer on island, stingray shuffle all summer long."

As she left the restroom, she heard her name called out and the woman handed her a hot cup. "Enjoy."

Taking a cup that weighed about two pounds, Vicki felt like a starving, stubborn dog, a mutt walking the streets. She sipped the coffee, and then shut her eyes. The voices in her head shouted, *Victoria, Victoria.* She drowned them in another sip. After her coffee, she went out to eat at a restaurant Grandma had taken her to many times, and then after breakfast, she stopped to say hello to a parrot.

"Hello," she said.

There was no reply from the parrot.

"Hello."

The bird looked away.

"Come on, now. Isn't hello usually the first thing they teach you birds?"

There was still no reply.

"Boo!" She said. "Peekaboo!" She played with it. "Polly want a cracker? A biscotti instead?"

The bird just stared.

"What? You don't like small talk? You think I'm shallow? Well, I'm not. What do you want to discuss. You tell me."

"Take island job. Take island job," the colorful bird replied. "You'd be a fool not to, a fool, a fool."

Vicki looked around to see if anyone else might have heard what she had just heard. No witnesses, just the other macaws, parrots, and cockatoos on display. Unless the parrot was talking about its own job offer, she was convinced it was a message, perhaps from Grandma, who had loved to talk to the caged birds. She walked away, laughing, and the bird laughed, too.

Thanks to divine intervention working through a bird, she now knew she had to accept the job on the island, but first, she needed sleep. She knew she wouldn't get any, so instead she opted for an attempt at rest and relaxation, and going to a concert at Centennial Park in Fort Myers would give her something to do, an excuse to stay up late.

"This will sure get his attention," a woman sitting on a blanket said to her husband as she drew "We Love you B. J. Thomas" in thick red marker on poster board.

Vicki unfolded her blanket, spread it on the lawn, and sat down next to the couple. She missed her family and knew they would have loved to be here with her. She grew up on this music and had seen this guy many times in concerts back home.

To pass time before the concert started, Vicki walked over to the bridge and looked out at the Caloosahatchee River below. She pulled her camera out of her purse and peered through it, waiting for the clouds to shift before snapping the picture. It had to be just right. She always did this. She always tried taking perfect pictures, as if one day they might hang in a museum.

But the clouds weren't moving. "Oh well," she mumbled under her breath. "*Hasta luego.*" And she took the camera down from her face.

"Would you like me to take a picture with you in it?" A man in his late twenties wearing sporty sunglasses got off a black bike with no kickstand and laid it down on the cement.

"No thank you," she said.

"Are you sure?"

"Well, okay." She handed him the disposable camera she had bought the day Rebecca wanted to take photos of a frozen Lake Michigan. Now she felt eager to use up all the pictures and get them developed, hoping she would have at least one shot of her friend in the twenty-four exposures.

As she stood in front of the setting sun, her eyes burned. It didn't help that she had poured an ocean of eyedrops into them before the concert. She opened her eyes extra wide in an effort to hide the signs of sleep deprivation that might show up through the lens of the camera. She didn't want the good-looking man taking the photo to notice the bags under her eyes. He didn't. Good.

"Do you speak Spanish, or is *hasta luego* your main phrase?" he asked.

"I'm learning."

"*Muy bien,*" he replied.

"You speak Spanish?" she asked.

"My parents are missionaries. I spent some time in South America as a kid."

"Well, that sounds interesting," she said with a smile. He took a few steps back and turned the camera, making it a vertical picture. "Oh, the music is starting. I don't want to miss the opening."

On "opening" he snapped the photo and handed the camera back to Vicki. The sun setting behind him made his sandy brown hair glow, and she noticed how gorgeous he was, like a Roman prince of sorts. The only thing missing was his halo. He wore a deep green T-shirt and black shorts. And he rode a black bike, not a flying white horse. *If he's a B. J. Thomas fan, Dad will give us permission to elope.*

"My name is Ben O'Connor," he said.

"Nice to meet you. I'm Vicki. You live around here?"

"I do," he said. "And I bike just about everywhere, except when I'm working." He handed the camera back to her.

"Well, thanks for taking the picture."

"So what do you do? Are you in school, or do you work?"

"I'm in school in Michigan. I'm on summer break."

"Michigan? Never been there. Nice state?"

"Great. They grow lots of Christmas trees, and the whole state has about fifty-four thousand farms." She couldn't believe her answer, although she knew his looks had caught her completely off guard, but she didn't want to have an intelligent conversation. She wanted to stare. Maybe she could have *written* a great answer to his question, but it wasn't an essay contest, just a conversational question. Grandma would have loved this one in a letter.

"Pride in one's state. I like that," he said.

She felt a smile stretching from ear to ear, and her face growing hot. "I'm only here for the summer, and I've got to find a job, quickly," she added.

"Good luck."

"Thanks. Do you work around here?" Her sentences were becoming choppy. She couldn't breathe.

"I'm a commercial architect here in Fort Myers. I moved down from Mississippi after I finished school."

"You like it here?"

"Love it. Oh, turn around, you've got to see the size of the sun now."

"It's blinding. Hey, I better go. The concert is starting."

"Would you like to have a drink with me after the concert? There's a piano bar just across the street."

"Thanks, but I'm a bit under the weather right now. Lack of sleep."

"Well, maybe we'll meet again." He shook her hand lightly.

"Maybe."

Vicki sang along with the words being sung on stage as she walked back over to the blanket, "Life has had its hard times when I felt the chill of winter—can't forget the night when my sweet Jesus slipped away."

The man next to her kneeled in the grass and videotaped the stage. The woman with the sign swayed back and forth.

"Here, do us a favor, will you? Bring these flowers up to him now, on this song. I love this song," the woman, who looked about her mother's age, whispered in her ear. She handed Vicki a bouquet of lilies, but Vicki handed them back. "Gosh, no. I can't walk up there in front of all these people."

"Go on. You're a young woman, full of life—go for it."

"They're your flowers. You bring them up."

"I can't. I have bad knees and don't want to fall on the way. Please! It would mean so much to me. My husband's busy with his camera, and I just want B. J. to get the flowers. I don't care if they come directly from me. I can live vicariously through you for a moment."

"Okay. I'll do it, I guess."

"You'll be glad you did. Why is it we always regret the things we didn't do in life more than the things we did? You won't regret this."

As Vicki walked up to the stage, she could feel her heart dancing in rhythm with the music, and she feared that walking too close to the speakers might trigger the pain. She didn't want to die, not now, not tomorrow, not ever. And especially not with the beautiful man on his bike watching her from across the street. As she carefully walked around the blankets spread across the grass, so as not to step on any fingers, she glanced at the lilies in her hand. They wore natural purple, blue, and white suits with ruffled blouses underneath. Somehow the lilies, once alive in the fields, reminded her not to worry about tomorrow, for tomorrow will worry about itself. She was also reminded that tulips belong to the lily family.

"Thank you," B. J. Thomas said softly into the microphone, and his voice echoed through all of downtown Fort Myers. His song had ended, and he bent down, hugged her, and took the flowers.

The crowd screamed, the woman cried, her husband kept videotaping, and Ben sat on his bike watching from the road. Later, Ben showed up at her blanket and handed her his phone number. "It's too loud to talk now, but I'd love to go out. Call me if you'd like, if you're not dating B. J Thomas, that is." He laughed.

Vicki watched Ben take off on his bike. He was the sort of man she was attracted to, but she didn't want to meet Mr. Right too soon in life. Admittedly, she viewed men as obstacles to all the things she wanted to do in life, before settling down. Then again, Ben was the type of man who would look quite sexy, even eating a Buffalo wing.

They spent every day together for the next several weeks. Their favorite thing was to walk the beach, and they did this for hours, always starting at the Sanibel Lighthouse. Sometimes they walked knee-deep in the water and sometimes on the white, crunchy shoreline, shuffling their feet as they went, forewarning stingrays to swim away. It was the same beach evening after evening, but each time it looked different, just as a painting on the wall looked different with the lights turned off and the shades shut, compared to when the lights were on or the sun was striking it from the window.

As they walked and held hands, Ben distracted her with frequent kisses. Each kiss felt like lightning, an electrical discharge between two clouds, and she liked being a cloud. They took a late afternoon Saturday bike ride through the J. N. "Ding" Darling National Wildlife Refuge and spotted alligators everywhere on the 4.5-mile, one-way road. Once, a gator decided to slowly cross the road in front of them, so they stopped and waited for as long as it took, as if waiting for a train to pass. They rented canoes and paddled the two-mile Commodore Creek canoe trail, beginning at Tarpon Bay, the heart of the refuge. They saw egrets, pelicans, and herons above and hermit and horseshoe crabs below.

Later they stopped for a treat at the Bubble Room on Captiva Island, and with every bite of the Red Velvet Cake she ate, Vicki moaned. Each forkful became a moment spent in instant bliss and carried her to some faraway world, a winter wonderland of sorts where no one worried about anything, a place in her dreams where whimsical characters pranced around to Christmas carols while stuffing stockings with toys and candy. She noticed Ben staring at her, so she stopped moaning, but continued eating the cake until the very last red crumb was gone, and then she licked the cream cheese frosting left on her plate. When she finished, she felt full, too full for guilt. Could this be the recipe for instant gratification her grandmother had promised to give her?

They enjoyed a theatrical and musical performance at the local theater, followed by dancing at a local club.

One day, as they walked the beach of Sanibel, they noticed the sand dollars, once buried out in the sand bars, were now arriving in the water near the shore to mate. This quietly reminded Vicki that time was moving on, and she would need to take a job quickly.

The more time she spent with Ben, the less she wanted to leave for the job on Tarpon Key and so she blew it off, not bothering to call the island. She no longer cared if they gave the job to someone else. The busier she kept herself, the less she thought about Rebecca's death. The more she experienced her shortness of breath and other symptoms, the more doctors she visited. They ruled out hypoglycemia, hyperthyroidism, and suggested she go off caffeine.

Enough time passed for her to wean herself from coffee, develop a withdrawal headache, overcome that headache, switch to herbal tea, realize that her symptoms continued and life wasn't as good without coffee, and reintroduce that glorious cup of morning coffee and a biscotti to her daily routine.

One night, as she and Ben sat on a blanket, listening to a band of retired jazz players in the same downtown Fort Myers Park where they had first met, she knew she needed to act soon. Ruth had left a message on her answering machine regarding the island opportunity. There was someone else interested in the job, so she would have to respond immediately if she still wanted it. Vicki never mentioned it to Ben. He knew nothing about her interview on the island.

As she picked a handful of grass, she noticed it was longer than when she sat here at the B. J. Thomas concert. She felt a new urgency to take the offer she had on the island. On the other hand, she noticed herself saying good night to Ben, and then counting down the hours until they met again. How dare Mr. Right sit next to her? She hadn't planned on him showing up for years yet, after she accomplished all her other goals. Somehow she'd discover a flaw in him, something to remove him immediately from the Mr. Right category.

"Ben, there are things I want to do in my life, lots of things. What if I don't do them? What if I lose control and never accomplish any of my dreams?" They lay on a blanket on their backs, looking up at the darkening Florida sky.

"You are in control. You make choices every day, right? He asked, massaging her hand.

She nodded.

"We're all forced to make daily choices, and these choices either bring us a step closer or a step further from our goals."

"What if I die before getting there?"

"Getting where?"

"Getting to where I want to be in life? Achieving my goals."

"Vicki, you might kick the bucket before reaching your goals. I might die before reaching mine. We all might. That's why the journey toward our goals, the daily steps, must mean something more."

"You're so philosophical," she said.

"Do you like philosophy?"

"Yes."

"Then I'll continue. Make the steps toward your goals count and make them fun."

"How?"

"I'd love for you to meet my mother one of these days. She would tell you to hop, skip, jump, run backward, or walk passionately toward your goals. Those steps should add pleasure to your daily life, and if they don't, well, maybe you should reevaluate your goals to begin with."

She liked his answer. She liked him. So much so that he suddenly looked like a roadblock, standing between her and all her dreams. She would disqualify him quickly and toss him into her Sea of Forgetfulness. "Do you foresee traveling in your future?"

"Vicki, I've lived all over the country, the world for that matter."

"But have you seen all you want to see?"

"For now, yes. With my parents working as missionaries, I grew up living all over South America. We spent most of our time in Peru and Brazil. I've asked my parents to send my photo albums, so I can show you. You won't believe the way in which people out there live. They have no idea what a department store is or even a car, yet they're deeply happy and it's a different kind of happy. There's a certain happiness about them that has nothing to do with the walls in which they live or the car they drive. It still blows my mind today, thinking about the people I've met. We would share our faith, they'd accept it as though they were grabbing onto a tree branch while standing in sinking sand, then they'd go on to eventually teach us about faith. I guess they grasped it so easily because so much of who they were came from the inside, and that's where faith is."

Vicki was in awe. She wanted him to go on and on, telling her stories about these people who lived along the Amazon River, not in homes, but in huts. She begged him to tell her as much as he could remember about growing up as a missionary in South America. The more she heard, the more she wanted to know. She listened until he could no longer think of anything else to say.

"Will you show me your pictures?" asked Vicki. "I want to see these people."

"Of course. I'll show them to you this summer. It's going to be a good summer, spending it with you," he said. "And fall will be good, too, because of you."

Why hadn't she told him about her plans for going to Spain come fall? Maybe she wouldn't go without Rebecca. She didn't know whether she could take off for the international adventure that her now-deceased friend would have died for. Surely she should tell Ben of her friend's death and her reaction to it, and of her breathing troubles, her panic attacks. No, she couldn't let Ben think her crazy. Was that why she didn't tell him? She took pride in always having life under control and, lately, she couldn't understand how her mind could be crazy enough to cause the shortness of breath episodes. She feared she might be losing touch with her saneness. She didn't want to disclose everything and scare Ben away. The night sky was clear, and she didn't feel like introducing any rain just yet.

"Are you sure you're done traveling, seeing the world?" Her Mr. Right would surely want to travel.

"Done. Here to stay. I need to belong somewhere, to establish friends that live in stationary homes, not huts that float down the Amazon. It's tough saying good-bye every time you really start caring for someone."

She liked him. She liked his answer, only she had things she wanted to see in the world, many things. All at once, she knew she had to say good-bye.

Dear Grandma,

It might not be the right decision, but I've made it. I'm leaving for an island in the morning. And that's all I'm going to say about that.
The realization that I'm not going to live on this earth forever, that my life here is not permanent, shocked me. I've never thought about death before. I never gave it any status in my future list of things to do. Now, I watch Bugs Bunny falling off a cliff, and I have a panic attack.

Just one more thing, Grandma. I never wrote about the day Rebecca cried in front of the mirror for an hour because she cut her own hair uneven and, inch by inch, she tried to fix it, only to be left with more hair on the floor than on her head. I stepped in with tissues, a fresh can of hair spray, and a curling iron, but the damage was done. She was upset because she had a date. Rebecca never could see the beauty in her naturally thick hair, whether long or short. She could see the beauty in everything else, including months of Michigan's dark, gloomy skies and dirty snow, but she could never see the beauty in herself. That's all.

P.S. I don't feel sorry for you at all, Grandma. You are with God. I guess I feel sorry for myself, and how badly I wish you were here with me instead.

CHAPTER SEVEN

AS SHE STOOD UNDER the bamboo hut, waiting for the boat to arrive, she felt like jumping up and down over her decision to take the job on the island. She wanted to shout with excitement at leaving behind her insomnia and all that came with it.

The silence now reminded her of her past weeks spent with Ben. She should have told him about her decision to take a job and to live on a remote island. She had planned on telling him in person, but then he flew to a last-minute business meeting with investors in Miami. She would ask around on the island for a laptop so she could send him an email. No, she would tell him in person on one of her days off.

Taking the dock master's hand and stepping onto the boat at Island Marina felt like déjà vu, but this time she had a couple of suitcases with her.

As they pulled away from the dock, Vicki stared until she could no longer see the bamboo hut. She felt a panic attack coming on and didn't know what to blame – the speed of the boat, the wind hitting her face, or the what-if scenario playing itself out in her mind. Breathing deeply, she could taste the salty air on her tongue. What if the boat tipped over? What if it ran into another boat? What if it sank for no reason at all?

None of that happened. Instead, the boat pulled up to the remote island of Tarpon Key, where a man standing under a crooked, petite key lime tree walked up to the dock to greet them.

"Hello there, and welcome to Tarpon Key. My name is Denver. I'll get your stuff and take ya on a tour that leads to the staff house."

Without allowing Vicki to lift a finger, the skinny man wearing a tight, black Bad Company T-shirt loaded her suitcases from the boat onto a golf cart. He wore his hair pulled back into a long, frizzy black ponytail with split ends sticking out everywhere.

"Is this here all the stuff you got?" he asked. "You gotta see what all these waitresses bring out here with them. You got nothing compared to them."

Exactly, she thought. She'd planned to pack lightly for her first days on the island. That way she could easily grab onto the helicopter rescue ropes in the middle of the night if needed.

"The tour starts right here at the boathouse," he said, helping her into the cart, which was parked behind the red brick building. "This is where everyone arrives. Yep, this is where everyone's journey begins."

A grandmother sat in a white wooden rocking chair on the shady side of the boathouse, humming to a crying baby, his nose running and his fist in his mouth.

"Just as you arrived here, you'll also leave here, rocking on arrival and rocking on departure," he said as the golf cart took off at full speed past the boathouse, then the restaurant, then down a winding sandy pathway through the subtropical jungle. They slowed down as they once again drew near to the water and approached a cozy-looking lean-to stocked with roasting sticks and giant-sized striped sitting cushions.

"We've reached no-no point," he said as he slowed the cart near a pile of logs next to the lean-to.

"Did you say no-no point?" She asked. Perhaps her decision to come out here was all part of some boisterous joke.

"Yep, a major destination. It's time to learn what you can and cannot do. Do *not* build a fire here in the summer. If you *do* build a fire, do *not* dump the empty marshmallow bags on the ground. I repeat, do *not* build a fire here in the summer. If you *do*, do *not* consume alcoholic beverages while building a fire here in the summer. If you do drink while building a fire here in the summer, do not drink to get drunk. If you do get drunk while building a summertime fire, do not burn the island down. If it looks like ya might burn the island down, you're just a few feet from the water, so grab some buckets from under the lean-to and run like hotcakes to the water."

"You just totally confused..."

"What? Ya don't know what hotcakes are?"

"Of course I do, but why..."

"Watch it. No talking back, ya hear?" said the scrawny man, on a power trip with his golf cart and his warnings.

The cart picked up speed again, leaving sight of the water and heading toward the center of the island, passing a shaded picnic table where a woman dipped into a picnic basket for a bottle of wine. The man beside her was kissing her neck.

"Love is in the air," sang Denver, stopping right in front of the couple. "As you spend time here, just be sure you're with the right person. It's better to picnic alone than to picnic with the wrong person, if ya know what I mean."

The couple stared, and Denver stared right back at them, before starting the cart again. Vicki could see the faded red brick lighthouse tower growing larger before them. To her surprise, it wasn't as large as it looked. It was simply built on a hill.

"What can I say at this point? It's the middle of the island," he said, tossing his hands into the air, which meant they were no longer steering the cart. "At this point we must distinguish between dreams and obsessions."

As the golf cart left the island's midpoint, Vicki noticed Denver was hardly holding onto the wheel, as if the cart made its own way on the path, naturally arriving at each destination.

"How many paths are on the island?" asked Vicki.

"Just one, and you're on it. Of course, you can venture off the path at any time," he said. "You like music?"

"Yes. Why?"

"I play the guitar. I sing too. Write my own lyrics. I'll sing for ya later, but not now because we've gotta venture off the path for a minute."

Vicki bounced up and down, biting her tongue and holding onto the side of the golf cart as if she were on a roller coaster ride. "Keep your arms and hands in the car at all times," shouted Denver with the kind of authority in his voice that a lifeguard uses to stop a swimmer from passing the buoy. "I repeat, keep loose limbs inside the cart."

Within two minutes they had arrived at a bungalow on stilts. It looked like a tree house that neighborhood kids had teamed together to build, with only a little help from their parents. "This is our next stop. It's not a required stop, just a choice that's off the beaten path," said Denver as he parked the golf cart under the stilted structure. "It's an option, and you've chosen it. Welcome."

"What is it?"

"The staff house. We call him Old Mr. Two-Face. His east side faces the trees and gets a little sunrise peeking through the branches. His west side faces the Gulf of Mexico and gets the sunset. We don't know which side is happier."

"Well, the sunset and the water side must be happier," she said as they walked around to the west side, with its faded green paint falling off like skin after an exfoliation treatment and just a few tiny, round windows that looked like sunglasses. "Then again, it's a mess. Too much time in the afternoon sun. It needs a serious paint job."

They walked around to the east side. "Maybe this side is the happy side," stated Denver. They could barely see the paint through the massive tree branches that were slapping it in the face. For a moment, when the breeze pushed one particular branch out of the way, they could see a deep green paint job that still looked fresh, without any sun damage. The windows were oval, and larger than those on the other side, but could hardly be seen, like eyes covered by out-of-control hair.

"This side certainly has the younger-looking skin and the bigger eyes, but it's so dark back here. My guess is that the other side is happier." Then it struck her. Were they really judging which side of the bungalow, a nonliving object, was happier?

They walked around to the side of the building, and Denver carried her suitcase up the steps.

"Meet Mr. Screened Front Door," he said, stopping at the top of the flight of stairs. "There's an island squirrel that loves to sneak in from time to time, so we don't lock Mr. S.F.D. You just gotta give him a light push, like this. He don't like to be kicked too hard now."

He kicked the door open with his foot and stepped on a walnut, cracking its shell. "We keep that bowl of nuts there on the floor at all times for Mr. Squirrel," he added.

Glancing at the filthy, sandy floors, Vicki looked around for a female to convince her she wasn't living in a staff house full of men. "*Mr.* Two-face, *Mr.* Front Door, and *Mr.* Squirrel. Are there any women objects here?" she asked.

"Oh no, we don't objectify women here. Is that one of those female lib test questions?"

"Well, I was hoping to see something female."

"Will this do? I wasn't sure if I was going to introduce you or not, but, this here is the public bathroom. We call her Miss Juanita. Don't worry. You're gonna have one in your bedroom." Denver slammed the toilet seat shut with his foot.

"Sounds like you've given this tour many times." Vicki coughed, allergic to something and perhaps everything.

"Every few months, people, they're coming and going." With a laid back slouch, Denver slowly made his way down the long hallway like a piece of wood floating down a river, and each time he came to a door he'd stop as if getting stuck for a brief moment on a branch at the side of the riverbed.

"This is my room," he said, then continued on. "And this is Ray, the bartender's room. He spends most of his time at the other staff house," he said, and continued again. "Way on the end is Howard the potato peeler's room, and up those stairs is the attic. It's bigger than our rooms and spooky, because it has a window on both the east and west. Some say it's Mr. Two-Faces' two personalities combined into one big monster. It's vacant right now, but we'll fill it soon."

"Why is this place coed?" It disturbed her. She didn't want to live in a staff house with the same men she'd be working with, men she didn't know.

"Yeah, there's, um, I'd say, um, let me count, and let me use my fingers to count. Three, four, okay, there's about six of us living in this staff house, and the rest live in the other one. We call that one Two- Faced Junior. Mainly the cooks are over in Two-Faced Junior." He tossed his cigarette on the tile floor and stomped it.

"I think it's dead," said Vicki.

"Gotta be sure with all this trash on the floor. Can't let a single spark go."

"So, where's my room?"

"Hark! Your room is down the hall. I'm guessing you're ready to drop your anchor about now." Denver slipped on a torn magazine page lying on the floor, but his reflexes were surprisingly agile, and he continued floating onward. She had to bend down to make it through the splintered wooden door, painted the color of an old dock. Inside, the walls were painted the color of a swamp coated with light moss or mold.

"This is your boat slip," said Denver.

"What are you talking about? This is my room? There's no furniture!"

She ran over to the one and only tiny round window and glanced out. "Thank God!" she declared. "I'm on the side facing the water and the sunset."

"The newcomer always starts with just a mattress. The next time someone quits and leaves the island, we hold a sort of auction based on good old seniority. You'll get to grab one piece of furniture just as soon as someone else leaves the island."

"Oh. There are no sheets on the mattress." Vicki pointed to the mattress on the floor, then looked down at her sandals. She could barely see her plum-colored toenail polish hidden under the sand. "And they don't supply us with towels? I should have asked more questions during the interview."

"Don't worry. I've got an extra sheet and pillowcase you can use. I'll bring it to ya later. It ain't any problem at all!" Denver flipped the mattress over to hide yellow-and-brown stains. "You don't want to sleep on that side. The springs are popping out."

"Oh, dear Lord." She knew that if she said such a thing, she owed God the respect of saying a prayer. *Oh dear Lord, I should have declined this job. I would be happier had I not taken this opportunity. I want to trust in You. Did You put me here, or did I put me here? That is what I struggle with most. How do I know if You are leading me or if I'm making wrong decisions completely on my own? Well, regardless, I'm begging You for help.*

"Please don't leave me," she whined.

"I don't have to leave ya. I can stay a bit longer," said Denver, plopping himself down on her mattress. "Ya like your room?"

She held her breath a moment because, when she inhaled, her heart ripped. She could only blame herself for not asking more questions when she was interviewed, and for lying to Ruth about the tour she never took.

"Denver, you never showed me the staff house the day I was interviewed."

"You never asked," he replied.

"So, do we get to vote people off this island?"

"Hey," he said. "You don't have to like me, but ya better like Mr. Two-Face. He knows when someone doesn't like him."

"Mr. Two-Face is a bungalow! It's not a person!"

"I'm warning you. Be nice to him," he whispered.

"I don't know what kind of medication you're taking, but this is an inanimate object that we're in. I don't know why we are talking about him, it, whatever, in the first place, as if it was alive."

"You better say something nice about him, or he might scare ya. You've gotta see the good in things, even when it's hard to see, or your fears will really scare ya."

"My, isn't that profound!" she declared.

"Well? Can't you give a compliment?"

"I like his long legs. I've never lived in a house on stilts before. We don't have stilted homes where I come from. Although a lock on my door would be nice," she said, examining her exfoliated bedroom door.

"Trust me, now."

"Trust you? I don't know you."

"You'll be safe. We're all courteous here. And don't mind the floors.

Without pavement on the island, they can't stay clean. No one's to blame for it. Are you the clean type?"

"You could say that." She wasn't going to tell him that as a kid she'd dust the head of every doll and vacuum her own carpet once a week. "I'm an extreme neat-freak. In fact, I had this horrible habit for a while."

"Sure, I understand. Alcohol? Drugs?"

"No, nothing like that!" Dressed in a pastel-colored floral print sundress, she stared around the room as she spoke. "We're talking about cleaning, aren't we? I used to spray my light bulbs with Windex until they'd explode. That's before I learned to turn them off and let them cool before spraying them."

"Yeah, reminds me of rehab. This might take some getting used to. But hey, I better get my bones back to the kitchen. You just make yourself at home here. Oh, been meaning to ask, are you from England or something? What's that sweet sound to your voice?"

"Oh, it's probably my Dutch accent. I'm from Holland. Thanks for the ride and showing me around. You've been accommodating!"

She inwardly scolded herself for always acting overly courteous to strangers, like a Dutch dancer welcoming tourists to the Tulip Time Festival.

"Whoa! You've come a long, long ways," said Denver. "Welcome to America. I hope Mr. Two-Face shares his wisdom with you."

"I don't mean the Holland in Europe. I'm from this country. Holland, Michigan. Have you ever heard of Michigan? It's a state in this country."

"I'll bet my brother was there. I've got a brother who has gone every place you could imagine. We don't have much in common. I don't like his life, and he disagrees with mine."

She found herself ignoring the scrawny man standing before her. She could care less about his lifestyle, or his brother's, and only wanted to think about all that she had left behind. She forced herself to yawn, which always meant stolen incoming oxygen. She opened her suitcases, paused, and decided to leave her clothes where they were. Ruth expected her in the restaurant for training.

Ruth lived on the island, but not in the staff house. Instead, the owners provided her with her own tiny cottage, somewhere on the island off the beaten path. She handled everything from scheduling the wait staff to conducting employee meetings to controlling inventory. Above the Jimmy Buffet music, she matter-of-factly explained everything—from the potato salad or coleslaw choice, to telling customers, "Yes, the shrimp deluxe is served hot and in the shells, so you'll need to peel them."

Vicki periodically glanced out at the Gulf of Mexico, topped with bobbing boats, then returned to taking notes with the intensity of a reporter gathering something newsworthy.

"You're a type-A like I was once. I can see it in you, but hey, you don't need to write all this down." Ruth looked her straight in the eyes.

"Shorthand. Learned it in college," replied Vicki. "So you *were* a Type-A. And you're not anymore?"

"Nope. Gave it up. Bad for the heart."

"Ruth, if you don't mind my asking, what made you come out to this island? I'm curious."

"Well, first, tell me why *you* decided to come here."

"Money. I needed a job."

Ruth laughed. "Of course you did, but there are more convenient jobs than this. Let's dig a bit deeper now. Why are you standing on a remote, primitive mangrove in the middle of nowhere when you could be waiting tables at one of a zillion places back in civilization?"

"I have no idea. I'm surprised by it myself. Maybe because this place is so gorgeous that I couldn't turn down the offer." In reality, Ben was the gorgeous object she had trouble turning down, and escaping to an island only made it easier.

"Wrong answer, definitely wrong answer. When is the last time you stopped what you were doing and allowed yourself to truly breathe?"

"I breathe daily. I just don't stop what I'm doing to breathe."

Ruth laughed. "We need to stop and breathe. Sure, it sounds odd because breathing is natural but, really, we need to breathe deeper than we are accustomed to."

"Who has time to actually stop and breathe, Ruth?"

"No one. We have to make time. Listen, if you're interested, I practice yoga every night at midnight on the deck of the old houseboat down by the dock—the dock located on the back of the island, the one no one uses. Just follow the trail back there, and you can't miss it. I invite anyone who feels like joining me. Sometimes it's just me. Other times I have up to five people showing up."

"Thanks, but I'm not a yoga person. I think it would completely bore me."

"Are you a perfectionist as well as a Type-A?"

"Yes, I guess I am."

"Well, that's quite arrogant of you to admit."

"What do you mean by that?"

"First, you are far from perfect and never will be. Second, you are measuring your perfection based on what the world claims to be perfect, and that is a shallow measuring device. Give me an example of your so-called perfectionist efforts."

"That's easy. I keep my apartment immaculate, meaning not a single sofa cushion can be out of place, and when it does get messy, I clean it immediately, before relaxing if I'm tired and before eating if I'm hungry."

"The world will never reward you enough for your attempted perfection because it will continuously demand more on a daily basis, so you may as well surrender your quest for perfection now, at this age, before you become a slave to pleasing something that will never be pleased. You will burn yourself out, leaving no time for true joy."

"Ruth?"

"Yes, dear?"

"I simply asked you why you came to the island."

"Join me for an hour of yoga one of these nights, and I'll show you. We all have our stories, and we all like sharing them."

She knew there was only one path on the entire island, and she had already traveled it once with Denver, and again on her way to the restaurant. It would be simple to walk in the dark, she thought, but the others had warned her differently, and now she knew what they meant. The path seemed much longer in the dark. It felt like it took a couple of years to walk from the restaurant to the bonfire site, then another couple of decades to pass the picnic table, and another forty years to reach the lighthouse tower, and then she had to leave the path to venture to the staff house. "It's a choice," she mumbled to herself, recalling what Denver had told her. "It's not a stop on the path. It's a choice *off* the beaten path, and it's a choice I've made."

Her arms, shoulders, back, and legs ached as if she had just run the senior citizen's four-hundred-meter low hurdles and skidded into the finish line. As she walked up the steps to Old Mr. Two-face, she trembled because, at night, with the black shadows from the moving palms hitting its back and the rippling reflection of the gulf hitting its front side, he looked more like Old Mr. Schizophrenic.

Once inside her room, she shut her door and, for a moment, felt safe, like a bug hiding inside an azalea's fuchsia petals just before they open. Then she turned the lights on and saw the hideous-colored room, so she turned them off again and lit a candle instead. She walked over to the tiny round window and peeked out at the black water. From the tiny piece of land she stood on, she stared way out into the Gulf of Mexico, which at night looked very dark. She hoped there weren't any big waves out there, waves big enough to wash over the island and kill Old. Mr. Two-face.

Looking out at the water made her feel so small and out of control that she knew she'd be happier in a room on the other side of the staff house, facing the trees instead.

She couldn't control her insomnia or her breathing or her ever-so-urgent desire to get down on her hands and knees and scrub the dirty floor of her new room.

She walked into the bathroom in search of a mop or broom that might serve the purpose, but after standing there, staring at nothing but ants in bumper-to-bumper traffic from the floor to the sink, she changed her plans.

She plopped down onto the mattress on the floor and slowly pulled Denver's torn bed sheet over the yellow-stained mattress. She opened the never-ending letter to her grandmother.

Dear Grandma,

Here I am, my first night on this island called Tarpon Key. I feel lonely, and all I have are my own annoying thoughts to keep me company. Is there no escaping ourselves? With no lock on my door, I also feel threatened and somewhat paranoid, as if I can't protect that same self that annoys me. I hear a lot of voices down the hall, but I plan to stick to myself out here and just make money. I don't want, or need, to get close to these people.

I'll learn their names, and that's all. I do believe a woman can be an island of her own, and I will prove so this summer.

As for my crazy panic symptoms, I thought that if I kept busy and forgot about my fear of death, they'd go away. Well, life is one big trial and error, so I'm still looking for something that might work.

Now I hear someone playing the guitar. It must be Denver. He works in the kitchen, washing dishes and cleaning. His lyrics are kind of redundant. He's singing over and over that, "Life is so hard, life is so hard." I wonder why life is so hard for him? I also wonder if these people ever sleep? I guess I don't mind if they don't! Goodness, I should love people who don't sleep. In my own freaky manner, I'm one of them.

Today, a few of the cooks and Ray the bartender made similar comments to me. One, who has a wild-looking black mustache, said I look so "clean-cut." Another called me "proper." I've never thought of myself as clean-cut and proper. Then again, I've never been around so many men with ponytails and wild mustaches. Well, I'll just stay in my room with my door shut every night, and they'll think I'm sleeping.

Hey, I really am on a remote tropical island!

P.S. Will you be my guardian angel? I understand man is above angels in the heavenly hierarchy and God employs the angels, but will you ask God for a favor? Ask him if you can be my angel for a while. Thanks, Gram.

Vicki closed the letter then and, as if preparing for an exam, she reread all the watering notes she had taken from Ruth before memorizing the dinner menu, which featured fresh broiled fish and shrimp steamed in beer, and entrees ranging from sixteen to twenty dollars. There was no printed menu. Instead, the wait staff recited it by memory to the guests. She practiced out loud several times, unsure how to pronounce halibut, and started to walk down the hall to knock on someone's door for help, but then she turned around. She didn't want to be with anyone right now, so she settled on her own pronunciation.

She tried to fall asleep but knew she wouldn't, so with a few minutes left before midnight, she grabbed a flashlight and ran out Mr. Front Door. She picked up the trail like one might the subway. She got off at the very next stop, the old dock at the back end of the island, a stop that Denver claimed to be yet another major step on the journey.

Even in the dark of night, with nothing but a flashlight and help from the moon, the dock looked weak and frail, something only a ghost could safely stand on.

"Hi, Ruth. I'm accepting your invitation," she said as she carefully stepped onto the dock. There were boards missing here and there, and it stood a couple of inches above the black, murky water.

"Well, that was sooner than I expected. Here, I'll give you a hand," said Ruth.

"This is the boat you practice yoga on? Will it actually hold two people?"

It looked like a piece of cardboard floating in the water. Ruth stood confidently on it, belonging there the way a fish belongs in an aquarium.

"It's old, wobbly, and hopefully safe. It will challenge your balance," said Ruth as she held her hand out to Vicki. "The story goes that this boat belonged to John Bark and his wife when they first arrived on the island. Apparently, they slept on it while building their home. I'm sure it looked like a houseboat back then. The house part of it has since been removed, and no one wants to get rid of the rest. It's a part of the island, and a great spot for yoga."

Ruth grabbed a mat and unrolled it a few feet away. "On nights like to-night, we have the full moon to light our way. Sometimes, when it's cloudy, I'll practice yoga out here with nothing but a few candles lit," she said. "Now let's get started."

Ruth stretched her arms like the branches of a tree swaying in a gentle breeze, leaning to the left to listen to a secret, then leaning to the right to share that secret, not saying a thing, just making a whispery sound in her throat. Vicki imitated the movements to the best of her ability, self-conscious that there were no mirrors to look into for reassurance.

"Do what feels best for you. Use me as a guide, but don't try to do exactly as I am doing," said Ruth. "I don't use mirrors when I practice yoga because I like to focus on how I feel, not look."

As she stretched her arms slowly over her head, Vicki's mind rushed from thoughts of her dirty room to items she needed to buy back on the mainland to the greasy hamburger she had eaten for dinner. She promised she would bleach the floor tomorrow night, buy potpourri on her days off and skip the key lime pie tomorrow night.

"Hold this pose, and close your eyes, Vicki, and bring your awareness inward, thinking about who you are, who you want to be, not what the world wants of you. There is much wasted energy in our minds. Our thoughts can become out of control at times. Yoga helps you quiet your mind from this over-flooding of chitter-chatter. This will, in turn, relax your body."

Vicki noticed an unstoppable conveyor belt of thoughts moving quickly through her mind. She tried stopping the conveyor belt and the thoughts, but it must have been running on Duracell batteries that wouldn't die. Her twenties were full of pressures to discover who she was in life, what she would do professionally, how she was going to survive financially, how she would stay fit physically, and who she would end up with romantically.

She saw her past decisions making their way like cereal boxes down the conveyor belt, and she noticed herself yanking many of them off before they reached the cashier. There were so many brands to choose from that it made her shopping an overwhelming experience. She looked forward to her thirties because, by then, she would hopefully have a few favorite cereals and the decisions would be over. She'd have her career, her income, her workout regime, and her husband.

"We cannot always control life, but we can always control our breathing, said Ruth. "Now this is the Standing Forward Bend," she added softly. "Never stop breathing. Close your mouth and breathe through your nose, making a quiet sound in your throat. That's it. Making this sound will help you control the flow of your breath. Very good."

Vicki wanted badly to open her mouth and breathe, fearful that she might suffocate with it shut. She wasn't a fish, and she didn't have gills, so why should she breathe with her mouth shut? Was Ruth trying to kill her? As she attempted the sound in the back of her throat that Ruth wanted her to make, she felt an allergic reaction to yoga and a hypersensitivity to her own breathing. She had to stop, or it might kill her.

"Listen to the sound of your breath, Vicki. It should be constant. Inhale as we raise our arms, and exhale as we lower. Try not to breathe out too quickly. Avoid the slightest strain and don't push too hard."

Vicki felt like a tree standing on a sand dune on the brink of immediate erosion, her branches shaking and her trunk devoured by ants. She glanced at Ruth, grounded and still, and felt concerned that if she fell out of pose, so too might it disrupt Ruth.

"Get to know your breath, because it will tell you about yourself. Some days your breathing pace will be shorter and other days it will be faster," said Ruth calmly, as she bent down and let her arms hang toward the wooden floor of the houseboat. "Try to coordinate your movement with your breathing pace. Now doesn't that feel good, natural?"

Vicki could stand it no longer. The movements were simple, but the combination of the breathing and the attention given to it made her feel like a key lime tree carrying coconuts. "No!" she blurted out, in a tone as sour as an immature key lime. She fell out of the pose and collapsed on the ground as hard as a coconut falls. "I don't feel good, Ruth. I think I'm sick. I've got a headache. I can't do this anymore."

Ruth came out of her pose without looking alarmed or disappointed at all.

"I feel ridiculous," added Vicki. "I don't know why I have trouble with the breathing part. I guess the slow breathing was a shock to my system."

"My guess is that you're always speeding through life. Am I right?"

"Yes," she answered, a conductor confident that her interpretation of life and the speed at which to live it had been the *only* interpretation. Slowing down had never crossed her mind.

"How would you describe your daily life? First thing that comes to mind." Ruth sat on the floor with her legs twisted like roots of a banyon tree.

"A dot-to-dot from one errand to the next on a never-ending daily list of things to do."

"What a place to live!"

"What do you mean by *place*?"

"We build our own dwellings, Vicki. We can live inside a shack that is constantly threatened by this and that and always in danger of tumbling down, or we can live in a fortress."

Vicki laughed. "What are you talking about? You live in that old bungalow I passed on the trail."

"No, Vicki, I live in a castle, but I once lived in a shack."

"I'm listening, Ruth. I'm trying to understand this one," mused Vicki.

"I worked many years on Wall Street."

"A stockbroker?"

"No, administrative assistant to a group of stockbrokers in a gorgeous skyscraper. I answered phones and took messages with the same intensity you see in my scrubbing tables. The piles on my desk formed skyscrapers of their own, and I never turned down a single task. I didn't know how to say 'no,' and that went for both my private and career lives. There was never an end to the things I had to do. My back ached from the inactivity of sitting at a desk all day. Soak in a nice hot bath? Forget it. Enjoy lunch outside on a park bench? No way. What were the colors of a sunset? I couldn't tell you back then. I used to show up in my cubicle before the sun rose, and I'd leave after it set. My eyes burned from staring into a computer screen for hours. I was the superhero Java Queen, until one day I started feeling achy all over, and it didn't go away. I went to doctors without getting any diagnosis, and it stressed me because I didn't have time for that, my health, of all things. I had too much to do. It didn't strike me until I got out here that I was spending my health making money, then spending my money getting my health back."

"So you escaped it all and fled to this paradise getaway? That's awesome."

"Not quite. I was getting far behind at work, and one day I kicked my feet up on my desk and glanced down at a tiny blurb in the *New York Times*. It mentioned that Tarpon Key is the kind of island that, when discovered, makes you want to do a little dance. A dance? Ha! So I took vacation days and showed up here, having no intention of taking this management position. I returned to New York, quit my job, sold my belongings, and have been living out here ever since."

"Ruth, it still looks like a bungalow to me, and not that much better than the tree house I'm living in."

"Physically, I do live in a bungalow, and physically, the west side of old Mr. Two-Face does need a face-lift."

"A face-lift?" asked Vicki boldly. "I'd say a blood transfusion, a hip replacement, and a skin graft might do for starters."

"Vicki, when I started the job out here, granted, my surroundings were a paradise, but soon enough I noticed myself once again saying 'yes' to this and that and every request coming my way. I found myself again working sixty hours a week, and I'm ashamed to admit, I still had no idea what a sunrise looked like. You see, I was an ignorant bug flying right back into the same web. You could have put me in any given situation in life, and I would still have been a miserable person with no time for anything relaxing or pleasurable in life. Believe me, the word 'yoga' alone would have caused a panic attack."

"Well, you look like you're enjoying yourself here. I haven't seen any signs of stress on your face yet."

"It wasn't my jobs, where I was living, or who I was living with that continuously caused me stress in life. Rather, it was me. I was not setting boundaries and limits. Demands, requests, and errands can hit you like a bulldozer, tearing down the walls that surround you. If you allow it, they will destroy your own peace of mind. Now I find myself tossing out the word 'no' as if I'm swinging a baseball bat and hitting a ball headed right for the place in which I live."

"The bungalow?"

"No. I live in a castle with walls made of boundaries, and nothing is going to tear the walls down unless I allow it to happen."

"What if I can't find the time or energy to build such a fortress?"

"If you live life trying to be perfect, you won't have any energy left for peace, joy, and things like that. Where do you want to spend all of your energy?"

"I don't know."

"It's quite simple. Make time for yourself and, as they say on Wall Street, put yourself into your budget. You will be constructing your fortress without ever realizing it. And choose to invest. The more you do so over a long period of time, the more your fortress has the potential to grow."

"Ruth."

"Yes, Vicki?"

"I think I'll give yoga another try. It's worth the risk."

CHAPTER EIGHT

ON HER SECOND NIGHT waiting tables, Ruth informed Vicki of a reservation that would require extra special attention.

Porter Smith is an elderly, well-established ship captain who will be bringing in a party of nine gentlemen tonight. Actually, they'll be docking any minute now." Ruth stood at the hostess desk and scribbled off the last name from the reservation book. "He is *extremely* well respected, one of our regulars for dinner, so we like to make everything just right for his table," she whispered professionally to Vicki. She was no drill sergeant, but spoke sternly, and the employees respected her for this.

"Waiting tables is showbiz, Vicki. No matter how you're feeling on the inside, you need to smile on the outside," prepped Ruth. "However, life is not. Remember that."

"I'll do my best." Vicki stared out the screen door. She couldn't tell where the water ended and the sky started, nor could she distinguish between the stars and the lights of approaching boats as she waited for the arrival of a guy she imagined might be wearing the white captain suit of a Miami-based cruise ship. She spotted lights approaching the island. They weren't bright, festive, cruising lights, but rather plain old spotlights, used solely to light the way in the night. *A simple boat. Maybe the captain left his cruise ship home for the night.*

"That might be them now," said Vicki.

"Yes, and keep in mind there's no telling how late they'll stay. Remember to offer them Brazilian coffees with their key lime pies."

"Okay, and up-charge them from iced tea to Long Island tea." Vicki laughed, and returned to her only other table of the night. During the day, the staff waited on up to ten tables at a time, but at dinner, two proved plenty. Evening customers loved to talk and dine for hours.

The dinner room glowed dimly, lit only by kerosene lanterns on each table. Earlier in the night, a man with long, curly hair had arrived on the island with a guitar. He played songs from the Dave Matthews Band and now sat on a stool in the bar singing "Riders on the Storm" and other Doors music. In between songs, he reminisced to Vicki about the concert in New Haven, Connecticut, many years ago when Jim Morrison got arrested and pulled off the stage. He said he liked Morrison and could relate to his lyrics. They made his blood dance in a weird way.

When the time came to service the ten-top, Vicki took a deep breath and approached the captain's table.

"Hello. Welcome to Tarpon Key. I'm Vicki." She struck a match and relit the wick inside the glass jar on their long wooden table.

"Hello, Vicki," said the man at the end, holding a pipe. "Mind giving me a light?"

"Oh," she said, surprised by his request. "Um, do you mind lighting it yourself? Unless, is it the same as a cigarette? Because I've lit cigarettes before, well, not for myself, but, anyway, I've not lit a pipe." Nervous and ridiculous behavior, she knew. But fearful she'd set his pipe on fire, she held the book of matches in the air, inviting the man on the end to do it himself.

"You've not lit a pipe before? Watch me, it's easy," he said and there was silence at the table as he lit his pipe. All the while, he looked at her with smiling eyes, and when he was done he puffed, then said, "Hello, dear, I'm Captain Porter Smith. So nice to meet you."

"Nice to meet all of you as well. So, you're a captain? Of which cruise ship?"

The captain laughed as he stuffed her matches in the pocket of his white jacket. "Oh no, no cruise ship. I'm not that type of captain. I'm a fisherman. We're all fishermen." He offered no more information.

Vicki recovered, giving a salute with her hand, then returned to business, recommending the infamous Silver King Sipper—a piña colada with Frangelico. Seven of the men took her up on the offer, and Ruth, watching from the corner of the room, hand-gestured an okay signal and disappeared to do paperwork in the back office. One man ordered a bottle of Joseph Drouhin. She hated opening wine. She could open a can of beer with no problem, but had a learning disability of sorts when it came to opening bottles of wine.

"Have you ever played poker?" asked one.

"No, why?"

"Don't. You'd lose. Your facial expressions are too honest. Would you prefer we all order that island special instead of wine?"

They laughed boisterously, like pirates. "It was the way your nose scrunched up when I ordered the wine."

"Oh no, wine is fine. Oh, goodness, you're the customers, whatever you want. It's no problem. Really! I've got this modern wine opener here. It came with the job. I'll be right back with your bottle of wine."

She fished through the liquor closet for the right wine label. Rodney Strong, Sonoma County Cabernet Sauvignon, Beaujolais Village. When she found the bottle of Joseph Drouhin, she kissed *it*, her enemy, the wine, and returned to the table. Like a blonde on *The Price Is Right*, she modeled the $85.00 bottle as everyone gawked. Then she pierced its cork with the modernized silver point.

"Methinks she caught a fine one. Let's see if she can reel it in," said a fisherman sitting next to the captain.

She smiled and rotated the bottle. Holding the cork steady, she attempted the opposite: holding the bottle steady. She couldn't remember which had worked best during her last disastrous attempt. She unhooked it, then re-hooked it and started over. All eyes studied her struggle. A camera flashed. She had become someone's souvenir. She heard cheers and laughs. They were teasing her, as if she were catching her first fish. She both hated and respected the catch, the bottle, at the same time. She started reeling it in, but the fish, no, the cork, crumbled. Only half came out with the hook, no, the modern silver corkscrew. Someone handed her a knife, and she scraped the rest of the broken cork onto a bread plate, hoping Ruth wouldn't see. An inhumane catch—she had mutilated it and felt unethical for doing so. Ashamed, she poured red wine with tiny cork crumbles into the clean, clear glass of the man who had ordered it.

He held the glass close to the table, lit by the kerosene lantern. All became silent, but for the overhead wooden fans. "I must assess its hue, clarity, depth, and intensity. This is important. Studying a wine's color helps me detect its age, as well as the way it was made," he spoke as if conducting a seminar.

Vicki wanted to take the glass in the kitchen for a minute, to strain out the tiny specks floating on the surface. Some had sunk to the bottom.

He held the base of the glass, rotating it gently. "This swirling action exposes more of the wine to air and helps it release substances that form its bouquet, which will concentrate in the top of the glass."

Lifting the glass to his nose, he took sharp, shallow sniffs. "Ahhh, the more complex scent of this older wine is revealed!" He raised the glass to his lips and took a mouthful of wine, about a tablespoon. Tilting his head forward, he pursed his lips and drew air through the wine in his mouth, holding his head rigid. He exhaled the air through his nose, keeping his lips closed and then moved his jaw in a chewing motion.

"I've had wine with him before," said the captain. "He's letting the wine flow around his mouth and come in contact with his tongue and the membrane lining the palate. Now, comes the part we've all been waiting for. He'll either swallow or spit!"

He swallowed to everyone's surprise and pronounced his verdict. "Earthy, muscular, mature, corky. Just how I like it." No one commented on the floating cork fragments after that, but Vicki noticed one man spitting casually into his white cloth napkin. The guy next to him picked some out of his teeth.

"I'm sorry about that," she whispered in his ear as he laughed.

"But I'm curious. Where did you learn such a routine?" she asked the man who had ordered the wine.

"I own a winery in Napa Valley."

"Oh."

"He is very passionate about wines," added the captain, "and the gentleman on the end owns a cigar shop in New York. Bob, the big muscle man over there, opened a health food store with massage therapists, chiropractors, everything you can imagine that's good for your health. It's his passion." The captain shifted in his seat as if ready to watch a good performance. "Tell us," he said to Vicki. "What is your passion in life?"

There was silence, and the silence made Vicki feel uneasy. She tried to quickly search inside herself for some form of passion, but all she saw were empty rooms and it made her feel like an old woman living alone in a mansion, yet having no furniture, or decorations to fill the space. The men were staring, waiting to hear about her passion in life, but she could think of nothing. And then she remembered Ruth telling her that waiting tables is showbiz.

"Passion. Let me tell you what I'm passionate about," she said slowly, loudly, like a woman in an old and dramatic black-and-white film. "I'm passionate about coffee." She picked up one of the men's cups of coffee and, with a gleam in her eyes, took a whiff.

"Treating it? Roasting it?" asked one.

"No, drinking it." She could tell by the looks on their faces that her answer didn't measure up. "And I'm passionate about Red Velvet Cake from the Bubble Room."

" My wife has been searching around for that recipe. Have you got it?"

"Oh no. I don't make Red Velvet Cake. I just eat it." She didn't like the silence or the stares or the fact that this kind of showbiz was impromptu. Where was her script? Where were her memorized lines? She felt her face turning as red as the cake.

"But I'll tell you my biggest passion," she continued, wondering what might impress them most—these, her customers, and she, their waitress. "Cleanliness and personal hygiene. I'm a neat freak."

Why did she blurt that out? Hopefully it might gain her a better tip and impress Ruth who was standing nearby. "Yes," she continued. "I sing the entire 'Happy Birthday to Me' song every single time I scrub and wash my hands." Secretly, she knew she never sang the entire song. She only quickly sang, "Happy birthday to me, happy," then dried her hands. Who had time to sing the entire song every time they washed their hands?

When her show ended, there was no applause. By the time the party cleared the table and headed for the door, she felt tremendous relief. But, as she started to clear the dirty table, Captain Porter Smith returned. "Vicki, you're a real trooper. We had a wonderful dinner and a lot of fun. Don't run out the next time I show up. We're not always this rowdy."

"I enjoyed our conversations," she said, unaware of whether her answer came from showbiz or real life.

"Where are you from, dear?"

"Holland."

"The country?"

"No, Holland, Michigan."

"Ah, Lake Michigan. Some fine catches there. I fished the Great Lakes a long, long time ago."

"Did you catch anything?"

"Of course. I always catch something. How about you?"

"Okay, yes, well, not with a fishing pole, but with a stick. I caught a disgusting, slimy vine of sorts."

"Oh, if only I were thirty years younger, I would have married you for your charm, young lady!" He laughed loudly for everyone to hear. "Vicki, I take people from all over the world fishing. How would you like to go late-night tarpon fishing with me?"

"Tarpon fishing? Sure. I'd love to sometime."

"No, I mean tonight. I'm dropping my group off at the marina, then I'll swing back to Tarpon Key and pick you up."

"So late?"

"Absolutely! Eleven o'clock. Be on the front dock."

"Okay. Why thank you. I look forward to it!"

She walked into Ruth's office. "I think I did something politically incorrect or perhaps dangerous. I don't know which."

"What did you do?"

"I told the captain I'd go fishing with him. Tonight."

Ruth stared. "Why of course you should. That's not wrong! He's a respected man around here, and he's taken celebrities and famous people from all over the world out fishing. Do *not* miss an opportunity to go fishing with Porter. You'd be a fool!"

God put those stars up there to separate day from night, Vicki thought as she looked overhead, mesmerized. Like staring into a fire, she could hardly drag herself to blink, and she hardly noticed where the boat headed. With not a cloud in the navy blue sky, the stars sparkled like a broken chain of scattered diamonds, and her neck ached from looking up. She had never noticed the sky before. She knew the basics, that the sky wore blue on sunny days and gray on cloudy days, but now, because she was taking the time to truly notice it, she saw that the sky wore more, accessories.

She looked around, studying the boat. No cruise ship, but in the realm of fishing boats, this captain kept his boat in top-notch shape. Like the napkin holders in her parent's shop, the silver rims of his vessel sparkled in the moonlight, as if freshly wiped with Windex. *Pride of ownership.*

"We're entering Boca Grande Pass, the world's best spot for tarpon fishing." Captain Smith had one hand on the wheel and the other on a tropical drink garnished with a piece of pineapple.

"Boca Grande means big mouth in Spanish, I think," said Vicki, dipping her hand over the edge of the boat to tap the dark, somewhat warm water below.

"Yes. This is the mouth of the Charlotte Harbor, and it's one of Florida's deepest natural inlets. The Calusa Indians loved its rich fishing grounds. Tarpon love it too. They usually hang out in warm, coastal waters."

"Do you think we'll catch anything tonight?"

"I *guarantee* you're going to catch a tarpon, and we won't leave until you do!" The saltwater guru sipped his drink. "We're not on a deadline here. We don't want to rush anything, but you *will* catch a tarpon. *When* I don't know yet. Tonight? This morning? Absolutely!"

"But how do you know I'll catch a *tarpon*? Aren't there other fish out here too?"

"Oh yes, there are others – grouper, snapper, cobia, mackerel, sheep's head, and pampano."

"Goodness! There's as many fish as there are bottles of wine!" The boat stopped, and he unleashed the anchor.

"A bottle of wine to go with every fish."

"What sort of wine would you order with tarpon?"

"Oh no, we're not out here to bring a tarpon home with us. In all my forty-eight years of fishing, I've *never* killed a tarpon. They're the most prized of all saltwater fish, and there's a no-kill law. No, there's no reason to kill these game fish. No one *wants* to eat a silver king, Vicki."

"So, basically, we're here to hook it and let it go? That sounds simple."

"I wouldn't say simple. Keep in mind that we're aiming for tarpon, tournament-size tarpon. Nothing less, nothing more, and tarpon is what you'll catch. They can reach more than six feet in length and one hundred and fifty pounds in weight, and no fish is more unpredictable than the tarpon." He attached small, live crabs to a fishing line and cast it out, before handing the pole to Vicki.

It was men's moonlight madness as boats shopped the dark, deep water, searching frantically, though displaying the calmness of men who shop. Everyone had his own space, no shoving, but fighting for the same sweater. Everyone owned part of the water. Just one more fish of the night, one more, then it's time to go home. As if the men had pushed the mute button on the remote control, it proved a quiet sale, almost silent enough to hear a dolphin breathing or gulls calling. Vicki and Porter didn't have to talk much. Though they were strangers, they felt comfortable with the silence of the event. She liked his comfort zone.

"There. Listen. *Shhhhh* - a rolling tarpon, a half mile down."

"A what?"

"Tarpon breathe air from the atmosphere like we do. They rise to the surface, exhale, inhale, and roll under. If all is quiet enough, you can hear it."

"I do." In the silent darkness they could hear the tarpon rolling and crashing about, porpoising in order to breathe air into its swim bladder. The fish rolled slowly with a soft, lazy sigh, sinking two feet below the surface. The captain attached live, finger-size mullet to the line on another pole and handed it to Vicki, taking the pole she had been holding for an hour. She cast it out, and the mullet stayed on the surface. The boat kept drifting.

"I feel it! I think we've hooked a fish!" Vicki's bait was sucked under, and her line went tight. She could feel the weight of something big, a tarpon tugging.

"Dip the rod to the surface to create controlled slack, Vicki." The captain stood there, calmly calling out commands. It all happened just below the surface, softness, not jerking, almost in slow motion. "Wait for your rod to bend sharply, Vicki. Tell me when you feel the full weight of the fish."

"Oh, dear God! I feel it. Help!" She wore her long blue skirt and white blouse from dinner, and didn't feel like embarking on the battle alone.

"Okay, now sharply sweep the rod sideways. A tarpon's mouth is as hard as concrete. You can do it. Steady, strong, pull on the rod. Keep constant pressure on the hook."

"Help! I'm going to need your help!"

Something silver exploded in the black water. The tarpon jumped, stung by the hook. In a wild scene, it jumped out of the water into the air. When it hit the water again, a flying wave of salty water slapped Vicki. "Please, grab onto my belt so I don't go overboard with this fish!"

"Okay, looks like you might get pulled. Need help now?"

"No! I can do it. I've got to do it!"

"Okay, ease the pressure and enjoy. You're now fully engaged in a battle with a silver king, Vicki."

By now the weight of the tarpon had pulled her feet to the edge of the boat. Her arms felt shaky, as if she had just lifted weights in the gym. Her blouse dripped with water, and she anticipated going overboard. A good twenty minutes passed, and she was still fully engaged in a stubborn battle with the powerful, acrobatic silver fish. The water below acted nervous as the scale-encased muscle danced around the boat. Her mind fought too. She couldn't give up now. She felt ready to battle, ready to face her fears head-on—fears that felt too big for life, fears of death. She didn't know how to battle her panic attacks, or her fears, but engaging in this physical battle with a fish felt good.

The captain took a Polaroid picture, then moved in to help. He took the pole over and lifted the fish to the gaffer. She could finally see its bright silver belly and sides against its dark blue back.

"Well, how do you feel? You've just caught an eighty-five pound tarpon. "

"Like I've experienced one of the wonders of the universe. Wow! I guess that sounds pretty dramatic, doesn't it?"

"People compare it to all kinds of things. One gentleman said it sparked the same kind of determination he needed during the interview process to land his dream job. A woman actually said it reminded her of labor and her two hours of pushing. It means something different to everyone. It's personal."

"Captain, why do you do it? I mean, has it ever lost that first-time appeal?"

"Every baby born to a woman is given a life. But oxygen, and the capacity to breathe, the elements of scientific living, they don't bring a person to life. Each person must decide if they want to live. Does this make sense?"

"I'm not sure."

"We can go through life living and breathing, but this has nothing to do with truly living."

"Oh."

"Dear, we all have our domains: a rider on his horse, a dancer on the stage, a pianist at the piano, a fisherman on his boat. Our domains are one thing: the horse, stage, piano, or boat. What we do with our domains is another. We gallop, dance, play the piano, and fish. Only we don't just go through the motions. We crave it, feel it, escape to it, savor it, and forget everything else in life. We get tired, we sleep, and we wake up and long to return to our domains. Only we bring more and more to them, and we get better and better, and learn more and more about our domains. In this age of information we are only human, overwhelmed. We can't learn it all and never will. We can, however, learn all we want about our domains, the things that make us trot, sing, dance, and catch fish. There are a lot of lost

people out there, people without domains. Find a domain and bring passion to your life."

"Captain Smith?"

"Yes?"

"I tried hard to come up with a passion back in the restaurant tonight.
I searched my thoughts, and nothing came up."

"Did we search for that tarpon tonight?"

"No, we didn't. We sat there listening for it to breathe."

"You want to find your passion in life?"

"I do."

"Be still and listen."

"How does a woman, scrambling for a job, identity, and purpose have
time to sit still and listen for a passion in her life?"

"Searching for a passion runs parallel to life. Don't make it a perpen-
dicular search. It shouldn't interfere, and it should never become stressful.
Be as confident as I was that I knew we would catch a fish tonight. Never
rush it. I didn't start fishing until sometime in my thirties. John didn't
open his health food place until his fifties. Don't push your life aside, just
be receptive."

Vicki understood now his reputation for being the best charter boat
captain around. She assumed he had told this story to others, to people
who had come from all over the world for the tarpon-catching experience.
Well, maybe he told it only to people who asked the simple question, *Why
do you fish, Porter?*

At the rusty pay phone located on the side of the boathouse, the side
that stood on the dock, she squeezed her dress and let the water drip freely onto the wooden planks. "Hello, Ben. I miss you," she said into the bat-
tered phone.

"Anything new and exciting in your life?" he asked from the hotel
room he was staying at in Miami.

She slapped at a swarm of mosquitoes feasting off her arms and legs.
"Yes, I just caught an eighty-five-pound silver king. We battled a good
two hours before I won." She knew she embellished the story a bit, but

hey, the fish story belonged to her, her first fish tale. "I've got a Polaroid picture of our struggle. It looks a lot smaller in the picture. It was huge in real life, and he did back flips about ten feet into the air."

"You went fishing? That's interesting. I can't picture you fishing."

"Can you picture me working?" She looked at the ripples of water slapping against the wooden posts of the dock.

"You found a job?"

"Yes, yes I have. And it's a unique one, quite unique."

"Congratulations. Where?"

"Well, I'm waiting tables on a remote island in the Gulf of Mexico. You can come see me any time you want, but you'll need to charter a boat because it's a few miles out, and there's no bridge, no roads, no anything. In fact I'm talking to you on a pay phone, outside on the dock."

"You've got to be kidding me."

"No, I'm not."

"Oh." There was silence. "You're living on this island, this remote island with no bridge, you said?"

"I am."

"When can I see you?"

"I work several days in a row, then leave the island for a couple of days off."

"So, you're working and sleeping there."

"Yes, and it's paradise out here, really."

"That's nice, Vicki. I'm glad you found paradise. I guess it's all perspective, what one considers to be paradise."

"Then tell me, what is your perspective of paradise?" she asked, suddenly feeling as if she were playing a game of chess.

"Oh, I don't know. You and me together, maybe."

"Ben, I can still see you on my days off," she answered strategically.

"Okay. Sure, give me a call before you leave for Michigan."

"Ben, I won't be going back there in the fall. I've been struggling with a decision. I'm going to Madrid for the fall semester, I think. I didn't want to say anything. I guess I've been confused lately, but I realize I want to travel."

"Well, thanks for telling me. Anything else new?" He laughed, and then there was silence.

She didn't like where this game was going. "No. That's all."

His turn to move. He hesitated. "Ah, thank you for calling me and giving me this information. You take care out there, and I'll talk to you later. Bye."

Ouch, she thought. *I don't think I captured the king.* She wanted to tell him she cared for him, that he came so close to fitting her Mr. Right profile, but the game had ended, checkmate. She would tell him next time. He had hung up.

CHAPTER NINE

SHE SAT ON THE MATTRESS in her sandy-floored room and let her mind wander dangerously. She had lived and worked on the island for ten days, and suddenly started feeling claustrophobic, like a plastic figurine in a glass dome with fake snow falling down about her. Did those figures ever want to break the glass and escape? Probably not, she decided. The dome housed their comfort zone. A nice world for plastic figurines, that is, until some clumsy child dropped it, shattering the glass. No, she was no figurine, just a minute, insignificant being living within the intestines of Old Mr. Two-Face on a small island in the large Gulf of Mexico. And, to make matters worse, she could think of no way to get off the island.

She peered out the tiny, round window and felt like an old, grumpy woman hiding behind her dark sunglasses. She could see nothing but darkness and a small stretch of the water, lit by the moon. It made her feel that much more sequestered, isolated, remote, stranded, a prisoner on Alcatraz, a shipwrecked sailor like Robinson Crusoe, a proper British schoolboy who might revert to savage brutality in a struggle for power and survival. No, this wasn't like what it was in *Lord of the Flies*. She couldn't call this an island of survival—just an island, like Great Britain, like Cuba, like Ireland, only smaller, *much* smaller. But, what if she got a chocolate craving and there were no grocery stores? Or worse, what if her heart pains returned and she had to get to a hospital? She declared that dilemma a thing of the past, unless, of course, she let it return. Then it *did* return, proving mind over matter was a powerful thing, and she wanted more than anything to switch rooms with someone on the other side of the building.

Just the *thought* of heart pains gave her brain blaring signals that life-threatening danger lurked nearby. Her autonomic nervous system started pumping adrenaline and cortisol, the hormones that made her heart pound harder and her fingers itch. As her arms shook, she decided they were recovering from the tarpon battle a few nights ago. She felt pain in her heart and a nerve reacting in her leg. No, it couldn't *possibly* be a nerve. Instead, it was something climbing over her leg! After springing up, she reached for the light. Two red cockroaches quickly scrambled into the mattress hole near her toes. They justified her decision not to fall asleep nor to turn off the light. She swore she would bring this sanitary issue to Ruth's attention come morning, and she wouldn't allow Ruth to tell her that some invisible wall would keep them out.

She watched another red bug sprint across the sandy tile floor before grabbing an old coffeepot that served no purpose—it was just an accepted part of the room—and trapped the creature. Watching it jump around under the glass pot disgusted her, so she threw a dirty towel over it. That still didn't satisfy her. She remembered her own feelings of claustrophobia and let the thing go. She felt pity for it, because it was ugly. How could people *not* hate cockroaches? If only it looked like a butterfly she'd make the effort to free it outside. Instead, she wanted it dead, but hated the crunching sound that had come from the last one she murdered. She wished it were a spider. They are simple to kill – a *smush*, not a crunch.

The music from down the hall grew louder, so she put her ear against the door and listened for words. It grew louder again and sounded like Tom Petty giving a concert in the staff house.

"She's a good girl, loves her mama, loves Jesus and America too," Vicki sang along quietly. "She's a good girl, crazy about Elvis, loves horses . . "

She stood with her ear to the door, relating to the words. She didn't move. But then, after the Tom Petty song, an old favorite came on, the Gloria Gaynor song that stirred her like a cup of coffee.

She looked at the cockroaches scrambling around the floor, having fun, and she started to dance, alone in her room. She closed her eyes as she moved and sang, carefree. "I've spent oh so many nights just feeling sorry for myself . . ."

It didn't matter that Gloria's voice came from speakers down the hall. She felt part of a party in her own room. With every twist and turn she felt the stress and burdening worries twirling away. She spun, leaped and spun again, then hopped over the coffeepot. Dancing gave her positive energy. It released the negative. With no one to see her, she could let her emotions control her movements. If it had a name, it would be called the "emotional-stress-relief dance."

After burning at least four thousand calories, she stopped. She couldn't help but miss Rebecca, who loved this song, and Grandma, who also danced behind closed doors. Grandma couldn't contain herself when Elvis came on.

With no one to talk to and no way to sleep with cockroaches on the prowl, she took out her purple, powder-scented journal, which was hidden under her underwear, still in a suitcase.

Dear Grandma,

If I'm going to be an island, I'd better get used to solitude of thought. Instead, I'm feeling stranded and lonely. I feel caught between two worlds—one that was comfortable and one that is new. When I close my eyes, I'm back in my old Michigan bedroom, looking out the window. I see Kid and Bay Pacer trotting through the yard below. When I open my eyes, I hope that once Mom and Dad find a home to buy, they will get the horses here to Florida. Again with my eyes closed, my mind tricks me into thinking I'm back in the twin bed next to your petite body. I open my eyes and regret that I never recorded your stories. I close my eyes again and smell Mom's homemade chicken noodle soup. I open them and realize I've hardly seen my mom this summer. So I close them again, and I'm suddenly on my old bike. I'm pedaling back from the beach with Ann in our bathing suits. We're in a hurry because we have to get to work at the ice-cream shop. We're hoping Dad doesn't notice the sand on our toes. I open my eyes and tell myself I will someday get out west to visit Ann. I close my eyes once more.

"Now, now, now! Pull yourself together," I can hear you scolding me.

"Okay, Grandma," I actually say out loud. "I need to live in the present, not the past.

P.S. Say hello to Grandpa for me. I know he no longer has his back pain. I know he now glides through time and space with ease as if possessing the enormous, powerful wings of the brown pelican.

She closed her letter and her eyes, and could see the bridge that linked the present with the past. She stood on the side, with tulips opening in the sun and Lake Michigan glistening in the background. She longed to sit close enough to smell their sweet perfume and to admire their satin costumes. Instead, she forced herself onto the wooden bridge and crossed back into the present. As she walked, she could hear a voice from history. "Every man is a piece of the continent, a part of the main."

She agreed now with John Donne—no man is an island complete in itself—so she walked down the hall toward Denver's laid-back voice as it repeatedly and pathetically sang the same lyrics, "Life is so hard, life is so hard." She noticed the cook's door was closed and assumed he was sleeping. He kept completely to himself. The bartender's room was empty. He was probably still at work. Vicki poked her head into Denver's room, and when she saw the walls painted in royal blue ocean waves and posters of every imaginable boat hanging above the painted waves, and the ceiling painted in white, billowing clouds, she couldn't resist. She had to ask if she could join this man who lived in a room as bright as an ocean on a sunny day, this man who sang such depressing lyrics, he surely didn't belong in an uplifting room, a room that also faced the water, like hers.

"You can come in, but only if ya sip this Silver King Sipper," said Denver, handing her a cream-colored drink with the liquor sunk to the bottom. "Come on now, don't be shy. I've got four more of those there piña coladas with Frangelico mixed into them."

"I know, I know. The island special. Thank you very much."

"Okay, babe. Take a sip. It's time to dance." He tossed his cigarette onto the floor, stomped on it, examined it closely, and stomped on it again. Then he grabbed her hand.

"Wait a minute," she said. "If you want to be friends with me, call me Vicki, not babe, okay?" She had no desire to dance with a man who was half her weight and bordered on being drunk.

"Sorry, chick. Listen. I'm so laid-back right now that I'm about to slip into a coma. I *gotta* dance!"

She knew how to say "no," how to scream, how to run out and how to just plain not do anything she didn't want to do. She knew all that, and she knew some fantastic moves from the movie *The Matrix*, to go with it all. She knew Denver belonged to another puzzle, and didn't match any of the pieces of her own puzzle, but something inside her suddenly craved new design to her puzzle. She felt curious about why someone could hang out on a little island, work in a kitchen, and sit alone in his room, drinking and playing pathetic songs on his guitar. Her curiosity drew her into a kind of ballroom-type dance with him as he invented new steps to Bad Company music playing on the classic rock station on the stereo. Next, came Tesla, then Damn Yankees. Except for the spins and dips, during which Denver almost collapsed, Vicki didn't mind. They danced a long time. He sang to all the songs, and his angelic-sounding voice surprised her. She complimented him on it, but he didn't hear. Instead, he psychologically sank deeper within himself, dancing with his partner all the while. He inspired her to study psychiatry instead of psychology, so she could find him someday and write him a scrip for an antidepressant. Then again, maybe he needed good counseling.

He spun her in the proximity of the stereo, then, still dancing, he reached over and cranked up the volume.

"Shut up in there," a voice called from down the hall. "Some of us are trying to sleep."

"Don't listen to him," said Denver. "He likes to breeze through life with the perfect amount of sleep, the healthiest kinds of food, the best wardrobe for any weather. He gets annoyed at anyone who keeps him up five minutes past bedtime or offers him a sip of something unhealthy."

"Well, he's great during the lunch crowds. He handles more tables than any of us can," replied Vicki. "He doesn't tire like the rest of us."

"Of course not. He follows the same course that the wind is blowing. He's a sailboat," said Denver. "He gets stressed over anyone who gets in his way."

"Did you say he was a sailboat?"

"Yep. This staff house is a harbor full of vessels. There's a lifeboat in the room next to you. She's a strong boat, designed for rescuing ship-wrecked persons or persons abandoning ship. Man does she have buoyancy and stability about her, a self-bailing capability. That chick could move forward in the stormiest of waters. Yeah, she could capsize and turn herself upright again."

Vicki smiled, aware that she was carrying on a deep conversation with a man who classified people as vessels. She blamed her psychology background for making her want to understand the vessel, the personality type she was still dancing with.

"And the day cook," continued Denver. "He's a houseboat, designed for use in sheltered waters. What you see is what you get with him. Damn, he's a shallow-draft vessel."

Vicki recovered from another of his lethargic spins and replied, "We certainly live and work with interesting people."

"Oh, wait a minute. Oh, good song. I like this here song! After midnight, we gonna let it all hang down," sang Denver in perfect harmony with Eric Clapton. "I like this song, but I gotta turn it off now. Yeah, I gotta do it again, one more time today, tonight, this morning, whatever zone we're in."

Denver led Vicki over to the orange armchair and nodded at her to sit down. Then he picked up a maroon-colored guitar, leaned his back against the wall, and stroked chords as he slid down to his butt on the sandy floor.

"Life is so hard, life is so hard." As he shut his eyes, it was as if his spirit took over, singing its song through Denver's lips.

"I had it all, lost it all, it came, it went, it's gone. Oh, hell, oh damn, oh hellish damn, life is so hard, life is so hard, life is so bad, life is so bad. I had it all, then lost it all, it came, it went, and it's gone. Oh, life is so hard, life is so hard, life is so bad, yes, life is so bad."

Vicki nursed her drinks and listened to his songs until around three-thirty in the morning. She preferred this to anxiety attacks in bed, but couldn't help but wonder why this pathetic individual sang such words over and over again. Perhaps she might bring him up as a case study back at school. She walked over to his tiny round window and glanced out at the same view she got from her own window: a frightening chunk of the mammoth Gulf of Mexico.

"You own a tiny lit-up portion of it too, of the Gulf of Mexico. We all do. We all own a part of it," she declared. "That little section, or at least the view, belongs to you. What are you going to do with it? What am I going to do with mine?" she asked.

"I see. You're one of those philosopher types when ya drink. Me? I get grumpy, so go philosophize in your own room. Party's over in my room. I'll pound on your door in the morning. There'll be no oversleeping here."

Denver took a final swig of Jim Beam from his plastic cup, and then tossed it into the closet.

"Denver, where'd you get a singing voice like that? It's too good to be human."

He walked over to the window and stared out. "I ain't got a clue. I always sing. I love to sing."

"Why is life so hard for you?"

"Damn, you like your questions, don't ya?"

"Your song is sad."

"Well, ya know, like I was saying, we're all vessels. And gosh, there are so darn many sorts of vessels. You gotta figure out what sort of vessel you are in life, and I'm guessing you haven't the slightest idea yet what you are. Why, me, I'm just a makeshift raft that keeps falling apart all the time. I'm in need of major repair."

"What makes you a makeshift raft?"

"The kind of vessel you are is a personal thing, ya know. I mean, it's who ya are in life. I don't try to be a yacht or anything. I mean, I guess a makeshift raft could turn into a yacht with lots of effort and all, but ya know what? I'm a happy raft. I just need to keep myself together next time around."

"Hmmm. Classifying people as vessels. It's a brilliant concept, Denver. But you're right. I have no idea what sort of vessel I am."

He stared her directly in the eyes and pointed at her as if threatening her. "Don't cruise any further until you know what sort of vessel you are. I can't give ya any better advice than that, girlie."

"Tell me why your song is so sad."

"Why can't I be sad? What, don't worry-be happy? Listen, if something happens in life, and you feel sad, I'm not gonna tell ya to rent a funny movie. You know why? That movie's gonna end and you're gonna feel sad again. No, let yourself feel down. It's okay to feel down. I'm sick of this world not letting people feel down. The theme of our world is be happy, but I think we all need to have days, weeks and sometimes months of feeling sad. I think it's part of life, that's what I think. We're gonna go through dark water, and sometimes we can't make it out in one day, it's too big."

"Have you been in dark water long?"

"Hey, it's bedtime. That means lights out, music off, band getting grouchy."

Denver made his way over to the lamp, first bumping into the wall, then turned out the light. In the dark, he knocked over a couple things and probably hurt himself in the process, but Vicki knew he'd pull himself together again in time for work in the morning.

"Thanks, Denver. That was the best drink I've ever had."

CHAPTER TEN

FLORIDA'S SKY MODELED SEVERAL fashions. Some nights it looked starched and smooth, except for delicate rhinestones sprinkled across the heavens. Other nights it looked organized, with white clouds ironed into sheets of navy blue fabric. Then there were the sweet, light blue nights dotted in puffs of low-hanging clouds, and angry black-and-blue nights when darts of lightning ripped through wrinkled folds. On angry nights, inky colors stained the sky. The sky dressed as it liked, not minding the events or occasions below. It dressed as its Maker told it to, not caring to please anyone.

Several nights were spent sitting in the old lantern room on the top of the lighthouse, and the view from the top gave her the same thrill as taking the elevator to the top of the John Hancock Building in Chicago. Only instead of an overhead view of manmade skyscrapers, she got to see God's skyscrapers. The towering palm trees formed a city of their own, but looking down at the tops of their heads sure beat looking down at rooftops.

She liked the breeze that made its way into the lantern room and understood why no one ever replaced the broken-out windows. She liked where she sat, her nest of privacy, and didn't feel like sharing it with Howard, a different breed of bird. The sky spread itself sweetly in baby blues tonight, the colors of a nursery, and she liked sitting under the friendly sky. She stared at the light blue canopy overhead just as someone shook a pillowcase and a star fell out. She wanted to ask Howard if he saw it too, but Howard didn't talk much. No one on the island knew much about the fifty-something man, just that he worked in the kitchen making real key-lime pie—the kind that is yellow, not green—and doing prep work and existing in his own happy-go-lucky world.

His hair grew like a spiral staircase around his head and down his neck, branching outward as it reached his shoulder, and in the dark of night resembled a bonsai in desperate need of pruning and wiring. He wore the same straw hat all the time, and his scruffy auburn beard grew like vines up his face. His conversations with the staff were limited because he spoke his own quirky language. Now, he sat in the lighthouse tower, way past dark, yet he sat with a paintbrush in hand, making strokes on a canvas.

"I wonder if we'll see another shooting star," Vicki finally said to break the silence, her voice like a coin dropping during a performance and rolling down the aisles. "But then again, you're busy painting, so you probably didn't see the last star." After another minute of silence, she added, "Yet you're painting on a dark night without a light, so I'm confused."

"Hey, Dude, would be kind of cool, Dude, cool to see another." He tossed a twig over the side of the lighthouse tower and watched it drop. Then he made quick strokes on his canvas.

She wanted to bring out a normal side to Howard and a simple question might do just that. "So, Howard, tell me, where are you from?"

"Whoa, Dude, I'm from the Creator." Dude was his word of the day. Some days it was "yo, man," and other days, "whopper," Vicki had observed.

"I'm from the same one who created that there ladybug sitting on your shirt," he continued. "I noticed it in the dark. I can almost see its red shell-back and how it's painted with little black dots—perfectly round. I couldn't draw a perfect circle if I tried."

He dabbed his finger in paint and dotted his canvas.

She picked the little creature off her shirt and tossed it over the side of the rail, wondering if he had escaped some cult. "So you, I, and the bug come from the same creator, Howard."

"That, that, that, that's right!" he said in a Tony the Tiger voice.

She wanted to tell him he was crazy, but not knowing the chemical status of his brain, she didn't want to trigger some violent reaction. "Interesting," she said.

Howard rubbed paint on his lips, kissed the canvas in front of him, and then wiped his lips on his tropical-flowered button-up shirt. "Who do you think I am?"

"I don't know. An artist gone mad?" She laughed.

"No, but hey, Dude, let me tell you something about art," he said. "We're all artists. Yeah, that's right. Every living person has the ability. Listen to me now. We wake every morning with a clean, white canvas before us. As the day progresses, we paint that canvas with the words we use, the gestures we make and the thoughts we think. And Dude, by the end of the day, our canvas might look horribly disturbing, or it might be a masterpiece. It's all up to us, you see," he continued. "We paint our own pictures. Now, who do you think I am?"

She didn't want to answer. She wanted to think about her canvas. What color has it been for the past several months? What color is it on a daily basis? She couldn't wait until morning to start with a fresh canvas, to paint something beautiful.

"Oh, come on now, don't get serious on me. Who am I?" he asked again.

"I don't know, Howard. Ah, a criminal on *America's Most Wanted*?"

"Ho, ho, ho, no, no, no," he laughed. "Try, try again."

"Okay, my second guess. Uh, someone in the witness protection plan?"

"You are far off. I consider myself an antique. Old, ordinary, forgotten, and worth a fortune. But in the world according to Denver, I'm a caravel."

"A caravel? What's that?" she asked.

"It's a sailing ship, typical of Portugal and Spain. When I'm peeling potatoes, as I do almost three hours a day, I'm the *Santa Maria*. Sometimes when I paint, I'm the *Niña*, and right now, as I'm here talking with you, I'm the *Pinta*. Just depends on my mood and what I'm doing. I mean, how can we go through life as just one vessel? We're constantly changing."

"Oh, so you're the three ships that Columbus took to America. Okay, and to think, the others on the island, they all told me you only talk jab-berwocky. How dare they?" She laughed. "You're a deep individual."

"It's not funny," he said. "I didn't come out here to get to know people or for them to get to know me."

"So why are you here and why are you talking to me?" asked Vicki.

He paused for a moment. "I'm here for therapy, and you're attempting to have an intelligent conversation, and I respect that."

"Therapy?"

"Yes. I'm dying."

"Oh." There was a moment of silence. "I had no idea."

Howard laughed. He laughed uncontrollably. He laughed until he cried. Eventually he wiped his eyes and smeared his canvas. "Oh please! We're all dying, you see. Yes, your mother, your father, your siblings if you have any, your friends, every one of us on this island, on this planet; we're all dying. Some people are already dead, and others have never lived at all. We were born to die, and every single day of life means one less day of our life."

"Oh."

"Come on now, you're the one who started talking to me," he said.

"Don't just sit there in that fearful silence. I'll tell ya, parents need to do a better job of telling and reminding their children that, someday, they're gonna die."

"Well, there's only so much time for the essentials, how to drive, bal-ance a checkbook, and how to . . ."

"Wouldn't this be a better world if children grew up aware of the fact that this life is quite short?"

"Well, it might frighten them."

"Bah, humbug! Why should death frighten anyone?"

"It scares me, Howard."

"Why? Tell me why!" Howard squashed a bug on his arm. "Every-thing lives and dies. Why should it frighten anyone?"

"It means separation from loved ones, it's unknown it's . . ."

"The separation from loved ones is temporary. It's like going away on a trip, saying good-bye, but not forever. You're scared because the topic of death is taboo, and you're not prepared to handle it. You're an educated woman, preparing for a career, for a house and family someday, for wealth and vacations, but I'll bet you're not taking any time out to prepare for death."

"Prepare for death?"

"Yes. It's stupid and simple. All you have to do is live. I'm guessing you're book smart, and that is a fine thing to be. However, now you need to live, become world smart, experience the world. Take it from me, the exploration vessel."

"Well, since I'm talking with a caravel, I'll admit that I was planning to go to Spain in the fall, but I'm not sure it's a good idea now."

"Why not?"

"Well, I was going with a friend of mine, but things got in her way and now she can't go, and I don't want to go without her. I guess in a way, I feel guilty."

"Are you asking me for permission to set out for Spain?" He slid his eyeglasses back up onto his nose using his middle finger and looked as if he was about to peruse the *New York Times*.

"No, of course not." She couldn't help but laugh.

"Then it sounds like you need permission from your friend before you set off. Let me help you with that. Get past the guilt phase. Live your life. Your day to die will come. If she's a good friend, she'd want you to go; she'd want your dreams to come true."

"Howard, you're wise."

"Thank you."

"And easy to talk to. I've also got this anger."

"Forgive. You've got to push yourself out of your anger and your guilt. It might feel like walking a plank into dangerous water, but do it. Push yourself to move on."

Vicki tore a vein out of a fallen palm leaf. "I don't know that I'd feel comfortable going alone." She wrapped the leaf around her finger, looking only at her project as she spoke.

"I can give you a contact to look up when you get there."

"*You* know someone from Spain?"

"Quite well. I'll give you the contact information soon, not now, so don't rush me on it." He tore a jagged sliver of wood from the lighthouse and split it in two, as if fiercely competing in a turkey-wishbone contest. "When the time comes, go and explore new worlds, new people. Sail away to Spain. It should only take about five and a half weeks with a crew of ninety. Sail away, young woman! Sail away!"

"Fine. Thank you," she said to this eccentric character.

"But remember, no matter where you go in life, and I know you'll go far, please don't ignore the small things, the details. Pay them attention, notice them."

"Like what?"

"Look at that lizard over there, behind you." He laughed as he picked the lizard up by its tail, which subsequently fell off. "When cornered, did you know one type lizard sprays the intruder with blood from the corner of its eyes?"

"I had no idea. My college doesn't offer classes on lizards, Howard."

"And another sort of lizard, uh, the chuckwalla lizard—when he's being hunted down, he runs into a crevice of some sort and breathes extra air into his lungs, so he gets bigger and can't be pulled out of his small hiding space. Oh, and the alligator lizard—he's got scales as mean as armor. The poor old lizards that don't have rough scales, they can dart quickly, to hide behind things and escape. The chameleon, well, we all know they change colors."

"They're like artworks, detailed art," said Vicki, smacking a mosquito that landed on her arm. "Death comes to the mosquito, too."

"Yes, it does. And I hope I've answered your question, Vicki. I'm here on the island to notice things, smaller things in life. It is my own personal therapy right now. I'm here for one other significant reason, but it's personal."

His words echoed above the palm tree tops, and this she noticed. His words sounded refreshing, and she felt mad at all the thoughts she had allowed in her mind over the past several weeks; all the thoughts that smeared over her canvas in dark, dramatic, depressing colors. He got up and opened the trapdoor of the light room, then nodded for her to climb through. She carefully climbed down a ladder, and then down the black iron stairway. He followed.

"Howard, my canvas has been ugly lately. I'd like to paint a really fun picture tomorrow. Any tips on how to do this?" she called up to him.

"Yes, meet me at the dock tomorrow night after dark."

Her interest brewed strongly, like a pot of freshly ground Colombian coffee. She lived and worked with all sorts of vessels. There was the ferryboat. He usually operated over short distances and wore out before the end of the working day. Others had to pick up where he left off. There was the speedboat. She ran around from table to table with so much intensity. The afternoon rush thrilled her as much as a speedboat hitting bumps. It was the slow times she couldn't stand. These people were like vessels surrounding her in a crowded harbor, carrying secrets, stories and precious cargo.

Dear Grandma,

I've finally made my decision regarding Spain. I am definitely going! I find it difficult to make the big decisions in life, maybe because there are so many options to choose from. Were there really hundreds of cereal types to choose from when you were my age, Grandma? I could walk down that aisle for hours, reading all the nutritional information on those boxes before choosing the best-tasting, most nutritious one.

When I started school, I was sure that I wanted to become a meteorologist until one day I decided the Weather Channel simply brought me comfort. I didn't want to be the one standing out in the downpour, wearing the hooded jacket and trembling from the cold. Then I wanted to become a writer so I took a bunch of English classes and wrote for the school paper. Then I switched my major to Spanish, and that's what bonded Rebecca and me. Then I decided psychology is where I can leave a mark in this world. I would still go to Spain with Rebecca, like I promised, and I could possibly counsel Spanish-speaking people. Anyways, I want to be a psychologist, and my scramble to decide exactly

*what I want to do in life is over. Now I'm scrambling to make it
happen.*

*When does the scrambling end? When can I just be me and not be some-
one working toward being something? At what age did you feel like you
were an adult? Did it happen once you got married? Had babies? I
know it didn't happen once you landed your career because you never
worked outside of the home. So did it happen once you and Grandpa
owned your first home? Once you learned to drive at age fifty? Did you
go crazy not having a car? Did you actually have time to sit with your
babies on the lawn in one of those inflatable baby pools in the summer?
I've got a picture that shows you did. How did you find the time to sit
and do that? Gosh, how did you ever find time to get married and have
babies? Did you belong to a gym and go to kick boxing? How did you
decide what you wanted to do with your life? Sometimes I feel like too
many choices are tougher than no choices at all. Oh Grandma, I feel like
a scrambled egg – still being scrambled, that is.*

*P.S. Don't feel bad. You aren't missing too much here. I can't begin to
imagine the sites and souls you are encountering there!*

CHAPTER ELEVEN

THE SUN AND MOON REPLACED clocks, and the crickets wildly warmed up as the island dressed for the occasion called night, so unlike daytime attire. But first it pranced around for a short yet comfortable time with its trousers from day not quite pulled down and its nightshirt not pulled over-head. There was only limited time before the sun set and the moon rose, and it was the most comfortable time of all.

Working lunches, then dinners, with no time but a water break and wardrobe change in between hadn't given her the opportunity to explore the rest of the island. She decided to do so before meeting Howard on the dock after dark. Perhaps this way she could come to him with a few ad-venturous colors already on her canvas.

"Knock, knock, knocking on Heaven's door. Can I come in?" Denver entered her room without knocking and collapsed onto the mattress as she was getting ready to sneak out alone. He always looked like he was phys-ically falling apart, and this time his ragged shoelace dragged on the floor and strands of long, frizzy hair poked down across his eyes.

"Make yourself at home." Vicki pulled her nightgown out from under him, stuffing it under her pillow. "I'm heading out," she said. "I want to explore the island a bit."

"Swift. You can go on two conditions. First, you spray this stuff all over you." He tossed her Skin So Soft. "And second, you take me with you."

"Oh," she said. "You can come."

"Swift," he replied again. "You better bring a lantern. There ain't no lights out there. And put real shoes on. You can't run in those things. They've got diamonds on them," he stated, pointing to her feet.

"They're not *real* diamonds. And run? Who says we're going to run?"

"Well, if you see a snake, you'll run. I guarantee!"

As they made their way on the rugged path that formed a circle—not a safe and perfect circle, but more of a twisted, curvy circle—around the plush two-mile island, Denver carried a tree branch, using all his power to dig it into the ground with each step.

"That over there is what ya call old age," said Denver as they walked over a hill and passed the old back dock with the houseboat that was creaking and cracking as it softly bumped the dock. "It's another major stop on the path. Ruth prances around on that old thing as if she were a weightless insect. I guess old age is what ya make of it."

"Ruth isn't that old," replied Vicki.

"Oh come on, can't ya see deeper than that? Don't ya get it? Does my tour of the island and my clues mean nothing to ya?"

"I appreciate you showing me around."

"You don't need me to show you around. The path naturally takes ya to each destination. But you do need to figure out how ya wanna reach each spot, what kind of fuel ya wanna use and what sorts of repairs you might need along the way," he said. "Oh, and how many times ya might wanna go off the path, and how far do ya wanna go?"

They made their way along the path as all the islanders in history had done before them. After the old dock and houseboat, the path took them inland over a small wooden arched bridge with dark, shallow water stagnantly standing below it. Vicki stopped on the top of the bridge and didn't feel like moving forward. It felt like a safe, comfortable spot to rest and she wanted to stay there. She shut her eyes and traveled back to the house she grew up in.

"Time to move on," interrupted Denver in an unusually loud voice. "It's up to you. You wanna move forward?"

She opened her eyes and replied, "Yes, of course." She felt the splintery wooden rail of the bridge. "Then, again, I really like standing here."

"Of course you do. It's the bridge. I repeat it's *the* bridge. Everyone likes stopping here, and some never make it to the other side. You wanna move on or go back?"

"You're a strange one," she laughed. "Let's go. I'd like to see the rest of the island."

As they moved forward on the path, low-hanging branches reached out to them, and the trees, standing tall and proud, peacefully, silently reigned, holding age-old secrets and accepting new.

"I'll tell you, it's funny seeing you making your way on this trail," Denver said as he pointed to a turtle, frozen in the sand. "You don't seem like the type to be living out here."

"Why not?" Vicki hopped over the hard-backed creature and bent down to knock lightly on its shell. "Hello in there. Can anybody hear me?"

"Well, you've been here a couple of weeks, and I've never seen your hair messy," he said. "You remind me of Ginger, you know, on *Gilligan's Island.*"

She looked at the top of the dark palm tree, its own mane blowing freely. It never bothered to tidy itself. The raccoons of the island didn't bother to brush their hair, and the spiders, well, their webs were a mess, always under construction. "I didn't realize I came across that way. I don't want to be Ginger! Marianne was always my favorite. I'll try to be her instead!" She was like a foreigner in a strange place and knew that in order for a place to become comfortable, it had to feel so with her. She respected this place and didn't want to be an intruder, overwhelming the salty scent of the air with her strong Red Door perfume.

"I bet you spend a ton of money at spas. I hear they've got tons of those spas in the Netherlands."

"I'm not from the Netherlands, Denver. I'm from Holland, Michigan. A city in the state of Michigan, the United States."

Denver used his walking stick to tear down a banana-colored spider spinning a huge web. The spider fell hopelessly, probably already beginning to plan where next to rebuild after the devastation caused by man. No wonder their webs were a mess out here. "Gosh, hope the Ginger comment didn't offend you. That's why I classify people as vessels—less offensive."

"Right. You told me you're a makeshift raft in need of repair. So, what sort of vessel do you think I am?"

"You? You're an underwater ballistic submarine."

That was definitely not the answer she expected. "Oh, how glamorous. I'd rather be Ginger. What kind of submarine did you say I was?"

"Underwater ballistic," he stated.

"Ballistic." She paused to look at him questioningly. "That does not sound like a compliment."

"Well, what were you hoping to be?"

"I don't know, a luxury liner or a cruise ship, like the Love Boat!"

"No, no way. You hide the imperfections of your life. Nothing bad shows on the surface. Your sadness is deep and, hey, I don't for a *single* minute believe your life is perfect. You look like you've got it all together, but you don't," he said in his rough, splintery voice that sounded nothing like his singing voice. "That's all I'm going to say about you as a vessel right now."

"But I don't know a thing about submarines. You've got to tell me more, *anything*."

"Nope. You need to work on yourself. I've got my own repairs to do," he replied, as if diagnosing a patient with an illness, and then telling them the recovery was completely up to them. There were parts to a person that were inaccessible to the naked eye, but Denver somehow saw through to those areas like an X-ray. Once he gave his diagnosis, his job was done.

"All I'll say is this. Most people don't realize what kind of vessel they are, or where they might need repairs, until it's too late."

"Too late for what?"

"We're back at the boathouse. End of the journey," he said as he reached into his pocket and pulled out quarters.

"And what's that red, glowing Coca-Cola machine? The light at the end of the tunnel?" teased Vicki.

"Hey! I like that. I think I'll plug that into my future tours. You're deeper than ya seem. Wanna go to the bar and get a bottle of rum for our

Coke?" asked the makeshift raft.

"No thanks. You go without me. I've got plans," said the underwater ballistic submarine.

She glanced up at the sky with a new appreciation of the moon. It was the governor of night. Tonight's yellow moon formed a perfect circle, unlike any she had ever drawn or traced. She had never taken notice of the moon before, at least not like this.

She didn't know what Howard had in mind, only that he had promised to turn her boring white canvas into something interesting. Having been told she was a submarine—and all she knew of subs was that they were ugly and gray—she felt desperate to brush new strokes of color onto her own canvas.

As she walked out onto the dock behind the boathouse, she held her lantern high in her right hand, like the Statue of Liberty, ready to declare her independence from living life like a dull, dark, depressing canvas. She joined the man with the scruffy auburn hair and together, lying on their backs with the ripples of water breaking against the moorings beneath them, they watched a lightning show overhead. Distant thunder rolled through the heavens like bowling balls striking pins. They could see dark, angry clouds mounting the horizon, and the Gulf turned murky and mean. For an instant, they spotted fireworks going off near Sanibel Island.

As they talked, they stared up at the gathering madness. Both enjoyed talking about deep things. Howard pointed out how scary the sky was, while Vicki explained what she knew about the enormous spiral nebula called the Milky Way Galaxy. Howard described gut instinct while Vicki described intuition. Howard shared his feelings of loss as Vicki discussed grief. Both talked of loss in their own words, but neither discussed what they had lost.

Howard sat up and threw a flat stone. They heard it hit somewhere out in the water. "So you said you wanted today's canvas to look fun."

"Yes, that's right."

"Then take off your clothes, and let's go swimming."

"Howard! Now that is rude. You brought me down here to skinny dip? Well, goodness, I'd love to see what sort of painting you'd be doing tonight."

"Relax, relax. I'm fooling around," he said, standing up. "You can swim in your jeans if you want. It's your choice. Well, hope ya don't mind if I take something off."

"Maybe I do. Keep your shorts on, please!"

He laughed as he took his straw hat off, tossing it to the side, and proceeded to pull his hair off. Vicki couldn't believe what she was seeing. His beard and sideburns came off too. "Your hair! It's a wig? You're bald?"

"I lost it at an early age. This here wig is great, sideburns, beard and all. I wear the hat to anchor it down."

"Okay. I guess this is what living is all about – swimming at night in your clothes and becoming world smart, not just book smart." She stood up and walked over to the edge of the dock.

Just then, someone, something stalked its way out from behind the bushes, shouting, "It's about time we talk, Howard!"

Howard reached for his wig and, in one quick flop, the long hair, sideburns and beard were nearly back in place, though a bit lopsided.

Vicki stopped herself from jumping into the black, mysterious water.

"Denver, don't do this," called Howard. "I don't have enough fuel in me for this. You know that. Besides, you're a raft now. Don't regress back to being a destroyer again."

"Well, I'm a destroyer tonight."

Denver, a destroyer, and fueled by alcohol, made his way out to the end of the dock and shoved Howard. Howard, by the saving power of adrenaline, picked Denver up and threw him over the dock into the shallow, marshy water below. He struggled in the tangled masses of arching roots and broke free. It was a collision between a destroyer and a caravel.

"Vicki, get back to the staff house, now!" Denver's voice rang out like a horn. "Hurry."

"I'll do as I like," she said as she walked away from the men. "I have no interest in listening to grown men fight."

She glanced back once, before turning onto a path that would take her in a different direction from the action, and it was then that she witnessed Denver climb out of the water and up and over the side of the dock. Sensing that it might become dangerous, she started to run but could hardly see the path without the lantern she had left back on the dock. She raced through spider webs and branches, twigs in the underbrush scraping her face. Somewhere near the bonfire area, she hit a small hole and twisted her ankle, falling to the ground. There, she kneeled behind the trunk of a palm tree and listened to the fight in the distance. So much for her beautiful canvas.

"You're nothing but a selfish, spoiled gay luxury liner," shouted Denver.

"Is that what this is about? You mean to tell me that after all these years you're stuck on the fact that I'm gay?" asked Howard.

There was a moment of silence. "No. I've moved past that."

"Then what? What now?"

"How dare you take off for the oceans of the world while I was stuck in the mud!" said Denver.

"You could have gone as far."

"No, I had forces working against me. You know that," yelled Denver.

"I don't believe that," he said. "You chose to drink just as you chose to gamble."

Denver shoved Howard in the shoulder. "You rich bastard."

"Yes, I'm richer now than I've ever been, and you know what? It's got nothing to do with green stuff," said Howard, quieting his voice.

"What are you doing peeling potatoes for Christ's sake? Why did you come out here? I was here first. Go find your own island."

"I'm here because, because I, uh, wanna help you."

"I don't get it," said Denver.

Howard cleared his voice and continued. "Listen. Listen carefully. A dying man is allowed one wish, is he not?"

"Yeah, okay," said Denver. "I can't argue with that."

"Okay, then take me seriously. You're the only family that's left," said Howard. "I've brought you money. You might call it a fortune. I've buried it just to the east of the trunk of that crooked palm tree, on the hill with the lighthouse. You know the tree."

"Yeah, yeah, I do," said Denver.

"Now when I'm gone," stated Howard, "I want you to take it and use it. Use it wisely. It's up to you."

"Gone? Oh come on, don't talk like that."

"Man, I'm going to be gone, and you've got to deal with it—in your own way."

"What do you want me to do with your money?"

"That's not for me to decide. You've got free will, and I won't interfere with that. It's the only way I know to help you, to give you a chance. Please don't screw up. It's my one wish."

"Wait. Listen. Did you hear that?" asked Denver.

Vicki stealthily backed up and walked carefully past the picnic table, then toward the staff house, her ankle hurting and her face smarting. More tree branches hit her in the face, rudely indicating wrong turns off the path. She kept stumbling, but made her way forward, telling herself she didn't need light or vision to guide her way. She was a submarine, cruising deep in the dark depths of night. But then she heard something loud moving ahead of her. She knew by its sound that it wasn't a lizard. Its magnitude resembled a lurching human more. Denver! He jumped in front of her. Shining his flashlight into her face, he grabbed hold of her arms with his free hand.

"Denver, you scared me to death! What are you doing? Where's Howard?" She maneuvered herself back, releasing his grip.

"Vicki, we told you to get back to the staff house," said Denver. "What have you been doing?" His hand felt greasy, like machinery.

"Everyone said this path was simple, that it would take me where I need to go. Yeah, right," she complained. "I'd do better walking blindfolded down Michigan Avenue in Chicago."

"The path will take ya there, but no one said it would be easy along the way," claimed Denver. "No one said ya might not get hurt or lost along the way." He lit his cigarette and used the lighter to help them see.

He no longer moved like a destroyer but now limped onward, smelling of salt and sweat. He walked like a starving, grungy mutt living in the streets of Mexico.

"Hey, did you hear the argument between Howard and me?" he asked.

"No. Couldn't hear a thing. Why? What happened?" She couldn't breathe.

"Tell me what you heard," he said.

"I told you, I didn't hear a thing," she lied. "I've been trying to find my way back, and all I hear is my body making its way through branches. What happened after he pushed you in the water? Are you okay? You poor thing!" They walked under the stilted staff house that resembled a nest at night, something that a dozen different breeds of birds might build in a failed attempt at teamwork. Just then, they heard someone coming along the path toward the staff house.

"It must be Howard," slurred the slightly muddy, bloody, rabid-looking man. "I've had enough. I'm in pain, and I don't feel like dealing with him any more tonight." He pulled himself up the stairs and into the staff house. Vicki followed, aware that most of Denver's injuries were self- inflicted.

"Where are you going?" she asked.

"Your room. I told you I don't want to deal with him right now," he said.

They walked into her room and, within minutes, Howard burst in.

"Oh come on, guys, my bedroom is not the Colosseum. I'm not going to allow gladiatorial contests to occur in here. Find another place for your wild-animal show," said Vicki.

Howard shook his head. "I admit. We got out of hand on that dock. No more fighting." He laughed. "You don't need us fighting to make your room any uglier than it already is. Besides, I'm a lover not a fighter."

"And that disgusts me," declared Denver.

"Denver, get over it. I'm your friend. I'm not your enemy."

"Howard, I want badly to hate you, man."

"You're doing a good job of it," said Howard.

"I'm not. I don't hate you."

"Then where's your hate coming from?"

"My own life. I've been stuck in the mangroves too long. I hate what I've made of my life. But I don't hate you. I've never hated you," said Denver.

"You could have fooled me." The sarcasm in Howard's voice softened. "Look, I know you don't hate me. I came here to help you. I came here so you could have a second chance. You can do it this time. You've spent enough time living within your mistake. You're the one who once told me we have to move through the mistakes we make, not live within them. Work your way out of the mangrove. Think. Think real hard about what you want to do with the money this time. Change your life and change your soul. You can do it."

Howard turned and walked out of the room.

"I've gotta clean myself up. Sorry for putting ya through this, Vicki," said Denver as he headed for the door.

"Wait, Denver. I need to ask you something."

"I'm not gonna say anything else about the fight, so don't ask," he said.

"No, I want to know about your song."

The man with the torn clothing and the muddy, bloody face walked over, plopping himself down on her mattress. He resembled a Halloween costume. "What do you wanna know? When my album is being released, so you can say ya knew me back when?"

She laughed. "No. I mean, yes, you probably will have an album some-day, and maybe you can mix the island sounds into it."

"You mean the clanging pots and pans of the kitchen and the eggs fry-ing on the pan in the morning, things like that?"

"No, of course not. The birds, the rippling water under the dock, the voices at the bar. But hey, tell me about your song and why the words are so sad. What did you lose in life?"

He stood up a moment to pull his cigarettes from his back pocket, and squinted his eyes as if looking for water down a long, empty well. "I smoked the last darn one. Life is tough, and I'm going to tell you some-thing I learned the hard way. I had me a business, cleaning boats. I worked real hard at it. Saved every penny I ever made and carried that money with me for years—nothing to spend it on. I lived simple but had an overabun-dance saved. Saved for what? I don't know. It just kept growing and grow-ing, sitting around. Took me a trip to visit a friend in Northern California. From there we went to Reno. Did some gambling. Started on the three-dollar blackjack table, nothing major. Each time I lost, I thought I'd win it back on the next round. Those casinos are pretty clever. They don't put windows or clocks in the rooms so you never know when day turns to night and then back to day again. Before long, I moved on to a twenty-five-dollar table. Started throwing down a hundred here and there. The dealer didn't like me. Hell, I got real angry when I lost five hundred dollars because he got twenty-one and I got thirty. I'm not the best counter. I made frequent trips to the debit machine, my fuel supply to continue, and kept moving on to new tables, all the while telling myself, 'I'm a loser, I'm a loser.' I couldn't stop and didn't realize until later how serious my addiction had become. I dumped my entire load in a matter of days. Yep, that's right. I left Reno with no money."

"What did you do?"

"I didn't know anyone and couldn't find anyone I knew so I walked out of the last casino, a destroyer who wanted nothing more than to sink to the bottom of the ocean. It took quite some time for me to want to help myself. Now I'm a raft made of twigs, trying to survive the rough elements."

"How do you and Howard know each other?"

"It's amazing how a lady gives birth to two babies. One grows up to be a destroyer, advancing to a makeshift raft, and the other is a caravel, who travels the world accumulating gold and silver. I don't know why we take such different routes. I only know our mother gave us the basic materials and sent us off into the waters of this world. It was up to us to create the sort of vessels we wanted to be."

"You're brothers?"

"Yep. For years I haunted him, calling him my sister. Just couldn't come to terms with his lifestyle. I was in denial when he told me, so I disowned him and went my own way. He went his own way and made it big – a career in interior design, a good salary, meaningful relationships. The family was proud of him, and I just couldn't accept that. Hey, did I tell ya he's the one who decorated my room? Yeah, he surprised me when I came back from my days off."

"Maybe he'll do mine next. So, what are you going to do now?" She didn't breathe a word about the money she knew Howard had hidden. She knew it would be best to stay out of that.

"It took me a long time, but I made a choice. I could continue to destroy, or I could start to repair. That is why I came here, and, just in time, my brother shows up to lend some tools, some very expensive tools. I don't deserve help, and it doesn't take much money to repair a raft. I guess I just need to figure out what to do with those tools and, in doing so, repair myself. That's all I'm gonna say about that. Now let's get some sleep, and when we go to breakfast in the morning we won't remember a thing about none of this. Ya hear this? Now good night."

After he walked out, she glanced at the clock. Three o'clock. Vicki wasn't ready to sleep yet. She went over to her window and peeked out. She could do whatever she wanted with that small piece of water. Maybe she would take a cruise ship out there and anchor for some time. She could throw a huge party. Or she'd just take a raft out there alone and a volley ball or something for company. It was hers to do with as she liked. The sea no longer looked enormous and overwhelming. Sure, it was big, real big, but she only needed to embrace a piece of it.

She climbed onto her mattress with her clothes still on. Then she slipped out of bed again to brush her teeth. Squeezing the toothpaste from the bottom of the tube, she stared in disbelief at the tiny red speck- les oozing out. Ants, millions of active miniature red ants, made their way through the sticky white paste. She dropped her toothbrush and strangled a scream. She didn't want to wake the rest of the staff house.

CHAPTER TWELVE

EACH DAY BROUGHT A NEW tub of potatoes. As Howard sat peeling them on a bucket turned upside down in the kitchen, Denver washed dish after dish with the sprayer, and Vicki ran in and out of the kitchen carrying trays with clean dishes, and trays with dirty dishes. They chatted here and there, quickly, as time allowed. Howard would ask about her canvas. Denver would share a vessel statistic, or tell her about a gorgeous submarine located somewhere out in Asia. Vicki would mutter Spanish and ask them how her accent sounded. No one mentioned the night on the dock, or the hidden money. They pretended it had never happened. She knew better than to ask any questions. She knew this story didn't belong to her.

Each night brought a new adventure or revelation about life, death, and things worth doing. She found herself meeting Ruth on the old houseboat several midnights in a row, and, slowly, practicing yoga became more natural. Others were coming for yoga, too. Some nights Ruth had an entire class. Other nights one or two people showed up.

"The stresses of daily life wreak havoc on the way in which we breathe. Through yoga, we are repairing our natural breath as well as the walls in which we live. Each time you practice, Vicki and Howard, find the slowest breathing pace you can comfortably sustain," said Ruth, while in what she called the "Bridge Pose." "Inhale to expand and exhale to contract."

"Ruth, I still find myself thinking about a million things while doing some of the poses," said Vicki. "How do I get rid of all my thoughts?"

"Don't scold your wandering mind. Accept it, then focus on your breath and the pose and the type of palace you'd like to live in. Eventually, you'll be able to eliminate the chatter from your mind."

"I'll try."

"I'm living proof that you can," said Ruth, once an off-shore racing boat, thundering across water at over one hundred and seventy miles per hour on its way from the Atlantic Ocean to the Gulf of Mexico, competing against other boats, wind, waves and weather, only to discover that life's real competition is against yourself. Vicki wanted to enjoy breathing. She wanted to learn how to calm her breath, and in doing so, relax her body at any given moment. Each pose was both a mental discipline and a physical posture, a working together of the mind and body. It was up to her to learn how to take care of herself, but she also accepted that this might take time.

Midnight stood as the border between two worlds, night and day. Night no longer meant time to fall asleep, thus no more futile attempts to drift off or struggles *not* to drift off. She celebrated that she no longer just had until midnight.

When she left the island for her two days off, she felt confident her anxiety was a phase now cured by the night therapy found on the island where she could stop and think. Wrong. Her mind stubbornly controlled her body and wouldn't let go. On the way home from the marina, she felt dizzy and nervous driving over the Causeway Bridge.

Her car collided with a butterfly, killing it, and it bothered her that death came suddenly, even to a bug. She noticed construction vehicles working on the other side of the median, and they looked like monstrous creatures with long black antennae and silver claws, mechanically moving like predators in a horror flick. Engrossed in fearful thoughts, heart palpitations, shortness of breath, and near fainting, she held both hands on the wheel, not trusting herself.

The end of the bridge was in sight, and she slowed her car down, but honking horns behind her pressured her to accelerate. She put her emergency lights on and could see the end of the bridge, but feared she would never make it. She would ram her car into the side and go over.

No, that won't happen. None of it will happen. I do have a fear—a fear of dying in my sleep. I am not about to let it become a phobia, an intense and persistent fear of a situation, specific object or activity. I am fully aware that my fear is irrational and way out of proportion, yet I also recognize my free-spirited imagination, which becomes dangerous when out of control.

But despite her psychosomatic diagnosis, still she secretly believed that she too lived with an undetected heart problem. Whatever the cause, her sleepless nights were pushing her to the edge, an edge that was dropping off into a chronic state of sleep deprivation, perhaps leading to insanity.

This latest attack led her directly to the Sanibel Library, where she found a section on grief. By now she had learned that she had a choice. She could either be passively grief-stricken and a victim of grief, or she could actively grieve and move toward healing. She read that the grieving process often included four stages: fear, guilt, rage, and sadness. She felt stuck in fear.

She moved her way to the self-help section and read that the episodes she was experiencing were commonly referred to as "panic attacks" and that millions of Americans at some moment or other have felt such periods of sheer fear. For some, the fear goes away. For others, it takes over their entire lives. It becomes debilitating, making their lives impossible. Fear is expressed in many ways. Some can't face crowds; others, heights or bridges or water.

As she read that anxiety is the fearful anticipation of impending danger, the source of which is unknown or unrecognized, she felt sharp pains dart through the left side of her chest. She read more, relating to the words on the pages. *The central feature of anxiety is intense mental discomfort, a feeling that one will not be able to master future events.* Yes, in her case, the night. She needed to survive each night so that she could live to see day again. *Physical symptoms include sweaty palms, muscle tension, shortness of breath, feelings of faintness and a pounding heart.*

She left the library and quickly found that days away from Tarpon Key meant a return to the things-to-do world that revolved around a wristwatch as she obediently checked off errand after errand on her to-do list. She got her passport photo taken, registered by mail for classes at the University of Madrid, and shopped for clothes for Spain. While opening a pile of mail, she discovered she had been awarded an academic scholarship and decided it would be a great reason to give Ruth when it came time to leave her job at the end of summer.

That night, she called Ben, and they drove to Captiva Island for dinner at a place located on the beach. As she sat across from him, she pictured what their children might look like. One would surely have his blue eyes, and the other her brown. Hold on! Come autumn, she'd leave the country, and after that, she'd return to Michigan. Mr. Right wasn't supposed to show up, not yet.

Ben playfully stepped on her shoes under the table, as always. "So tell me, what's this island life like? What sort of people go off to live and work on a small island with nothing to do?" He casually folded his cocktail napkin into an airplane.

"It's intriguing, Ben. I guess they're people who want to step back from this hectic world for a moment. Those who need to stop, catch their breath. All sorts." She took several gulps of white zinfandel.

"Then why are *you* out there?" he asked, shooting the paper airplane he had folded directly past her.

"It's refreshing. I can breathe out there." She rubbed her eyes, hoping it was just hair spray, but she knew it wasn't. She knew her anxiety was taking over, blurring her vision. Ben went out of focus, and she felt dizzy. She bent down to pick up his plane once she noticed her shortness of breath. Why, at a calm moment, would this occur? She had many hours left until bedtime, until midnight. Not wanting him to see her struggle to breathe, she knocked her purse to the floor and bent down to gather it up. It seemed that bending down helped to clear her airways. Sometimes she'd tie her shoes or fix the cuff on her pants.

"And you can't breathe here?"

"Well, sometimes we all need to take time out to live on an island."

"Hello, Vicki. What do you think Sanibel and Captiva are?"

"Islands." She wanted to tell him that now, even as she spoke, she was thinking of impending danger, of a heart attack. She wanted to tell him of her psychosomatic illness, her phobia of dying in her sleep, and the panic attacks that crept up on her during most of their dates and almost all of her nights.

"So why are you out on that island when you can live here on these islands?"

She needed more air, but didn't want him to see her gasping. How could an attack come at a calm, relaxing moment, one that provided absolutely nothing to justify a panic attack?

"At this particular time in my life, I need even more of an island," she answered.

"*More* of an island?"

"Ben, I want to tell you something. I need to."

"Yes, I'm listening, my little high-maintenance princess," he laughed. She stole a few more sips of wine, assuring herself that all was safe and nothing life-threatening was going to happen. She looked around for escape routes like the bathroom. Then she reminded herself that she was an imaginative person, and that her imagination loved to tease her.

"I need more space, more solitude, more time away from things," she said.

"We have spent so much time together, and there is much I know about you and much I don't," he said, taking her hands into his and massaging them. "I want to understand why a woman living on an island feels a need to leave for an even farther island. I'd love to know what a woman gains from time spent on a remote piece of land in the middle of nowhere, with no shops, hardly any phones, no roads, no cars, no link to the mainland, no desirable men. Women thrive on all of these things and can't survive without them."

"A woman can survive without those things, Ben."

"Oh?"

"Yes, and a woman craves time alone, time to do absolutely nothing."

"Really?"

"Yes," she said, and then thought of tulips and how they need four to six months of cold dormancy to flower.

"I knew women crave things like chocolate and shopping but didn't know they crave being alone and doing nothing."

"Do you know anything about tulips?" she asked.

"Not a thing," he said. "Why?"

"Well, coming from Holland, Michigan, I know a lot about tulips. Too much, in fact. A tulip needs morning sun to open," she said. "And as much as that tulip needs morning sun, a woman needs time alone. She discovers immense power from within, power she never knew she had, once she spends a moment with herself."

She arrived at the condo and climbed into bed by one o'clock in the morning, not ready to sleep. *How could death be so cruel? How unfair to take Rebecca in her sleep, and Grandma too! Who next?* Her pillow felt damp, as if someone on the beach had stood over it, shaking their wet, salty body. She longed to have coffee with Rebecca, or paste together seashell mirrors with her grandmother.

She couldn't help but think about Grandma, who came unglued after her husband died. Grandma's mourning had turned into depression, and she started to live most of her days in the past, in their home. She had raised her family in that home, in that neighborhood, in that comfort zone. After Grandpa died, she crossed a bridge back to her glory days and never fully returned to the present.

She sat up to stop the stabbing but didn't have the patience to counsel her breathing. She let it go untamed, and the battle took its course.

She closed her eyes and took several deep breaths. When she opened her eyes, she glanced down and saw the pile of mail she had neglected to open. She opened a yellow envelope postmarked from Holland. Reading just the first line was like reading an affidavit. It validated, in writing, what she had refused to believe after all this time. She stopped after the first sentence because her hands began to shake, so for a moment, she held it and kissed it, then continued to read.

Dear Vicki,

Doctors say Rebecca had a heart condition that we never knew she had. She suffered several minor heart attacks in the months leading up to her death.

I haven't been sleeping or eating or smiling or doing anything pleasant at all. Why couldn't it have happened to me instead? A mother only wants the best for her children. Why am I stuck here in this world filled with holidays, parties, and parades, in a world that pressures us to celebrate, smile, and socialize? Since Rebecca's death I have been trying hard to create a world for myself in which I don't have to do any of these things. I've been sitting at her graveside for hours at a time. I bring flowers, but their colors clash with the ugly brown ground. Suddenly, one day, as I brought a bouquet of yellow roses, I could almost hear Rebecca telling me to leave her grave site and take the flowers with me. It confused me, so I stood there a moment with my eyes shut. I swear I heard her telling me she didn't want me sitting there on the ground any longer. She'd rather see her mother bringing flowers to a party, smiling, socializing with others. She told me a daughter also wants the best for her mother and that it would bring her much peace to see me happy again. I whispered that I didn't feel that I had any reason to socialize or smile, or party for that matter, and she told me I was wrong. She told me I had great reason to celebrate. She told me to continue buying flowers, but instead of dropping them here on the ground, to keep them, or give them to Dad or her sisters, and to party every day. Now that sounded strange, and I had to laugh. Then she told me, "Mom, go and celebrate your life. It won't last forever. Your time will come as well, so make sure you live the life you have been given."

Vicki, let's celebrate life. It's not going to happen immediately. But let's try.

Love,
Rebecca's Mom

CHAPTER THIRTEEN

RETURNING TO THE ISLAND meant stepping into a world without pressed dresses. The color of the sky on a particular day mattered more than the color of clothes she chose to wear. The humidity on her skin meant more than the sweat that came from working out in a gym. She enjoyed walking the rugged, sandy path more than sweeping and mopping the kitchen floor back home, where things like sand and turtles surely didn't belong. Stepping foot on the island meant returning to a world where errands didn't matter. She felt like a person removed from the developed world, from malls and grocery stores, gas stations and traffic. Here, everything was simple—not boring, just simple. She felt a sense of elation after returning to the island, her kingdom of Narnia, as if life off the island tossed her one too many things to do.

The island represented a newly discovered mentality, something she was capable of embracing anywhere and anytime. She would charter a boat out to some island any time her list of things to do became overwhelming.

Some people never needed to make a list in their lives. They stored details in their memories, not knowing why they felt agitated and stressed. These people needed to visit an island. Vicki was one of those who write down every item of every day's agenda, including things that might be natural instinct—wake up, eat breakfast (Quaker Oats Life cereal, something from the fruit family, plain yogurt), shower, bank, post office, etc.

This at least gave her brain a break from having to store it all.

On the other hand, she was a perfectionist *and* a list maker, and that combination—along with a strong work ethic and a Type-A personality—threatened to drive her to the edge of sanity. Such people needed to make perfectly *beautiful* lists, and if they screwed up one word, or the order of their errands, they felt compelled to crumple them up and start over again. Making lists coincided with a profile on obsessive behavior, but Vicki's reasons for making lists were entirely practical—a disorganized list meant a disorganized day, and a disorganized day naturally led to a frazzled, unproductive mind.

Island life required no lists. Life just happened there, like the weather. Rain arrived whenever it pleased. Its timing didn't matter. It could hit in the midst of an outdoor party and not care that it was falling on guests' expensive hairdos and drenching their designer gowns. Let them worry about that. And this they surely did! If rain took into consideration all the events, it might ruin on any given day or night, the world might shrivel up into dryness because the rain worried so much.

Tarpon Key was a small mangrove and didn't allow much room for worry. Lists, whether mental or written, would fall through the branches into the murky water. Life there stayed rudimentary. And it forced Vicki to notice smaller things, like a roseate spoonbill pacing deliberately in slow motion. Or the smaller oystercatcher, with its long, curving beak and dainty steps or anhingas perched in the mangroves to dry their wings, while the great and little blue herons stalked crustaceans and small fish in the shallows.

Vicki worked lunch, then walked briskly back to the staff house to change her clothes for dinner. Denver had told her a new vessel had arrived, and Vicki couldn't wait to meet the new waitress.

There were lines on her face, tracks, but not the railroad type created for a purpose—more like the bad kind of tracks, not meant to be there; the kind left behind after a heavy suitcase is pulled across a hardwood floor that someone would love to hide, but redoing the floor might cost a fortune. Her cheekbones were as pale and sunken as a collapsed sand dune falling into a lake. Thick black mascara enclosed her eyes like a barbed wire fence, warning people not to get too close. Only her long, curly brown hair added feminine softness, and it fell around her face like a flag torn by the wind. Her name was Evelyn, and she was assigned Old. Mr. Two-Face's spookiest room—the attic way up the steep stairs.

The ceiling hung low, forcing the women to duck as they stumbled up and down the stairs like Halloween guests scurrying through a haunted house. Together, they cleaned out the piles of old newspapers, empty cigarette boxes, and beer cans stashed in the closet. They brushed the cobwebs off the gray paneled walls. As Evelyn washed the window facing the east, tree branches slapped against it like the hands of an abusive partner.

"I feel more at home with this window than I do with the one overlooking that enormous body of water," said the woman, jumping back as a large branch slammed against the glass. "Yeah, I'd rather have just this one window. The window overlooking the water reminds me I can't swim."

"Well, I just hope you'll get a glimpse of the sunrise through those tree branches," said Vicki.

The woman stood like a hunchback in the low-ceilinged attic. "You look like a college-educated gal; am I right?" she asked.

"You could say that, yes," replied Vicki. "So tell me, Evelyn, why are you here on the island?" She tossed the last two beer cans into a Hefty bag.

"I'm in hiding. But I'll tell ya about that some other time. For starters, I was wondering about your birthday. When is it?" Evelyn tucked her cleaning rag into the waist of her jeans and opened the window facing the east for air.

"*My* birthday? Why?"

"A birthday tells me more than a name. When's your birthday?"

"December 18."

"Nice to meet you, my little arrow-shooting centaur."

"What?"

"You're a Sagittarius. We'll talk later."

Evelyn certainly didn't require much training. She said she had waited tables her entire life – except for the decade when she danced topless in a bar near a beach. Despite her curiosity, Vicki left the woman alone her first few nights on the island, assuming she might want initial privacy, the kind she herself had wanted weeks ago when she first arrived, before agreeing with John Donne that no man was meant to be an island.

There was a strange glow in Old. Mr. Two-Face's eyes, and Vicki noticed it as she approached the staff house after a busy night of waiting tables. She planned on sitting outside on the wooden steps for a few minutes, something she often did when insomnia struck, but tonight the glow from the newcomer's window caught her curiosity. She altered course and made her way up the narrow, steep stairs and peeked into Evelyn's room. Kerosene lanterns, belonging in the restaurant, were glowing everywhere. The woman sat Indian-style on the sandy floor. In the flickering red light, her facial lines showed up as more embittered than they appeared in daylight.

"It's dark in there," whispered Vicki.

"I don't mind darkness, but the window is totally freaking me out," said Evelyn.

"I see why. It sounds like the tree branches are going to break right through."

"I'm used to the branches slamming against that window. It's still the other window that freaks me out the most."

"Why?"

"All I see is water. I'm not even going to look out it. I feel like a small bug that can't swim."

"How can you find your way to the window, let alone see what you're playing in this dark room?" whispered Vicki, noticing a deck of cards in her hands.

"Oh, my little college-educated girl, welcome, welcome," said Evelyn. "Come on in now, out of that doorway. Come on."

"Let me guess. You're playing a lonely, desolate game of solitaire," said Vicki, squinting at the cards.

Evelyn laughed, "Oh no, not solitaire, and I'm not *playing*, honey. This is serious stuff. Here, shuffle this deck and draw eight cards. Come on. Don't be a scaredy-cat."

A horrible shuffler, Vicki clumsily moved the cards through her hands, while looking at the weird and colorful pictures on their backs. Candlesticks, men with wings, other men with horns, gold wine cups, ladders. She selected eight cards and handed them to Evelyn.

"These are Tarot cards, and they're going to tell *me* about *you*. About your past, your present, and if they feel comfortable, your future."

"Why would I need cards telling me about my past and present? I already know about them. I would, however, like to know about my future, my immediate future."

"What do you want to know?"

"Am I going to die anytime soon?" She knew she had asked a serious question, but she put no belief in the cards, or in what Evelyn was saying.

"The cards will tell me what *they* want you to know. I have no control over that, babe." Evelyn laid the eight chosen cards in two rows on the floor and studied them seriously for a moment. "Now this is your past. They want to tell me about your past, maybe so you'll believe in them more. You were comfortable, surrounded in comfort. I get a strong sense of home, belonging, comfort in people and places you loved all around you, and -"

"Wait, stop," interrupted Vicki, rubbing the goose bumps on her arms. "I don't get it. Where are you getting this information? You don't know me, anything about me!"

"It's not coming from *me*, doll. The information is coming from the *cards*, the spirits working through the cards."

"Spirits?"

"Yes, I thought I told you that. I'm just reading what the spirits want you to know." Evelyn flipped another card from the deck and said, "More recently, you feel guilty you didn't go to her funeral, don't you?"

"*What?* I've never said that out loud to anyone. What are you talking about?" Her tongue caught a warm, salty tear before it dribbled toward her chin. And she wished she hadn't stopped at this lighthouse, because nothing about it felt safe. She longed to be sitting on the staff house steps instead. Why didn't she stay on course?

"Moving on," said Evelyn without emotion. "Writing. I see writing."

"Sure. Letters. I write letters to my grandmother. My letters keep her going." Vicki crossed her arms, not in defense, but to shield her from a sudden chill.

"Yes. Keep writing those letters. They may turn into something more someday."

"Okay! Stop." She felt as if her immune system had weakened, like a head cold coming on quickly.

"We've gotta finish, baby cakes. Touch as many cards in the deck as possible, then choose four more."

Vicki did as she was told, her hands trembling.

"You asked about death. Well, I can't get any specifics on that, but you are your own worst enemy. Does that make sense?"

"I think I've had enough. This is too weird. I'm done."

She left the attic, making her way down the steep steps and the long hallway to the front door. It felt good to leave Old Mr. Two-Face and walk the path to the dock and the houseboat. But as strange as the tarot card experience was, she found herself curious, wanting more.

"Often, we rush through our days at an accelerated rate," said Ruth, while in the so-called Cat Pose. "Then, we plop ourselves into bed, expecting to fall fast asleep. We do nothing to make this a natural transition, and we get frustrated with our minds and bodies if they don't fall quickly to sleep."

Vicki closed her eyes while in position, and began to pray, thanking God for her mind, her body, and her breath. She looked forward to her years here on Earth, and to her never-ending years in Heaven as well.

"Ruth," she said after finishing her prayer, "I find myself thinking more positively when I practice yoga. I find myself craving healthy foods. I find that my body doesn't ache as much after carrying those heavy trays. I find myself praying more deeply, whereas before I would pray only briefly because things interrupted my concentration."

"Vicki," Ruth said from a balance pose, "are you feeling at all seasick?"

"No. Why?"

"You haven't noticed that the waves are picking up and the boat is rocking heavily back and forth?"

"Not at all."

"Nice. You're focusing inwardly. You're grounding yourself, preparing for future attacks."

"Future attacks?" asked Vicki.

"Yes, any one or thing that might attempt to tear down the peaceful fortress in which you live."

"Okay."

"Before, you might have felt weakened by the boat rocking back and forth, just as any stressful incident might have made you weak. Yes, your walls are becoming stronger, and that is good."

The next day during lunch, a man carrying a dozen red roses arrived on the island by charter. Without coming into the restaurant, he yelled to Vicki through the screen.

"Hey, do me a big favor, will you? Ask Evelyn to step outside. Tell her there's a surprise out here." Everyone, including customers having lunch, heard him ask his favor and watched curiously as Vicki ran into the kitchen.

"Evelyn, hurry! There's a surprise for you outside. Quick!"

"For *me*? Oh gosh, oh shit! I mean, a *surprise*?" She walked out the front door and looked around.

Like a jack in the box, the man was whistling from behind a palm tree, and as Evelyn walked outside, he popped out. "Marry me, Evelyn!" he shouted.

She jumped into his arms crying as he spun her round and round, sending chills through Vicki. Customers clapped. One lady wiped her eyes with her napkin. No one knew Evelyn had a boyfriend. She had only talked about her future, and that of everyone else.

Nights came and went, some plain and others fancy. Some were casual, and some were dressy. Some were damp, wrinkled, and in need of ironing, while others were dry, smooth, and simply hung out like a sheet on a line, absorbing the scent of the air. On one particular night, she started worrying about Spain come fall and all her big and little worries wouldn't go away. She felt as if the darks and lights were tossing together, their colors bleeding, and she felt too exhausted to separate them. Walking the trail, she felt like a load of wash stuck on a never-ending hot cycle, shrinking from every exotic sound and sweating from the extreme humidity. So this was how one felt when worried over everything.

As she entered the lighthouse area, she felt drained. She stopped for a moment, remembering the money Howard had hidden to the east of the crooked palm, and wanted it as much as one might a twenty-dollar bill stuck in the pocket of a pair of jeans about to enter the wash cycle. She could quickly yank it out, dig it up in the dark. No, I'm too tired. It's not worth the effort, she told herself and started to walk again.

Next she heard voices cheering her on to join the gold rush headed west, then came a bell, the insistent kind that rang on a slot machine when someone became a jackpot winner. No, too much publicity, so it then turned into a silent sound, someone handing her an envelope donated from an anonymously generous admirer, urging her to accept the money, to use it at spas and on cruises—anything for herself. Yes, she'd have to yank the money right out of the blue jeans' pockets before the wash cycle kicked in. No, she couldn't do such a thing. The jeans and the money belonged to someone else.

She started to walk away from the crooked palm once more when suddenly she noticed a light coming from a lantern a few feet away. She stared, trying to focus on who was carrying the lantern but saw nothing and no one. She walked toward the light and wanted to say something to the man she could now see holding the lantern. She wanted to tell him that his shirt was see-through. He really needed an undershirt.

As she continued staring at him, his shirt mesmerized her. It had a photograph of a palm tree on it, and the more she stared at the palm tree, the more the picture on his shirt kept changing scenes every time he moved—first to one tree, then another. She was absolutely astonished that a shirt could do such a thing, but then it struck her, with as much of an electrifying impact as a woman ironing and reaching into the hot, sudsy water of the wash cycle at the same time, that this was no ordinary man. She looked at him again and saw right through him. Never in her life had she seen through a man the way she was seeing through this man, right now. Maybe it wasn't a man at all. Maybe it was simply someone's shirt hanging on a line to dry, she told herself as she walked closer and waved her hand through it, not feeling anything. She pinched herself because she remembered how mentally tired she had felt tonight, so much so that she had made the decision to walk the path in total darkness, not bothering to carry a light, like a sleepwalker who could let her subconscious mind work for her and knew where to walk.

Now fully awake, she laughed at herself and at this crazy dream acting itself out in front of her, at this ghostlike figure, this man, fluttering before her and carrying a lantern. She stopped laughing and started shaking, like a sheet, still warm, taken out of the dryer and shaken fiercely to remove wrinkles. She wanted to be folded and put away in a quiet closet with the other sleeping linen.

Instead, she found herself tossed on the dirty ground, and, on her hands and knees, she did as the man signaled her to do. She began digging into the mound of dirt east of the crooked tree. He made her do it. He floated above her, lighting her way with his lantern. It wasn't she who wanted to dig up the money. It was he, the ghost of John Bark, enslaving her as he allegedly had enslaved his wife.

Yes, this was the story she would give Denver or Howard, or anyone who might catch her on her hands and knees on the hill of the lighthouse, digging in the dirt at midnight with no light. No one would ever believe her, and at first, she didn't believe it either. But now, just as she knew for sure that a rayon shirt must be dry-cleaned, she also knew that this man was indeed a ghost. Fear. That was why she continued to dig, despite utter exhaustion. She dug for as long as it would take to wash three loads of wash, then dry them, fold them, and put them away, and she felt just as tired as someone who actually did that work.

She wanted to take her own dress off before it got really filthy, but the man signaled her to keep digging. Suddenly her fingers felt something. She pulled an object out of the dirt and brushed it off. The man held the light closer now, close enough for her to identify the object as pottery. She pulled out more and soon had enough relics and items to open a small museum.

"And people said this was just a hill," she said to the ghost. "It's an ancient Indian mound, isn't it?"

He nodded in agreement.

She instantly liked this man who agreed with her and who helped her find these priceless relics. She liked the man, who was wearing an incredibly sexy white linen shirt and who held the lantern for her and fluttered before her as if wanting to dance. He was too good to be true, but he was hers.

"Those aren't yours," he said.

"Oh? You've given me a gift and now you want it back?"

"Those aren't mine. They belong here on the island. Bury them over there, so no one will find them."

She immediately did as she was told and, after digging a hole, deeper and faster than she had ever dug a hole in her life, she took the precious Indian relics and hid them so no one else would ever find them. She hid them with the passion of a woman who had found a great item at the store and didn't have the money to buy it, so she hid it so no one else could find it. By the time she had finished, she was confident no one would ever find what belonged on the island. Denver could shop around all he wanted and would leave with nothing but the money his brother had hidden for him to the east of the palm.

"Sure enough, you use me, then vanish," she muttered, looking around for the man in sheets.

CHAPTER FOURTEEN

VICKI'S BODY ACHED AFTER work, and she blamed it on the heavy dinner trays she had carried all evening. Just as one usually hates the taste and experience of trying sushi for the first time, then goes back again and again until soon they crave it as they might their daily cup of morning coffee, so too did Vicki crave yoga now. She headed to the houseboat at around midnight. To her surprise, there were bodies already lying on the extra mats. Not wanting to disturb their moment of peace, Vicki quietly joined them on her own towel. She was pleasantly surprised to notice Evelyn relaxing next to her and Howard a few bodies down. He liked yoga and practiced it often on his own.

"Now that we're all lying down," said Ruth calmly, "rest your legs apart comfortably and place your arms about one foot from your sides, palms facing up. Relax your body parts."

"Damn, these darn no-see-um bugs," interrupted Evelyn loudly, scratching and squirming.

"Bring your attention inward," responded Ruth. "Place one hand on your lower abdomen and the other on the lower part of your chest. Feel your chest and abdomen move as you breathe."

"Eyes opened or closed?" asked Evelyn.

"Closed. Focus inward." A moment of silence passed.

"I can't. I can't focus. What am I supposed to see inwardly?"

"Your third eye," said Howard.

"What the hell are you talking about?" asked Evelyn.

"Shut up," he said.

"Howard," said Ruth. "We're all at different levels. It's okay. We will be doing poses that date back a couple of thousand years; however, we will be adapting them to meet your individual needs tonight."

"So, how do I touch my toes while holding a cigarette at the same time?" laughed Evelyn, "Because that's what I need right now."

"Please, shut up," declared Howard once more.

"Howard, block out the external interruptions if you can," said Ruth. "And Evelyn, calm down. Yoga can help you discover a pleasant, peaceful place within yourself."

"Ruth, no one's gonna find a pleasant, peaceful place inside this here body. I guarantee you of that, and hey, inside me is the very last place I feel like being. I'm trying to escape me. Why would I wanna go further into me?" She fell out of her pose. "See everyone back at work tomorrow."

The next night, after dinner, Vicki walked alone to the staff house.

Several islanders needed days off at the same time, leaving Vicki and Evelyn to carry the load for the next couple of days and nights. Tonight, those who weren't on days off were either fishing near Boca Grande or island hopping.

Old Mr. Two-Face didn't look lonely at all. Instead, he looked tired tonight, as if he had been standing on those tall, skinny legs a very long time. Rather than missing the noise and excitement from everyone, he looked at peace, as if he didn't mind his empty nest.

As she kicked open Mr. Screened Front Door, a small furry body with a full, feathered tail ran out the door carrying a walnut in its mouth. A lizard with half a tail followed. Vicki jumped twice, then stepped into an atmosphere twenty degrees warmer than the eighty-degree night outside, and she knew now that Old. Mr. Two-Face suffered a severe fever!

She staggered down the hall, a human tossed into a snake cage. It didn't take a heating-and-cooling expert to diagnose a broken air conditioner. She called out for Denver, despite the fact that he wouldn't be back until morning. He liked to repair things and people, and perhaps fixing things helped him fix himself.

Unlike the dry Midwest summer nights and Florida's typical humid warmth, this heat was overbearing. Vicki began dripping sweat so profusely that she felt as if her head were hanging over a pot of boiling water on the stove. She headed for the door to go tell Ruth, but turned around again. It was too late for anyone to call a technician. Besides, he had to come by boat, and it would be morning before he could get here. "Hey, Kool-Aid Man," she cried, "where are you when a gal needs refreshment?" But he only appeared to children.

The tiny round window in her room provided no air, and she felt as though she were locked in a sauna, unable to breathe. She glanced outside to make sure the Gulf of Mexico hadn't picked up and left. She was concerned because she couldn't hear the gentle lap of the sea stroking the shore in front of the staff house that she typically heard through her window. Her breathing became more labored. She had dumped her paper bag weeks ago, determined to combat the ridiculous problem without it. Now she needed it as a claustrophobic needs to break free from a seat belt as it tightens against her or him during a sudden stop in traffic. Frantic feelings tumbled about loudly inside her like tennis shoes in a dryer. She wanted a window, a refrigerator she could climb into, a frozen margarita, anything for relief. She tried to stay calm and slowly inhaled one breath at a time.

"Girl, pack a bag 'cuz you and me are going to have a slumber party," called Evelyn from down the hallway.

"I thought you went island hopping and dancing with everyone else," Vicki hollered back. "Is this heat making you sick, too?"

"Sweetie, this heat's going to dehydrate us like lizards and kill us in our sleep. But don't fret, babe. We're leaving this place."

Evelyn tossed her cigarette butt into the toilet as soon as she entered Vicki's room and reached into her back pocket for another.

"I don't have a better solution myself, so I'm game. Should I get dressed?"

"No time for wardrobe and makeup. We need to get our bodies outside where the temperature will be only one hundred degrees, a breathable, survivable temperature. This environment is for the lizards, not humans.

I feel like I'm in a smarmy aquarium."

The women set out, carrying pillows, blankets and a bag of melted candy bars. Holding Vicki's hand firmly, Evelyn led the way, skipping and singing, "Lizards and spiders and snakes, oh, my! Lizards and spiders and snakes, oh, my!" She sang her rendition of *Wizard of Oz* lyrics for a good five minutes before Vicki caught on and joined in.

They skipped all the way, stopping on the wooden bridge as Evelyn looked down at the murky water below. "I remember when I was a little girl and I'd get to ride the pony next door. Those were the happiest days of my life. I'd trot around the yard on that thing, free from everything. I miss being that age. I miss everything about my life back then."

"Evelyn, stop looking back. Come on. You've got to move forward," said Vicki, pulling the woman off the bridge. "Back to the present."

"I hate my present life."

"Then why not change what you hate about it?" asked Vicki.

"I don't want to. As bad as it is, I'm comfortable with it," said Evelyn.

"Golly damn, I'm living in Hell, and I'm comfortable with it. Is that sick or what?"

They picked up speed and didn't stop until they were right below a window to the restaurant. The glass was still broken from a time when Howard was picking key limes off a tree and tossed one several feet farther than where his bucket was sitting. Ruth hadn't gotten around to fixing it yet. "Who is skinnier? You or me?" asked Evelyn.

"It doesn't matter," said Vicki. "We're not supposed to be in the restaurant after closing. Don't look at me like that. I'm not squeezing through there."

"Then give me a hand, come on," said Evelyn, stepping onto Vicki's reluctant hand. "We have no choice. We need fluid in our bodies. I'll be back with refreshments in a minute. It's a matter of life or death."

She made her way through the tiny window frame like a spider disappearing through a crack.

Vicki waited outside the darkened window until she suddenly heard a bloodcurdling scream followed by what sounded like someone practicing the drums, only there was nothing musical about it.

"Clear the way," yelled Evelyn's voice from inside. Just then, a small, dark figure came hurtling out the window and right over Vicki's head. "A flying rat," screamed Evelyn. "Take cover."

Vicki screamed the way a woman might if a flying rat were just over head. In fact, that's exactly what was happening, only she didn't know if the thing was alive or dead, nor exactly where it had landed.

"Okay, so now I'm a rat murderer," said Evelyn, poking her head out the window. "Here, catch." She tossed a bag of marshmallows followed by heavy logs and a bottle of rum out the window with the same velocity as she had thrown the rat. Vicki caught the bottle of rum and let the rest of the items crash into a pile on the sand.

"Evelyn! Where's the ice tea? Where's the ice? What's all of this?" she asked.

"Trust me," answered Evelyn.

"Why should I trust you?" she asked in disbelief. "Follow me," said Evelyn.

"I don't know if I want to." But she did, and they caught the trail to the spot where Denver had told them not to light a bonfire. Evelyn bent down and tossed some logs in place.

"Why are there logs here if we're not to build a fire?" Vicki asked.

"Who knows. Nothing in life makes any sense to me," said Evelyn as she pulled a hidden container of lighter fluid out from under her pajama shirt. She poured it onto the logs, then pulled matches out from her pocket. Within minutes, the women were roasting marshmallows over a horribly weak bonfire on an unbearably hot Florida summer night.

"If we get caught, we'll get kicked off the island," said Vicki.

"How are we gonna get caught? This fire is no bigger than the smoke from my cigarette."

"That's true, but the fact that we're standing here roasting marshmallows over a cigarette-sized bonfire is absolutely nuts," declared Vicki as she opened a Hershey's bar and smeared it onto her marshmallow. "I already knew you were crazy, but now I'm starting to think I'm crazy."

"Well, don't look at me. I'm just a chick with PMS. It's the only time I eat chocolate. It's the only time I eat anything the least bit sweet. I hate sweet stuff."

Vicki stared for a moment at Evelyn and started to laugh. She couldn't stop. Tired, irritated from bugs and from heat and now from the summer bonfire that might get them both kicked off the island, she couldn't stop laughing. Tears rolled down her cheeks and her stomach hurt. Evelyn stared at her with a smile, then lit her cigarette in the fire.

"Babe, you're still in the sweet stage."

"What?" Vicki wiped the tears from her eyes.

"The sweet stage. Tell me something—how do you like your coffee?"

"My coffee?" asked Vicki, landing from her flight of laughter as she answered.

"Yeah, your coffee, and be specific. Order it like you'd order it in one of those coffee shops."

"Okay." She stared into the fire, not sure where this was leading. "Well, come on. We don't have all night," snapped Evelyn.

"I'm in line," said Vicki. "I'm at a coffee shop, right?"

"It's two o'clock in the morning, and you think there's a line for coffee?"

"Okay. I'll have a tall, nonfat mocha with whipped cream, please."

"Ya want extra chocolate?" Evelyn asked in a fake tone.

"Chocolate shavings on top will do just fine, and a few chocolate- covered espresso beans, please."

"Evelyn pretended to be fixing a make-believe cup of coffee, then reached over to hand Vicki the bottle of rum, looking like the old lady handing over the goods in Hansel and Gretel.

"No lid. I eat the whipped cream right away."

Evelyn rolled her eyes in frustration. "What else, dearie? Any added sugar?" she asked sarcastically.

"Yes, one blue packet. I'll add it myself. Oh, and a chocolate-covered almond biscotti. That's all."

"I knew it. I knew it." Evelyn grabbed the bottle back and took a swig. "Let me tell you something, babe. I drink Folgers, and I drink it black. I brew, pour, and drink. Nothing more. You see, life, like coffee, progresses. And as you grow older and move through life, you'll eventually skip the sugar, the chocolate, and the whipped cream, all in stages. You'll go to that one or two percent milk and you'll only drink non-flavored beans, the more bitter the better. But hey, it's all part of growing old. But soon, you'll tolerate it less and less sweet, and come to my age, you'll drink black coffee and you'll like it."

"I haven't ordered a caffè mocha in months. I don't even remember switching to caffè lattes."

"Told ya. It's happening already," said Evelyn.

"In fact, whenever I brew my own coffee, I don't squeeze chocolate in it anymore."

"You're on the fast track to being bitter," added Evelyn. "Your taste buds are changing. Me? I skipped the sweet stage altogether."

"Evelyn, you said earlier, when we were on the bridge, that your present life is Hell. Let's figure out some way to make your life better."

"Oh, shut up! What are you going to do? Plop some whipped cream in my coffee?"

"That's not what I had in mind," said Vicki.

"No, I don't deserve better. When I was a little girl I dreamed of Prince Charming picking me up on his pony and taking me off to Fort Myers Beach and all. I wanted to live in a mansion with hanging glass chandeliers someday."

"Evelyn, you *can* live within that mansion. You can build it yourself, one brick at a time," said Vicki.

"Oh yeah? You sound like Ruth. She says I can surround myself with positive people and build peaceful, beautiful walls around myself. I told her I prefer surrounding myself with angry, dangerous men. I like living within the crumbled-down walls of a dump."

"I do not believe you. I don't think you like how or where you're living," said Vicki.

"Yeah, well, I've never had much to offer. No brains, no money, no education."

"Tell me, when did those cards of yours stop predicting your future and instead start dictating it?"

"Whoa! You like getting kind of deep. Couldn't tell ya that."

"Evelyn, you deserve peace of mind, happiness. You deserve to be treated well, nothing less. It's your right to be treated like a person."

"And how do I make men treat me like a person?"

"Treat yourself like that first, and set some protective boundaries."

"Ahh, get a grip, my little romanticist. You still believe in those rosy little happily ever after tales, don't you? My prince came for me in a broken-down truck. Yep, he tied me up and tossed me in. *Ha, ha, ha, ha, ha, ha*. Oh, come on. I'm teasing."

"I don't think it's that funny."

"Girl, you've never been treated badly by a man in your life, so what do you want to say to me?"

"Oh, I don't know. You will survive!" Now she knew that dancing and singing to Gloria Gaynor's music with Rebecca did serve a higher purpose.

"You think so?" asked Evelyn. "You think I'll survive?"

"Sure. You will survive. I'm assuming that at first you were afraid, you were petrified, I mean, how he did you wrong, and how to get along," She said, quoting from the song.

Evelyn stared with interest, so she continued, "And now he's back, from outer space."

"He sure is, babe. And it's not even Mars," added Evelyn. "There's gotta be a planet way far out there that these men come from, and it's definitely not Mars. It's worse."

"Well, you should have changed that stupid lock," recited Vicki. "If you had known for just one second he'd be back to bother you."

"True," added Evelyn. "But I was falling apart mentally, you know, at him trying to get to me."

"Of course, you thought you'd crumble," she said, still quoting. "You thought you'd lie down and die."

"Exactly. That's exactly how I felt."

"Oh no, not you, Evelyn! You're not that chained-up little person."

"I don't want to be," she said.

"You're not! And ya know, why? You're saving all your loving for someone who will love you!"

Evelyn wiped her nose and sniffled. "Vicki?"

"Yes, Evelyn?"

"We're building a bonfire in summer, and we're drunk."

"Speak for yourself. I'm not drunk," said Vicki. "And you're the one who built the fire."

"Then I'm drunk, and I built a summer bonfire, and now it's growing. Did Denver give you that strange tour of the island?" she asked.

"He sure did. According to Denver, this bonfire spot is the 'no-no' point."

"I don't know how deep an individual you are, but I'm pretty deep," said Evelyn. "I figured his tour out. The boathouse is both birth and death. This is the toddler stage where we learn what we can and cannot do in life. The picnic table symbolizes falling in love, and the lighthouse is like a midlife crisis, where we put to rest some of the things we wanted to do in life and continue on with others."

"And the bridge is that point in life when we all look back," added Vicki.

"Hey, I didn't catch on to that one. You're good," she said. "But Denver, he's a strange one."

"He is who he is," said Vicki. "He'd probably call you and me two disobedient toddlers playing with fire."

"Probably, and our fire is growing, you know. Maybe we better kill it before it burns the island down."

"How?" asked Vicki. "How are you going to put it out?"

"I don't know. You gotta go pee?"

"Don't even think about it," said Vicki.

"Relax, just kidding," she said. "We'll pour the rest of the rum over it."

The next night Old Mr. Two-Face's fever was gone, but he looked unusually dark and lonely, perhaps because Simon had taken Ruth, Howard, Denver, and the others by boat to Captiva Island to go dancing. Vicki felt tired and once again planned a quiet, restful night alone as she kicked open Mr. Screened Front Door. As she walked down the hall, she could hear Evelyn ranting and raving, her voice ringing out like a lighthouse foghorn gone mad.

"Vicki, is that you? Girl, you've gotta help me!" she cried out from her room upstairs.

Vicki ran up the narrow flight of stairs leading into Evelyn's attic to find her frantically hanging a pillowcase over the window facing the water with thumbtacks.

"I hate this window. I hate what I see when I look out."

"What do you see?"

"Too much. Way too much."

"It's just water," said Vicki.

"Wide-open water," added Evelyn.

Once the last thumbtack was secured, Evelyn rushed over to her closet and began searching the insides of her shoes. "Oh, honey, we're all in danger. You, me, everyone living here." Her mascara streaked her face and made her look like a rabid zebra. "Oh, damn, where's my sage? I brought a ton of it out here so I could burn it and rid this place of negative energy."

Vicki walked over to the dresser and spotted the deck of cards. "Tarot cards, O Tarot cards, tell us, where is Evelyn's sage?" She waited. "Evelyn, they're telling me it's under the bed."

Evelyn jumped up from the closet floor, then walked over to the bed and lifted the bed skirt, peeking under. "Well honey, I sure ain't looking for *this*, although it could come in handy!"

She pulled a huge knife out from under the bed. It resembled a sword from medieval days and might have been a souvenir from a Renaissance Fair.

"Evelyn! What are you *doing* with that thing?"

"This might just save my life, your life, and everyone's on the island life," she said, sliding the weapon back under her bed. "But that's not what I'm looking for. Help me! My sage has gotta be in here somewhere, unless someone stole it."

"Sage is for cooking," said Vicki. "What are you going to make?"

"I'm not cooking a thing. I already told you. It's for cleansing the air of negative energies."

"What kind of negative energies?"

"I don't know, but I sense a lot of negativity up here in this old attic. I also sense my crazy boyfriend may come to the island and do us all harm."

Together, they continued searching each of Evelyn's shoes and eventually found the bag of sage stuffed inside her smelly white tennis shoe.

"Honey, you seem uptight. Before we rid this place of evil, I think you need a reading," said Evelyn, grabbing her deck of cards.

"I don't know," said Vicki. "I've given it thought and don't feel good looking to a deck of cards for information concerning my life, my future."

Evelyn sat down on the floor and dumped her deck of cards out of the box. "You crossed paths with me for a reason," she told Vicki. "I have access to the spirits, working through these cards, and I believe I am supposed to give you an important message. This is probably why you and I have met in the first place. Let's begin."

Vicki fidgeted with the tiny gold cross hanging around her neck and, for a moment, felt ashamed that it shared the chain with a shark tooth. "Should I be thinking about anything right now?" asked Vicki, taking the cards in her hands.

"Yes. As you shuffle, I want you to think about something you want an answer about."

As the cards flipped through Vicki's hands, her mind began to silently pray. *Dear Heavenly Father, I want to trust in you. I want to face uncertainty in life like a confident vessel moving forward through dark waters. I also want to know when storms are coming my way so I don't get hit. How can I turn around or take another route in time if I don't even know they're approaching? This is why I am sitting here on the floor touching these cards.*

Suddenly, in an attempt to form a bridge with the pictorial cards, Vicki missed, and they flew all over.

"Now, now, girl, shuffling ain't your talent, so don't try overachieving." Evelyn laughed raucously.

Starting over, Vicki shuffled conservatively; no bridges this time. Evelyn took the large deck—fifty-six suit cards plus twenty-two cards with special images—and arranged the cards on the floor.

"These pictures represent the forces of nature and virtues and vices of humanity," she explained. "Okay, according to this first card, hmm. That's odd. There seems to be a block on you tonight."

"What kind of block?" asked Vicki.

"A *spiritual* force of some sort, honey."

"What else are they saying?"

"Nothing, but I'm getting a powerful feeling that we're done with the cards tonight. Who's Jeremy?"

"I don't know a Jeremy. Are the cards telling you that?"

"No, it's not coming from the cards. I'm just getting an urge to tell you the name Jeremy will come to mean something to you."

"Nope. I don't know a Jeremy and never have."

"Doesn't matter. You will soon. That's all. Your reading is done for now."

Evelyn jumped up, walked over to her bed, and picked up the bag of sage. She pulled it out of the bag, struck a match, and lit it. Once the tip of the sage had begun to burn, she lightly blew out the fire and let it smoke. She broke off a smoking piece of the sage and handed it to Vicki.

"Here. Walk around the room with me as you hold up this burning sage."

"What?"

"Just do it, quickly, before it burns out. It'll rid the room of negativity."

Evelyn opened a tiny box on top of her nightstand and pulled out a flash card. "This is a picture of Michael the Archangel. I'm going to hold it as I walk so he can guide us."

Together the women walked to each of the corners of the room, holding the burning sage high above their heads as they went.

"This stuff smells a whole lot better atop a turkey," said Vicki. "Or is it rosemary that goes on turkey?"

"Quiet. Concentrate on getting rid of the negative energies. Michael the Archangel will help us."

"Evelyn," said Vicki a minute later. "Open that drawer over there."

"What drawer?"

"That bottom one," stated Vicki.

"Why?"

"There's a Bible in it."

"I didn't bring any Bible out here."

"Doesn't matter. There's one in there."

"How do you know?" asked Evelyn.

"There's almost always a Bible in a nightstand drawer."

Evelyn set her flashcard of Michael the Archangel down on the floor, knelt down, and opened the drawer next to her bed. She tossed a pile of old magazines on the floor and, under used tissues, found a red Bible.

"Have you been snooping in my room?" she asked Vicki.

"Of course not. Here, let me see it," Vicki said, taking the Bible from Evelyn, then placing it on the floor. With her right arm holding the burning sage high up in the air, she closed her eyes and flipped the Bible open randomly with her left hand. She opened her eyes, glanced down and read out loud Jeremiah 44:33-34 for the first time in her life: "'They provoked me to anger by burning incense and by worshipping other gods that neither they nor you nor your fathers ever knew. Again and again I sent my servants and the prophets, who said, "Do not do this detestable thing that I hate!"' "

Vicki could feel her mouth falling open and tears forming in her eyes.

"Evelyn, come with me. We've got to rinse this incense immediately. We're not supposed to be doing this. God loves us, and apparently He doesn't want us burning this to some entity we do not know."

"Holy shit," said Evelyn as she followed Vicki downstairs to Miss Juanita. The women quickly ran the burning sage under the faucet and then tossed it in the trash.

"I know you couldn't have opened the Bible to that page on purpose," mused Evelyn as they walked back upstairs. "Your eyes were closed, and you did it with one hand," she said, glancing back at Vicki.

"Evelyn, I've got to ask you something serious. Have the cards ever really helped your life in any way?"

"My life. Ha. Let me tell you 'bout my life, my endless cycle of Hell. Just name it and I've experienced it—rape, abuse, near starvation from no money and no food, and divorce. Did I mention spouse abuse? Got so bad I had to have surgery. It happened with both husbands and two boyfriends." She plopped down on her bed.

"Evelyn, you take advice from a deck of cards, or the spirits working through the cards, but who are these spirits?"

"How am I supposed to know who they are? They only give me information that I interpret. They don't talk about themselves."

"This is why it's far safer to just talk to God."

"God doesn't want anything to do with me. I can guarantee that."

"Oh, I wouldn't say that at all. God loves you no matter what you have done."

"No, he doesn't love me. I mean, I don't even know how to talk to Him."

"It's easy. It's the easiest thing in the world." Vicki started praying to God, and Evelyn closed her eyes and listened.

"Amen," said Vicki a few minutes later.

"Amen," said Evelyn. "Amen."

The women talked and Evelyn shared how she had been abused by men in several different relationships. They cried because these men that abused Evelyn were like pirates, enemies to all of womankind.

"What about your fiancé and your engagement?" asked Vicki.

"I can't marry that man. He hurts me all the time."

"But Evelyn, the proposal, the tears?"

"Yeah, yeah, yeah. Tears of fear! It was all an act to save my life, babe. You're such a naive romanticist. I didn't want to disappoint you by telling ya that the men in my life are as dangerous as worldwide ozone depletion. You were happy for me. How could I tell you the good old truth? You couldn't handle it."

"Why'd you say yes to his proposal?"

"Call it acting, my dear, acting. I'm good, aren't I? Yeah, that was all a big act. I came to the island to hide from him. He said he was going to kill me because I tried breaking up. Believe me, he *will* kill me! I escaped to this island without telling a soul, not even my daughter. I hoped to stay out here long enough—I don't know how long, just long enough for him to get on with his life. But he found me. I don't know how. The whole proposal scene, it was done publicly because he knew it would be the only way to get close to me. As he swung me around, he whispered in my ear that he'd kill me if I didn't return. I told him I had to finish my week at work in order to get any pay at all."

"Do you think he might show up here again?" asked Vicki.

"Yes, with his gun! I've seen his gun close up. Believe me, I've almost felt its bullets. It would be just like him to charter a boat out here and show up at night when we're all sleeping. There's no way I'm gonna sleep tonight, and neither should you—for your life's sake, keep your eyes open all . . . night . . . long!"

With no locks on the front door of the staff house, or on her own bedroom door, Vicki didn't need Evelyn to tell her to stay awake. She finally understood Evelyn's anger, her attitude, the toughness of her voice, and the lines on her face. She remembered all the case studies of domestic violence that had been discussed in her psychology class, and knew the potentially life-threatening situation it often posed for anyone involved.

Hours passed, and Vicki tried returning to her room, but Evelyn begged her to stay. "I'm scared to death to go to bed, babe. He might kill me while I'm sleeping. Oh, this is probably all so strange to you. Tell me more about God."

Dear Grandma,

Everyone has fears in life. Some fear the future. Some fear not measuring up to what this world declares a success. Some fear not making their dreams and goals come true by the exact age at which they fantasized them to be a reality. Some fear not having a fortune in the bank by the age of thirty or not owning a house by thirty-five. I have been meeting some new fears, some I have never been introduced to before. Now I realize that some fear physical threats. Some fear addictions. Some fear love. Some fear financial starvation or homelessness. At first, I was afraid of these strangers I had to live with on this island. Now, I like them. We are meant to be here, living and breathing together at this time and place. There's nothing more exciting in life than converting strangers into friends. It's worth staying up late for.

Instead of relying on Tarot cards, I need to patiently live out God's timeline in my life. Why would I let a deck of cards, or the unknown spirits at work in them, dictate my future? What if they told me one thing when in reality another thing was supposed to happen? As a result, their advice could make me stray from my real destiny. The cards, or the person reading the cards, might predict some pretty strong things, and it might change the whole course of my life. The joke would be on me then, because I let them steer me.

P.S. I know you're not dead. How dare I conceptualize you as dead? Oh Grandma, you are more alive than ever, I'm sure!

"Wake up, child! We gotta get ready for work."

"Are we late?" asked Vicki, looking around to reorient herself.

"No, not yet, but no time for dillydallying." Evelyn's eyes searched out the round window of her attic room, the one facing the sunrise and the trees, like a child watching for Santa Claus.

"Evelyn, how did you wake up without an alarm clock?"

"Never slept," she announced matter-of-factly, pacing back and forth from window to window. The pillowcase that had hung on the west window the night before now rested on the floor, and the Bible lay open.

"Did you read more of the Bible after I fell asleep?" asked Vicki.

"Yeah, but if you really wanna know why I couldn't sleep, there was this enormous lizard sitting on your back. The thing was huge."

"An iguana? Bright green?"

"Yep. I took it upon myself to keep an eye on it for you. Who knows what it could have done to you while you slept."

"You do think of anything to stay awake, don't you?" mused Vicki.

Vicki could still feel the puffiness around her eyes that night when she waited tables for dinner. A couple had chartered Simon's boat out to the island's rustic kerosene-lit restaurant for their thirtieth wedding anniversary.

"This may sound strange," the man said to Vicki as she handed him a plate with a piece of key lime pie. "I don't know why I am supposed to tell you this," he added.

"Yes? What is it?" asked Vicki.

"Do you have a Bible out here?"

"Yes, why?"

"I'm supposed to tell you to read Jeremiah, chapter forty-four, but I don't know why."

Vicki stared. She held the woman's plate with the key lime pie long enough for the woman to reach up and take it from her.

"Have you been talking with Evelyn, the other waitress? Did she tell you to say that to me?"

"No, dear, we haven't spoken to anyone," said his wife.

"Then why did you tell me that? What does that mean?"

"I don't know," he said. "I was praying to God during the boat ride over here, and when you first walked over to our table to take our order, I felt an overwhelming urge to blurt that out to you, but I didn't."

"My husband kept asking me if he should say something to you. I told him he should. Does it make any sense to you?"

Vicki sat down and explained the burning sage story to the couple. "Yes, it makes a lot of sense. Thank you," she said. "The name Jeremy now means something to me, and I've heard the warning three times now."

Toward the end of their dinner, she felt tempted to leave the island with the nice-looking, normal couple. They resembled lifeboats, and she would feel safe getting a ride back to the mainland with them. They could take her to shore. But, no, she couldn't go back. She had to stay.

"Hey, Vicki," said Evelyn after closing. "I've got a decision to make."

"Oh? What is it?"

"It's private. Usually, when I have this kind of a decision to make in life, I ask my tarot cards. Now I'm wondering, what to do. Do I ask God?"

"Absolutely. You can go to God in prayer about anything at all. Remember, it's simple. Start by saying anything, just talking. Be yourself. You don't have to be formal."

"I've got to remember that," said Evelyn. "Does He like certain prayers best?"

"Here, come with me and we'll write something out for you." The women sat down at a table and Vicki wrote out the "Lord's Prayer" on the back of a paper placemat.

"Thy Kingdom come, thy will be done, on earth as it is in Heaven," they read together.

CHAPTER FIFTEEN

LIKE READING ENTRIES IN her journal, the days flipped by quickly. Some days hardly got the descriptive entries they deserved, but recording life in the form of a letter was becoming a preoccupation for Vicki. Just how obsessive could a diary or an ongoing letter to her grandmother truly become? Well, for the detail-oriented perfectionist that she was—as a creator of daily lists of things to do that had to be artistically and grammatically correct—any correspondence, no matter how short and insignificant, became a novel in the making.

So much of life never got put down in ink and as a result was forgotten as soon as one's memory faded or the person who experienced it died. Vicki wrote about the things that mattered most to her, of the personalities and issues facing the strangers on the island. In doing so, she could feel her circle of comfort growing wider as did her worldview. This was reflected in her collection of shoes.

Some shoes fit. They weren't necessarily her style or from stores she'd ever shop at, but they did fit. She made them fit. If it meant putting on eight pairs of socks, this she would do. But some styles felt so out of proportion to her own feet that she couldn't get them on even when she tried, socks or no socks. These were the times she wore wooden shoes, not minding that others wore flip-flops.

Why write of shoes? *Grandma would surely relate to such a metaphor*, Vicki wrote. *Her tile sandals, allowing her toes to get wet, walked her down the beaches of Sanibel Island each spring when Vicki and her sister came for a visit. Her red satin slippers escorted her to plays at the Red Barn Playhouse in Saugatuck, easily sliding off when the lights were dim and her toes requested freedom. The Indian moccasins slowly and silently walked her to Loaf-N-Mug Deli for coffee each summer morning in Saugatuck and then quickly walked her home, fueled by caffeine. Those thick rubber white gym shoes that matched perfectly with her bulky gray jogging suit trekked her comfortably to the family reunion in Michigan one cold Christmas. The grandchildren had wanted badly to rescue Grandma's tiny body from that oversized sweat suit. Finally, her furry pink slippers—they went to Marro's for pizza and danced to Elvis in her apartment. Perhaps they took her the farthest.*

Nights passed swiftly, as fast as it took to tie a shoestring. Vicki wore cream-colored sandals for a date with Ben. He picked her up at her grandmother's condominium, and they packed snacks and sandwiches, then continued on to catch a sunset near Blind Pass Bridge.

Once they found their spot in the sand, she slipped her sandals off and spread the blanket out close to the water. The waves looked like white-winged planes smoothly flying across the low, flat horizon, landing on shore one after the next. And small flocks of sanderlings were there to greet those waves and to pick up the colorful coquina clams. Every new rush of water brought more clams and they were as colorful as tourists wearing tropical shirts.

"I've come to a significant conclusion regarding my job, my life," said Ben, as he picked up an Olive Shell and rubbed its smooth exterior. "I think I'm going to take time off. A year or two."

Carefully packed sand and a few seashells into the shape of a building on the beach next to the blanket.

"Why?"

"Why not?"

"Well, what would you do with that time?" Vicki opened a package of wheat crackers and started spreading one with dip.

"A lot of significant things."

"Like what?" She stared out at the sun. Only half of it left.

"My part in preserving this awesome world we live in," he laughed, popping a grape in his mouth. "Just things like that."

"Ben, what are you talking about?"

"I've been researching save-the-planet-type organizations and projects. There are all kinds of interesting opportunities out there, and it's something I feel compelled to do."

"Compelled?"

"Sure. Did you know that in some countries people are required to put one year's worth of time in the military?"

"One year is a long time." There were only minutes left before the sun would be gone completely.

"One year is nothing. It's nothing," he said dryly.

"But you have so many career aspirations. You said you wanted to start your own firm and -"

"I know, and I will probably reach that goal, but life doesn't start once you reach your goal. It starts now. Who knows what the future holds? We can set endless goals, then die before reaching them."

"Thanks for the morbid reminder. You didn't have to say that."

"That is why we enjoy the process leading up to our goals. That is why we must enjoy the journey toward our goals as much as and perhaps more than the moment we reach them. More people die on the way down from the mountain than they do going up."

As he leaned over and sweetly kissed her, she couldn't help but think about the complexity of Ben and his newly revealed idea. Just as a good beer offers more flavors each time the glass is raised – one moment dry and the next sweet – Ben too continued to surprise her. And like a great beer, his kiss left a long, lingering aftertaste.

"So you're not worried about taking a year off from your career?" she asked, pointing to the horizon and the descending sun.

"It'll always be there, and who would dare *not* hire me simply because I took a year off to help preserve part of our planet?"

"Can you afford that much time off?" Only half of the sun was left, and before he answered, only a quarter was left.

"No, but these sorts of things are never convenient. If I go through life saying I can't financially afford to help generate awareness over ozone depletion, or I don't have enough vacation days to help preserve the rain for-est, I would go through life doing absolutely nothing for this world in which I live."

They watched a green fringe appearing on the upper edge of the sun. "You sound like a commercial on public TV."

He laughed. "Just call this my own little secret. I've been pondering it for a long time now."

Just then, the last of the sun vanished and a brilliant, greenish light could be seen on the horizon.

"Did you see that?"

"I saw it. This planet is amazing!" exclaimed Ben.

"If you pursue your idea, where would you go?"

"There are projects I could do locally, in the Everglades. I could stay right here."

It was a busy morning, and she had much to do before catching the staff boat back to Tarpon Key. She spent a couple of hours cleaning the condo, then rushing to the bank to cash her check, shopping for ameni-ties, followed by dropping her dresses off at the dry cleaners before head-ing to the travel agent to pick up her round-trip plane tickets to Madrid. They cost twelve hundred dollars, and she paid with her own cash—her summer goal met.

Ben had tried getting together with her several times throughout the morning, but she kept telling him she would call him back once she fin-ished her errands. Eventually he showed up at the condo, right as she was ready to leave for the marina. He offered to drive her there, and she accepted.

"Ben, you're quiet. Is everything okay?" she asked as they waited under the bamboo hut for the boat to arrive.

"I've been thinking about you on that island. Are you okay living out there?"

"Ben, I love it out there. We've discussed this before."

Just then, she could hear the distant sound of the boat's motor making its way to dock. There were two bodies standing on it, probably leaving for their days off, but she couldn't decipher who it was.

He took her in his arms and held her close. "The closer I get to you, the more I dread the horrible good-bye ahead of us," he said. "Vicki, you're living on a remote mangrove in the middle of nowhere. Wouldn't you rather spend your evenings at the jazz club with me?"

"I love my nights with you."

"Then how about tonight? You don't have to get on that boat. You could leave with me now, and tonight you and I could watch another sunset, see another green flash."

"That's a once-in-a lifetime sight," she whispered in his ear.

"Yes, and we saw it together," he added, then kissed her. "What does that mean?"

"Oh, Ben, I can't leave with you now. I'm working through a few things in my life, and this place is like therapy to me." She waved at the approaching boat.

"C'mon. I've only got you for the summer, then you're off to Spain."

"And after Spain, I'll be back to Holland for school. Who knows where I'll go from there? There are so many places yet to see. We've gone over it again and again. I can't let anything get in the way of my goals."

"Yes, but remember, you have to enjoy the journey there."

A little girl ran past them, skipping and hopping, and for a moment, they stopped and laughed. "Vicki, you've gotta hop, skip, and jump toward your goals, enjoying the process as much as the destination."

"You're right." She wanted to tell him he was right for her, but the words just stopped. She kissed him passionately, convinced that loving an American man was much better than ever falling for a Spaniard.

"Tell me this," she said as she picked her bag up and started walking toward the boat. "Do you still want to travel?"

"At this point in my life, I don't want to go far. I want to stay put in my comfortable world, where I've already established close friends. That happens after one spends their growing-up years living with tribes in South America," he said, and laughed. "I've had my share of adventure. Believe me, I was content when my parents decided to settle back in Mississippi. They reached a point in life where they needed to find a home. We've all left enough friends and family, moving from one place to the next."

As she stepped onto the boat, a woman with a huge sword only half hidden in her partially open suitcase stepped off the boat.

"Evelyn, I didn't think it was time for your days off just yet," Vicki said.

"It is, babe" replied Evelyn. "I've got swimming lessons."

"You're going to learn how to swim?"

"Something like that. You know the window in my room? The one that totally spooked me?"

"Yeah, the west window, the one facing the water," said Vicki.

"Yep, that's the one. I walked right up to it and dared myself to look out."

"And?"

"I saw something new, something I never noticed before."

"What?"

"Opportunity and desire."

"So you're going to learn to swim."

"Sort of, babe. I saw a bunch of water, and now I'm ready to do something with it. I don't have the time to stand here chatting. I gotta get going. Bye." She rushed off.

"Bye."

Vicki took her seat on the boat and blew a kiss to Ben. He waved, then turned and started walking toward his car. He didn't wait for the boat to leave.

The Mississippi steamboat left. Every time it picked up a load of passengers in life and got to know them, it would have to drop them off again. She felt tempted to stay with it, to become the longest-lasting passenger it had ever had, but she knew she couldn't. Soon she would be leaving for Spain, and the steamboat couldn't make it to the Mediterranean Sea. Sure, steam-powered vessels do indeed cross the ocean, but the operating costs were high. The owner of this steamboat wasn't willing to pay those costs. Only the submarine could go this time, and it would go solo. It needed to go much further than the rivers at this stage in its life.

CHAPTER SIXTEEN

CONNIE REPLACED EVELYN, WHO never returned after her days off. The others said she spent her last day on the island staring out her tiny attic window at the water for hours. The new waitress arrived on the island carrying an enormous, pale blue suitcase, the shade women wore on their eyes in the sixties. Denver was busy unloading new kitchen plates off the staff boat so Vicki showed the new woman to her room.

As Connie opened the trunk before her, Vicki paused in the doorway and stared at the contents. There was a condensed stack of T-shirts, each shirt identical but for its color, twelve pairs of rainbow socks tucked and rolled into balls, like cookie dough carefully placed on a pan, first aid supplies, including a box of smiley face Band-Aids, as well as perfectly folded dresses. It looked as if the woman spent days—perhaps months— planning, preparing, and packing the suitcase, as if drafting a will.

"I have never seen underwear folded that neatly," Vicki said in awe. "It looks like you've brought nearly forty pairs."

"Can't go anywhere without clean undies."

"Yes, that's exactly what my mom used to tell me."

"Then just call me Mom," Connie answered as she unfolded navy-striped sheets and began tucking them into the mattress on her floor.

"Is that your teddy bear?" asked Vicki in amusement, as a worn, torn, stuffed animal fell from the folded sheet. "Don't be embarrassed. I've got a tiger."

The woman quickly picked the bear up off the floor, brushed sand off its nose, then held it close to her face, smelling it and rubbing its head. "Snuffy, oh Snuffy!! How did you get in here?"

"Either he felt left out when you were busy packing, so he hopped in when you weren't looking, or you put him in there yourself but are in complete denial," teased Vicki.

"Bedtime without Snuffy is awful," Connie admitted.

"Well, it doesn't matter, because you won't get much sleep around here with or without Snuffy."

"I wouldn't say that. You are presently looking at the world's most sleep-deprived woman. Believe me, I bet I'll get more sleep out here than I've had in the last ten years combined," Connie said, pulling a torn flannel nightgown from her suitcase and placing it under her pillow. "I'd love to talk more, but I better get myself to the restaurant. Ruth wants me to get started right away."

It didn't matter that Connie's hips and behind carried a good fifteen pounds of extra weight and that she wore no make-up except for lip gloss. As she ran from table to table, she had every male customer falling in love with her the moment she laughed, and almost anything triggered her laugh. She had the resonant sort of sound that echoes across a room, making everyone wish they were over chatting with her. Her laughs exploded as uninhibited outbursts from the gut, and they were contagious. A single laugh ranged from high to low tones and came out sounding so friendly that it made Vicki re-evaluate her own laughing style.

Goodness, if only I could laugh that boldly, that boisterously, she thought. Every bit of stress shot right out Connie's body every time she laughed. She used her forefinger to delicately wipe tears from her eyes, tears of laughter. Men laughed with her, even if they were sitting across the room.

"I can't believe I'm out here," she would tell every table. "I can't believe I'm actually waiting tables on an island. Pinch me, someone. Am I really here?"

"Either you're here, or there's a ghost carrying that tray with our burgers," one man joked.

"You pinch me first, and I'll pinch you," teased another.

"I like you. You're certainly not taking paradise for granted," noted another. "My rich, spoiled girlfriend went to the bathroom to powder her nose *again*. How about we leave her there, and you and I take off in my yacht? Something tells me you'd appreciate the beauty out there more than she does."

Connie didn't mind getting dirty and wore more food on her T-shirt than she carried on her trays. It didn't matter. She had fifteen more shirts just like it, all primary dark colors. In the course of the day and into the evening she helped the cooks, several times, smelling the potato salad for spoilage and tasting the lemonade for sweetness.

"She is a well-balanced individual," commented Ruth. "She handles a zillion tasks at once without slacking on anything."

"What are you talking about?" asked Denver as he filled the kitchen basin with hot water. "She's bobbing up and down, barely surviving. Buoys never sink. They bob. Yep, she's a buoy. You just don't see it."

It was only her first day on the island, and Connie could take drink orders within one minute of customers sitting down. Even with a table of fifteen, she smiled her way through their shouting demands, as if she were a professional demand handler. She delivered appetizers in a timely manner, before delivering the lunches, and she picked up excess straw or cracker wrappers, dirty plates, and any other items cluttering the tables as the customers ate. The thing that amazed her coworkers the most was Connie's ability to carry on a stimulating conversation with the guests she served, and she did so with a look in her eye, the kind that says "this woman has been sitting in a silent library one hour too long and is now absolutely craving discussion, the louder the better, with anyone." People liked Connie and, like a boomerang, she liked them right back.

"Well, you've survived your first day and evening waiting tables on this mangrove out in no-man's-land," said Vicki. "Nice job."

"I've done it. I'm actually here. I can't believe it," laughed Connie. "I think I like no-man's-land."

"Well, it sure likes you. Do you always have so many men flirting with you?"

"No, no. Oh, absolutely not," she replied in an offended manner. "I have no intentions with these men, none at all. I'll have adult conversation with anyone who feels like talking. Although, I admit, the attention does feel kinda nice."

"Well, if you're up to it, why don't you join me on the chairs out in front? I'll just be sitting out there catching my breath from the hectic night. It's a nice way to unwind," said Vicki after her last table walked out the door and into the darkness. "I'm taking a mug of hot chocolate out there with me. It feels a bit breezy tonight. Help yourself to some."

"That sounds great, but maybe I'll add a dose of Bacardi," answered Connie. "I haven't had a drink in, gosh, how many years? Do I dare? Should I have a drink?"

"I don't know. Do you have a problem with it?" asked Vicki.

"Do I sound like I do?" asked Connie. "Because no, I don't. I'm just a woman in need of a drink who has gone too long without, nothing more. Don't make me laugh again. Gosh, last time I almost peed my pants."

"Please, refrain. When your last guest is gone, meet me outside." Vicki waved to the few stragglers hanging out at the bar as the aroma of prime rib from the kitchen followed her outside.

The white wooden chairs felt cold against her bare legs, and the night wind kept stubbornly blowing her hair wildly across her face, interrupting her view of the navy blue water with its bobbing boats. There were no stars, no clouds, and the moon was barely visible. Just black outer space and serene surroundings.

Vicki loved being outdoors, but she had never enjoyed it the way she did here, under the stars and on the water off the coast of Florida. She couldn't remember ever closing her eyes while standing outside in Michigan, in the yard, or anywhere. Why didn't she do this before? *What does Michigan's air smell like? What does it feel like? Do its stars differ from these stars? Does the moon look different from Michigan than it does here in Florida?*

She regretted never taking the time to savor her own state's environment and longed to stand outside in her yard in Saugatuck: to close her eyes, to smell, to feel, and to tear a leaf off a tree and hold it in her hand. She would do that when she returned. She promised herself that she would notice all of nature more, feel it and enjoy it. Even if it meant doing an angel in the snow, she would do it. She tasted the salty tang of the air as she took in a breath and felt the warmth of the night's temperature on her arms. She looked up, saw no stars, then closed her eyes and inhaled deeply. She could *breathe*.

"Vicki, that prime rib smell is like an aromatherapy treatment. My pores are eating it up." The wooden screen door slammed behind Connie, then a second later it slammed again.

Two male guests left the bar in trail behind and took it upon themselves to join the women.

"We hope you ladies like history," said one. "We love it," said Connie.

"Speak for yourself," Vicki said. "I'm more of a language buff."

"Hi, I'm Hank, and this is George. We're history professors, sailing for the summer, trying hard to keep our conversations off the subject of world wars, the Declaration of Independence, and the Great Awakening," said the man, whose skin made him look as if he had spent the last thirty years swimming in a slow cooker.

"That's right. Maybe you two can help divert our endlessly long discussion concerning the French Revolution as portrayed in a recent Hollywood movie," chimed in George.

"Yes, you do need rescuing," joked in Vicki. "So, which boat is yours?"

"It's out that way about fifty yards. It's a forty-foot sailboat."

"We took a small inflatable dinghy here for dinner, and we're anchoring right where we're at tonight," said the other as he downed his drink. "Hey, have you ladies heard of Spook Island?"

"Oh yes, actually, my customers talk about it all the time." Vicki sipped her hot chocolate. "From what I hear, everyone who has ever tried getting there has run into difficulty."

"Well, we think we know where it is, not too far from here. What do you say, would you two like to venture out and give it a try?"

"Stranger danger," Connie whispered to Vicki.

"What did you say?" Vicki glanced at the woman sitting beside her. How could a woman who packed a bear named Snuffy and said things like "stranger danger" make it out to an island like this in the first place?

"On second thought, we'd love to discover Spook Island," Connie stated loudly, with no fear. "Yes, we accept your invitation!"

"Are you crazy?" asked Vicki. "It's black out there tonight." "Not with this flashlight," offered Hank.

"How are we going to get there?"

"Our dinghy. It's durable enough. Come on," said George, setting his drink on the grass, then standing up to offer his hands to Connie. "Let's not waste any time."

"I'm game," said Connie as she let the man pull her up from her chair.

"I don't know, Connie," said Vicki. "It's late. Shouldn't we find it during daylight?"

"Vicki, it's called *Spook Island*. Any place with a name like that requires a night search," laughed her newfound friend. Again, her laughter got completely out of control, and all four adults were totally engrossed in hysterics for about five minutes. The chorus of laughter allowed Vicki a moment to study and imitate its style, and no one noticed as her laugh started blending with that of her new friend.

"I can't believe I'm doing this. Am I crazy? Am I really here?" Connie asked the others, now cramped in a rubber life raft made for two.

"You're here, you're here, for real," three voices chimed together. Their flashlight lit only a small circle of the dark, rippling water ahead, and they had paddled about one hundred yards from Tarpon Key when the sky god, Zeus, tossed wind and rain at them. Cold waves splashed their faces and awoke Vicki to the realization of where she was and what she was doing. She felt a moment of panic as she glanced down at the black water that housed all creatures great and small, toothless and non-toothless, full and hungry, all down under.

"My toes are cold," she said. "I'm thinking of dipping them in my hot chocolate."

"Mind if I lick it off?" asked Hank, who, perhaps on purpose, but hopefully by accident, had just squeezed her behind.

"Ugh," replied Vicki, glancing over at Connie to see if she had found that gross as well. The night was too black for facial expressions to be visible, and the gusty wind carried droplets of saltwater into their now burning eyes.

"Ugh," she said again, in part because she wanted to clearly send the signal that she wasn't at all interested in the history professors, and because she now felt cold, tired, cramped, and nervous about the men and the weather, which was like an unpredictable, unknown beast that showed up out of nowhere. How could she have been so stupid as to actually set sail for, no, to actually set dinghy for Spook Island with these two strangers, or as her new friend, Connie, initially referred to them as, "stranger dangers"?

"Connie?"

"Yes, Vicki."

"Is your first opinion of people usually accurate?"

"Yes, always. My problem is that I never go with my gut reaction. Why do you ask, Vicki?"

"Never mind," she said. "Too late now," she mumbled under her breath.

"I think we had better reroute to our sailboat," stated George. "Not because her toes are cold, but these waves are starting to hit us. Where did this come from?"

"I've got an idea." Vicki massaged her toes where they stuck out of her sandals. "Let's return to Tarpon Key and call it a night. Great attempt, but, hey, looks like our quest to discover Spook Island is triggering a mysterious storm."

"We're closer to the boat," said Hank. "We're not going to make it much longer in this dinghy, not with these waves and this wind."

It was true. The sky had started out navy blue and progressed into black. The water had also started out as navy and now looked like wet tar.

"Take us to your boat, then. Safety is number one," said Connie, still nursing her mug of hot chocolate with Bacardi.

"You've still got that drink? If it was a to-go cup, I'd say keep it, but that heavy mug is going to weigh us down," said Vicki, only half teasing. Her other half didn't like the ride any more.

"Toss the mug," shouted Hank. "Take your last swig and toss."

Despite the waves, the water splashing in their faces and weather arriving in an unknown manner, the group laughed as Connie downed the last of her drink and threw the ceramic mug overboard into the blackness.

"I'm queen of the world," shouted Connie with her arms up. "I can't believe I'm here. What a change in routine."

They made it to the boat, but, according to the radio, the winds gave no indication of dying down. "You're history experts, so tell me," said Connie as she sat cuddled in a blanket on the couch. "Did Pocahontas really save John Smith's life?"

They discussed the fearless leader of the Jamestown colony captured by Powhatan's Indians for a good hour as the waves swayed the sailboat, and it tugged and strained on the lines to its anchor below. With no sign of the wind calming, the men opened a bottle of wine, drank it, then opened another and another. The women each had one glass, but turned down the continuous offers after that.

"Let's have fun now," slurred George as he reached over and kissed Connie's neck. "There's not a whole lot of privacy here, but you women don't mind."

"You've got that wrong," said Vicki.

"You sure do," added Connie. Her tone became more authorative. "We'd like to go back to the island now. We both have to work early, and it's well after midnight."

"Well, ladies, we'll take you back in the morning, but we're not going out in the dinghy in this weather. Besides, we didn't take you out here to chat about Pocahontas and to catch some z's."

"Sorry if we gave you the wrong impression," said Vicki. "But we want to go back now."

"That's right," said Connie. "In fact, my husband would die if he knew where I was and what I was doing right now. He'd -"

"That's a good one," said George. "Where's your ring?"

"It's usually right here. See? You can see somewhat of a white mark from not getting any sun there." Connie pointed.

"We told you once, we're not taking you back. There's too much wind."

"But this is a *sail* boat. These boats love wind, don't they? I'd like to go back now," said Vicki.

"This isn't *wind*, this is a *storm*, and we're *not* going to take you back. Not tonight." George walked over to the kitchen drawer and pulled out the corkscrew once again.

"I'd really like to go back to Tarpon Key now!"

"You heard what she said, she wants to go back to Tarpon Key now, so either you'll take us, or we'll dinghy ourselves back!" Connie blurted out.

"Be our guests. Take the dinghy and your lives, you two dingbats!"

Connie threw the blanket on the floor and took Vicki's hands. "Come on, honey. We got ourselves into this, and we're gonna get ourselves out."

"What?" whispered Vicki. "How?"

"We have to get out of here. I don't like the look of this. This isn't good."

As they made their way up the narrow steps to the door leading to the deck, the women clutched arms and tried blocking out the sounds of the drunk men, laughing and watching them from below.

"I should have taken that blanket with us," said Connie. "I didn't know it could get so cold out here in the summer."

"Are we really going to do this?"

"Vicki, I don't know about you, but I have to. I think I've been hit with a cold wave. I can't believe I'm out here. I'm married."

The women carefully lowered the boarding ladder and settled into the wet dinghy. Within seconds they began paddling like crazy, steering in the direction of the island.

"Vicki, I've been wanting to come out to this island now for months. I saw the ad in the paper one Sunday when I was clipping coupons," Connie said. "I cut it out and hid it away in a junk drawer. I don't know why I did that."

"And you started packing, didn't you?"

"Yes. I've had my suitcase packed and hidden under our bed for weeks, adding to it almost daily. Gosh, I haven't been on a vacation in a long time."

"So this is your vacation?"

"I'm so ashamed. I told my husband I needed a week alone at my mother's house, and I've worked out a crazy story so I won't get caught."

"Do you love this guy you're married to?"

"Of course. We've been married almost eleven years. I've never loved anyone else. This isn't about me being unhappy with him."

"Then what is it? You wanted a trip, and he doesn't like traveling?"

"No," laughed Connie. "We've got four kids, all under the age of seven."

"Four?"

"Yes."

"I don't want to change the subject, especially not now, but I've got to ask. Do you know how to steer this thing? Because I sure don't."

"Oh sure, like I drive my sons to preschool every day in a dinghy. Yeah, we prefer it over the minivan."

"Well, the dinghy should follow the same course as the wind is blowing. It's blowing toward the island. Good God!" Vicki suddenly coughed on a wave that hit her in the face. Covering her mouth, she dropped one of the plastic oars. "Oh no, quick! Help! Use your hands, Connie!"

"No, don't lean over. This thing is filling with water. We'll have to let it go."

"I'm drenched. Are you?"

"Vicki, look what we're sitting in! Five inches of water!"

"What if a shark goes by? Are we safe, Connie?"

"No, but steer zigzag, and we should be fine. They can't chase us if we steer zigzag. My seven-year-old, Tommy, loves shark facts." Connie paddled with her hand, trying not to lean too far over.

"I think you mean alligators. Alligators have eyes that can't move in the zigzag manner. Sharks have better eyes. Then again, I heard that was a myth. It's not even true."

"Well, I thought it was sharks. See what I mean? I don't even listen to my own kids I'm so overwhelmed," said Connie, gulping a wave. "Don't get me wrong, I'm absolutely in love with my family, and my role as stay-at-home mom, but I'm so tired. I haven't thought my own thoughts in seven years. I used to paint. I don't do that anymore. Vicki, I've lost myself. I don't know who I am any more."

"Well, don't ask Denver."

"He's kind of strange. He called me a buoy today. I don't know what he meant by that."

"We both look like a buoy out here tonight, bobbing up and down, but who knows what Denver had in mind when he said that. He sees people in an unusual manner."

"Ruth invited me to yoga."

"Are you thinking of trying it?"

"At midnight? I was hoping I could be in bed by eleven, but look at me, already, my first night, and I'm up past midnight paddling my way in a dinghy. It's just like me to do this. At home, on rare occasions, when all four kids are asleep before ten o'clock, I would suddenly find myself folding laundry, which then led to cleaning my closet, then my bathroom."

"Who is home with your kids now that you're gone?"

"My husband. Times have gotten pretty bad for us. He took a risk with a venture capital company, and it filed for bankruptcy. He's been home for weeks calling around for a new job. Our house is small, cramped, and always a mess, and I just lost it. I knew he'd never let me leave for some island, so I just left—and here I am."

"How long do you plan to stay?" asked Vicki, feeling like soggy cereal.

"I'd love to stay for a month, but I miss my kids already. And I miss my husband horribly. I don't know what to do. I'm afraid if I return, I'll start feeling the same way as before, buried under grocery shopping, cleaning, cooking, changing endless diapers, and being awakened every night at least once by each child. That means being awakened at least four times a night; therefore, I'm only actually asleep for a couple hours a night. I don't want to bore you with the details."

"Well, unless we start seeing some clues as to where we're paddling, you'll be wishing you were home ironing, safe, dry, and alive," said Vicki, surveying the area around them for signs of the island. "Wait. What's that?"

She pointed to a light that had appeared out of nowhere. It shone again, long enough for the women to catch a glimpse of the island.

"It can't be. Tarpon Key's lighthouse has never had a light," said Connie.

The women stared at the beam of white light in the night, two flashes every thirty seconds. "I know, but it is," said Vicki. "Come on, let's start paddling faster and in that direction."

"Thank you, madman John Bark. Thank you!" whispered Vicki. The waves had become so high that she lay down in the dinghy for a moment of shelter.

The direction of the waves worked to their advantage, and they noticed the current carrying them toward the light—and toward their island. Both were hugging each other under the slanting rain—in part for comfort, but also so that neither would fall out of the deflating dinghy. At this point, the dinghy had reduced its services to those of a kickboard, and it was no longer something they could sit in. Instead, with both arms holding onto it, they used leg power to kick their way back to Tarpon Key. Vicki's foot cramped into a charley horse, but they did reach the back side of the island, near the old houseboat.

With the hair on their arms standing straight up from the cold, they left the dinghy and splashed ashore, dragging the collapsed rubber boat up the bank and leaving it there. They found the trail and started following it toward the staff house, not realizing they were doing so without flashlight, kerosene lantern, or moon in sight. Connie clung onto Vicki's arm all the way.

"You're dream was not in vain, John Bark," Vicki whispered as they ran past the fixed, immovable, dependable structure, but there was no longer any flashing light coming from the lighthouse tower. It stood there innocently, a relic of an era gone by, the object of one man's skill, mastery, and passion.

"I think I'm going home tomorrow," said Connie as they passed Ruth's bungalow.

"Couldn't you stay a bit longer? Can they survive without you for a couple more days?"

"Yes, they probably can, but I picture my three-year-old, Lizzy. She has the toughest time sleeping without Snuffy. She must have slipped him into my suitcase because she wanted me to have someone special to cuddle while I was away."

"But everyone comes out here for a reason. Do you think you've gained anything from the island yet?"

"I feel like I'm a person again. I'm carrying on adult conversations. I've hardly said the word 'boo-boo' once all day, except when Howard sliced his finger with the potato peeler. Men, I think, have found me interesting and fun to talk with, even though I have absolutely no interest in anyone but my hubby."

"What is going to be different for you when you return?" asked Vicki, her skin stinging from saltwater and her finger joints stiff from the cold.

"I don't know. I honestly don't know."

"Then we can't go back to the staff house. You can't go to bed, not yet. Time is of the essence. You've got to get more out of this island experience." They passed the staff house and continued on to the restaurant, dripping wet.

They entered the dark, kerosene-lit bar, surrounded by postcards of lighthouses that hung on the walls and were surprised to see so many strangers on the stools at this time of the night, or morning, they didn't know which. The same band that played during dinner was still singing more great hits from the Doors as well as songs from the Dave Matthews Band. For a moment, they watched men talking together at the bar. Some were millionaires of the mannequin sort—their complexions as clear and pampered-looking as their wives'—and others were plain old rugged-looking anglers. They had all arrived from different walks of life and had different stories. Vicki couldn't help but hear their voices like the tides drifting in and out of her hearing range.

"I killed a five-foot-long alligator here on the island once," said one man. "Yeah, that's right. Cooked it for dinner. Tasted great."

After a few sips of Chianti, she heard that same voice add, "I also caught this shark." He held up a tooth he wore on a gold chain around his neck.

"*You* caught a shark?" asked a lady sitting at the end, also overhearing his story. "On purpose or by accident?"

"I set out shark fishing for the night. Caught it on purpose," he answered.

Just then Simon took notice of the women standing near the fireplace, drying their wet dresses. "What happened to you two? Looks like you were caught out in this storm," he said.

"We didn't know there was a storm coming," replied Connie.

"None of us did. These guests have been stranded in the bar all night, drinking and talking. Nothing better than that," he laughed. "Come on over. Join in."

They took a seat on each side of Simon, and he put his arms around them both. "Are you two enjoying this magnificent mangrove as much as I am?" he asked.

"Oh yes, we are."

"Good, because I have a lot of pride in this area. It's in my blood, my history," he said. "And the Calusa Indians, the Spanish Conquistadors, they all loved this magnificent area as well."

"Hey, Vicki, looks like you could use a rum and pineapple juice. It's the drink of the night," said Ray from behind the bar.

"Sure. I'm getting kind of tired of red wine and that whole French paradox thing," she replied. "Connie would probably like one too."

"You got that one right."

Ray stabbed a pineapple with a plastic sword and set a drink before Vicki. "Simon and these gentlemen were all just discussing life's journeys."

"That's right," added Simon. "Tell us, what's one of *your* greatest journeys in life?" he asked the newcomers.

"I don't have one."

"I don't either."

"My dears, you've got to have one, both of you."

"No, I don't."

"I agree."

At that point, Howard and his three-piece wig, which nested an inch too far to the left, walked into the bar and signaled Vicki to meet him at the dartboard. "Oh, I'm horrible at darts," she said, then walked away from the life-journey conversation to join Howard.

"Listen to me," he whispered, aiming a dart at the board. "Remember that Spanish contact I told you about?"

He threw the dart, making bull's-eye. "Here's his name and number. He lives in Madrid. His name is Ignacio. Call him Nacho for short. He's about your age. Look him up when you get there."

"But, will he -"

"No questions. Just look him up," said Howard as he handed Vicki the darts and started walking out of the bar in a hurry. "Oh, one more thing. Promise me you'll ask him to play the piano for you."

"The piano?"

"Yes, remember the piano." Howard left the bar, and Vicki stood there with nothing to do but toss the darts. She missed the board altogether and almost hit Ruth, who just walked in.

"Hey, everyone! How about some coffee? We'll put Kahlúa in it, on the house." Ruth walked up to Connie and felt her cold, wet hair.

"Hey, I bet you didn't know getting caught in a storm was part of the job description."

"Ruth," Connie said seriously. "I don't know if I'm going to make it out here."

"Oh? Could it be the feeling-stranded-on-a-remote-island phase? Vicki, you felt that when you first arrived. Tell Connie about it."

"No, it's much more than feeling stranded." As Connie downed her rum and pineapple juice, she started laughing. She laughed until tears rolled down her cheeks. The laugh differed from her usual one. It was a pathetic sound, as if she knew she should be crying instead of laughing, or as if her emotions were taking control and playing nasty tricks on her. Like a watershed, her tears kept pouring. Everyone stared.

"I left my four wonderful babies and my incredible husband to come here. They don't know I'm here," said Connie, crashing out of her emotional ride. "I was barely keeping my head above water. I was losing myself. I felt like I was existing simply to keep everyone else on track."

"I told ya she's a buoy, bobbing up and down," stated Denver from across the bar, the first words he had spoken all night. They all stared at him for a moment.

"And I told Connie," said Vicki, "that if she left too soon, she might be pushing herself against the wind, and that she might only wind up back where she started from—confused and in need of another island escape."

Both Ruth and Simon were now very much focused on Connie's emotions.

"Yes, in part, you are right," said Simon. "She will find herself in need of another escape; however, not everyone can pick up and actually leave for a real island."

"I escaped here because we're so low on money, that I figured I could at least escape to paradise and work at the same time," added Connie. "If I return, I don't have the money to leave again for another island."

Ruth nodded in understanding. "This has absolutely nothing to do with real money, but you need to treat yourself as if you were a monthly bill. You need to pay yourself first. By that, I mean you must somehow find time to do something special for yourself every single day, despite the household demands that are screaming out to you. If you do not pay yourself first, you will soon die, emotionally. Children want their moms to be happy."

"That's right. Ruth spent years on Wall Street. She gives great financial advice." Simon smiled. "And Connie, you need to discover a more realistic island, one that naturally fits into your life."

"I once needed to escape my life, so I did," added Ruth. "I physically fled. I upped and left New York City. I did not have to leave, but back then I only knew how to run. I'm here and I love it, so I've decided to stay, but you see, had I known then what I know now, I would have simply built a fortress there. It can be done anywhere. You don't need to run from your life. You simply need to make it more beautiful, add walls adorned with flowers and a garden, have a sanctuary to peacefully sit in once a day, or more. It's all up to you."

"I say that everyone needs to discover an island. I repeat, it doesn't have to be a real island," said Simon. "It just has to be a time and place where you can stop and think."

"It can be on a cozy chair by your favorite window, or a bench at your favorite park, or the local coffee shop," said Ruth. "Then, you need to think about what sorts of boundaries and limits you can build in your life so that you're living in a peaceful palace."

"There are islands everywhere just waiting to be discovered," said Simon. "And Vicki, you say you have never been on a journey, dear? You have never been unemployed, unable to land a job? You have never said good-bye to someone you love? You have never lost something precious? You have never feared anything in life? You have never felt under the weather or like you were drowning?"

"I sure have," interrupted Connie.

"Yes, me too," said Vicki. "I've spent endless night wondering if I'd ever see the light of day."

"Then you have both gone on journeys. Don't ever underestimate the journeys you've been on. They don't have to be geographical or physical journeys. Everyone has their dark days of life when the storms feel never-ending."

"Often, these journeys make up the women that you are and the ones you are becoming," said Ruth.

Just then, the band, also stranded by the storm, went on break and, for a moment, the voices of everyone living on the island and visiting the island blended like a symphony. The colors and stories added many notes. The kerosene light was now so dim that the bodies could hardly be seen. It was a room of voices, of stories, of lives anchoring for a moment, long enough for a drink and maybe more. Someone offered Vicki another drink, and when she turned around, Connie had left.

Would she follow the advice given? Would she return to her life and the endless cycle of her everyday existence, the joys of motherhood blended with the eclipse of who she was and who she used to be and who she wanted to become? Basically, Vicki mused, would she do as Simon said?

CHAPTER SEVENTEEN

MUCH HAPPENS BETWEEN THE hours of sunset and sunrise. Sometimes, issues become clear in late-night conversations or spells of insomnia or prayers. Other times, they work themselves out in our dreams, as if our brains surrender to another existence, and in the morning, our subconscious minds have it all figured out for us.

In the morning the restaurant sounded boring without Connie's laughter, and Howard no longer sat on the upside-down bucket in the kitchen. Someone said he had caught his own private charter off the island in the middle of the night, and they had seen him carrying Connie's gigantic blue suitcase.

Vicki stopped in for a coffee to go, then left on the morning boat for her two days off. As the boat took off at high speed, she glanced back at the island that was shrinking into a tiny speck, and then it vanished. Several dolphins playfully escorted them for the rest of their ride. When she turned to look forward again, she could see Ben sitting on the edge of the dock waiting for her. She felt like a person living a dual life between "on the island" and "off the island."

She liked this part of her world, the one with Ben in it. They spent the morning sipping coffee while sitting outside near the fountain at the Bell Tower shops in Fort Myers.

"I'm sorry. Did it burn you?" she asked as she knocked her large latte over and onto his lap. "I can't believe I did that."

"Why are you always dropping things? The bottle of wine into the sand last time we saw the sunset, the lightbulb last time I picked you up at the condo, the suit—"

"I know, I know," she interrupted. "My suitcase was in the water when you picked me up at the marina." She didn't want to admit that love was playing a hilarious joke on her every time she saw him, but she knew she loved him, and the sound of his voice made her drop some- thing every time.

Later, Ben had to meet up with a contractor to discuss plans for a high-rise they were designing in Naples, and Vicki left to pick up her father at the airport.

The business situation in Michigan would demand more time, but he was returning to Florida for a few days to handle additional details on this end. She spotted him instantly and gave him a big hug. They spent a couple of hours eating and talking together at a restaurant on Sanibel.

"So how was Michigan, Dad?" she asked as she sipped her chocolate shake.

"The new owners are now selling hot dogs in the shop. I don't know that it goes that great with ice cream," he said.

"Ugh."

"And they painted the front door a much darker pink."

"I liked the old pale pink. It was always a pale pink," she said.

"Yeah, I know. Couldn't believe it."

"What else did they change?" she asked.

"They're redecorating Mom's guest rooms upstairs."

"No. You're kidding. They can't! We wallpapered those together, all of us."

"Yeah. Wait till they find all the letters you girls scribbled in marker on the walls under the paper."

"Hey, they're still carrying the same flavors, aren't they?"

"Yep, but they added sorbet down on the end," he said.

"That's no good. No, they shouldn't start getting complex like that."

"Tell me about it. And you know how you girls used to draw the daily special in chalk on the chalkboard?"

"Yeah, what happened to the board?"

"They were going to dump it."

"How could they? Customers loved those chalk drawings."

"I know. I've got the board in my suitcase. It still has your parfait picture on it. Some of the whipped cream smeared off, but we'll preserve the rest of it." He sipped his creamy coffee.

"Sounds like you miss the place, Dad."

"I do. I admit it. My mind still smells the waffle-cone batter heating up on the griddle every morning," he laughed. "Looking ahead now, how are you preparing for Spain?"

"Well, I do need to start reading. There's a list of assigned books. The first is, *A World History of Our Own Times*—a five-hundred-and-seventy-one-page history book."

"Do you have time out there?" He bit into his cheeseburger, loaded with hand-sliced onions and tomatoes.

"I'll make time. I've got five more books just like it lying on my sandy floor. My foreign language academic counselor said that, as an American representative in Spain, I should be able to answer intelligently any political or historical questions people may ask me concerning the U.S."

"Yikes. That could be scary for our country!" he teased.

"Hey, I could tell them what sorts of fish we have in our waters. Now isn't that a lot more interesting?" she asked.

"Yes, but can you tell them in Spanish? That is the real question," her father asked.

"No, I don't think so. Hey, Dad, tell me, what types of fish live in Lake Michigan?"

"I'll be darned!" He laughed. "My daughter is asking about fish?"

"I'm sort of curious."

"Okay. There's perch, bass, catfish, tuna, smelt, sturgeon. Do you want me to go on?"

"No, that's good enough."

"That reminds me." He reached into his wallet and pulled out a small photo. "You asked for it. You got it. Here's a picture of Holland's lighthouse."

"Thank you, Dad."

"Not a problem. When you called and asked me to drive out to there and take a picture of it, I didn't think I could find the time," he said. "But I did, and after quickly snapping the photo, I found myself sitting there, for a good hour at least. The water, the lighthouse, it got me thinking about the journey Mom and I have taken, from the Midwest to the South, and now what? It was then that I realized we need to operate another business of our own. I miss pride of ownership. I miss our old comfort zone. We raised you girls there. All our memories are there. It's been tough on us, leaving it all behind."

"I know it has, Dad."

"But we'll find something new," he said. "A new adventure. We've got to. That's what people do when they leave behind the life they loved. They find new things."

"You will, Dad. I know you will."

On her second day off work, Vicki awoke with a strong craving. And because there is a time for everything—a time to be silent and a time to speak—she knew it was okay to spend the day silently alone. After weeks of being in the company of and listening to the stories of others, she now wanted to listen to herself. And she longed for this personal time as much as one might a day at the spa. She needed the silence as does a woman balancing on a trapeze. The slightest noise might distract or throw her off course, sending her and the thoughts she needed to think into midair, then crashing to the ground. She neither knew nor cared what she might say to herself, nor what she might hear in her day of solitude. She only knew she needed to mentally pamper herself for existing in a constantly changing world. There was no harm in pampering one's soul from time to time, acknowledging its journey.

She packed her bag with books on seashells, then drove to the west end of Sanibel and over Blind Pass Bridge to Captiva Island, the narrow piece of land with the Gulf of Mexico on one side and the bay a couple of feet away on the other, and then she drove as far as she could go, toward the end of Captiva. She needed to go there. She had walked around the tip of Captiva many times throughout her life, with her grandmother, her sister, her family and felt that area calling her back.

Older and now alone, she grabbed a handful of the sizzling-hot white sand and let it sift through her fingers. She tossed broken shell chips into the water and started walking along the crunchy seashore, a forced emporium. At first, she noticed the shells in a detached sort of way. Florida Fighting Conch—three-inch-long shells, rich in orange and brown to deep mahogany shades—seemed to be the majority. They shared the sand with scallops that looked like stone fans, and whelks, which were orange, white and brown, like little pounding tools. Fragmented seashells that once were whole and gorgeous somewhere out in the Gulf of Mexico were now getting smaller with every foot she walked along the beach. She stayed selective. The shells of dead mollusks went carefully in her bag. Seashells with living, slimy creatures inside were pitched into the waves. As for the starfish and sand dollars, it was hard to tell if they were alive or dead, so she tossed them back into the water. Her eyes followed the flying, fuzzy starfish until they hit the water and sank.

She walked for miles, her neck aching from hunching over and looking down. But she felt her immune system strengthening with every step and breath she took. Searching for seashells calls a person's attention to the immediate present, a therapeutic place to be.

When she glanced up, she spotted an old lady walking the shore toward her. The lady, white and freckled, and wearing a hat topped with colorful feathers, looked more like a nearly extinct, precious and treasured bird species.

"I like your hat," Vicki said.

"Why, thank you," replied the woman.

"It looks like something my grandmother would have worn. Purple was her favorite color. She loved to walk these beaches daily."

"I'm a local here. Perhaps I knew your grandmother?"

"Betty Jann."

"Yes, come to think of it, I did! We met at a meeting to raise awareness for manatees. There was a lunch afterward, and your grandmother and I sat at the same table. In fact, I told her I had the recipe to instant gratification."

"You did?"

"Yes. I took her address and promised I would send it to her."

"I can't believe this. I've been wondering about that recipe. What is it? She was going to send it to me, but never told me what it was."

"Oh, you've got to have it. Everyone needs a little instant gratification in life, dear. How about I send it to you?"

"Okay. I would love that."

"Are you at your grandmother's address?"

"Yes."

"Good. I never throw out an address. I'll send it to you. I feel bad I never got around to sending it to your grandmother, but I'll send it to you right away!"

"Thank you."

"No problem. Have a nice day."

"You too."

She continued walking, feeling a closeness with her grandmother and her past. And then she squinted as she looked across the channel, past northern Captiva Island. Somewhere out there, too far to see was Tarpon Key, her present. Soon the summer would be over, and she would leave that mangrove and Florida behind, just as she had done with Michigan. The very thought of leaving another comfort zone made her feel queasy. It was as if there newly hatching caterpillars in her gut, and they were nibbling on their eggshells.

CHAPTER EIGHTEEN

WHEN VICKI RETURNED TO the island, she missed Denver. "Ruth, where is Denver this morning?" she asked.

He left. He left for good, Vicki. He said he had inherited money. Seventy-five thousand dollars, so he claimed. Like I really believe that! Oh well, you know Denver."

Ruth took a white filter off the shelf and started measuring five tablespoons of coffee grinds.

"Add a few zeros, and you'll have the accurate amount," mumbled Vicki. She had heard more of their fight that night than she had fessed up to. "I wonder what he's going to do with that kind of money?"

"I don't think he was telling the truth, Vicki. It's a nice fantasy, and I'm glad to see he's got a good imagination. I couldn't help but laugh when he told me, though. It was kind of amusing, and creative."

"I hope he anchored here long enough to repair himself. I hope he spends it wisely."

"What?"

"Nothing. I'd better get ready for work."

Nothing ever changed on Tarpon Key—except its visitors. They were always coming and going, like ships—anchoring for a moment and gone the next. It seemed as if everyone should at one point or another make a journey in search of an island, to stop, to think, and to relearn who they were and what was important in relation to the ever-evolving world around them. Ruth, Simon, and some of the island cooks made Tarpon Key more than a pilgrimage site. They made it their home, staying there many years as artists at their crafts, broiling halibut and baking key lime pie day after day, to the utmost perfection. They liked the kitchen, their domain. This didn't excuse them from needing, at times, to discover yet a further, more remote island, one where they could simply put their work aside and notice the beauty surrounding them.

Every day, Old. Mr. Two-face looked different, or maybe it was Vicki's perspective that was changing. She no longer noticed his skin, wrinkled from age, and his eyes, which once looked small to her, had become incredible windows offering a glimpse of awesome opportunity. His dark side now looked more lonely than spooky, and she no longer wanted a room on the other side because it wasn't better over there, facing the trees.

Having worked lunch, Vicki ran back to the staff house and changed into an evening dress. With time to spare before the dinner guests arrived, she plopped herself down on the mattress, wiping her eyes with the corner of the pillowcase. She missed Denver, the makeshift raft who had stopped long enough to gather twigs to fix his weak spots. He was the kind who would arrive at his next destination stronger than a tanker.

She prayed that Evelyn wasn't victim to any more abuse. Someday she might realize she deserved a good life, and that she was as much of a person as anyone else. Hopefully she would leave her crazy and dangerous comfort zone, despite the discomfort that leaving caused. But first, she needed to get to know and trust God, not the unknown spirits speaking through a deck of cards. What had they offered her thus far? They wouldn't even reveal who they were.

Howard remained the mystery of all mysteries. After his disappearance that morning with Connie, no one spoke of him again. Vicki couldn't wait to look up his Spanish contact. Maybe he could offer clues concerning this caravel.

Connie sent a postcard stating that she would definitely discover an island closer to home but that the timing and location of her last voyage hadn't felt right. She lived like a buoy, bobbing up and down for breath, barely hanging in there.

The world itself could lose value as people came and went suddenly. High school students in Colorado were shot down in class. John F. Kennedy, Jr., his wife and sister-in-law crashed into the waters off Martha's Vineyard while on their way to a wedding. Office workers were shot down in Atlanta, Georgia. A train wreck in India took hundreds of lives. Midwesterners died of summer heatstroke. Over twelve thousand people died in an earthquake that shook Turkey during the night. The quake itself lasted forty-five seconds. Mourning and grief for all these victims would last for years. And the most shocking of terrorist attacks came on U.S. soil—both towers of the World Trade Center and one wing of the Pentagon destroyed in explosions of fire as they collapsed in clouds of debris. Who would ever forget the hideous TV pictures, repeated over and over again? Planes hijacked and turned into diving bombs aimed at America's universal symbols of freedom, fortresses of power and economic might. More than three thousand people disappeared with no trace – flight crews, passengers, innocent tenants, military personnel – mothers, fathers, children, brothers, sisters, sweethearts and friends. Death had come in a cruel manner, manifesting itself in many costumes. These people, many young in age, had come and gone so quickly, too quickly.

As the world collectively mourned such public losses, individuals everywhere mourned silently and alone for lost loved ones of their own. Many embarked on journeys in search of something comfortable and soothing to fill their voids. Some dared to venture far enough, to find that one special place, not necessarily a real island like Sanibel or Captiva, but something more remote, like a Tarpon Key, their own lost continent of Atlantis, a place of recovery. And many didn't need to venture that far. What they were looking for to fill their void and comfort their loss was with them all along.

Also in this season, the artists in Saugatuck were looking to the leaves, masters of color, as they prepared for their annual autumn exhibit. The proud branches would soon model bold, vibrant, yet perennial oranges, purples and reds, but only for a season. Then they would shed everything without question, and the locals would decorate the naked winter branches with more than five hundred thousand Christmas lights. Couples, wrapped in warm blankets and riding through the village in horse-drawn carriages, would marvel at the trees, not dead, just asleep, yet looking so awake.

Back in Holland, they were strategically planting tulip bulbs four to eight inches deep and six to ten inches apart in the cool soil, and students were buying their books and returning to campus where classes would be starting soon. Vicki tried imagining herself walking the campus – its perfect comforts of life and its pristine charm and the bright young faces. She instead felt thankful for her living, breathing lessons on the island. Although she couldn't picture herself a part of university life now, her mind rushed her through its seasons, and she longed to rake the lawn and smell the burning piles of orange, crunchy leaves on the side of the road leading to her classes. She craved a mug of hot chocolate with marshmallows while warming her toes in front of the residence fireplace. She wanted to feel the first snowflakes of the season land on her eyelashes. Suddenly, everything went gray like a landslide burying her thoughts of both the future and the past.

She tried hard, but in no way could she imagine herself in Madrid. She couldn't picture anything about Madrid, a place that seemed so far away; a place she had never seen. She blocked out all anticipation and allowed herself no expectations. She reminded herself to live only in the present and opened her letter to Grandma.

Dear Grandma,

I've met a lot of interesting "ships" (short for friendships) this summer. It is good to anchor, every so often, in life. Eventually, anchorage spots become comfort zones, where we fill up on wisdom, stories and interesting relationships. We need to rest in one place before we can fuel ourselves to move onward again.

Yes, we're all like ships coming and going, and we're all propelled through life by different things. Some make their way by oar and sails, and others by paddles and poles. Some have steam engines and boilers, and some internal-combustion engines or outboard motors. Some go through life in a purely recreational manner while others stay practical. If a vessel is determined enough to stay on course, it will be strong enough to resist the waves banging against it. Some of us take on water and sink from time to time, while others constantly work to stay afloat. I've met all of these vessels.

It doesn't matter where they come from, or where they are going. The waters of the lakes can be as unpredictable as the waters of the sea, and both have caused many shipwrecks.

I haven't begun to prepare for my journey to Spain. Why should I? I'd rather live the moment, and the moment is still anchored at Tarpon Key. I'll think about Spain when the time comes to set sail.

That night during dinner, Ruth called her into the office. "Vicki, I'm sorry. This letter came for you today, and I forgot to give it to you. Please forgive me. It's been so busy around here."

"Thank you."

Vicki delivered a basket of warm lemon poppy seed muffins to a couple, then took a seat at a table in the empty front room. She tore open the letter and held it close to the flame of the lantern.

Dearest Vicki,

I wanted this to arrive romantically, as a letter in a bottle, but the post office wouldn't deliver it that way, and I can't control the currents of nature. Who knows where the bottle would have ended up if I just tossed it in the water and wished it toward Tarpon Key? Anyway, right now, I'm sitting at the marina writing this to you. I know you're a few miles out there, but without a boat, it feels further. This fact has frustrated me many nights. Once I woke up in a sweat. In my dream I held on to a log and tried making my way out to see you, but the log broke, and I woke up choking for air.

Anyway, I got a call from my father telling me my mother is not well, and it would be wise if I came home to see her. I think it might be serious, so I'm taking off right away. My flight leaves in two hours.

This is not a letter of good-bye. I know I won't see you again before your trip to Spain, but still, I am not writing to say good- bye. I can't bring myself to do that. I love you and always will. You know where to find me if the currents in your future lead you back here.

If ever I decide to travel again, I will certainly let you know. Perhaps, someday, we can cruise the seas together on a floating hut. They're really cozy!

Love,
Ben

P.S. I tried calling you, but I know that darn pay phone on the dock is the only phone you're supposed to use for personal calls. I left a couple messages in the bar, but you never called. Maybe you never got my messages.

She wiped her eyes with the letter, smearing the ink on a few words. She ran outside and stared up at the sky, spinning around for a moment, searching for the moon. Sure enough, the moon and its fullness stood above, controlling the night. She looked out across the water and tried imagining Ben sitting on the dock, miles away at the marina, but the night was black and she could only see the flickering white of a few sailboats anchored past the island. She glanced at her watch and knew he had already landed in Mississippi. She looked back at the restaurant windows, warmly glowing in the light from lanterns inside, and remembered she had customers waiting for their dinners. She reminded herself his letter did not mean good-bye. They were merely moving on with their lives. She stepped into the ice-cream freezer in her mind. She had to. She had customers who were hungry and paying a lot of money for their once-in- a-lifetime dinner on a remote island in the middle of nowhere.

Her stomach felt funny again, as it did that day on Captiva when she thought about summer nearing its end. But this time, it was as if there were a caterpillar in her stomach and it was wandering around in search of a sheltered area where it could rest and cocoon. The letter from Ben made her want to do that now, to rest and cocoon. But she had to keep going.

CHAPTER NINETEEN

VICKI AWOKE EXTRA EARLY to the sound of rain beating down on the staff house roof. It had never rained in the morning before, so she intended to enjoy this downpour. Ignoring the sudden rush of blood to her head, she bolted upright and bounded out of bed, only to feel dizzy and almost fall to the ground. All summer she had wanted to shower in the rain. Now was her chance. She forced herself up and squeezed into her bathing suit, then grabbed her bottles of shampoo and conditioner, and a bar of soap.

Outside, despite the cloudburst, a miraculous slice of sunshine streamed through the green fronds of the palm trees, producing a tiny rainbow. She knew exactly where she wanted to shower, but it was way off the beaten path. She had to close her eyes because the rain was coming down hard. After she made her way to the special, secret spot, she raised her arms in triumph and, laughing with joy, began doing an imitation of a rain dance in honor of the Native Americans who had once inhabited this land. No one could see her. She had made sure to look around. Besides, who woke up this early in the morning? This was an island of night people and late sleepers. She lathered her hair and rinsed it. The rain provided ample water. She looked down, and her imprints in the mound started to flood. She looked up, but the force of the rain pounding on her tender eyelids hurt. Rain in Michigan would have to pound for forty days and forty nights to equal one day of rainfall in this tropical area of Florida.

She opened her mouth and gulped from the torrents of water streaming down her body. The rain was hitting so hard that she couldn't tell that she was actually crying for the young woman who would never feel the accomplishment of standing as a professor before her first class of students, or bake another batch of chocolate-chip cookies, or kiss another man, or walk down the aisle arm in arm with her father. Rebecca would never be a grandmother rocking in her chair, reminiscing about things of the past. She would never be a mother either. Her tears joined the rain drenching her.

The pain washed down Vicki's face and joined the mud now burying her feet.

Had she made the most of her summer at Tarpon Key? Did she appreciate the songbirds that proudly sang every morning? Did she truly listen to the strangers around her? Did she convert them into friends? Did she touch their lives as much as they did hers? Did she learn from them?

She felt as if a doctor had granted her one more day to live, and she wanted to savor everything—the saltwater air that so often blew her hair into her eyes, the afternoon wind, the squirrels running down the sandy trail in front of her, the view from the top of the lighthouse tower—all these things and more. Time ticked by too quickly, and she felt frantic—frantic because she would never be this age again. That time had come and gone; nothing would be the same and nothing could match it, ever. She already envied her younger self, just starting her adventure on the island three months ago.

It was then that she had left behind the comforts of her hometown, her family business, and her friend. She left on an adventurous journey through dark, wavy, unfamiliar waters. But worse than the mystery of the waters, she didn't know herself or what class of vessel she was. It took Denver to tell her that. As she rinsed the conditioner from her hair, she remembered those dark days of not knowing how to grieve or handle death or deal with loss or change or new things to come, whatever they might be. She also realized she had moved on.

The sand dollars were no longer found along the warmer, shallow shores of the beaches. Instead they returned to the deeper waters, as they do in early fall, and later that day she would be leaving on the three o'clock staff boat. She looked around as the downpour switched to dribbles and shadows fluttering about her caught her attention. She looked up to find five white doves flying overhead. Their feathers were as smooth as the petals of white tulips as they nestled on higher ground, away from the mud. She had never seen doves around the island and felt her spirits soar as she listened to them cooing, one to the other. She thanked God for lending her Rebecca's angels for the summer. Perhaps they might now help someone else in need.

The doves lifted their wings and, in the twinkling of an eye, disappeared behind a palm tree.

Before the lunch crowds arrived, she had piled her suitcases in a closet in the restaurant. Now, in the bar, she took the picture of Holland's lighthouse from her purse, grabbed a black magic marker, and wrote on the back: *Ships come and go, anchoring for a moment—Vicki Brightman.* She handed it to the new bartender and ordered a beer. He laughed as he taped it to the ceiling of the bar. Next, she signed the guest book at the hostess stand: *Tarpon Key, a magnificent place, definitely worth a second visit.*

Once her last table of customers was gone, she gathered her suitcases and said farewell to the bartender, the cooks, then Ruth, standing at the hostess stand by the front door.

"I'll be back to visit," said Vicki.

"I won't be here," answered Ruth.

"Why not? Where will you be?"

"New York. I'm headed back home."

"You're leaving paradise?" asked Vicki.

"No, I'm taking it with me. I'm ready to return home again."

"Then this really is good-bye" Vicki put her arms out. .

"Go! Don't even think about getting a hug from me. Get out of here, Vicki."

She walked out, letting the screen door slam shut gently behind her. Like a dragonfly, with its legs attached just behind its head, walking felt nearly impossible to her.

"Remember, Vicki, if you budget your time," Ruth called after her, "you'll be able to afford a castle well beyond your expectations."

Without looking behind her, Vicki kissed two of her fingers, then extended her arm behind and waved just as Grandma always did at the airport in the fall. It was the authentic good-bye wave. The only thing missing was Grandma's tinted black sunglasses, which she always put on first thing in the morning on the days of Vicki's departures. She made her way slowly down the sandy trail to the boathouse, where she had once arrived on the island and where she would now leave the island.

Simon started the staff boat and, for a minute, Vicki could feel the eyes of the dock master on her. Ignoring his compassionate regard, she sat, tearfully savoring the smell of the salty air. One of the nation's bald eagles swept above her in search of a channel marker to land on. For a moment, she felt sure she saw the national bird, endangered or threatened, she didn't know which, flying in sync with its cousin, the osprey. Donning her sunglasses, she watched Tarpon Key grow smaller and smaller as the boat sped away at top speed. She didn't think for very long about the pelicans and laughing gulls following the boat. Instead, she found herself already mourning the tropical mangrove located at a channel marker in the Intracoastal Waterway, several miles south of Charlotte Harbor. She didn't know which she loved more, the people or the place.

She noticed the boat slowing down sooner than usual.

"Dear, you must read some of Hemingway's works," said Simon. "Please, I can't stress enough how magnificent you will find them. Especially now that you've lived in the tropics and you're off to Spain. You will appreciate his magnificent writing. *Death in the Afternoon* can help prepare you for a bullfight. Do be open-minded when you go."

"I will. When Simon says to read Hemingway, I'll do it, just for you, Simon. You've helped me understand a lot this summer, and I promise I'll try to be open-minded at a bullfight."

"Dear, it's been magnificent having you on Tarpon Key. I know you'll move on with your life." He had a sparkle in his eye. "But I also know this place will remain in your heart forever. Do come back and visit. You owe that to yourself."

"Thank you for that first boat ride to the island. I didn't know if I should take the job or not, but you convinced me. Thank you."

After a moment of silence, she asked him, "What if my life gets busy again, and I live in a place that has no islands?"

"The island is symbolic. I told you that when you first called for directions. I tell that to everyone, dear."

"I think I understand now."

"You'll understand it better someday when you do live far away from a Tarpon Key or a Sanibel or Captiva. You'll realize it when you create your own island, when you take time out for yourself and go somewhere by yourself, and do nothing but stop and think. Often we keep ourselves so busy that we never allow ourselves to sit and think. Sometimes errands only bury the things we don't want to think about. That is why we must find islands, moments without errands."

"Maybe I should stay a bit longer."

"Vicki, you have such a bittersweet look on your face right now. What do you think that means?"

"I don't want to leave but I'm ready," she answered. "Yes, Spain. It's time to think of Spain now."

He nodded. "You'll do well, dear. Just remember what Simon says." It took all her willpower not to hug him.

CHAPTER TWENTY

THE MUCH-SOUGHT-AFTER mangrove cuckoos, easiest to find in late spring and summer, were nowhere to be seen, and they too probably looked bittersweet when fall gave them the hint to leave.

"I feel like a mangrove cuckoo," she whispered softly in the reflection of a window at the airport in Fort Myers. "But just as there is a time for everything, well, it's time to move onward. Yes, you've got to think Spain now," she told herself.

It had been raining off and on since she woke that morning, but now the rain was pouring down as if the angels above were tossing water balloons. Suddenly, like a child standing on the tip of the high diving board, she changed her mind and didn't want to jump. The water below looked dark, and the journey there quite long.

She wanted another day on Sanibel Island with her family. Her mother was thinking the same. "I wish we had had time for coffee," she said, just as a bolt of lightning lit up the window and an explosion of thunder blasted from a heavenly microphone. There was a line of people behind her, waiting to board.

"I wish I had decided on the later flight. I wish we had ten more minutes."

Her father didn't offer the many fatherly cautions typical of him. "What can I say? You're going to another country today. At this point, I can only tell you to use your common sense, and I know you will," he said.

"Oh, and perhaps most importantly, do not carry luggage or anything on the plane for anyone else."

"I've got too much of my own luggage, Dad." Now she envied those who backpacked through Europe with nothing but a pair of Levis and a white T-shirt. She wasn't that type. Packing for the trip had become Operation Pack for Spain. She began drafting her plan, her list of items she would bring, way back on her first days off the island. She then edited and added to the list throughout the entire summer. Packing enough clothes for a semester in Madrid used a special portion of the brain, the same area one tapped into in times of crisis, when trying to fit thousands of passengers into lifeboats that could only hold hundreds while the ship was quickly sinking.

"Women and children first. Underwear and bras first," she had decided.

"Get out of there," she told her oversized, royal blue robe. "You're too big and heavy. You can't go."

"We need you," she had said to her pair of brown hiking shoes. "Yes, you will be of much help."

"Okay. I did say women go first, so hop right in," she had said to her sexy black high-heeled sandals.

"Well, I can't separate the two of you," she had said as she threw the sexy black cocktail dress in. "I'll do my best to keep dresses and matching shoes together."

"Me, me, me," shouted her slippers. "Forget it. A pair of socks takes up less room."

"Enough. I can't fit anything else in this lifeboat. Hey, Dad, can you help me close this suitcase?" she had called out. "There's only two lifeboats left. I wonder who should be the ones to go," she said as she looked around her room at the piles of blue jeans, sweaters, shorts and dresses. Suddenly something came over her like a wool sweater on a cold night, and she remembered Rebecca's team of angels.

"You're lightweight and don't take up much room. Would you all come with me? Please come with me," she had whispered softly as she sat on her bed for a moment's rest. "I was supposed to return you to Rebecca once we met up at the airport, but why don't you stick around with me? I'll show you all a nice time."

She heard the last call for boarding the plane and knew her moment to jump from the high dive had come. She walked to the tip of the board and mentally prepared herself, ready to perform the infamous backward good-bye wave. It would take both coordination and confidence to twist her right arm backward, wave her fingers, and look straight ahead. Not many people could successfully pull this move off, but she would try.

Something went wrong in midair. She glanced behind her, failing the backward good-bye wave, and spotted her mother in tears, arm in arm with her father. Her eyes filled up quickly, and once she could find a moment to catch her breath, she said, "I'm not sure I want to go. I was starting to feel comfortable on that island. I could stay and work longer."

"Vicki, it's good to leave your comfort zones," said her father.

"Yes, and discover adventure," added her mother. "We love you."

She got right back up and boarded the plane. She hated good-byes. She didn't mind a good-bye meant for a short amount of time, but she couldn't control time or death, so how was she to know the outcome of any good-bye?

As she tucked her large carry-on bag under the seat in front of her, she remembered that she had forgotten to pack the most important thing in her life—Rebecca. Her friend and walking, talking Spanish dictionary. Suddenly she missed Rebecca with an unbearable longing. This was why she couldn't stop crying. They were supposed to be going to Spain together today. She was supposed to be meeting her at her layover in New York. That was the plan.

She fidgeted with a seat belt that first felt too tight, then too loose. She could control her breathing, but not the plane. No, the pilot would control the plane. She considered walking up front to meet him, but the flight attendant started talking on the microphone so she stayed put. She again bent down, this time pretending to fuss with the purse under her seat. She caught a little air that way, but not enough. She reached up to redirect the air control, aiming it in her face, and asked the people on both sides of her if she could turn their air controls toward her too. For the first time, she carefully watched the flight attendant describe the oxygen-mask procedure.

The darn creatures in her gut decided to rehearse again, but the plane's takeoff disturbed their choreography, and they scattered about inside her. She felt dizzy, as if the earth were whirling around the sun. Faster and faster it went. But it couldn't be. That would cheat our calendar days. No fair. The earth must take its full three hundred and sixty five point two days to rotate fully. No speeding allowed.

Dear Grandma,

Here I sit at La Guardia Airport in New York. Rebecca hasn't arrived yet, but she's always late and me, well, I'm the early bird. Oh, who's kidding whom? I know she's not coming. I've kept my end of the deal, and I've even brought her team of angels with me. I sure wish she could have kept her end. I don't feel like boarding this plane without her. I just traded in American money for euros, but I don't understand how the two relate to one another. I gave one hundred dollars and got a hundred and ten euros. What a deal, I think?! Oh well, if I didn't have a ton to learn, this wouldn't be a learning experience.

P.S. I feel alone, but I know we are not alone for a single moment. We are surrounded by beings we cannot see. How I would love to put on glasses that allowed me to see their mammoth white wings glistening and surrounding me like bodyguards!

CHAPTER TWENTY-ONE

AT BARAJAS AIRPORT, NINE miles outside Madrid, Vicki showed the taxi driver the address she had carefully tucked away in her purse. She silently applauded herself for having written it down in advance and rewarded herself by sitting peacefully and passively in the backseat of the taxi, no verbal effort needed. She had also decided to keep a pad of paper and a crayon in her purse at all times, hoping she could simply scribble pictures of whatever she might need. The crayon reminded her of Rebecca and the goals they had scribbled together on the white paper tablecloth that night. Now, in the backseat of the taxi, Vicki used the crayon to draw a toilet, then a stick figure sipping a glass of water. Well done. Her most urgent, yet basic needs jotted down on flash cards, stored in her purse, just in case her Dutch accent dominated and perhaps trampled over her classroom-learned Spanish accent.

The taxi turned off a busy metropolitan street and pulled up to the curb of a narrow street, lined with meat markets, bread shops and tall apartment buildings decorated with black cast-iron balconies. A woman in her late sixties stood on the curb holding a long, thin loaf of white bread. Vicki wondered if it might be Rosario, the *señora* she would be living with. Her college had assigned her a Spanish family and given her their address, as well as the names of the family members.

The woman watched Vicki carelessly toss the taxi driver money, and after the taxi driver deposited the luggage on the curb and drove away, she then walked up face-to-face with the American girl. "Vicki?" she asked, wiping her hands on her food-stained apron, then pushing fallen strands of dark gray hair back into the clip of her bun.

"*Si, si.* Rosario?" asked Vicki.

The Spanish woman nodded, then stepped closer and kissed her, once on each cheek. Vicki could smell the juice of freshly minced garlic on the woman's skin. Rosario placed the bread under her arm and grabbed two of the heaviest suitcases. Vicki felt embarrassed, as if the woman might be judging her a materialistic American, unable to leave home without everything she owned shoved into two large suitcases, one small carry-on suitcase and two more carry-on bags disguised as purses. She placed her hands over the *señora*'s hands that smelled of garlic. She wanted to carry her own luggage but, after a tug of war, she surrendered, allowing the woman to drag her load up four flights of stairs.

The climb up the stairs felt long. All the way up, the out-of-breath woman offered her new guest a fast flow of shouted words. The words came loud and fast, and there were no pauses between them. The words, sentences, and paragraphs went unrecognized and sounded like static in her mind. The words hit hard and fast, and with her hands full and her dictionary tucked away in her pocket, she felt as though she had been caught in the midst of a rainstorm with her umbrella at home.

"*Baño,*" Vicki said once inside the apartment. It triggered no response. "*Baño, necesito baño, por favor.*" She felt her bladder was ready to burst, like a water balloon hooked to the faucet, as big as it's going to get. Okay, if her words didn't sound familiar to Rosario, flash cards surely would, unless Spanish toilets were designed differently from American ones. As she flashed the crayon drawing of what looked like a stick figure sitting on a donut, Rosario took hold of her hand and pulled her down a long, dark, wood-floored hallway.

After the water balloon had been emptied, Vicki tried communicating again. "*Agua, por favor.*" No one could convince her that "*agua*" didn't mean water, yet Rosario again stared in misunderstanding.

"*¿Qué?*" asked the woman.

"*Agua? Agua, por favor.*" She had heard the word on *Sesame Street* her entire life, and the puppets pronounced "agua" no differently than she was saying it now. But then, they were American puppets. Would Spanish puppets say *agua* differently? How many ways could one possibly say it? After attempting some more unique pronunciations of the word, aware that her Spanish professor might expel her from being a Spanish major if he heard, she took out the picture of the stick figure sipping a glass of water. Proving the worth of pictures, Rosario hurried down the long hallway once more, this time to the room at the end, the kitchen.

"No hurry. It's not that urgent," Vicki mumbled to herself as the woman slid around the corner, returning with a glass of *agua*, which today meant, and had always meant in the past, water in Spanish. *"Agua, agua, agua,"* practiced Vicki out loud.

The tour of the apartment differed from the tour of the staff house. The place was as cozy as a bed-and-breakfast, and Rosario was as welcoming as an innkeeper. Vicki knew the woman spent most of her time cleaning to make the antique wooden table shine, the silver teacups in the hutch sparkle, and the bed linen smell like a breeze of fresh autumn air. For a moment she feared she might have felt claustrophobic in her new, windowless room—not much larger than a walk-in closet—but at least the ceiling was high. The colors of the apartment, mahogany, rust and shades of brown sang out calmness and peace, like the colors of crisp leaves. Anything bright or pink would clash like a tulip opening in October.

Rosario pulled a chair out from under the dining room table and, with dramatic hand movements, motioned for her to sit down. Then she shouted something about soap and twins over and over in Spanish, and "Victoria, Victoria, Victoria." It sounded as if she were saying there was a bar of soap that had a twin named Victoria. Beside herself, the woman dramatically turned on the television and waved toward the screen.

Oh my goodness gracious! I can't believe what I'm seeing! Vicki covered her mouth with her hand. *It's a Spanish soap opera, and I look exactly like the woman on the screen. Only she's Spanish and not a true blonde.*

Rosario shook her head in disbelief as well, staring at the television, then at Vicki. *"Victoria, Victoria, ¿sí? ¿sí?"* She walked up to Vicki and again kissed her once on each cheek, then joined her hands together as if saying a prayer. Vicki felt very welcome, as if this woman had been counting down the days until her arrival. For their first hour together, the Spanish *señora* and the American student sat at the dining room table eating marinated black olives and watching a soap opera called *Victoria*.

At supper, they broke bread and ate. Rosario's chair remained empty as she hurried back and forth into the kitchen for more courses to the meal. There were two other empty chairs as well, and Rosario said something about her two older sons who once sat there but now sat at their tables with their own families. Rosario had a keen eye for when her family wanted the next course, and only then would she introduce it to the table. It started with red table wine, white bread, and more olives. As she brought out a platter of anchovies stuffed with garlic and strips of pimento, she explained that life itself was meant to be savored, just like a meal. "Never rush any part of it," she said in Spanish, and Vicki proudly translated into English. "The appetizers are as important as the dessert. *Sí*, the beginning is as good as the end."

Her husband, *Señor* Lorenzo, sat at the end of the table, and it was hard not to notice his enormous stomach. Vicki wanted to look him in the eyes, but she couldn't keep her eyes from wandering down to his stomach. It was huge and hardly allowed him to push his chair close to the table, so he sat about a foot away from the table and leaned over to eat. Lorenzo was not at all intimidating. He didn't give off a man-of-the- house or head-of-the-table personality. He closed his eyes as he chewed, opening them only to glance and smirk at Isabella, his grown daughter sitting next to him.

Next Rosario brought out bowls of stuffed squid boiled in its ink, fried shrimp with cloves of garlic, and seafood soup.

As Vicki glanced down at the bowl of soup before her, nothing had prepared her for what she saw. Tiny black snails were squirming for life. Perhaps instead of all the grammar and history textbooks, her curriculum should have included a text on Spanish cuisine. Was this a cultural thing? The creatures must have been freshly dumped into the soup and hadn't boiled enough to be dead yet. They squiggled around frantically, taking cover under the hard-boiled eggs.

"My soup is alive! *Esta viviendo*, look!" Vicki screamed. "They're still moving!"

All eyes stared at her, the eyes of her new Spanish family, and the eyes of the snails in her bowl, as she stood up, covering her mouth with her hand. She couldn't possibly eat something slimy and still living. It had taken her several tries before liking sushi, and several more experiences before developing a craving for it, but the sushi she ordered was always dead, and didn't have little ears and eyes. She brainstormed her escape as she looked toward the door. She would take the bowl of living creatures with her. Surely there was a pond or a mud puddle somewhere. Maybe they came from the Mediterranean Sea. Regardless of where they came from and what they were, they were full of life, and she would set them free. But then she noticed them moving less and less. Too late. They now looked nearly dead and swallowing them might actually put them out of their misery, if they were feeling any. Then again, what were they? She had mentally referred to them as black snails, but had never seen anything quite like them before.

Standing up in the middle of a meal the way she had must have made her Spanish family nervous because they were still silently staring, so she started speaking a universal language—a game of charades.

She patted her stomach, shook her head, then covered her mouth. "Estoy, *um, estoy embarazada*." There, she said it, or at least something like it. She told them she was full, or maybe she said embarrassed. She didn't know which came out.

Silverware dropped, as did a half-chewed anchovy from the father's mouth. Rosario covered her mouth as she had many times during the soap opera, and they all started talking rapidly at once. Now she had a bowl of dying creatures and a Spanish family in an uproar, all because she had said she was full. It must have offended them.

"No, no. *Estoy lleno por que comi en el plano*." She gestured with her hands to demonstrate that she had eaten while up in the sky in the airplane.

Their daughter, Isabella, shouted something loudly, grabbed a maroon- colored velvet pillow off the sofa, and shoved it down her shirt and in front of her stomach. Señor Lorenzo pointed to his daughter's stuffed stomach, then to Vicki's.

"*Waaa, waaa,*" he cried out like a baby with a Spanish accent. No, "*Waaa, waaa,*" he cried out, like a grown Spanish man pretending to be a baby.

"Oh dear Lord, what did I say? No, I'm not pregnant. Oh no, misunderstanding. Wait, wait." Vicki slapped her stomach then flipped through the pages of her dictionary and, sure enough, the word *embarazada* meant pregnant.

Rosario and her husband forgave the misuse of language, but laughed and joked about it. Isabella didn't find it funny at all. She hardly ate anything and only played with her food throughout the dinner, despite pressure from her parents to eat more. The family talked for quite some time, but Vicki didn't know what they said and didn't try to understand. The physical trip to Spain had been accomplishment enough. Perhaps she'd try interpreting another time. Now, she needed a mental rest. She knew she would soon have to wake up and learn this language and this family. She longed to know what Isabella did for work. Was she dating anyone? How old was she? Simple questions in English, but quite complex to ask in a different language.

Soon, the anchovies were eaten, and Rosario brought out a pan with various cold sausages, pâtés, and small pieces of goat's milk and other cheeses. No one spoke a single word of English, and they all took turns speaking with their new arrival. After each of their questions, Vicki offered them little more than yes and no answers, but they were delighted and she felt like a grown-up bundle of joy, something a stork had dropped off.

Rosario's colorful meal continued as long as it would have taken for a family of five to go through the drive-through of a fast-food restaurant, eat, then go through and eat ten more times. Who had time for this? How did this family find the time to sit and savor food for hours?

Vicki could taste garlic, onion and tomatoes in the yellow rice topped with green peas and strips of red pepper. Señor Lorenzo took on the responsibility of educating Vicki on his wife's *comida*, slowly explaining that rice is a popular ingredient in Spanish cooking and that any firm, white fish can be used with this dish. He patted his wife's plump behind as she filled his plate, and everyone laughed. Then he picked up a mussel and a clam, and bragged that his wife had spent much of her day cleaning the ingredients for this dinner.

"Did the snails get a bath or shower?" she attempted to ask in Spanish. There was no reply. "Did the creatures enjoy their bath?"

The head of the table shouted something at his wife, and Rosario ran into the kitchen and returned with a bowl of shells, as if to show Vicki where the seafood originally came from.

"*Mas, mas,*" Señor Lorenzo urged as he broke off more white bread and dipped it in his rice. *Mas* meant more, so Vicki got a second helping and a third after that. After the ever-so-lively meal, Rosario brought out a bowl full of pears and apples, and they all continued to feast, proving the end was indeed as significant as the beginning.

CHAPTER TWENTY-TWO

AS THE SUN STARTED TO rise over the city of Madrid, so did the aroma of baking bread from the shops below. Both reached the cast-iron balcony of the apartment four floors up. The noise of the waking metropolitan city worked like an alarm clock each morning, drawing Vicki to the balcony. But Rosario scolded her for standing out there with bare feet, so this morning she put on a pair of socks and shoes, and headed down the long hallway to the kitchen for their morning ritual of cookies and milk.

As she headed toward the noise of Rosario clanging pots and pans, there was no evidence that her Spanish sister, Isabella, had been sleeping on the floor. Rosario always picked up her pillows and blankets as soon as her daughter rose each morning, and there seemed to be no resentment toward Vicki for having stolen her closet of a bedroom. Isabella was in her late twenties and still living at home, now sleeping on the floor, and she held a full-time job as manager of a boutique in the Salamanca District, known throughout Spain as the quintessential upper-bourgeois neighborhood. She worked during the day and enjoyed a social life in the city streets below at night. Some nights Vicki heard her sneak in at around three o'clock, but it never upset her parents. And by the time she awoke, Isabella had left for the day.

How did this woman spend her nights on the streets of Madrid? Was it anything like the nights on Tarpon Key? Vicki missed staying out late, but interpreting a foreign language took much energy, and she collapsed into bed each night. This didn't mean she fell asleep right away. Often she lay on her back, staring for hours at the high ceiling above her, wishing it were the Sistine Chapel so it would at least be interesting to stare at. But it was dull, painted in brown, and only her imagination turned it into something more. At times she saw ships coming and going, or tulips opening in intense colors, or a clean, white paper tablecloth, or a pure white canvas—she didn't know which. Her nights of staring up at the ceiling were long and agonizing, and she missed her old nights on the island, exciting and brilliant.

As she took her seat in the kitchen, Vicki felt tempted to ask many things. *Why does Rosario's husband, Lorenzo, have such a gigantic stomach? Why does everyone leave the house but Rosario? She cooks and cleans all day. Why is that dead animal hanging on a rope upside down in the kitchen with its head cut off, and blood dripping from its neck into a pan?*

Suddenly, as if she had finished listening to a motivational tape, or watching a year's worth of Oprah, she felt ambition joining forces with desire deep within herself and knew she had to turn those pictures on her ceiling into words that could be used in the kitchen with Rosario, in the city streets below, and in the classroom. She closed her eyes and made the decision to advance her language quickly. Yes, now it was time to learn. She would have to act quickly since she only had one semester, so she started by making it her goal to learn from Rosario in the kitchen each morning.

The *señora* poured warm milk into a mug and placed a roll of flat cookies on a plate next to a jar of marmalade. She never sat down with Vicki but instead wiped counters, scrubbed the floors, and poured more milk each time it got low. As the American woman nibbled on *galletas* and complimented Rosario on the marmalade every other bite, the Spanish woman poured out her life and boldly shared her opinions on everything.

Though barely understanding one another's native words, the women communicated. Vicki grew empathetic as Rosario's eyes saddened. She felt homesickness as Rosario's voice lowered. She felt anger as Rosario's hand wildly flailed in dramatic gestures, and she felt frustrated as Rosario wiped her dirty hands on her apron and closed her eyes in silence.

Vicki now appreciated the significance of the family tree exercise they once did in one of her Spanish classes as Rosario told her how she missed her aunts, uncles, cousins, sisters, brothers, nephews, nieces, brothers-in-law, sisters-in-law, great-uncles, great-aunts, second cousins - all living in Pamplona. She shared how her husband loved food so much that his stomach had grown bigger by the day, and how she worried about his ever-growing *estomago*. She mentioned how her life consisted of nothing but cooking and cleaning, and how the collapse of the Franco Regime had accelerated a social/sexual revolution in her country and how, along with the downfall of Franco, came a downfall of morals. The *señora* liked the fact that birth control, abortion, divorce, homosexuality, and adultery were all illegal under Franco. Now, *la gente* do all of these things—littered the streets, picked public flowers, skipped church, and sunbathed nude along the coastal beaches. She shook her head in a tempered disbelief as she spoke.

Was Rosario saying she missed *Francisco Franco?* A man who ruled the country with an iron fist for forty years? Vicki spread pear-flavored marmalade on another cookie and sipped her warm milk.

The mornings came and went as quickly as the marmalade in the jar disappeared, and the two women continued communicating in a way that demanded more than simply traditional talking and listening. It required a keen observation of tones, hand gestures, facial expressions, and body language. Vicki understood her *señora* well over morning breakfasts.

During the christening of a new jar of plum marmalade one morning, she slowly asked Rosario what she feared most in life.

"*Nada. No tengo ningun miedo*," replied the woman as she hit the jar against the counter to loosen the lid.

"You must fear something. Everyone fears something," said Vicki.

"Fear no, anger yes, *si, si*. If fears won't go away, get angry at them.

Drive them away because fears are the enemies!" shouted the Roman Catholic and believer in Christ.

"Do you ever fear or get angry at death?"

"No. Only those without God, without a plan for salvation, should fear death. Then and only then, it should be their biggest fear in life."

"Despite your faith in God, do you ever personally find yourself fearing death?" Vicki spread marmalade onto a cookie and took a bite.

"Only when my children were young. I feared that death might take me and leave them motherless," she answered. "*El muerto* should hold no terrors because it is only the beginning of eternal life with God."

"What would you say to someone who feared death?"

"Pray," she replied, then gave the sign of the cross and blew a kiss up to the ceiling.

Vicki missed the mornings with Rosario, but her next two weeks were spent sightseeing throughout Spain with a group of other American students from various Midwest colleges. The foreign studies program grouped them together initially to minimize culture shock and develop English-speaking contacts, should they be needed through the *semestre*.

Together they toured El Museo Del Prado and El Palacio Real. They drank pitchers of sangria and ate *tapas* in *masones*. They climbed to the top of the Roman aqueducts in Segovia and walked the Alcazon castle where Queen Isabella and King Ferdinand gave Christopher Columbus permission to go to the New World. It also claimed to be the castle that Walt Disney modeled his castle after. Their last few *dias* together were spent in and around Cantabria, a town lying along the Bay of Biscay, better known as El Mar Cantabrio. There they hiked the Picos de Europas—mountains in Northern Spain that rose to almost nine thou- sand feet—ate in exquisite restaurants, slept in bed-and-breakfasts and savored life.

Dear Grandma,

A mural of heaven! Someday, my dream is to own property in Los Picos de Europa, and on that property I'd like a Spanish-style inn. I can't take such magnificent nature for granted. As our bus trudged up the winding mountains, wild bulls crossed the dirt road in front of us. Let me tell you, bulls do have the right of way in Spain, and they can take as long as they like.

I also spotted a tiny, solitary fisherman standing on a stretch of sand at the foot of the immense weather-beaten cliff. I wonder what his catch options are in water like that. Tarpon? Shark? Whales? I'd love to go fishing with him. I hear those waters host the finest seafood in the world. Then again, I heard it from a boastful little old Spaniard who was chopping wood. These people are proud of what they have and of their magnificent country.

Hiking through the mountains was treacherous, and we got dizzy, but I felt like it was the highest and closest I've ever stood to Heaven. It began pouring, and I fell a distance, cutting my knee, but I still felt an exhilarating high. I felt in tune with God and His beauty, His art.

Then we stopped at the bottom of a waterfall. I stood to the side and put my hands in the crashing water. Its temperature pierced through me. It was then I realized there are several levels at which we can participate in life. So, despite the group looking at me as if I were just released from a mental asylum, I quickly pulled my shoes and socks off and started to wade in the icy pool. I then chose to hold my head under the falling water. But then, I decided to go one step further and walked under the waterfall, not minding that my clothes were also getting drenched.

Unfortunately, I slipped on a rock and fell like a child in the tub. I must not have looked hurt because within seconds, shoes, and socks were flying everywhere and the entire group joined me. Thankfully, the path led us to a sunny spot so we could dry ourselves off and tame our goose bumps.

I don't want to return to Madrid. It's a busy city! It's too much of a culture shock after the island. Maybe I'm in that purgatory stage, lingering between two comfort zones. Will I ever love Spain as much as I loved the island?

Anyway, I took photos of my seafood soup at night. In it were foreign-looking shells, far different from the shells of Sanibel Island.

P.S. How does it feel, Grandma, being cast back to your Maker? He loves you so much that he took you back!

After spending the night in a quaint valley inn situated in the mountains of Spain, Vicki dreaded leaving the next morning. She longed for more time to walk with the roosters of the country and to talk to the old, toothless, parch-faced farmers chopping wood in their backyards. The natives of the valley had an ignorance that tasted as pleasantly pure as honey from a hive. She wanted to sit in the geranium- and laundry-filled porches of the little inn and write letters to Grandma. She liked the cold, wet valley air that cleansed her pores. It reminded her for a moment of Michigan's chill. About this time of year the crispy leaves would start to fall, delicately covering the ground over Rebecca's grave site.

The tour bus left, and the group spent the next three nights at a luxurious three-star hotel in a city called Llanes. There they drank sangria and cedra and ate fried squid and tapas under the moon overlooking the sea. They swam the icy waves of the Mar Cantabrio. Vicki and other Americans lay down on their backs in the sand near the shore and let the waves rush over their bodies, stealing their breath away. They danced way past midnight at flashy *discotecas*. They lived a lot and slept little.

CHAPTER TWENTY-THREE

BACK IN MADRID, THE city felt cold, crowded, and dirty compared to the Spanish countryside, but Vicki knew it would only be a matter of time before she found that one special place—Sanibel Island's Lighthouse Beach, Tarpon Key's old dock and houseboat, or its rustic bar. It might be a challenge finding it in a metropolitan city, but she felt determined. She would eventually discover a place to think, to dwell, to escape, just as Simon had said she would. Such secret places made time go by more slowly and new places became a little more comfortable.

Rosario had two such places in life, the apartment and the church on the corner. She made daily stops at the meat market and bread shop but spent most of her time in the apartment or at mass.

The day before classes began, Vicki had mailed a letter to Ignacio Guillermo. She kept it brief, simply stating that she had met a friend of his family's while on a little island off the coast of Florida. His name was Howard. She included her Spanish family's phone number and suggested he call to arrange a time and place to meet.

Dear Grandma,

I especially feel drawn to the Prado Museum and the Centro de Arte Reina Sofia National Museum. I will return often. A museum has stories to tell. Every painting, every piece of art represents a story. When

I first stood outside the glass showcase of Picasso's final "La Guernica" at the museum, I could almost hear the voices of crying mothers with dead babies, soldiers screaming in pain, and dying horses. The twelve-foot-high, twenty-six-foot-long canvas shares a gruesome, destructive story of the Spanish Civil War.

Then the Spanish tour guide explained the symbolism behind it. The open mouths signal that the person is alive while the closed mouths mean the person is dead. The toro represents the country of Spain and hope for overcoming Fascism, while the arm holding the light points out the hope for Spain. The picture itself depicts the saturation bombing of a Basque village by German planes. I took a photograph of "La Guernica," and I don't think

I was supposed to do that. As the guard came running, I hid my camera under my shirt and took off.

And Palacio Real! What a great place to hold a wedding. But since the eighteenth century, its sole purpose has been to hold receptions for royal families and ambassadors. A few Spaniards asked me why there isn't royalty in the United States. I told them there are. We call them "celebrities," and they live in Hollywood.

Then they asked me about American castles. Well, mansions don't compete, so instead I told them we do have castles, but we call them "lighthouses."

As for culture shock? Well, I've grown up near Midwest cornfields and streets lined with tulips, and I've never taken a subway before. Now, I have to take a subway that announces the stops in Spanish. I guess I also tend to smile at everyone who walks past me in the city. Our tour guide noticed and told me not to be so friendly, that it could be "peligroso." It seems a bitterly cold thing to do, but I guess I'll smile less.

I'm also homesick and find myself quietly humming the national an-
them as I walk. I guess I feel patriotic because I'm far from home, and
I'm feeling like a complete foreigner. If I bumped into another Ameri-
can, I'd hug the person to death, simply for being an American.

P.S. You must love living in the eternal kingdom. I can't even imagine
the peace, the glamour, the beauty, the love you must feel for the place
where you dwell now. Nothing can destroy the city in which you live,
Grandma. Nothing can damage its people, and nothing can tear down
its walls.

With a less than typical smile, she proceeded to walk about a mile to Madrid's Complutense University for her first day of classes. Dressed in black
pants, a red-and-black Spanish-looking button-down sweater bought in
Florida, and new, black, pointy European shoes, she felt fashionably
dressed to go with the rest of the Spanish culture around her. Her blond
hair, with no dark roots, and her fair complexion were giveaways that she
was American as she walked the downtown streets, stopping along the
way for an espresso topped with milk and a thin, triangular tuna fish
sandwich on white bread. She poured a little milk into the espresso, no
longer desiring the amount of milk that a latte provided. As she walked,
male voices called out several *"rubias"* to her. This meant blonde, and she
knew they were only complimenting her. She looked like a Spanish soap
opera star. In America, she'd glare back, but in Spain she knew men were
only throwing out compliments as they shouted things at women walking
by, a cultural thing. As long as they didn't bark, or meow like a cat, she
didn't mind, so she smiled a "thank you" and continued walking, making
no eye contact. If truth were known, women hated men gawking, yet if
they didn't gawk, the women secretly wondered why.

Like the hour hand of a clock, she felt in sync with the hours of Madrid. Street life awoke at around eight in the morning, shut down for siesta from around two to four o'clock, then picked up again all afternoon and ticked well into the night. Restaurants overflowed with people between the dinner hours of nine-thirty and midnight, bars were packed by eleven-thirty, and traffic continued until three.

Her time for education had come. As she walked under a huge stone arch in the northwestern part of the city, she could see her destination, the campus, a couple of blocks ahead. Under the fresh colors of the morning sky, the campus appeared as a scribbled-down item on her life's list of goals. In a few minutes she'd be sitting in a classroom, officially a foreign student studying abroad. If she had a question, oh well. If she didn't understand something, oh well. Her professors didn't understand English. And if they did know a bit, they wouldn't let her know. While in *their* country, she had to speak *their* language. Those were the rules. She felt scholarly, so she dipped into her book bag and took out fake spectacles she had bought back home for five dollars. She didn't need glasses, but she liked them. They made her look studious. It's why she had bought them. She wanted to look studious for her semester abroad.

"*Perdoname, Señorita, perdoname.*"

She heard this voice louder than the other voices on the street, and woman's intuition told her he was talking to her. *Don't look, and definitely don't smile,* she reminded herself.

She tried hard to act in a PMS sort of way, both glaring and ignoring the voice from behind her. She put her spectacles on, stared straight ahead, and pushed her hair behind her ears in a bold, don't-mess-with- me manner.

"*Puedes ayudarme, por favor?*" The male voice was asking her for help.

She stopped to look in a bakery shop window but wasn't looking at croissants. In the reflection of the window, she could see a man in a car pulled up to the curb. Rolling down his front window, he beckoned to her. *Okay, he needs help. In times of potential crisis, a glance can't hurt.*

She turned and smiled.

"*A dónde está el Calle norte?*" He only needed directions to North Street.

She took full notice of the car, a Mercedes, and of its driver leaning out the front window. When he smiled, dimples overtook his face, making him look years younger than he probably was. She did feel a bit safer knowing he drove an expensive car. In a stereotypical way, it meant he might be educated, a professional. Maybe he enjoyed the prestige of owning classy transportation, or maybe he drove long distances to work from a home in the country, a hidden getaway, and needed a well-engineered car—her imagination took over. *Okay, he could have stolen it, or he could have smuggled drugs or something. Okay, you're analyzing things way too much,* she told herself. *You've already smiled, so the damage is done.*

"*Yo no hablo español.*" *Smart,* she sarcastically told herself.

"*Porque estas aqui, en Madrid?*"

Porque, estoy estudiando a la universidad de Madrid."

She pointed at the university campus straight ahead, feeling quite confident that she had constructed a solid sentence. Words came to mind and, one by one, they formed a complete sentence, probably not in the right conjugation, but they created a rough sentence. She felt pride, as much as one might while building a skyscraper one floor at a time, then standing below and looking up at what had been accomplished.

In a slow, educated Spanish dialect, he said, "*Un estudiante. Si, si. Pues, parlez-vous francais?*"

Did she speak French? *¡Oh, por favor!* She had just spoken the most perfect *español* of her *vida,* and now this man—with hair long enough to rest on his shoulders, too short to make a ponytail but long enough to curl slightly on his sharp black sweater—wanted to know if she also spoke French. Well, they weren't wasted moments after all, she told herself, the time spent washing her hair in the shower. She did know a little French because she spent every morning reciting and memorizing the French descriptions and "to use" instructions on the back of her hair conditioner bottles. Yes, she could speak French, as long as the conversation centered on shampoos and hair rinses. What did he use on his own brown hair? How did he slick it back to be as sexy as it looked?

Removing her fake spectacles after they fell down her nose, she replied, "*Si, la solucion demelante. Mode d'emploi. Appliquer sur les cheveux propes.*"

The man laughed, displaying once again dominating dimples, the kind that say this man is a doll, this man can only be a sweetheart, and even in times of anger he has a hard time hiding his softer side, thanks to his having dimples that large. He kept his glasses on. They were real, and he was real. He was no imposter. Those glasses belonged on his face. *"Tu eres Americana,"* he said.

She nodded and smiled. He had guessed that right. She looked and sounded American—whether speaking Spanish or French. She studied his eyes behind the eyeglasses—amused eyes—and felt curious about his story. Fine age lines only added to his appeal. Why did she understand his Spanish better than that of any other Spaniard she'd ever heard? His words came clearly and easily and, listening to him, she felt as comfortable as she might if standing in her favorite section of a bookstore. She understood his words as quickly as it took her to read the titles on the spine of a book. She didn't have to read the fine print; the title said it all. Maybe he spoke more slowly than the other Spaniards, out of courtesy.

She asked him if he spoke English, to double-check that their conversation couldn't just take place in English.

No. He spoke Spanish, Italian, and French, and explained that the people in his country tended to speak fast so she shouldn't get discouraged. He told her that soon she'd be dreaming in Spanish.

He put his car in park and opened the door. She suspected she had gone too far, and that she should never have smiled or stopped in the first place. Her tour guide had warned her, but she lived in Spain now and wanted to learn the culture. How could she do that without chatting with its people? The man getting out the car wore a black turtleneck with black, dressy, pleated pants. Did he iron them himself? He came up to her and stood too close, invading her comfort zone, making her feel like a small piece of tissue, a biopsy being examined for disease. She took a couple of steps backward, but he drew closer again, and she felt intoxicated by the smell of his cologne. She reminded herself to buy mints later, because Spaniards like standing face-to-face when they talked. They conversed with no fear of spitting or coffee breath. And, up close, they talked as loudly as Americans who stand several safe feet away from each other. She understood this about him, so he didn't offend her.

In Spanish, the stranger told her she spoke proper Spanish and started to laugh.

She stared at his eyes, a kaleidoscope of brown and green, and, feeling offended, she asked him why he was laughing. What had she said?

He confessed that her Spanish sounded quite antiquated, at least a few centuries old. He told her to imagine a Spaniard in the modern-day United States speaking Shakespeare.

"Great. Thou art a complete weirdo," she mumbled to herself. She had no idea that her choice of words included ancient verses only used in *libros*, though books were where she had learned most of her Spanish. She defended herself by telling him about the Ancient Spanish Literature class she had taken at school last semester. It's why her words sounded a bit outdated. But that was why she came to study in Spain, to transform words learned from a book into living, breathing conversation.

From her language style to her clothes, the observant, outspoken stranger sounded as if he were writing a commentary. She felt alienated and abducted, and wouldn't have been surprised if he had drawn out a silver needle to probe her next.

Instead, he asked about her red-and-black sweater. Where had she bought it?

She told him it came from a boutique in Florida.

Then he asked how she liked wearing the pointy shoes of *Europa*.

She desperately needed to complain to someone about the narrow eighty-dollar pair of shoes she had bought and felt like a native as she yelled at the black torture devices on her feet. She told him she couldn't wait until the end of the day so she could change into her comfortable American loafers. He bent down and touched her shoes, and that she found odd.

All this time, his car engine was running, so he excused himself, *un momento*, and returned with the keys. "*Perdoname, como se llames? ¿He sido hablando, pero no he preguntado su nombre?*"

She hesitated, understanding his question but debating whether she would actually give her name to a man in Spain, a stranger with a fascination for her clothes, her shoes and the ancient style of her language.

"Vicki," she replied.

"*¿Victoria?*"

"Vicki."

"*Victoria, que hermosa!*" He kissed her once on each cheek, then asked for her last name, too.

She felt each kiss, so close to her lips, yet far, intimate and somewhat daring, yet completely innocent and only friendly. She knew the double kiss was simply custom in this country, a place full of romance. For a teasing split second, it brought this man close up and, like a wild, edible plant, he was good enough to bite, but of course she'd never do such a thing.

"*Victoria. Victoria de los Estados de Unidos,*" she answered. He'd have to settle for that "*Quien esta?*" She asked his name to be polite.

He played along with her game. "*Yo soy Rafael. Rafael de Espana.*" She asked Rafael from Spain where in Spain he lived.

He explained that he came to Madrid frequently on business, but lived on a yacht in northern Spain. He worked as a fashion designer in Spain, Italy, and France.

Sure, she thought, suspiciously, feeling ahead of the game. *I've read Danielle Steele. He probably wishes he worked as one. What an innovative way to capture my attention! Imagine me, a young, naive Americana falling for a pretend European fashion designer. Please, Rafael, just be yourself. You're a nice hombre. Besides, I'm not attracted to you because you drive a Mercedes, nor because you dress well. These things don't make a person. Better yet, I'm not attracted to you at all. I just understand your Spanish better than anyone else's in this country. Normally, I go for personality, but I can't seem to translate personality yet. All Spaniards have the same personality to me at this elementary stage in my language interpretation.*

"*Que?*" She came out of her English-language daydream, realizing he had asked her something. Her mind took a moment to translate it. *Oh yes, what time does my class start?* She glanced at her watch, but, like a cruel joke, it looked as if it spoke another language as well. She was too nervous to figure out which dot meant what hour. That required more translating. She knew she shouldn't have bought a watch with dots.

Again, Rafael asked her what time her first *clase* started, and when she told him nine-thirty, he glanced at his black leather wristwatch and laughed, telling her it was now almost ten-thirty. They had been standing on the curb under the arch for an hour, speaking in Spanish.

"Oh no, no! My first class in Spain, oh, and my second too! *¡Tengo que ir!*"

"*Mañana,*" he declared.

"*Mañana?* Tomorrow? What do you mean?" she asked with disgust.

"*No te preocupes, hay mas clases mañana,*" he said.

"Of course there's more classes tomorrow, but today was my first day of classes. This is not good!" She knew her words had switched to English, but that happened under pressure.

"*Mañana, mañana, mañana, Victoria.*" He laughed, a laugh that normally would make her feel as if he were laughing at her, but those dimples pardoned him; then he pressed a button on his key chain and the trunk of his Mercedes popped open. Inside were piles of white blouses with opaque floral sleeves neatly placed over silky skirts. With his nod of approval, Vicki took a closer peek and touched the soft fabric of a pale pink blouse.

"*Te gustan las ropas, Victoria? Tu puedes tenerlos, si quieres!*"

Had he offered to give her the clothes? She felt sure he had said they would probably fit her, and that she could pick one or two for keeps. No, that would be an embarrassment if she didn't hear him correctly, so instead she shook her head and walked back to the sidewalk.

"*¿Te gustan? ¿Te gustan?*" he asked in the same tone Rosario used when she asked if Vicki liked dinner. He grabbed a blouse and held it up to her.

"*¡Si, me gusta mucho!*" She loved the clothes.

"*¿Victoria, por favor, me gustaria tomarte a un restarante, si quieres?*" He looked nothing like the European male stick man Rebecca had scribbled on the tablecloth that night. This figure had dimples, something stick men didn't have. And this figure certainly wasn't naked. No, he was gorgeously dressed. Yes, he was much better, so much more in-depth than the silly little scribble, so she accepted his gift and agreed to meet for dinner. First, he'd be in France on business, and said he wouldn't be back until early October. So they agreed to meet on October fourth at six-thirty in the evening.

He asked where he should pick her up, and she remembered that her Spanish family never had anyone up to the apartment. She didn't want to expose her Spanish family's apartment to some stranger. She was the one to stop, turn, smile, and talk in the first place, so she'd pay the consequences if this man turned out to be a foreign creep. She told him she'd meet him on the main corner of El Corte Inglés, the seven-story department store that stood a block from the family's apartment.

Rafael flipped throughout the pages of a black leather day planner and scribbled the date, time, and place, then drew a big heart and wrote "Victoria." He wrote the same on another page, ripped it out, and handed it to Vicki as a reminder.

Wow, that's quite a way to confirm a date! She had to admire his finesse.

As he drove away, he waved his hand out the window until he could no longer see as the American woman with books in hand turned in the opposite direction from the university, heading for the Prado Museum at the other end of Madrid.

Visiting the museum clicked. It immediately became her place—a comfort zone in a big city in a big country in a mammoth world. *The world is large and easily overwhelming, and that is why it must be broken down. That is why people of all ages need to find their hangouts, their escapes, and little hiding places in life*, she wrote to her grandmother later.

While staring at the works of sixteenth- to eighteenth-century Spanish artists on the main floor of the museum, Vicki felt guilty for skipping her first two classes in Madrid. She blamed Rafael partially for her first skipped class, but she had had plenty of time to make the rest of her classes. Instead, she had chosen one of the world's most famous art museums and convinced herself that she must live with such decisions. A museum could teach more than a classroom. Eventually, instead of feeling guilty, she felt risky, dangerous, and terribly adventurous. She told herself not to make eye contact next time, to keep walking, even if someone needed directions. Besides, who would dare ask a blonde with not a single dark root for directions in Madrid? *What a yahoo*, she decided. She couldn't wait to write Grandma all about this character, who seemed to have popped straight out of a romance novel. Yes, Grandma would love the details about Rafael.

She heard the tour guide say in Spanish that the broad spectrum of paintings reflected the personal tastes, religious beliefs, and political power of the Spanish Crown dating back to the reign of Ferdinand and Isabella. She listened, she learned, she thought. The Prado Museum became her place to stare and think. Who had time for staring and thinking? No one, but she made time.

She decided not to tell anyone of her encounter with Rafael. She had plenty of time to decide if she would dare meet up with this *hombre* on October fourth. He himself probably wouldn't remember her in two weeks, let alone their scheduled date. Would she actually stand on a corner waiting for such a man three weeks from now? Probably not, she decided later, while looking at Goya's works downstairs.

For the rest of the school week and the following week, she arrived early to reserve a front-row seat, and left each class with a severe headache. Listening and trying to recognize the Spanish words of her professors proved a strain. In one class, she was taught something about Spain consisting of two great kingdoms for two whole centuries of its history— Moors and Jews, if she heard right. Both had diverse dialects. The Spanish civilization during Moorish supremacy thrived. There were schools built, and many were free so that poor people could attend. She caught fragments of facts, nothing more.

As the days passed, her mind worked overtime listening, interpreting, and taking notes that flipped back and forth from Spanish to English. She felt confused, not knowing in which language she should make her notes. Her brain heard Spanish and tried to convert the Spanish into English. Should she take notes in Spanish or English? She worried that straining might create an indented fault line on her forehead. Late at night, she looked up the meanings of unknown words in her Spanish-English dictionary, and then studied her notes from class thoroughly.

After closing her dictionary, she would sit in bed late at night and noticed an old familiar problem returning. A terrible knifelike pain darted through her heart, accompanied by shortness of breath. Drained as she felt from interpreting her classes, she fought off sleep and stubbornly stayed awake for hours. She didn't mind not sleeping—she only wished she knew of something productive to make of the night, like tarpon fishing or chatting by the lighthouse. Soon, she promised herself, she would get to know Madrid at night.

Dear Grandma,

When I can't fall asleep at night, I look forward to the next day's siesta. This entire country naps a couple of hours a day. I always viewed napping as a sport for babies. Maybe some Spaniards throw tantrums, but probably not. Owners close up shop, business people keep sofas in the back of their offices for resting, and insomniacs refresh themselves. I love the concept and wonder if I might be influential enough to take the siesta back to America with me. But where would everyone go to nap? At least in Madrid they can walk home to their apartments, or lie on a bench in one of the many parks. I guess Americans in the corporate world could bring mats and nap in the hallways or conference rooms. The lights could go off, and there'd be blankets handed out and a stardust lady to tap naughty nap takers on the shoulder.

But no, only babies and cats nap, and for good reason. There'd be too many sexual harassment claims centered on naptime in America. People would have to lock their doors and sleep safely in their offices.

Could the United States handle closing down business for an hour every day? Naptime would have to be mutually declared and perhaps made into a law. The siesta could only work if everyone went down for a nap at the same time. Winston Churchill napped daily and claimed that when the war started, it was the only way he could cope with his responsibilities. If I were president, I would declare a war on stress and mandate every U.S. citizen to take a one-hour nap every day. I wish my country would wake up to the benefits of the siesta, especially because everyone might then have more energy for fiestas and for appreciating the night.

P.S. Do you ever sleep up there? Probably not. You are no longer limited by fatigue, aches and pains, disease, or mental worries, so why would you need sleep?

CHAPTER TWENTY-FOUR

AFTER THE NEXT DAY'S siesta, Howard's mysterious contact Ignacio
called.

He had received her letter and wanted to meet but had questions. At
first he spoke *rapidamente* like everyone else in Spain, but then he picked
up on Vicki's low level of Spanish comprehension and slowed down, reassuring her that she spoke Spanish quite nicely. Talking on *el telefono* was
always more *dificil* than talking in person.

She agreed. The phone made the language barrier more difficult, as if she
were standing in the United States and he in Spain, and they were divided by
an international border of barbed-wire fences, guards, and mean dogs.

He said that neither he nor his mother had any recollection of a man,
let alone a friend, named Howard and living in Florida. In fact, they didn't
have any American friends at all. After much hesitation, he decided to
meet her anyway, in case the name Howard might eventually ring a bell.

"*Lo siento*," she apologized. "I feel foolish. Let's forget the entire thing.
If you do not know an American man named Howard, there must be
a mistake."

"I do not want to forget," he said in Spanish.

"You must. There must be another Ignacio living in Madrid, and I probably messed up part of the telephone number. Please, accept my apology."

"I am not ready to accept it," he declared. "Call me Nacho for short."

"*Si, si*. That is exactly what Howard had told me to call you as well," she replied. "You must remember him."

"Friday night is best. You meet me then."

"*Sí, sí.* I will bring my friends," she said. Then again, she hadn't made any friends yet, but talking of them might lend the impression she was protected—the higher the number, the greater the protection.

"No!" He insisted she go alone.

What-ifs crowded her mind, as they had on that first boat ride to Tarpon Key. She imagined a strange plot, a kidnapping, a mugging, a mysterious plan set forth by both Howard and his strange European contact. "Nice talking to you, but *por favor*, forget the entire thing. It's no big deal."

"Wait!" he said, as if screaming across an ocean.

"What?" she asked. And then he tempted her with the one thing she had been craving for weeks.

"Have you seen Madrid at night?" he wanted to know.

"No," she told him. She'd been staying in the apartment with her *señora*, studying at night.

"So you know *nothing* of Madrid," he declared in Spanish.

"*No es la verdad,*" she said. "I do know some things. I'm taking several very intense classes, all taught in Spanish and by Spanish professors."

"*Sí*, but you are missing out on the one most precious aspect of Spanish life."

"The night?"

"*Sí, sí.* If you don't know the night, you don't know the people *de España*," he stated. "Madrid has *dos personalidades.* I heard another *Americana* say Madrid was schizophrenic, completely different night from day," he explained in his native tongue. "I want to introduce you to the side you do not know."

This sounded like Denver's introduction to good Old. Mr. Two-Face. Then she thought of tarpon fishing and late-night conversations and yoga at midnight, and knew that what he said was true.

"Okay. Night does have its value. Let's meet Friday night at six o'clock," she said.

"No," he told her, "night doesn't begin that early. Nine o'clock."

"We can meet at a café," she suggested.

"No," he said again. "We meet inside Madrid's Opera House. Friday night, nine o'clock, row ten, seat B."

"What? *¿Que?*" she asked, still uncertain if her translations were 100% accurate, or if her mind had turned reality into a surreal semblance of things she thought she had heard.

He said, "*Yo tengo dos* tickets to a visiting orchestra performance. I will have *uno de* those tickets waiting *para ti* at the ticket box when you arrive. You only need to give your *nombre* to the *persona* inside the box."

"No!" She was adamant. "I prefer to meet you outside the performance."

"No!" he shouted. "I will not stand outside, risking your tardiness."

She paused for a moment because his intensity reminded her of someone. She was the one who was always early. She was the one who stressed others not to be late.

"Okay. I'll meet you inside."

"The Opera House is located opposite the Palacio del Oriente. Do you know where that is?"

"*Si, si,*" she answered. Of course she knew of the Royal Palace, the second most stunning tourist attraction in Spain. How could she *not* know where Philip the something—in seventeen something—had built a home suitable for a Bourbon monarch? It did catch her eye every so often as she walked by, and she had gone for a tour with an English-speaking guide. Alfonso the something was the last person to live in the palace, yet Franco's body was still there today. Yes, she could certainly find Madrid's Opera House, just across from the palace, and she could probably find row ten, seat B.

"*Adios.*" "*Adios.*"

They hung up.

Dear Grandma,

There's something I will never again take for granted back in the United States, and I can only daydream wishfully about plugging it in, turning it on, filling it with water, and feeling the steam rise forth. Yes, ironing. It took me an hour to persuade Rosario that I needed to iron, let alone wash my clothes. After a fun game of charades, she took out the ironing board, but explained that I'd have to pay her first, and that I could use the washing machine only once a month.

I know I shouldn't complain. Life could be tougher than this, but it happened the same day that I was in the midst of shaving my legs in the shower when Isabella, my Spanish sister, shut the water off. She explained to me that shaving my legs was costing her family money and that I shouldn't do it daily, rather, like washing my clothes, I should shave monthly. Once she chased me out of the bathroom, she ran in there and stayed for quite some time. I think she might be sick. Her face looked so pale.

Well, I suppose if I am to live the Spanish life, I need to adhere to this Spanish family's rules. An attitude adjustment is needed. May the hair on my legs grow free and wild!

P.S. You all must laugh at the things that fluster us down here.

She thanked God that the hair on her legs hadn't grown too long by Friday night as she walked the couple of miles to Madrid's neoclassic Opera House. Why was this mystery man adamant about meeting inside? Was he that uptight about missing a single moment of the performance? It was only a visiting orchestra, and he was a *Madrileno.* They're the ones late for everything.

She followed his orders, telling the man in the box office her name, and he handed her a ticket for row ten, seat B. She went inside and found her seat, the second from the aisle. There was no Nacho. A woman sat on her right, but the seat to her left was empty. *Look who is early and look who is late*, she thought.

The lights dimmed, and she could hardly see a thing. Now she wouldn't be able to see what Ignacio looked like, at least not until the performance ended. That is, if he showed up.

He did. A man took the seat next to her nearly a quarter of the way through the first performance and made no apologies for his tardiness as he whispered into her ear. "Do not think I am interested in you romantically," he said in his native language. "I am not."

She didn't know what to say. She had felt a rude disconnection with this man the moment they first spoke on the phone, and she felt it more now.

"And I am not interested in you," she whispered back.

"You are offended?" he asked.

"Of course not. Let's listen to *la musica.*"

"*Si, si.* That is what the love of my life told me. She told me I must listen more."

"Are you married?"

"No. I am taking a rest from her. We have been together a long time, since I was a child. I need this time away, time to listen."

"I think that's a good idea. I think you should listen. You don't have to say another word to me. Let's both just listen then to *la musica,*" replied Vicki, aware that their whispering might upset the people sitting around them.

"I don't like the silence," he said when the music stopped and no one clapped.

"*¿Por que?*" She asked him why.

"*Porque,*" he whispered loudly. "I don't know what to do in the silence. I don't know how to feel."

She herself was glad when the music started up again, so the others wouldn't hear him whispering during the silent moments. But then she felt his shoulders jerking about and his hands flailing in the air, as if he were a conductor himself, or perhaps a crazy man controlled by the music, like a puppet on strings. He bounced about and it all made her quite nervous. She couldn't breathe. She felt anxious, like she wanted to escape, but she couldn't. She was also like a puppet controlled by invisible strings and there was nothing she wanted more than to cut her strings and those of the hyperactive character beside her. Then the two of them might run down the aisle and out the door. He could go his way and she hers. What a nice escape it would be.

"Wait," she said to Ignacio, who was standing up in the middle of the performance. "Where are you going?"

"Quiet," he said. "You must listen. Listen with your eyes shut, and you will hear things you don't hear with your eyes open. I go to the bathroom, and I will be back."

She closed her eyes and listened. It was true. She heard the music differently, and felt it surrounding her body like a powerful electromagnetic field. She felt stronger and healthier as if the music added strength to her immune system.

A good twenty minutes passed. Row ten, seat A remained vacant. She walked home alone.

A few days went by, and she began feeling uneasy about Nacho. Perhaps he got sick and had to take off. Perhaps he got mugged on the way to the bathroom, or he lost his ticket and they wouldn't let him back in. Maybe he was some whimsical figment of her imagination, her alter ego, the "her" she needed to get to know, the "her" who dumped men into a fierce Sea of Forgetfulness, and now she had been tossed overboard herself by someone who gave her no chance to be known, by someone who forced her to close her eyes and truly listen, not to others, but to music, and in doing so discovered new beauty. She didn't get mad. She became curious, and it drove her crazy not knowing how he could tell her to listen when he himself could hardly sit still. And it was rude to leave a woman alone and not escort her home. She called him up.

"*Hola.* You yourself hardly listened for five minutes. I haven't known you long – correction, I don't know you at all, but I agree with your girlfriend. You do need to listen more," she said slowly in Spanish.

"Girlfriend is too simple of a word. She is the love of my life," he answered in his native tongue.

"Then you should have taken her to the performance, not me," replied Vicki.

"I did. I was with her in my mind that night."

It had gone far enough, and she told him it was all too strange. "Let's forget we ever met," she told him. "This was all a big mistake. *Adios.*"

"*¡No!* I will pick you up at eight o'clock on the curb below your family's *apartmento.*"

She regretted ever giving him the address the first time they spoke on the phone. What had she been thinking?

"No," she said. "You won't."

"*Si, si, I will,*" he said in Spanish.

"I won't be there," she stated.

"I will be there."

"Adios."

"Adios. I see you then." He hung up.

"No you won't see me," she said to herself as she slammed the phone down. "*Loco.* This guy is crazy."

Dear Grandma,

The other night I was attempting to make my way through the dark hallway to the bathroom when I heard an awful noise. It grew louder and more ferocious with each step I took. Suddenly, the noise was right below me and, horrified, I discovered it was Señor Lorenzo. I had mistakenly routed myself into their bedroom and was standing over their bed. I've never heard such a snore in my entire life. It had a Spanish accent to it. I started to shake with laughter as I stood there, frozen and blinded, with my hands gagging my mouth.

P.S. Is thunder really some kind of noise from Heaven? I know it's not the angels bowling, but is it anything other than plain old weather acting out? I'm dying to know. Well, not "dying."

She stood outside on the balcony, looking down at the city street below, hoping and praying Ignacio wouldn't show up. Then, at around eight forty-five, he pulled up to the curb in an old-fashioned bright yellow car. As he got out, she saw his features better than she had at the darkened Opera

House. He was a semi-good-looking, short, stocky Spaniard with dark features inherited from Moorish invaders of long ago. He glanced up at her and tossed two kisses, waving his hand first to the left, then to the right.

She stared with disgust and disappeared into the apartment. Just then, Rosario flagged her into the kitchen with a look of excitement.

"*Mira, mira*," she said, pointing to a pot on the stove. "We eat this tonight," she said.

With a quick glance into the pot full of living, slimy creatures, Vicki knew she had no other options. "*Lo siento*," she replied, shaking her head.

"*Me voy*. I go out tonight, I go now. I am late."

"*No*," declared Lorenzo as he entered the kitchen. "Spaniards are always late. It is good to be late. You have enough time to eat a little."

"I'm already late so I would be way too late, very late, if I stayed to eat a little," she explained.

"They are ready to eat now." Rosario scooped snails onto a spoon. "I give you some now to enjoy before you go."

"*Si, si*. You stay," added Lorenzo. "It is good to be late in Spain. Early is bad."

"I am not early. I am late. I am very, *very* late, *muy, muy tarde. Me voy*," said Vicki as she rushed out of the kitchen.

Within seconds, she was down the flights of stairs and outside on the sidewalk with the mysteriously rude Spaniard. He served one purpose, and that was rescuing her from downing another bowl of living creatures.

They strolled to a nearby café in the heart of Madrid and drank a small glass of *chato*, a red wine, and ate tapas, or appetizers of fried fish, slices of sausage and prawns in butter. The café was crammed full of shouting Spaniards, and Nacho's voice blended in perfectly. His opinionated personality made him a sort of genius, except when it came to remembering whether or not his family knew a Howard from the United States. Vicki described Howard's physical appearance, his personality, and the island, but still nothing came to mind. Nacho declared the entire thing suspicious but said he didn't mind. He enjoyed meeting her anyway.

"Try this," he demanded in Spanish.

"Okay," she said as he fed her something off his fork.

"*Mas, mas*," he said before she finished chewing the first bite.

"*Delicioso*," she declared. "I like it."

"You like it?"

"I love it," she answered. "I'd like more."

"I give you more."

"*Gracias*," she said as she waited for him to feed her once more.

"What is it?"

"Bull's testicles," he answered in Spanish.

"No *mas*," she declared out loud. "*No mas, no mas*. I'll be right back," she choked, wishing she had stayed home to eat the snails. At least they slid right down on their own. "*Un momento, por favor.*" She exited quickly for the restroom and remained there a good ten minutes, rinsing her mouth obsessively. She swore she would never tell anyone what she had eaten. She would never admit to having a bull's testicle in her mouth, and, for the record, she had *never* declared anything about it to be delicious!

He lectured passionately about the Constitutional Monarchy, shouting out his own views, then wanted to know her views on political figures, domestic and international issues, literary authors, and more. His words flew out fast, like a human sneeze shooting stuff out at 100 miles per hour. He picked her brain and, frighteningly at times, he had a better understanding of her own country than she did. As he spoke and as he listened, his thick, bushy black eyebrows nervously twitched and arched in sync with the words.

Tranquilo, tranquilo, Vicki thought. She was glad he wasn't acting rude toward her, nor was he the least bit interested in her on a romantic basis. There was nothing fizzing and foaming and ready to burst inside any chemistry tubes. That was for sure!

He asked Vicki if she had seen the morning paper.

"*No, no he leido a nada. ¿Porque?*" Vicki had not seen it.

He handed Vicki the *El Pais* newspaper and pointed to a small article on the second page.

The article reported that Spaniards, and especially *Madrilenos*, sleep less than any of their European neighbors.

Espresso-intoxicated Spaniards still swarmed the café at one o'clock in the morning. A nearby table of students sat flipping through textbooks and highlighted notes. A woman across the room stood in a corner wiping her mascara-drenched face with a napkin as her friend shouted words of comfort at her. Young kids crowded a small table, trading CDs. For Vicki, keeping cafés open in Madrid long after midnight was an insomniac's Utopia. They were therapeutic refuges from the world, philosophical havens and retreats for modern-day mourning. She thrived in this city of night owls and looked forward to the next day's siesta to refresh.

All at once, as if the thought of insomnia triggered her problem, she felt short of breath, as if there wasn't enough oxygen for everyone in the cramped café to share. *I'm so sick of this*, she thought, and ordered *tequila* at the bar.

"Tequila should calm me down a bit," she announced in English, before downing the shot.

"*¿Que?*" asked Nacho.

"Oh, never mind. Tell me, what's the name of this café? Oh, wait, did I say that in English? I think I did." The shot of tequila was doing her no good."*¿El nombre de este cafe?*" she asked again, this time in Spanish.

"*Yo no lo se.*"

Vicki asked the woman sitting on a stool next to her the same question.

"*Yo no lo se,*" replied the woman.

"You don't know the name of this café either?" Vicki felt frustrated.

She liked this place, despite its close air, but she wanted to know its name. She then asked the bartender.

"*Yo no lo se,*" he replied confidently.

"*¿Que? ¿Que?* How can you *not* know the name of the place where you're working? That's absolutely nuts! *Mas tequila, por favor.*"

As she waited frantically for her next drink, Nacho told her there were more bars in Madrid than in any other city in the world. He said there were something like eight thousand bars.

"Oh, as if that's any excuse for not knowing the name of the bar you're in right now. Well, I don't know if this is a bar or a café. It serves both liquor and coffee."

She downed another shot of tequila, disgusted that everyone she asked, including the bartender, did not know the name of the bar, café, whatever it was that they were in. She waited for a thank you from her lungs, and within minutes they were so busy breathing normally that they didn't have time to thank her, and she was pleased. She wanted another, but also knew she didn't want to mask one problem with another. "Let's go, *vamanos*."

On their way toward the door of the crowded café, she stopped to ask one more intelligent-looking man the name of the place.

"*Yo no lo se*," he said.

"You do not know it either? *Estupido*," the Spanish-speaking tequila slurred from within her. She ran outside and looked at the sign on the door. It read, *Yo no lo se*. That's right. The name of the place was, "I don't know."

The next morning Vicki stared at the cookies and milk with the face of a woman who had just downed five shots of tequila and five worms. Rosario asked her guest what Americans eat for breakfast. Vicki liked the morning snack but could still taste the tequila from last night, so she answered honestly, "*Huevos*." In case the woman didn't understand, Vicki pantomined breaking an egg against the counter and pouring it into a pan.

"*¡Si, si, si! ¡Tortilla Española!*" responded Rosario, and she went to the refrigerator and took out three brown eggs. "The most widely eaten dish in my country," Rosario said in her native language. "Watch carefully. Take this recipe home with you. I teach you how to make the *tortilla*, or Spanish omelet."

As she chopped two medium-sized potatoes into fine matchsticks, Señora Rosario bragged that the French stole the idea of the tortilla from Spanish chefs at the court of Louis the something after he married the daughter of Philip the something in sixteen-something. Vicki understood most of what she said. Was the *señora* now speaking more slowly or was she herself understanding more than before? Then again, maybe Rosario didn't speak at all. Maybe her gestures spoke for her.

Rosario chopped a small onion in a manner that declared, "A mother knows things," and the way in which she tossed the onion's skin in the bucket said, "You need more than *galletas* for breakfast today."

Vicki hardly answered. It didn't matter. Often, the women in the kitchen watched each other more than they listened. Rosario rinsed her hands in the sink, then waved them in the direction of a picture of her daughter, Isabella, then held her hands up toward God in a way that said, "*Aye, Dios Mio.* Help her, dear God."

Vicki watched the woman's face, as if watching her soap opera, and made sure to accentuate her hand gestures because that too helped Rosario to better understand. This time she casually waved her hand in the air to say, "Isabella will be fine, don't worry about her." She didn't understand why Rosario worried about Isabella to begin with, only that she would be fine.

As she fried the potatoes and onion together slowly in oil, without browning, Rosario took the time to carefully and passionately watch Vicki's facial and hand gestures, as if watching someone directing traffic. Both only listened to ten percent of each other's words, but *las mujeres* communicated.

Rosario nodded, "*Si, si.*" She beat the eggs well, added them to the pan, and then let them fry for a moment.

She placed a plate on top of the omelet and turned the frying pan upside down, then slipped the *tortilla* back into the pan on the other side. She signaled to the American to stand up and take watch of the eggs and then left the kitchen. When she returned, she had a suitcase in hand.

"*Rosario, ¿adonde vas?*" Vicki asked where she was going.

"*Hoy, no, mañana, si.*" she said. "No place today, tomorrow, yes."

She turned the stove off and, for the first time, Rosario sat down, setting her chores aside as she spoke and cried. She was homesick. She missed her extended family in Pamplona. But her husband had a good job at the post office downtown, and they would never move back there, not now that the kids were grown and living in Madrid. Her children liked this modern world, their home, and moving back to Pamplona would mean leaving them behind.

Rosario's husband, Isabella, and her two married sons and their families made the trip to Pamplona only twice a year. Rosario and Isabella took a third trip each fall and would be leaving tomorrow for a short time. She bragged about Pamplona as if she herself had designed it. She described it as a prosperous city with high-rise apartment blocks, nice lawns, and factories, if Vicki understood correctly. She said Pamplona was so old that, from the tenth through the sixteenth centuries, it was the capital of the kingdom of Navarre. After the Civil War, she said her people had changed it into a flourishing city. She boasted that her people were hardworking, religious, and conservative.

As she wiped her eyes with her dishcloth, she said she loved that

city, but her husband was from Madrid. She said she often regretted having fallen in love with a man from another city because it forced her to choose between her man and her family, and her man would never leave Madrid. She chose Lorenzo, and ever since they had lived together happily in Madrid.

CHAPTER TWENTY-FIVE

ROSARIO WAS QUEEN OF the house and wore the crown of the kitchen. She peeled, sliced, and minced garlic like the CEO of a large corporation cutting out the waste and getting to the core of business. She monitored the amount of food in the pantry, inspecting the onions, red and green peppers, and making sure nothing went moldy, just as the head of a company watches for excess spending and costly items not being used. She walked around her kitchen with a confidence that declared this woman knew every nook and cranny, and every speck of dirt in need of cleaning. She knew when the dish towel needed a washing and when the window needed opening. She gave her kitchen the stream of fresh air it needed, exactly when it needed it. She knew darn well how to peel an onion without tears, but at times, perhaps like a CEO too passionately and emotionally connected to the corporation, she let it burn her eyes and she cried. The voluntary downsizing hurt worst, the day when both her sons left the nest. And sometimes she stayed awake at night,

calculating how much a new ironing board might cost or what ingredients she needed to make the world's best paella feast for her family. At other times she slept deeply, dreaming of a new apron.

Each morning she awoke refreshed and made her commute to work down the long hallway and into the kitchen, often stopping to pick up her daughter's red robe from the floor, then going forward when she saw her husband's green sweater just a few steps ahead.

At times, when she saw the yellow sun rising through the kitchen window, she slowed, then continued her commute down the hallway, not stopping to pick up the mess. Long before anyone else would wake, she would stand at that window, watching the sunrise while praying to her own superior. She gave thanks for the God-given products she had carefully found to feed her family throughout the years, nourishing them with nature's best, never purchasing anything with ingredients she didn't understand or couldn't pronounce.

At other times she simply needed a rest, and then she would return, noticing once again the gorgeous green avocado she had sliced for her husband's sandwich and the ripe, red tomatoes she chopped for the stew, and after pouring olive oil into the pan, she would rub a little extra into her hands, pampering herself in a secret, still moment. Every so often she ran her oily hands through her thick, long hair to moisturize its gray strands, then she quickly pinned it up in her daily bun, the bun she had begun wearing years ago when her hair still shone a deep black.

Perhaps the only thing that set her apart from a CEO was that she delegated nothing. She got down on her knees to clean the hardwood floors. She made several trips up and down the flights of stairs, carrying as many bags of food as she could fit securely in her arms. She washed her husband's and her daughter's clothes, and ironed them all without complaint. She played moderator when Isabella and her father discussed marriage. He loved his daughter but didn't hold back when it came to pressuring her regarding a husband and grandchildren. At times, Rosario—peacemaker, heart of the household—stepped between them and resolved the heated talks in an authoritative yet fair tone of voice, despite her own secret longing for her daughter to find the right man and get married.

Rosario made sure there were just enough pears and garbanzo beans and other food items to sustain her household before she left for Pamplona, but still, she didn't feel deserving of her getaway. She needed to trust that everything would run fine without her for a short time.

Her absence with the power she held triggered a sort of celebration of gluttony for her husband Lorenzo and, incidentally, for Vicki.

The rebellious fiesta began that night at supper, with a pitcher of fruit-filled sangria. Lorenzo insisted that Vicki write down the ingredients of his infamous sangria, made of *vino tinto*, liquor, brandy, sugar, pears and apples. He added the ingredients with pride, as if turning water into wine. Then he urged Vicki to make the second pitcher as he watched with the impish grin of a little boy, claiming that his wife had put this recipe to rest long ago.

As Vicki chopped the fruit, Lorenzo drank glass after glass, telling her he had fallen in love with his wife because she was from Pamplona and Pamplona had better fiestas than any other city in Spain. He said he later had been disappointed to learn that his wife never liked the annual fiesta in Pamplona. She found it overwhelming, but he would one day convert her into a party animal. He had said years ago that he and his father would have fiesta after fiesta, almost every day.

"Do you have a lot of fiestas today?" she asked in Spanish.

"*No, no mas*," he answered honestly.

"Would you rather live in Pamplona?"

"*Desde Madrid al Cielo*," he replied.

"*Si, si*," she said. "I've heard that phrase before from several others, that after Madrid, there is only one destination: Heaven."

Lorenzo admitted he felt guilty and knew his wife would not like the fiesta he was hosting, but he added that *la comida* and *bebida* (food and drink) were his only rebellions in life. He knew he acted in disobedience toward his wife, the domestic queen, but couldn't resist his passion and re-spect for food. As Evelyn would have said, Lorenzo had never outgrown the sweet stage of life. He diluted his coffee with sugar cubes and *leche* and the normally mellow, loving father couldn't harm a fly. He caught bugs in a glass, then let them free outside. He served as an all-around obedient husband who appreciated his wife's home-cooked meals of lentil soup, garbanzo beans with carrots and olive oil, octopus and Spain's best paella. He needed his sweets and sangria once in awhile, and knew that meant sneaking them. Rosario had long ago prohibited such indulgences out of worry over his mammoth stomach.

"When Rosario gets worried over *mi estomigo*, I say, come here, give me a hug," explained Lorenzo in Spanish. "I tell her one hug *cada dia* will add *muchos* years to my life. She hugs me with a smile every morning. I walk into her kitchen, and she stops everything. I know she has a lot of work to do. She drops everything to hug me. Then she returns to work. Ahhh, Rosario! This is why she is so good at her job. She is the heart of the household, the queen of our castle."

After the sangria, he opened a white paper bag full of an assortment of *galletas* and *dulces*—his favorite being nothing more than gourmet chips dipped in a candied glaze of chopped peanuts.

Between chomps he lazily sang, "*Da da da de da de da.*" To Vicki, it sounded like the tune from "If I Were a Rich Man."

She tried asking if he had seen *Fiddler on the Roof*, but the word "fiddler" wasn't in her *dictionario*. Still, she felt sure she heard this Spaniard mumbling the Jewish song.

"*Da de da dee da de da,*" he sang as he controlled the outpouring of the sangria. This fiesta wasn't about to end, not until the last drop was drunk.

"*Mas, mas, Victoria,*" he announced, as if he were a ruler. But he was no ruler, just a harmless, hard-working man who liked to party. But he made it clear that once he slurred his first word, he always stopped drinking.

"Are you saying you do not drink to get drunk?" asked Vicki.

"*Nunca, nunca! Yo no bebo demasiado porque los espanoles tienen la dignidad,*" he said. "Never! Spaniards only drink to enhance their perspective and wit, but once they get drunk, they've lost their dignity."

"*Tengo una pregunta,*" said Vicki. "Madrid is a major city." "*Si, si,*" he said.

"It's a big city, a successful city, a busy city."

"*Si, si, claro que si,*" he flagged her onward, eager for her question.

"Everyone naps every single day. They close down shops and put a halt to business."

"*Siesta, si.*"

"Well, if you add up all those siestas, do you know how many hours it takes away from business in a single year?" she asked as she downed sangria.

"*Si, muchos anos, si.*"

"Well, we can hardly fit in an hour lunch break back in the States, let alone a sit-down lunch, or a coffee in a real mug, not a to-go cup, but a real, breakable mug, so tell me, what is your secret? How can a city flourish despite the fact that professionals shut everything down to nap every single afternoon?"

"Divine intervention," he said in slightly slurred Spanish. "Divine intervention."

"Oh," she replied. "That explains it."

Lorenzo took advantage of his wife's absence for the rest of the week.

One fiesta after the next. Every night he'd open the little white bakery bag of goodies as if he were Santa Claus dipping into his sack of toys.

Despite these late-night indulgences, something significant clicked for Vicki during the day. As she sat in the front row of her History of Spanish Civilization class, she took notes in Spanish without thinking about translations, conjugations, or meanings. She no longer strained to interpret the professor. Without any delay in her mind, she now understood her classes, and her headaches disappeared.

She felt on top of the world. The pages of her Spanish grammar books had come alive. She felt immersed in Spain and its culture. At last, she could understand her professors, Lorenzo, and the people on the streets of Madrid, and that meant she had become fluent in Spanish. As if the joy of it all fueled her, she regularly left class and walked the streets of Madrid for hours; alone, yes, but as a loner, no. She needed time alone, time to think about herself in relation to the world around her. As Pablo Picasso once said, "Nothing can be accomplished without solitude; I have made a kind of solitude for myself."

She wanted to enjoy her own company. Why shouldn't she? She'd have to be with it the rest of her life. And still, after death, she'd again have to live with her mind, her soul, her spirit, herself. She walked under the luminous blue sky that Velazquez once painted and felt the warm air blanketing her skin.

Feeling peaceful and happy as she walked, she allowed herself to think, not letting anything get in the way of her true thoughts. There was a time when she didn't allow herself an activity like this, a time when she didn't have time for a bad mood or for sad thoughts that might surface, but now, as she walked, she didn't hold back. At first, her thoughts fluctuated like Picasso's erratic eras in painting. So, in the next minute, she felt outraged, in a dark blue mood. Deep down inside lurked despair. Grandma and Rebecca were no longer just a phone call away. Her parents' home in the country had been reduced to a memory. She could never scoop another ice-cream cone in her family business again. She felt far away from her sister. She felt furious, fed up with her breathing problem. Breathing was the source of life! She walked faster.

Others were walking, too. Punks with rebel hair, mothers with grocery bags and toddlers, and business people with briefcases followed the rhythm pulsing through the streets of Madrid. They strutted rather than walked. Into the darkness, people went. The nights belonged to everyone.

She walked through Gran Via, a major thoroughfare in Madrid, past cinemas, shops, and fast-food restaurants. After several miles, she knew her walking had become obsessive, like searching for seashells that day on the beach, but she could neither stop nor slow her pace.

But then she walked past a bucket and a gray bundle crunched up on the sidewalk outside the El Corte Inglés department store, and for a moment, felt guilty about her nightly fiestas with Señor Lorenzo. She had no money to donate to the bucket, so she sat down on the cold pavement and smiled at the ancient, sunken black eyes hidden inside a hooded flannel shawl. Still out of breath from her walk, she couldn't talk, and if she could, she didn't know what to say. She didn't know why she sat down next to this stranger who was busy with her hands. At first, she repeatedly twisted her gray hair, then switched to fondling a pebble on the sidewalk, or touching the sidewalk itself. For a long moment, Vicki heard silence, and she decided the homeless bundle, nobody's grandmother, might want to share her story. The woman kept touching anything in sight, as if to say, "I am lonely. I am starving for conversation. Please help me."

Unlike story-sharing on Tarpon Key, there was no wine or rippling currents, just an empty bottle of tequila and the sound of honking horns. But the woman, like every other homeless person, and every other living creature, had a story to share, and Vicki felt like listening.

Out from the black flannel, a scaly, wrinkled hand wiped a cold tear from her eye, but she said nothing. She assumed that wearing this woman's shoes must be horrible because typically in Spain, children, grandchildren and extended families don't allow their aging mothers to sit in rags begging for money. "This is my choice," said the woman, who wasn't wearing any shoes. "I want to be here, exactly where I am," she said in Spanish, and nothing else. After about five minutes, Vicki got up and walked away.

Like descending into Hell, the subway's escalating stairs took her deep into the earth, at least ten floors down. She learned slowly, but she learned. No eye contact. Look straight ahead. Which line to take? Sometimes she got confused. Attention Deficit Disorder, maybe. So she'd just ride. Any line, any color. Once she hopped on, and a little old man grabbed her, pulling her off before the doors shut and the subway took off. Whispering in Vicki's ear, he warned her about some *"peligroso"* stop. That meant dangerous. His eyes speckled with blue, green, brown, and yellow—an artist's palate—as he held her hand tightly, walking her to another stop. He nudged her to board. As he stood outside on the subway platform, he waved through the closing glass doors. His angelic eyes looked familiar. He then pulled out a straw hat with a hole in the top and put it on his head, laughing. It couldn't be Howard without the sideburns, without the beard. No, Howard wasn't that old. But he did have Howard's bluish-gray eyes. They waved until the subway car pulled away, and she could no longer see the stranger. Everyone has that one moment in life, in which they look back, wondering whether or not they have encountered an angel, and they try questioning the sparkle they saw in the eyes or the manner in which the stranger vanished after helping. Everyone wants to believe they bumped into an angel, and there's no reason not to believe, they decide, until they bump back into the same character a month later, and he's honking and swearing one car back from them in traffic. She wouldn't bump into this fellow again because she wanted to believe he was more.

She always power-walked over the bridge, then slowed as she passed the two fountains in the park, taking a favorite bench outside the Prado Museum. Here she tried to memorize the photographic grandeur of the fourteen mammoth white arches, sculpted with various statues, leading to the museum doors. She appreciated the art of the tall, slender black lanterns and the stone-carved figures surrounding her in the park.

She knew returning to visit Tarpon Key someday might be easier than it would be returning to one of the world's most famous art museums, with its collection of over 4,000 masterpieces, many of them acquired by Spanish kings. It might be difficult returning to this, so she wanted to remember everything. That way she could return in daydreams. As a submarine that had traveled from Lake Michigan to the Gulf of Mexico, and now the Mediterranean Sea, she never wanted to forget the route she had traveled and looked forward to the route ahead.

She closed her eyes and felt a cool, autumn Madrid breeze tickle the hair on her arms. She felt alive and in love. Yes, in love with life. She promised herself that when she returned to the United States, she would carry a blanket in her car at all times, and stop and sit in parks whenever time allowed.

Oops! Time would *never* allow such a thing, so she would have to *make* time instead. Sitting in a park would be a priority from now on, and she would cook more than microwave entrees. She would use fresh basil and olive oil and no more garlic powder. She would take time to use the real thing, to peel, then mince or chop or thinly slice its cloves, depending on the degree of flavor she would want. And she would walk into a church and pray, or take a long walk and pray. She would do all of these things and more. Now she knew why people said, "I'm going to *take* time and go on a vacation." They never said, "Time is *giving* me a vacation." So she would do these things, not because time had become more generous, but because she would become a bit more selfish and take a larger piece of time. No one is *given* time. It's up to people to find it, grab it, and take advantage of it in a wonderfully outlandish and selfish way.

Her daydreaming relaxed her like a catnap as her eyes settled on the white pillar of the museum, and she remembered that life was but a passing mist and nothing lasts forever. Sadness, anger, resentment, and worry pass like the clouds—some are just slower-moving storms.

"I've got no money," she said to a homeless man who sat down next to her.

"I have no intention of begging for *dinero* from you, *Americana*," he replied in Spanish. "Although I feel I am entitled to it."

"Oh? And why do you feel you are entitled to money?" she asked.

"I have a noble title in life," he boastfully claimed in a blend of Portuguese and Spanish. "My nobility dates back to the Middle Ages, to the time the Christians started reclaiming land from the Arab invaders."

"Then how can someone so noble end up homeless?" she wanted to know.

"*Aye*, everyone grabbed on to some noble title back then," he admitted with a grunt.

"You believe that every person in Spain has some nobility?"

"*Sí, sí.*" He nodded, then inched his way closer to her on the bench.

"It's hard to compete when the whole country is noble. This is why I am left homeless," he said. "I am homeless because I do not believe someone of noble title should work."

Having never met a more arrogant but charming bum, she got up and walked inside the museum for her fifth time that semester. Each time left her more entranced, more invigorated with confidence, determination and inspiration to accomplish something significant in life, but at this stage, she didn't know what. She refused to worry about her future now. She was in the moment, and the moment meant Spain. When it came time to do something significant in life, she would know. Ideas would come to her, doors would open, and people with a purpose would pop into her life. She would be ready, but for now, for today, she could only think about the moment, and the moment wasn't picking apples from an orchard in Michigan or eating a piece of Red Velvet Cake at the Bubble Room on Captiva Island, although she wouldn't mind a quick moment of that kind. Her moment was Spain—where her greatest present accomplishment might be doing laundry.

After spending hours in the museum, she walked the several miles back to her early-evening economics class. By then she had a decision to make. Either she could return to the apartment, or she could walk back to Calle Preciados and drop by the corner of El Corte Inglés at around six-thirty and see if a black Mercedes had showed up. After all, today was October fourth.

CHAPTER TWENTY-SIX

SHE CASUALLY STOOD OUTSIDE the doors of the crowded department store, which sold Levis for about ninety-three dollars a pair. Feeling indecisive, like a woman impulsively ready to spend money but also fearful of wasting that money, she started to walk away, then turned back once more, as if giving the black Mercedes one last chance. She remembered its driver saying that if the corner looked busy, he wouldn't park the car but would instead pull up along the curb so she could hop in. Did she really want to step into the car of an unknown foreign man? What would it cost her? Was there a return policy? Would he return her to the curb if things didn't work out?

Suddenly, she didn't want to invest anything of herself with this stranger, and she started to walk away. She felt proud and without regret, a woman choosing to leave the expensive clothes behind. Then she noticed the old woman in the same gray rags she had seen earlier., She was still sitting on the same piece of sidewalk square. Vicki changed her mind.

"Have you seen a man in a black Mercedes?" she asked in Spanish.

"No," replied the woman.

She wanted to better describe Rafael but didn't know the Spanish word for dimples, so, instead, she sat down next to the woman to wait, listening to the sound of coins dropping into the bucket every couple of seconds. Some coins landed with a splash. Others sounded like a single droplet of light rain. The bucket never went dry. The people of Spain wouldn't allow it to, and the old woman, probably noble, surely seemed to be surviving off a country that cared.

Vicki looked up as if giving Rafael one last chance. "He is just a man, a stranger," Vicki told the woman.

"Why would I get in a car and drive away with a man who doesn't speak English?" she asked, then, feeling horribly foolish for making plans with him in the first place, she quickly squeezed the cold hand next to her, stood up, and started crossing the street in the direction of the apartment. Why, of course he had forgotten about her, their encounter, their plans to meet on a crowded corner of all places! And she too would make it a forgotten moment, and him, a forgotten stranger.

As she reached the other side of the street, she felt someone yanking her sweater from behind. Her heart made a record-breaking leap over the high jump as she whirled around, ready to protect herself with a fist, but she couldn't hit the little old woman under the gray shawl, frantically flinging her cane in the air and pointing it toward the department store.

"*El hombre, el hombre,*" she cried. "*Gracias,*" said Vicki.

"*Vive!*" shouted the woman.

A black Mercedes had parked along the curb, and Rafael stood with a bouquet of purple, yellow, and red tulips on the corner. He held the flowers as if he understood where the American woman came from, as if he knew that tulips made her want to dance and scrub streets with buckets of cold water and old-fashioned brooms, and that tulips marked every corner of her hometown, and that now they might make her homesick. He formally held the flowers, yet casually looked around as if his fifty-five minutes of tardiness meant nothing at all.

The two women re-crossed the street together. The older took her seat on the sidewalk corner. The younger accepted the bouquet of tulips and got in the car.

They drove ten minutes to what Rafael kept calling *el museo de cera.* Vicki had no idea what the words meant nor where they were going. She didn't care as she softly caressed each of the silky petals.

"*Me gustan,*" she told him she liked the flowers. "How did you know that tulips are my favorite flower?" she asked in Spanish.

"*Son preciosas como ti.*" He told her they were as precious as she was. Then, he asked slowly in Spanish. "Of all the flowers in *el mundo*, why are they your favorite?"

She carefully laid out the correct Spanish words in her mind before speaking. "I'm from Holland, Michigan. It's a *ciudad en los Estados Unidos* that holds an entire festival for tulips."

"A festival of tulips? I've never heard of such a thing," said the Span ish stranger next to her.

She paused a moment to translate his words, then responded slowly. "People have been celebrating the flowers for hundreds of years, since 1632, when the interest in tulip growing exploded over in Holland, the country," she added, and tried hard to remember the words of her professor when he had lectured about the flowers.

"Tulip growing developed into a craze, and there was wild activity in tulip stock. People asked outrageous prices for a single bulb." She noticed him staring more at her than at the road he was driving down, so she stopped talking.

He waved for her to continue. "*Mas, mas. Quiero escuchar mas.*" He said he wanted to hear more.

She continued in fluent yet slow Spanish. "The tulip situation got out of control, and finally, after many Dutch people went bankrupt, the government stepped in to regulate the tulip trade."

He smiled and said in his native language, "And *Victoria*, after all of that, the tulips survived and still stand proud every spring."

"*Si, Si,*" she answered.

Following their drive, Rafael parked and they walked into a building where they were greeted by the king and queen of Spain. Vicki peeked into an anteroom and noticed Michael Jackson standing as he had on the cover of his *Thriller* album, then John Wayne. A distance away she noticed Mother Theresa. Had Vicki died and gone to Heaven? Then she glanced much further and saw Hitler! No, Hell. It struck her like a matador strikes a bull. *El museo de cera* meant wax museum.

They began their tour in the political room, walking past Hitler and other political figures, then they stopped in front of Franco.

"I was talking to a *señora*," said Vicki. "And she was telling me she missed Franco as ruler, that his collapse triggered a sort of social and sexual revolution, a downfall of morals."

"*Si, si*," answered Rafael. "Divorce, birth control, abortion, homosexuality, and adultery were all illegal under Franco."

"*Digame*," she said, wanting to know his views of this stern ruler. "*Rafael, ¿que piensas de Franco?*"

He spoke clearly and slowly, and it only took her mind a second to translate his Spanish words into her English words. In fact, she heard his Spanish words as English in her mind. He was better than any history book she had ever read and more interesting than any class she had ever taken.

"When Franco died, our country was reborn," he said, staring Franco in the eyes. "With his collapse, Spain jumped from dictatorship to democracy overnight, *Victoria*." As he spoke, he looked back and forth between Franco and his American guest. "It marked the last Fascist regime in Europe."

"*Mas, mas. Quiero eschuchar*," she said. "I told you about tulips. Now you tell me about Franco."

"Forty *anos* of dictatorship and order at the expense of freedom," he said, shaking his head as if scolding the wax figure in front of him. "My father, my cousins, anyone who protested against the restrictions on speech and press and assembly were disciplined."

"Your people must have been furious," she commented.

"*Si, la gente de mi pais* were afraid. You would be too, *Victoria*. But Franco had power, too much power. He was empowered by the army, church, and the Falange Party."

She knew now that Rafael and Rosario had different perspectives. Rosario missed the stern order Franco insisted upon for Spain. Rafael despised the man.

"*¿Su vida esta muy diferente sin Franco, no?*" She wanted to know if and how life changed when Franco no longer had power.

"*Ahhh, si, si*," he replied. "Franco limited the cultural and intellectual aspirations of my people. With Franco gone, the fashion industry flourished. Women used to wear mostly black. Without Franco, they immediately started wearing some of the most daring colors." He laughed. "What a statement—so modern—the models made as they walked down the European runways in wild colors for the first time. *Las mujeres* mostly dress daring in the city. Countrywomen are still conservative."

"*¿Por que?*" She wanted to know why they dressed in black in the country.

"*La muerte,*" he said. "Death is all over, *Victoria*. In the country, they mourn for several years after the death of family. Because they have such large *familias*, they're always mourning someone and always wearing black."

Might wearing black actually help someone overcome grief? Maybe she should have worn her black dress instead of that pastel bikini right after Rebecca died. Then again, neither Rebecca nor Grandma would have wanted her to go around wearing black for months. Rebecca once said that black darkened her eyes, and Grandma, well, she only wore purple.

"*Estamos de moda, Victoria,*" Rafael declared proudly, as he turned and walked toward the next room.

She couldn't argue. They did look like a country in style!

They entered the dark movie monster room where the damp coldness reminded Vicki of a cellar. They were the only ones touring, and she wished the museum had more customers. As Rafael took hold of her hand tightly, she felt sudden fear. Not from the mummies and monsters, but from the man wearing glasses, walking by her side and now holding her hand, the man wearing cologne she had never smelled before, a scent that said this man liked fine dining, red wine, and conversation, and romance to go along with it all. She could always tell much about a man based on the cologne he chose to wear.

Who was he? Why did she get in the car with him in the first place? How did it all start? What if he were married? Well, if he was, this luxurious man was a Titanic heading for disaster. Suddenly a sharp pain struck her chest like an iceberg. She couldn't breathe, and her legs shook. Her vision blurred, and she knew she was losing the mind-over-matter battle once more.

Her panic attack had begun. It would be a matter of minutes before she would start to hyperventilate. She tried to listen to Rafael's slow, clear Spanish narration of the tour. He knew a lot about wax figures, but did he know CPR? She dropped her purse so she could bend down and catch her breath, but Don Rafael insisted that he be the one to pick it up. She didn't want to die, not here in the wax museum, not here in Spain. The figures around her looked real—real and dead, as if they should be resting in coffins instead of standing around in a basement, staring into space.

As they entered another political room, Rafael's voice grew louder, filled with excitement. *"El es un amigo de mi padre, muy especial, Victoria. Y el tambien."* He pointed to a wax person. "Once, he and my father were friends, and look there! They too were friends! Now, they are dead. Now, they are wax sculptures in a museum."

She knew Rafael's father had important friends. Anyone made into wax after death is important. She knew Rafael's father was important. Anyone who is merely friends with wax sculptors must be important himself. She wanted to know more, but at this point she was only half concerned with the stories of the wax figures. Most of her attention went to talking herself out of a panic attack in the cold, dark, creepy museum. Not only was she standing in a spooky-looking room with a mysterious man, but she was with a man whose father had friends turned into wax!

She felt relieved when the tour ended, and they drove away. After a while they parked the car and walked to Café Gijon, located near the Plaza de Cibeles at the edge of the prestigious Barrio de Salamanca, a wealthier part of town. It was a chilly night, so once inside the warm café, cozily designed with polished paneling and gilt mirrors, Vicki didn't want to leave. It didn't matter that they both had already drunk two espressos. Neither felt ready to venture out into the windy night, and something about the century-old café stirred a desire for fine conversation.

They stayed in the café with its black and white tabletops for almost four hours, discussing a 1942 novel Vicki was reading for her Spanish literature class.

"So *Pascual Duarte* is your favorite novel," said Vicki. "I could hardly understand the plot, themes, and characters, but now it all makes sense to me!"

"Camilo Jose Cela won the Nobel Prize for literature back in 1989." Rafael waved his hands as he spoke, as if his gestures were part of Spain's language and as important as words. "It is my favorite book, and I've read it several times."

"I stayed up until three in the morning trying to make sense of it all," said Vicki. "I found it so sad."

"It is written in a type of realism known as *tremendismo*," said Rafael.

"Do you know what *tremendismo* means, *Victoria*?"

"No, *¿que significa?*" she asked.

"It features the antihero and an insistence on the ugly, harsh aspect of life."

"Why do you love such a depressing novel?" she asked him in Spanish.

"*Porque.*" He looked down. "I have had several depressing moments."

"*Digame.*" She told him she wanted to know more.

"*Mañana, mañana.*" He told her he'd tell her another time.

"That means you'd like us to meet again."

"*Si, si.* But we must carefully choose our cafés," he whispered, looking around at others who were sitting at nearby tables, some holding books, others looking over a stack of paper that looked like a manuscript.

"*¿Por que?* Why do we have to choose carefully?"

He shook his head. "*Victoria*, choosing a café in Spain is like favoring one political party over the other. Cafés have reputations. There are right-wing and left-wing cafés, cafés for artists and cafés for writers. There is a café for everything."

"Just like there is a time for everything," she added.

"*Claro.*"

"So what is this café known for?"

"What did we just discuss?" He asked in Spanish, but Vicki under-stood it like English.

"Literature."

He smiled, giving her a nod of approval, then responded slowly, "You have your answer. Hemingway loved this café."

When it came time for them to part, Rafael insisted she tell him where she was living so he could properly drop her off on the sidewalk below, but she refused. Despite the wonderful evening she had, she wanted to retain her privacy and that of her Spanish family, just in case, so she had him drop her off on the same corner where he had picked her up earlier that night. It was only a couple blocks from where she lived, and she never minded walking the city alone at night. In Madrid, a night without the moon meant nothing, thanks to the city lights.

"Then we meet next week, same time, same place," said Rafael.

"Yes, I will be here," she said. "And I will try *not* to be early this time."

Her fingers went numb as she climbed under the covers and lit a gardenia-scented candle beside her bed. The tiny apartment felt cold this late at night, but she couldn't resist. She had to write about her conversations with Rafael to her grandmother.

Dear Grandma,

I'll call him Rafael de España. He transforms Spanish into more than grammar off the pages of a book. He brings it to life for me. He takes the language barrier away. As he speaks to me, slowly and with-out shouting, I feel way beyond the culture shock and, I think, home-sickness. I think it's time to stop crossing off days in big black marker on my calendar. As I lie in bed and hear his views of Spain and fash-ion and his people in my mind, I am glad to be here. There is no place I would rather be at this given time. I love this country now. I start-ed loving it the moment I started breaking the language barrier. I love it a little better now that I have Rafael as a friend. This may sound dramatic, Grandma, but I know you love reading romance. And I don't mind living it.

P.S. Is there really such a thing as soul mates?

CHAPTER TWENTY-SEVEN

ON JULY 18, 1936, MANY *painful letters were written. The rightist revolt had been launched. The National Socialist parties of Italy and Germany fully supported the army and had decided to seize power and destroy the Second Republic. This decision began the Spanish Civil War. The Republicans set up camp in the urban areas of Madrid. The rebels, who called themselves the Nationalists, moved in from Morocco. They were led by General Francisco Franco as they entered Barcelona, establishing themselves in the provinces of Catalonia, Murcia, and Valencia,* explained the professor.

Like armies of rebels, ants moved their way through the veins inside Vicki's left arm, heading toward her shoulder. Then the professor explained that the death toll, an omen of sorrow for the Republicans, sounded early in 1939, when Franco's forces, after weeks of bitter siege, entered Barcelona.

A bow and arrow—no, it was a sword. No, the date was 1939. A *bullet* struck Vicki in the heart, and she bent over at her desk to catch her breath. She declared herself crazy. How could a lecture alone cause a panic attack?

The professor continued. *The Nationalists had control. They had disciplined, well-armed troops. They were led by experienced generals and had plenty of materials from abroad. Writers have described it as if they were on a sort of Holy Crusade to crush the infidels as they chanted, "Long Live Death!"*

Vicki's attempts to catch her breath became loud sighs of frustration and forced yawns. Sweat formed on her forehead, and she could no longer decipher the giant map of Madrid on the board in the front of class. The only thing that looked somewhat normal was the Pablo Picasso painting hanging on the wall next to her desk, and the more she listened and the worse her anxiety grew, the more his Cubist art made sense.

The battle lost, she nearly collapsed on the floor as she ran out of the classroom door, her conceived escape route. Alone on the sidewalk outside, perhaps where the Republicans once established their base of support, she felt ridiculous that such symptoms could be coming from her mind. These panic attacks were becoming a bad habit. Like a soldier wounded while simply listening to the history of the Spanish Civil War, she started running toward the big hospital she had seen a few blocks away. She allowed no time to talk herself out of this one. She was dying. Her mind had convinced itself of that.

She knew the word *corazon* meant heart, but her Spanish came out broken under pressure, as she explained her pain to the nurses. After sitting in a crowded waiting room for a good hour, the nurse led her into a bigger room with other sick people lying on beds, then told her to take her shirt off.

"I need a curtain, a door, a private room," she said, glancing around at the crowded room filled with dark-haired men. They wheeled in a divider.

A doctor with messed-up hair appeared completely overburdened with ill people seeking free medical care. Vicki felt like a pathetic character in the musical *Jesus Christ Superstar*—just one more body demanding the doc's attention. "Heal me, I'm hurting. Heal me, I'm bleeding. Heal me, I'm dying."

Unfortunately, none of the doctors on duty spoke her native language, and in a time of crisis, English would have been comforting.

The doctor's assistants hooked the ECG up to her chest. As they rapidly talked medical terminology, she lost all capacity for translating. Abducted by outer space aliens, she lay on the cold table looking up at the bright fluorescent light. Speaking their own language, they poked her and stuck her with things, then debated amongst themselves.

After the ECG, they led her in a wheelchair into a waiting room. An unfamiliar-looking man in a white coat asked her questions. He wanted to know her symptoms. She had a perfectly fluent Spanish conversation with Rafael, so why couldn't she have one now? Why hadn't she read the Spanish version of those medical encyclopedias? She had no idea how to say heart attack in Spanish. Then again, she did just leave the Spanish Civil War lecture, in which the professor used the words *golpe* for military attacks and the word *guerra* for war. Close enough. She'd give it a try.

"*Tengo un dalor en mi corazon, como un golpe o una guerra. Si, tengo un guerra en mi corazon.*"

She judged the doctor's silence as poor bedside manners. Then he started to laugh. He laughed from his gut, and tears streamed down his face. She lay on the hospital bed with stabbing sensations piercing her heart. She knew what she had said. She had told the young Spanish doctor that she had a war or militaristic attack on her heart. The more the doctor laughed, the younger he looked.

"Well, good, I'm glad I'm a stress relief for you. So can you treat wars of the heart, Doc?" She said it in English but didn't care. She cried, while the doctor laughed. "I'm feeling better, Doc. You must think I'm a hypochondriac wanting attention, and the hospital is the only place for me to get it."

Finally, he managed to pat her on the knee and ask her slow, simple questions requiring no more than a yes-or-no answer. She must have answered one too many no's because he then wheeled her into the same ECG room that she had been in with the nurses and began hooking her up again.

She felt like a child on a merry-go-round, lying that she had not yet been on the ride, and she felt guilty, but didn't know what to say to stop the ride from starting. It was too late to admit she already went through the ECG with the other little people in white suits.

"Worry no. I explore you," the doctor said in an attempt at speaking English.

"Explore me? Goodness, Doc, that's worse than me having a war of the heart."

Just then the nurse who hooked her up to the ECG the last time, returned.

"*Hola!*" said Vicki.

The nurse began waving her arms and shouting loudly at the doctor.

Both stared down at their abductee, so confused! She just answered "no" to the ECG question five minutes ago. Unhooking her, they took blood instead.

An hour later, the doctor explained something about stress and wished her well. She left the hospital alone, alive, and feeling like a soldier sent home from war, only there was no fanfare because she hadn't earned any medal for heroism. There was no one to greet her and no one to offer her counsel that comes with mental discharge. She stood on the sidewalk outside the hospital and felt lost, so she wandered to the corner of El Corte Inglés department store. She was an hour early for her date with Rafael and didn't want to be there. She had wanted to be late for him, a Spaniard who never let time get the best of him. He'd show up in an hour and fifteen minutes. well, probably an hour and a half. He didn't care about time. No one in Spain cared about time. What were they doing in those moments of tardiness? Were they having a hard time ending incredible conversations? Were they savoring those last mouthfuls of paella? Were they engaged in a moment of poetry, passion, and whatever else happened in moments of poetry and passion? Were they slowly sipping the last few drops of their coffee in breakable, non-transportable coffee cups while sitting still in one chair, doing nothing but sipping and talking?

Well, just as they were probably making the most of their moments of tardiness, she decided she would now make something of her moments of earliness. She had never had a homeless person as a friend before, nor tried making one a friend. They didn't exactly fill the streets back home in her part of the woods, and if they did, she had never noticed. There was a shelter, and it may have been full, but they never sat around on the streets, not that she observed, and they never begged for money. If they had, she had never given a penny.

She took a seat on the sidewalk next to the woman bundled in gray, the same one she had spoken to last time. The people back home would be dressing up like bums about this time of year. Greedy trick-or-treaters. she was always one of them.

They sat side by side in silence, as close yet distant as two pumpkins in a patch, one severely and recognizably bruised and the other ready to be picked with hidden dents. Then, in slow, clear terms, Vicki started talking about what she had lost and left behind. She spoke words in English but mostly in Spanish.

"Keeping myself busy and hiding my grief like that did me no good," she said slowly. "And my hidden pain manifested itself in the form of fear, that I too might die in my sleep, and that fear progressed into a phobia of falling asleep and, worse, into full-blown panic attacks."

She didn't care that her words came out a combination of Spanish and English at the same time, a form of *Spanglish*. It felt good talking about it, as if the seeds of a pumpkin were being scraped out of her.

The old woman, who constantly fidgeted with her dry, cracking hands, stopped her fidgeting and patted Vicki on the back, carving a smile on her face.

"*Gracias.*" Vicki didn't know what else to say. "*¿Come te llamas?*" asked Vicki. "What is your name?"

"*Triste,*" answered the woman. And Vicki interpreted it to mean sad, but if the woman wanted to be called Triste, she would call her that.

"Why do you sit here every day like this?" The smiling pumpkin with the no-longer-hidden dent asked the uncarved pumpkin covered in bruises.

"*Tengo muchos anos*, I am very old," she answered. "The churches, they tried taking me in. I am *muy* proud of *España*. I never have hunger. *La gente de españa*, they fill my bucket *cada dia.*"

As she spoke, she never smiled or looked Vicki in the eyes. "I am a woman, very stubborn. I don't want strangers to take me in. If I had *familia, si,* I'd go in. *Pero* I have no *familia.* As a young woman I watched my country go mad."

Vicki had heard about the destruction and wastage of the Spanish Civil War in class, but now she saw the emotional bruises all over this woman.

"Franco and his war killed my parents, my brothers, my newlywed husband. It killed my grandfather and uncles and everyone I loved. I have been mourning ever since, *muchos anos*."

She stared at the people walking by and continued. "I have come far. I went from wearing a black shawl to wearing a gray shawl. People called me *loco*. They told me to stop mourning. I told them 'no!' The tragedy of my country has wounded my soul for life. I made a decision. I chose to mourn one year for each of my loved ones lost in that war. Then, I decided to mourn for every Spaniard who died in the battle. I sentenced myself to mourning for life. Now, an old woman on the sidewalk, I am proud of the years I have put into full-time mourning. I sit on the sidewalk, watch strangers go by, and pray for them. I pray that *España* will never divide in such an animalistic manner again. *Si,* I will pray and mourn until the day I die. It is my purpose in life."

"Well, blessed are those who mourn," said Vicki, reciting Jesus' words and the Sermon on the Mountain. "Blessed are those who mourn, for they will be comforted."

The woman reached within the dark blanket wrapped around her and pulled out an embroidered purple handkerchief, saying it had at one time belonged to her mother. It was the only thing she grabbed the day her mother died, and now it had years of tears soaked into it.

"Go," said Triste, flagging the handkerchief in the air. "You want me to leave?" asked Vicki.

"Go," said the woman. "Get on with your life."

"I want to."

"Get on with your life," she said again. "Live life."

"I will."

"Live life. Live life now."

"I want to live life now," answered Vicki. "I will live now. Thank you."

The words made sense to her, and she was not only a smiling pumpkin, but someone had lit a candle and placed it inside of her.

And then a paper bill floated down, landing in the bucket like an autumn leaf falling from a brittle branch, and Rafael reached his arm out to Vicki, helping her up from the sidewalk like someone salvaging a fallen apple. She squeezed his hand tightly as she stood up. She didn't realize until she stood up how long she had been sitting there. Her buttocks felt achy and cold from the cement, but she felt alive. There was only a minor sore spot from where she had sat, and it was already healing.

They drove, then walked, discussing projects Rafael was working on. He had met with another designer in Paris, and the two would be joining together to create a line of dressy yet casual jeans that can go anywhere, that can walk a person right across international boundaries, if she interpreted him correctly—whatever that meant. He told her about his other line, which had a tag of Spain's flag sewn on the back left pocket, and told her that earlier in the day he had met up with sales representatives who call on clothing stores located around the Calle de Serrano and Calle Ortega y Gasse in the Salamanca District, best known for Spanish names. They usually placed the new designs in this area first, and the store owners there enjoyed being the first to introduce the new items.

They stopped outside a high-rise hotel on a busy street, and he looked accused of wrongful action as he urged her inside the lobby. "*Una sorpresa* for you on the top floor, *nada mas*," he explained in Spanish. "Nothing more."

They took the elevator to the twenty-sixth floor and stepped out onto a balcony glowing from candlelit tables and stars overhead. Three men were playing instruments: one, the tambourine; the second, a bagpipe; and the third, castanets. She felt like a voyager arriving in another world, another life. As one waiter led them to an intimate corner table, another poured red wine into their glasses almost before they had sat down.

She hadn't eaten anything all day, and now the live instrumental music became as intoxicating as the wine she was sipping. Under its influence, everything possessed extra vitality, and she couldn't help but notice the details all around her. She swished the velvety wine around her glass and nibbled on assorted cheeses, cubes of yellow, orange, and white. Looking down at Madrid gave her the same sort of feeling she had experienced sitting atop the lighthouse tower, looking down on the island. But instead of palm tree tops, these were rooftops. The lights from the city below looked like white Christmas-tree bulbs.

Her toes tingled as she felt tipsy from just a few sips of wine on her empty stomach. "Do you know, Rafael, where light comes from?"

"*Digame,*" he said, aware of the trick question.

"Those lights you see below us, the city lights, they're lightning bugs reincarnated," she continued under the influence of the wine that had overtaken her mind.

"*¿Que?*" He didn't understand.

She switched to English and slurred slightly. "Bullies once stomped on the fortunate little things and smeared them against the cement. Now they're shining so brightly again. I toured the Edison home back in Fort Myers, but I know the truth. It was really just a reincarnated lightning bug factory."

"*Tu eres una mujer muy interesante.*" He said she was an interesting woman, although he didn't understand a thing she had said.

"*Gracias.*" She felt dramatic, a woman in a black-and-white movie, as she tried to decipher where the man-made window lights of the city ended and where the large celestial bodies composed of gravitationally contained hot gases emitting electromagnetic radiation started. Music and another sip of strong wine influenced her imagination, so she decided not to take another sip until she had real food in her stomach. She no longer had to promise herself to live for the moment; she was living the moment, and she appreciated it, every detail.

"*Te quiero, voy a ir a America y casarme con tu,*" Rafael broke the silence by telling her he loved her, he was going to America with her, and he wanted to marry her.

She ignored his comments, at least for a moment. She needed another cube of cheese, several cubes. She downed them quickly, knowing she had to take back her mind and drown out the little alcoholic grapes that wanted badly to speak for her tonight, to marry this man, to run away with him, and to have a good time. As always, she understood his Spanish well, even with a few glasses of wine in her, so she didn't have to double-guess what he had just said, all in a single sentence, completely out of the blue. Had Rafael, her friend and tour guide, turned himself into the stereotypical romantic male Spaniard? They hadn't yet kissed, and now he wanted to marry her?

"*No, no mas,*" she said to the waiter trying to pour more red wine into her glass.

"*Si, si, mas,*" Rafael told the waiter trying to pour more red wine into his glass.

"*Si, si, mas,*" she said to the other waiter carrying the silver tray of cheese cubes.

"*No, no mas,*" he said to the waiter carrying the silver tray of cheese cubes.

Suddenly, she decided she had no intention of kissing him, ever. Second, she told herself, she didn't want him in that sort of way. She wanted him as a friend, a conversationalist, a companion, a shoulder to lean on in times of foreign distress, a man who could teach her about this country, its people, their passions and fears. She wanted him for all of these things, but not for Mr. Right. She was still waiting for the right timing for Mr. Right.

She let his words linger in midair as the wine spoke to her mind. As she stared at the miles of city lights, she pretended she was a queen, looking down upon her kingdom. The wine spoke in a deep, romantic tone, telling her to consider his proposal. She would switch to white wine, something with a dry voice. No wonder Spaniards drank the red. It was so much fuller and livelier. She was having a difficult time standing up to its overpowering and seductive voice. She needed an American friend right now so that together they could laugh at Rafael's proposal. She needed a pen and paper to write Grandma a letter. Grandma would surely tell her, "Now, now, now, forget it, young lady! Stick to your senses! Your father would kill you, but keep writing me letters, and don't leave out a single detail! And oh, those dimples!"

The waiter set down a platter of *bacalao a la vizcaina,* which she recognized as cod, tomato, thyme, red pepper, bay leaf, onion, garlic, and fried croutons.

Rafael, the king, took her hand and, in his native romance language, continued with his poetic proposals. "I will design you a wardrobe. I will brand name it 'Victoria.' I have already begun to create the skirt, pants, and blouse with you, my *preciosa,* in mind. Now, I only need to measure your waist, and I will do that after dinner."

"No," she said in English. "No," she said in Spanish. "No," she said in French. No, being universal in almost any language, he understood. No man was going to put a tape measure around her waist.

Why can't he make you the wardrobe without measurements? asked the wine from deep within.

She peered deeply into his eyes and said once more, "No!" "*¿Porque?*" He dared to ask why.

"*Por que.*" She answered, "Because." Then she asked him how anyone could ever fit into the clothes he designed if they feasted so much.

"Victoria, you eat plentiful. Eat food from God, nature's food. Limit *papas fritas*, food in packages, food with chemicals and man-made ingredients. Eat only God-given food because it brings beauty both inside and out - eggs, avocados, tomatoes, lemons, grapes, olives, beans, fish, rice, basil, vinegar, potatoes, espresso beans, and more, and combine those one-worded, simple ingredients into creations *muy delicioso*. I don't understand why Americans want to drink coffee in paper cups in their cars. Take time out for food so you can savor every bite and enjoy every sip. Food demands time, time to prepare and time to enjoy. When life gets too busy to prepare food in a healthy manner, and to sit and slowly savor it, then life is not good. Then one needs to make emergency changes. This, Victoria, is what I tell the models for whom I fashion my clothes. Never starve or binge and never make your job more important then enjoying one of life's greatest pleasures—food."

He sounded like a sexy, romantic, yet sensible electronic grocery list that talked and she felt a desire to return to the States to publish a new diet, a new lifestyle approach to food, a new way of making time in one's life in order that healthy food might become a priority. She would call it, "The Rafael Diet."

She swigged more of the seductive, speaking wine, then bent down, not to catch her breath, but to reach into her purse on the floor and pull out a red crayon. Rafael closed his eyes, as if savoring his bite of food, and Vicki started to write on the white linen tablecloth. In English, she scribbled down, "Home."

Writing it on the tablecloth now turned it into a visualized goal. Just as a ballet dancer stops herself from getting dizzy by focusing her eyes on one thing, she would focus on home, and in turn, she wouldn't allow his proposal to throw her off balance or make her dizzy. Then again, was home Michigan or Florida? She did not know. She would figure that out later. Home definitely meant the United States of America, and that was good enough for now.

Rafael opened his eyes and for a moment stared at her scribbles, then grabbed the crayon from her. Just as the waiter approached the table, he quickly covered the red markings with his bread plate. When the waiter walked away, he asked, "*¿Escribe?* You wrote on the table? What did you write? *¿Porque?*"

She felt a battle within her. The cheese and fried croutons teamed together to overtake the red wine, but the wine had some strength left.

"Sometimes I like to write out my goals. Americans do this all the time. It brings them to life, gives them personality," she said. "Oh, Rafael, you have no idea! Life in America is so hectic that we drink nothing but coffee in to-go cups, and we drive and drink at the same time, burning our hands. This is why some designer has recently become very wealthy creating a—I forget what it's called—wraparound skirt, I guess you might say, a *cardboard* wraparound skirt that fits snugly around a hot cup of coffee to go," she said.

"Sounds very sexy," added Rafael.

"Oh no! It's very sad how we rely on that coffee to get us through our never-ending lists of errands, but without the list, we hang out on the sofa eating chips and pop. We go to pieces without a list of things to accomplish."

"*Ahh, si, si, Americana,*" he said. "But why a list on the tablecloth? *¿Por que* not on paper, *Victoria?*"

"It's an American custom," the croutons within lied in her defense. "*Lo siento.* I didn't realize the Spaniards do it differently."

He lifted his bread plate and scribbled down, "*Ser feliz.*" He moved the plate over the words, hiding them from the waiter.

Vicki translated it as, "To be happy."

She slid the candle centerpiece over and wrote, "To return to America, alone." She understood why woodpeckers carved out holes in tree trunks, left, and then returned to the same hole year after year. There was something about the concept of going home that sounded right.

He took the crayon and wrote, *Ser feliz con Victoria*—to be happy with Vicki.

Next, they feasted on *cochinillo a la segoviana*, suckling pig roasted over a wood fire and basted with lard and seasoning. Once the food overpowered the wine, she turned the conversation over to more intelligent things, like the religion of Spain.

"Does everyone in Spain practice Catholicism, Rafael?" She was back in reign over her body, her thoughts, and her conversation.

"Franco had forced it upon us all. But today, we worship in whichever denomination we choose."

"What have you chosen?"

"Because it was once forced upon my family, I am still confused. I know many who struggle with this, still today."

As he pulled up to the corner of El Corte Inglés, he took out his black planner and flipped to the end of the week.

"I like you. I like our conversations. But Rafael, your proposals at dinner made me nervous, you understand that, right?"

"*Si, si.* I understand. I will continue to wine and dine you, *Victoria.*"

"Oh?"

"And you will fall in love with me soon," he said.

"How soon?" she wanted to know.

"You will fall in love with me tomorrow. *¡Mañana!*"

"No Rafael, that is *not* the goal of our meeting. I will *not* let that happen. As I said, I enjoy talking with you. I enjoy you as a friend."

She knew she could love him as more than a friend, and she knew it the moment he innocently kissed her on each cheek the first time they met. Well, back then, she didn't know she could love him as a friend because she didn't know a thing about him. She only saw his dimples and colorful eyes that lived carefully hidden under those glasses, the kind she only wished she needed a prescription for, the kind that made an ordinary person look mysterious, intelligent and potentially sexy all in one.

"My friend and *nada mas*." He said sadly. "*Nada mas*," she stated.

"And you do not enjoy romance? How sad, *que triste*."

"Yes, I like romance, but not now. I have to leave Spain in a few months, and I cannot allow myself to fall in love."

"Is it my age? I am only a few years older. American women appreciate older men like they appreciate older wine, no?"

"You are more than just a few years older than me. Yes, your age has something to do with it," she said.

"Oh, Victoria. That is not fair. A man cannot control time, but he can control how he changes with time."

"Then tell me, Rafael, how do you change with time?"

"I grow wiser and better physically, mentally, and spiritually. I was good to start with, but soon, with such improvements, you will fall in love with me. You will love me very soon."

"Impossible," she declared. "There will be no 'soon' for us. I've got so much to do. I need to graduate and move close to my family and friends again. Spain is only temporary for me."

She grabbed his day planner and flipped it forward three more weeks. She'd meet him then, no sooner.

"If Spain is only temporary for you, then I am only temporary."

"*Si, si*, you are. So am I. Everything is temporary, Rafael." She got out of his car and started to walk down the sidewalk.

"Then what do you want from me that is permanent?" he called out the window.

She walked beside his car as he slowly drove. "Your friendship for now and your memories for later."

"And what do you want from me that is temporary?" he asked.

"Tell me your last name. For now, all I want is your last name." "*Rafael de España*," he said.

"Oh, well. Don't you want to know my last name?" she asked.

"I know it. *Victoria* precious angel, *Victoria de los Estados Unidos*."

He drove away, leaving her to stand on the street corner, a tulip standing tall and proud, waiting for the photographer to snap its photo, but then the man with the camera drove away. With him gone, she wanted his attention, she wanted him to pick her, to take her home and place her in a beautiful vase and give her water and care for her, admire her. She stood alone now, without his interesting facts, his sophisticated Spanish, the smell of his foreign cologne, his romantic little sayings, his coming on to her. She wilted and walked away, realizing she was just one flower in a world full of beautiful petals. Three weeks seemed a long time, and surely many others would bloom before him in that time. She might be forgotten. Yes, she might never see him again, and it was her own doing.

She climbed in bed and lit a candle because she didn't want to wake her family by putting a light on that could be seen under the curtain of a door. She picked up a book she had been meaning to read for quite some time, *A Death in the Afternoon*, a documentary study of bullfighting by Ernest Hemingway.

CHAPTER TWENTY-EIGHT

Dear Grandma,

It was a holiday for me. My entire Spanish family left me alone. They had something to go to in some nearby town and kissed and hugged me good-bye a million times before leaving.

As soon as they left, I shaved my legs and ironed all my clothes. I feel guilty for all the water and electricity I must have used. At least I didn't wash my clothes. Washing clothes means I would then have to hang my underwear outside on the rope overlooking metropolitan Madrid. Rosario does the entire family's underwear once a month, all in one huge, collective load. Then it hangs outside for a good two days after that. Lorenzo had a colorful pair so big I thought it was the Spanish flag. I guess I wouldn't mind my undergarments hanging in the country, but in the city? No way! Not mine! Had I known they'd hang publicly like flags, I wouldn't have packed my hot pink bikini pairs.

Spain and Tarpon Key certainly have something in common: Night life. For the islanders, it's tarpon fishing or dock chatting. For the Spaniards, it's walking the city streets or hanging out in cafés all night. I'm not saying all insomniacs need to relocate to a remote island or Spain, but they should certainly keep in mind that not everyone in this world goes to sleep at nine o'clock. Maybe as they sit in their recliners or pace down their hallways they can think of such places, knowing they're not the only people awake at odd hours.

P.S. I heard it in class and agree. This world is a stage, and we are the actors. I'm so convinced. I'm shifting my perspective because I prefer comedy.

Mañanas came and went. She knew this because she had originally packed over twenty pairs of underwear for the trip and was now down to two clean pairs. As she crossed the corner of El Corte Inglés department store carrying a bag full of new underwear, she looked around for Rafael. He wouldn't show up. They had no plans. Why hadn't she at least got his number? Why hadn't she insisted on getting his last name? Why hadn't she given him hers? Where exactly did he work? She kicked herself about Rafael from Spain, her secret source. That's all she knew. She kept him her secret, never telling anyone about him, not even Rosario.

As her Spanish improved, she discovered things she never knew about Nacho. He had normal friends, ones who weren't as intense as he appeared to be. They were childhood friends, dating back to infancy. They were all carrying guitars and backpacks as they picked her up on the street below her family's apartment and together took the Metro to the Lago stop, then walked to Caso de Campo, miles of parkland filled with pines lying south of the Royal Palace across the Manzanares River. It was once royal hunting grounds, and they pointed out the gate through which the kings rode out of the palace grounds on horseback or in carriages. Now it had a zoo, an amusement park, and plenty of scrubland.

"Javier, Michaelangelo, and I sing this song in the English language all the time," Jesus told Vicki in his national tongue as they sat down on the grass near the lake filled with rowers. "It's about four women. We want to sing it for you. It is very famous, and we think you will like it."

As she listened to the three Spaniards singing, she wanted to laugh.

She wanted to cry.

"Guys," she said in Spanish after their song had ended. "Do you know what winter, spring, summer, and fall means?"

"*Si, claro que si*," replied Javier. "Names of women."

"No, no."

"We sing this song all the time. Of course we are singing about four women," said Jesus. "It's a very romantic song."

"*Invierno, primavera, verano, y otono*," she said. "Names of seasons."

"I could have told you that," stated Nacho with a laugh. He was the only one without a guitar and who hadn't sung.

"Yeah, right," said Jesus.

As they continued singing songs from Crosby, Stills, and Nash, then the Beatles, in English, but with strong Spanish accents, Vicki laughed until she cried. She no longer felt embarrassed about her weak Spanish skills upon her arrival to their country. At least she could differentiate seasons from names.

As if a wonderfully exciting storm had arrived, the men, all but Nacho, quickly excused themselves, then returned twenty minutes later wearing navy embroidered suits—performance costumes.

"We are taking you someplace special. We will bring you back tomorrow," Nacho told Vicki.

"Tomorrow? Where are we going? *¿Adonde vamos?*" Vicki asked the men, passionate as storm chasers.

"*Mis amigos* are *muy* popular, and tonight they have a concert. We want to take you," explained Nacho. "I am proud of them and of their music."

They took the metro, then the *autobus* to the *pueblo*. With three hours until the concert, they drank wine and ate bits of skewered meats, omelets, olives, and ham in a nearby, noisy bar. Waiters were clinking glasses. Everyone was heavily engaged in laughing and shouting. The television in the corner served no purpose, but it stayed on, adding to the noise.

"What's up with your girl?" Nacho asked his friend, sitting next to him.

"She told me 'no,' " shouted Michaelangelo to the group. "I asked her to marry me, and she declined again."

"You two have more love than a flock of lovebirds. Did she tell you why she refuses to marry you?" asked Javier in Spanish.

"I didn't say she 'refused' to marry me. I said she said 'no.' There is a difference."

"Did she say why she said 'no' to marrying you?" asked Nacho.

"*Si, si*, she told me why." He wiped a tear from his face, and then bit the head off a sardine. "Her career. I get in the way of her career."

"I don't get it," said Jesus. "Men work, and they get married. They've done this for centuries. Now women want to work. Why don't they want to get married and work? They can have both."

"It's not marriage that gets in the way," added Javier. He had brown, curly hair, huge brown eyes and wore a yellow-flowered tie under his navy suit. "It's the babies."

"Why can't she marry you and wait a few years to have babies? Women are having them now in their forties," said Vicki.

"How could she wait that long? I would get her pregnant before then."

"What about birth control?" asked Vicki.

"Speak up," whispered Michaelangelo in her ear.

"*Si, si*. We can't hear you," shouted Javier.

"I said, what about birth control?" she yelled across the table.

"She doesn't believe it's right. She says if God wants her to have a baby, she will get pregnant. If He doesn't, she won't. The only way she thinks she can control it is not to marry me yet."

"So she still wants to marry you," said Nacho.

"*Si, si*, of course," he added. "Once she gets her job and works it for awhile."

"How long?" asked Vicki, pushing the platter of sardines away from her and down the table toward Nacho.

"I don't know. I don't think she knows. A year, five years."

"How long does it take a woman to tire of what she's doing? How long until a woman gets tired of the world out there and feels like having a husband, and staying home to take care of a baby?" asked Michaelangelo.

"Well, don't look at me," said Vicki. "I don't have the answers. I am, however, wondering about something. Who is this love of Nacho's life that I've heard much about but never met?"

For a moment, no one said anything.

Nacho rolled his eyes at her. "I told you, Vicki," he said. "I love her dearly. We were becoming too emotionally connected and needed time apart. There's nothing more to it."

"That's right," added Jesus. "Nacho was no longer spending time with all of us. We're glad to have him back for now."

"For now, *si, si*," said Nacho. "I am back for now, but a part of me is missing. It's only a matter of time before I return to her. Enough of this talk."

"So what can I give her to make marrying me, having a baby, and staying home sound good to her?" asked Michaelangelo.

"Can you give her a prestigious title, a salary higher than your own, and the respect that comes from operating a priceless corporation?" asked Jesus. "And a chef and a maid to go with it all?"

"She doesn't want you giving her anything," declared Nacho. "She wants to go out there and get it for herself."

"*Es la verdad*," said Vicki. "There are things a woman wants in life. Things she wants from life and from herself, and they are things she must go after herself."

"Then where does a man fit into it all?" asked Michaelangelo. "And what about babies?"

"A woman is a remarkable organizer," said Vicki. "She's just got a lot to organize right now, and all at once."

"So what are you going to do now?" asked Nacho.

"I'm going to ask her to marry me tomorrow," answered Michaelangelo. "*Mañana*. But it's time. We must warm up."

Outside, the stage stood decorated in festive, brightly colored paper ornaments. Sausage and tortilla *bocadillas* were being prepared on an open grill and three hundred-year-old-looking women were dancing hand in hand next to a group of young, rowdy teens. Two little boys were throwing a dried chicken foot at a screaming girl, who picked it up and whipped it back. The men in the navy embroidered suits took their places on the stage, and soon everyone was singing, dancing, and clapping to their music.

They pulled several people from the audience up on stage, and an old woman caught in the crowd grabbed onto Vicki's sleeve, pulling her along. They tried publicly teaching her how to flamenco dance to their modern Spanish rock, but she had never moved her body in these contortions before and felt her face turning red hot.

"The apple concept," she heard from a male voice. "It's the apple concept."

She glanced down and a redhead standing on the ground, directly below where she was on the stage, caught her attention immediately. He stood out like a carrot in a pitcher of sangria. "Are you American?" he asked as she managed to bend down long enough.

"Yes, from Florida. Well, Michigan," she shouted.

"Me, Connecticut. Listen, flamenco is as simple as reaching up to pick an apple, then twisting and bringing it down toward your mouth, taking a bite, then another twist, and tossing it to the ground. I've been pulled up on stage many times, and it took me much embarrassment to learn."

"Wait, pick apple, bite apple, toss apple to ground?" she repeated.

The century-old grandmother yanked her upward, and the crowd cheered as Vicki made sense of the apple concept. *Pick, twist, bite, twist, and toss.* It was that simple. Together, everyone picked, twisted, bit, twisted and tossed over and over again until there couldn't possibly be any apples left. And if there were, she surely couldn't bite another. By the time she made her way off the stage, she looked around for the American. She felt a patriotic unity with him and wanted to thank him for helping her, but she couldn't find him.

As if the hours of pigging out and dancing weren't enough, after the concert at around one o'clock in the morning, they caught a taxi to Palacio de Gaviria, an aristocratic, nineteenth-century palace converted into a *discoteca*, where they met up with more friends. As they stood in a long line for one club, Vicki noticed her Spanish sister Isabella and a man getting into a taxi.

"Wait, Isabella, Isabella," she called out.

Vicki was positive she saw Isabella turn and look at her, and for a moment, the women stared eye to eye, then Isabella hopped in the taxi and drove away.

"Do you and your friends ever tire?" she shouted to Nacho in the middle of the dance floor at three o'clock in the morning. He pulled her aside and asked if she felt tired.

"¿Estas cansadas, Victoria?"

"No, estoy bien. Me gusta la noche."

They wandered through a sequence of extravagant Baroque salons, part of the dance club. "La madrugada," he shouted.

"La what?" she asked.

"La madrugada. It's what Spaniards call the hours from midnight to morning.

"Oh."

"Do you like it?" he asked in Spanish.

Of course she did. Once a woman lying in bed staring up at a ceiling, and now a woman picking apples on stage and dancing all night.

What was there not to like?

"Often, when la madrugada passes unnoticed into la mañana," he added, "there's no point going to bed."

When they walked out the door of the discoteca, the city street was alive with music and laughter, and there was hardly an empty taxi to be caught anywhere. At four o'clock in the morning there were traffic jams, so they walked to the Chocolateria de San Gines and ate strips of fried dough called churros dipped in melted chocolate. When they left the chocolateria, the city street was quiet again, and each caught their own taxi on their first attempts and rode away: one toward the east and the rising sun, one toward the west where it had set the night before, one toward the north, and one toward the south.

Isabella pulled up to the apartment in a taxi at the same moment as Vicki. Her eyes were red, and Vicki asked if she was okay, but Isabella signaled for silence. The women said nothing as they quietly tiptoed up the wooden stairs to Isabella's parents' apartment. The exciting night had ended, and they were tired.

Siesta time came every day at the same time, as predictable as Florida's daily summer rain. No one dared to control it, or alter the details of this national tradition, but instead respected it and closed down shop and halted business until it ended each day. Vicki respected the siesta in Spain and always dozed off as peacefully and simply as a person put to sleep by falling rain.

She needed this hour of sleep. It became the momentum necessary to stay awake through the nights in Madrid, a city that possessed two personalities, and she didn't know which she liked better: Madrid by day or Madrid by night, the siestas or the fiestas. A night out with the Spaniards felt like getting sucked up in a tornado and blown through the city streets in a sensational pattern. Madrid's younger generation, which had enjoyed a new period of personal and artistic liberty after the death of Franco, termed it *la movida*—the late-night scene. They took their nights of eating, drinking, talking until sunrise, dancing, and riding the streets in taxis seriously, probably more so than their next day at work. But they never got drunk or did anything illegal or stupid. They lived the nights like storm chasers, lustfully and passionately, making the most of such fast-passing moments.

As sure as a tornado warning, she knew *la movida* would suck her up again, and it did. Nacho picked her up at seven o'clock, and they spent time sipping espresso and talking at a small table outside in La Puerta del Sol, an oval plaza surrounded on all sides by cream-colored eighteenth-century buildings and the most popular meeting spot, basically, of the café society of Madrid. It was noisy and crowded, but she liked it. Ben would like it too. Maybe someday they might find themselves standing under the same clouds and in the same rain again. She missed him.

Later, they walked the *tapa* circuit, all the way from La Puerta del Sol to the Prado Museum, and down the streets Carrera de San Jeronimo and Atocha, stopping along the way and chomping on bloodred *chorizos*, mushrooms in oil, potatoes with garlic mayonnaise and manchego cheese.

Afterward, they drove to Old Madrid and walked along the narrowed cobble streets lined with wrought-iron balconies until they came to a cave-like neon-lit bar. Inside the bar, the whites of everyone's eyes, as well as the drinks, glowed a shamrock green.

Nacho started a game of pool with a stranger, and Vicki leaned against the brick wall, studying his face and his constantly twitching black eyebrows.

As she watched him hit three solid balls into some holes, she wasn't ill or tipsy, but felt dizzy and confused to the point of frustration thinking about how Howard must have known Nacho's family. Had Nacho lied to her? There was no reason for him not to remember an American friend of the family. As much as she tried telling herself it didn't matter anymore, it drove her crazy, and her frustration clashed with the black-and-white checkered floor beneath her pointy, black, buckled Spanish shoes. The beat of the music made her mind jump back and forth, rehashing every word Howard had said to her, trying to pin down some sort of clue.

Nacho studied the table seriously, but glanced at Vicki each time before shooting, raising an eyebrow without a smile. She started fidgeting with a gaudy silver ring she had bought in Toledo when suddenly it hit her, the way the blue ball had just hit the red ball. The piano! Howard had said she must ask Nacho to play the piano for him! It was around three o'clock in the morning when she yelled out, "*El piano*," and Nacho hit the red ball so hard it flew across the room and cracked down onto the floor.

No one picked it up. Instead, he signaled her to follow, and they headed for the door. Outside she asked Nacho if he was any good at the piano. His demeanor signaled the mysterious rush of a category three hurricane making a dangerous turn at the last moment. "Yes, I am good," he answered brusquely. "Why does it matter you?"

"Wait a minute, Nacho! Did you just say that in English? No? Yes, I think you did!"

"*Si, si*. I speak very little *inglés*."

"Little? No. I don't think so. You speak fluent English, don't you? I mean, that sounded pretty good to me."

"No, please, don't compliment."

"Nacho! How *could* you not tell me something so important? You said you don't speak any English. Why would you lie to me about that?"

"In my country, we speak my language. If you don't learn the language, you don't learn the people," he shouted behind him to Vicki, who was almost running down the cobblestone street to catch up.

"I've hardly said a word in English to anyone since I've been in Spain," she said in English. "I'm learning your language, and I'm learning about nights in Madrid. I'm getting to know the people, Nacho. But I don't know you. You are a stranger to me." There was silence, and they kept walking. "Did you understand what I just said?" she asked.

"No." He stopped and turned around. "*Si, si,* I understand you very good," he said with a smile.

"Nacho," she called out to him, nearly out of breath. "Just think of all the good conversations we could have had by now if you had only told me sooner you speak English."

He stopped again in the middle of the narrow street, raising his arms toward the black sky above. "What, what do you want to talk about?" He looked at his watch. "We talk now."

She stepped up to him, eye to eye. "The piano. Play the piano for me. Let's find a piano."

"*No se.* It has been a long time."

"So it's true. You do play the piano?"

"*Si.* I once play every day, every *minuto,* but these days, no. Today I don't play anymore."

"Nacho, *por favor.* I am leaving your country soon. I beg you to play for me."

He rolled his eyes as he opened the car door for her. "*Vamos.* We go to the apartment of my mama. She is not home tonight, and I respect her. If she were home, we would not go there now. But because she is not there, I take you. I will take you. I am taking you," he spoke English with a sense of pride, having nearly mastered it, yet wanting to practice it and now was his chance. "Yeah, that's right. I take you. No, I will take you. We go now to my piano. My piano is at the apartment that is my mama. No, that belongs to my mama. Yeah, that's right. *Vamos.*"

As he sped down the cramped and curvy roads in his bright yellow car, Vicki sat in silence, shocked at the discovery that her mysterious friend spoke English and proud of herself for remembering the key that might unlock his secret. She felt as impressed as the time on the island when

Howard of all people switched from jabberwocky to perfectly fluent Spanish and an intelligent conversation.

Asking people why they had come to Tarpon Key had once proved fascinating. She now tried a new question with Nacho, hoping to achieve similar results. "Nacho, why do you play the piano?"

"Stupid question," he replied with his lips and with hand gestures that always danced in tune with his emotions and that meant they hardly stayed put on the steering wheel.

"No. Don't say that. It's not stupid," said Vicki. "I don't come from a musical background. Music isn't my domain. Do you understand me? I am envious of people with a talent for music. I just wonder why you hit the ball across the room when I said the word 'piano.' "

"*Tranquilo, tranquilo.* You wait." His eyes frantically traveled from her eyes to the rearview mirror to the radio, but never to the road ahead, it seemed. She decided not to talk any further until they had arrived safely, and she could step out of this carnival ride.

If there were a ticket booth outside his mother's apartment, people would purchase tickets to get in. Art sculptors, statues on white rugs stood upright and still, making Vicki self-conscious of her own posture upon entering. As in a painting, the dark object caught her attention immediately, the only dark item in the elegant living room.

"My piano. I introduce you to my piano," said Nacho as he walked over to the black object and softly touched it with his fingertips, as if caressing a woman's body. Then he pulled his black sweater over his head and set it on a chair. He walked over to a mini-bar and poured himself a glass of dry sherry, took a few sips, then closed the window blinds, shutting off any outside view, dimmed the lights, lit a candle, and cracked his knuckles before taking a seat on the piano bench.

He sat there a moment, closing his eyes, and took a deep breath. "This is my piano," he said as he opened his eyes. "I told you we were taking time apart. That time has now ended. Vicki, I would like you to meet the love of my life."

As she stood in the center of the white room, she felt a chill, similar to that which entered the dorm room before Rebecca had died. "It's my pleasure," she said and nodded.

He didn't answer. As if he had forgotten he had a one-person, informal audience standing before him, his fingers hit the keys, and his nervous facial glitches and eyebrow twitches danced in tune with the notes. As if the piano contained mysterious electricity, it jolted him. The lines on his forehead deepened, and his eyes closed.

As she stood alone in the large room, Vicki felt fear. The death of her friend frightened her. She too would die some day. Her other loved ones might also die. She had no control over its timing. It would arrive when it liked, a thief in the night.

His music switched keys, and now she felt guilty. She should have stayed in Michigan long enough to attend the funeral, to comfort the family, to wear black. She should have met Rebecca twice a week for coffee instead of once a week. Sure, they studied together nightly, but she should have insisted they have more fun together. She should have told Rebecca how much she loved her as a friend. She should have this and that. She should have, she should have.

The music exploded into storms of octaves echoing each other as Nacho's hands pounded the keys, almost violently now. She felt anger bursting from the keys or going into them—she didn't know which. Rebecca had left her at a very bad time, just before their semester in Spain. She had never said good-bye. How rude! Vicki felt angry at life ending without warning, mad that God had made it all part of some plan. Nacho also looked angry as he too looked afraid, then guilty. They both seemed to be taking similar journeys.

His music slowed, and she felt sad. She wanted to block out the music, but it demanded sensitive listening.

Sweat dripped from Nacho's face, and she felt exhausted watching him, tired from going through the stages of grief. When his fingers stopped, the room filled with a lonely quiet. The silence ached, so she had to say something, but she self-consciously knew that her voice sounded ugly after such gorgeous notes. She stood still, alone, in the center of the room, her arms hanging awkwardly beside her.

"Nacho, who did you lose?"

"My father," he said, and then slammed his hands down on the keys.

She jumped. "Why don't you play the piano anymore?" "I told you. We were too emotionally one, connected."

"That was the most incredible thing I have ever heard, Nacho. Your music is beautiful."

"*Gracias*. There is something you do not know about me," he said. "There is," she replied.

"I was child prodigy," he continued. "*Mi padre*, he became ill and died not long ago. That is when I stopped playing. He was my, how you say it, *mi maestro, mentor de la musica*."

"He taught you how to play the piano?"

"*Si, si*, when I was three years old. My piano, we have been together since I was a child."

"Thank you for playing for me."

"No! I no play for you!" he pounded the keys again. "I play for *mi papa*, for his spirit."

"*Lo siento*."

"No! I am sorry. I am sorry I did not know my father as a man. I knew him as a father and as a teacher, but not as a man. I did not accept him as a friend, and now it is too late." Nacho closed his eyes and struck the keys some more.

"Who's Howard?" she asked quietly.

Nacho stopped playing. "My father's lover," he answered. "I did not know where Howard was leaving to, only that he was grief-stricken when he left. I did not know him well. That was my decision then, not to know him. In making that decision, I missed out on knowing my father as well."

"Nacho, you speak English well."

CHAPTER TWENTY-NINE

SHE COULD HEAR OPERA music blaring from Rafael's Mercedes as he pulled up to the well-lit commercialized corner of El Corte Inglés. European shoppers with bags full of expensive clothes, perfumes and cosmetics scurried about the corner, and at times it seemed that the mutter of their voices rang louder than the blaring traffic noises.

Vicki looked at her wristwatch. It was nine forty-five. This time Rafael was only ten minutes late, but she no longer minded his typical tardiness, or the entire country's lateness for that matter. A culture that runs behind schedule allowed her to do things she might not normally make time to do. But, since Rafael had shown up only ten minutes late, it left her no time to chat with her homeless friend, who again sat on the same sidewalk square between the same two sidewalk cracks.

Vicki waved to the woman who still mourned the damage Franco had done to her country and people during his autocratic rule and said hello to the man who celebrated the fashion and freedom that came to his country following Franco's death.

"*No te preocupes. ¡Vive!*" The woman's voice rang out like cathedral bells as she told her not to worry, but live. Go live life!

Rafael wore a black turtleneck and gray dress slacks. His shoes shone and his cologne always smelled good. Vicki didn't recognize it, but knew it meant a night full of conversation, rich food, red wine and culture.

They left the skyscrapers and city traffic behind and drove fifteen miles into country hills filled with ancient tall pines.

"Rafael, *no te gusta Franco, ¿no?*" She was learning about Franco in a history class, but preferred learning directly from the people of Spain.

"Some give credit to Franco," Rafael answered in Spanish. "After all, he never opened Spain to Hitler and that is positive. But I give him very little credit. I made a mistake in life many years ago, a mistake very horrible. Because of Franco, I've had to live with that mistake, and my life has not been good."

Vicki unrolled her window so she could feel the cool air hit her in the face as they drove. "*Digame?* What sort of mistake?"

As they pulled up to a ranch-style restaurant, Rafael put his fingers to his lips and shushed the topic, giving Vicki a subtle indication not to ask again. "This restaurant, where I am taking you, received five forks, *cinco!*"

"Five forks? *¿Que significa?*"

"It means I only take Victoria to the best." He answered in Spanish. "*En España*, we rate restaurants on a scale of one to five forks, based on the quality and price."

A hostess greeted Rafael by name and led them to a candlelit table on a glassed-in porch on the side of a cliff overlooking nearby chestnut trees and evergreen oaks in the distance.

A wandering flamenco dancer dressed in orange, purple and yellow stopped in front of their table to perform, and Rafael leaned over to Vicki to whisper loudly his opinion of the dancer. "This dancer is emotionally uninhibited. She is more concerned with experiencing the very moment than with anything else in life," said Rafael.

Vicki didn't understand. She only saw a dancer. "Do you know her?"

"No. Watch the flamenco. Watch her moves. She is completely carefree and has an attitude toward *la vida. La musica* and dance are her ways to express it." Rafael sat silent for a moment, but the song and dance felt never-ending to Vicki.

"*¿Que piensas? Digame, Victoria. Digame in inglés.*" He asked her what she saw in the dancer, but asked her to describe it in English, not Spanish.

"Describe what I see? in English?"

"*Si, si, en inglés, Victoria. Inglés.*"

"Okay, sure. I can do that but you won't be able to understand what I'm saying," she replied. "Oh, well, I'll describe what I see. I see a dancer. A dancer in a colorful costume who's getting a great aerobic work."

Rafael interrupted by gently pushing her chin toward the dancer. "*Mira.* Look at the dancer, not me," he urged in Spanish.

"*Si, si,* I see a dancer, one who has a story to tell. It's a long story because she's been dancing a long time now. She wants to share her story. She wants to express it. This woman is expressing a story about, uh, death. She has some things to say about life and death and things worth doing."

Vicki forgot about the man sitting beside her, and instead only noticed the lines on the gypsy's forehead deepen as her voice turned rough, like sandpaper. "Oh dear, this song is tormenting. She is looking, her eyes shut now. It's regret. it must be."

As her neck jolted and her eyes rolled around, the woman didn't notice the couple at the table. "She's looking back on her life, the hardships, the frustrations, and how she handled them, or how she let them handle her. What else can it be? She's dancing through the dark moments of her life," announced Vicki, who could feel her own face responding to the scene before her. "And she's not afraid to show her torment, her stress, her emotions."

Then the gypsy's teeth showed and her forehead crevices disappeared.

"Peace," declared Vicki. "She has found peace in the present. She is going to focus on things worth doing, things she can control, her attitude toward hardships."

"I thought flamenco was happy-go-lucky," continued Vicki. "I thought flamenco was simply a reach, pick, twist, and toss. I was wrong. This woman is releasing every stress she's ever had, I'm sure of it. This is an emotional outburst, and she's not afraid to express herself. I want to learn from her. I want to express myself. If I'm having a bad day, I don't want to smile. I want to feel. Then, I can genuinely move past it."

"*Muy bien,*" said Rafael as the flamenco dancer moved to another table. "Rafael?"

She took his hands in hers and smiled, staring him in the eyes. "*Gra-*

cias," she said. "I'm glad you showed me that. I'm glad I chose to really see. Flamenco dance is wonderful."

"*Algun dia*, someday," he told her. "I'd like you to do your tulip dance for me."

Vicki laughed. "Oh, my Dutch dance? Okay, someday. I need my wooden shoes to do it."

Three waiters catered to their table. One opened a bottle of red wine, another laid cloth napkins on their laps, and the third opened their menus. As Rafael raised his glass of dry sherry to his mouth, she caught a glimpse of his gold wristwatch that whispered five minutes until midnight.

Suddenly, she wanted to know why Rafael had never told her his last name. Who was this man sitting next to her?

They picked at the plate of cold *serano* ham, sausage and shellfish. Rafael ordered a bottle of sparkling *cava*, Spanish champagne. She demanded his last name.

"Rafael. *Yo soy Rafael de España*," he replied.

"Okay, Rafael from Spain, disclose a bit more, please. *Mas, mas*."

"*¿Quien eres, Victoria?*"

"Who am I? *Yo soy Victoria de los Estados Unidos*." Two could play this game.

He poked his long, tiny fork in his plate of octopus salad. "Would you consider staying in Spain *mas de solamente un semester?*"

"No," she said.

"There is no place better than Madrid, except Heaven." He held a fork of baby eels dripping garlic butter sauce up to her mouth, urging her to taste. She tasted, and he urged her to taste more.

"*Mas, mas*," he insisted.

She tasted more. He sampled the grilled crayfish off her plate. "You could travel around all of Europe and the world."

"No. *Yo no puedo, Rafael*," she stated boldly. "I can't travel the world, as much as I would love to. I have my studies waiting for me in Michigan."

"*Si, si, entiendo*." He said he understood. "But you would have a far superior education with me. The world has more to offer than a textbook, *un libro*. You see the world with me."

"*Por favor,* stop with all your offers. I've read all about Don Juan men like you, so stop trying to convince me."

"*No te preocupes, mi preciosa.* I can come to *los Estados Unidos.* You teach me English."

She laughed.

"I build a home in America, but I still have to travel much to *Europa* on business. As long as I have your precious face, I can design clothing anywhere in the world."

"Wait, wait, wait! *Un momento, Rafael!*" She had no problem being firm with her words. She told him there would be no relocating to the United States for him and that they shared a friendship, and a special one, but nothing more! If he couldn't accept that, this would be their last night together. She stood up and walked to the bathroom.

As she passed a table where the flamenco dancer now performed, she noticed a young woman wiping her eyes while watching the dancer. A man held her tight in his arms. As the woman dropped the napkin from her eyes, Vicki stopped. It was Isabella. The women spotted each other at the same moment, and Isabella looked like a deer caught in the headlights of an oncoming car, but why?

As Vicki walked over to her Spanish sister's table, Isabella quickly stood up, kissing her two times. "*Hola, Isabella.*"

"*Hola,* Vicki, *hola.*"

The young man generously pulled up a chair, offering her a seat. "Hello," he said.

"You speak English," said Vicki.

"I'm a lawyer from New York. My name is Ron." He laughed and then kissed Isabella on the cheek, wiping a falling tear.

"Isabella, are you all right?" she asked in Spanish, taking a seat.

"*Estoy bien,* you two speak your own language, go ahead," she flagged them on to speak freely in English.

"Isabella refuses to learn English, but one of these days, I'll teach her," said on. "Oddly, beyond my understanding, she feels it might be disloyal to her mama."

"Why is she crying?" asked Vicki.

"She gets absorbed in watching the flamenco dancers. Did you know those songs and dances are made up of Arabic, Sephardic Jewish, and African music?"

"No, I had no idea, but I found the dance quite moving myself. She was at our table earlier."

"Everyone proudly says the flamenco reflects the region's multicultural heritage. I know that's what Isabella loves most about it, anyway, the multicultural heritage."

"Isabella, *estas bien?*" asked Vicki, careful not to leave her Spanish sister out of the English conversation.

"*Si, si.*" She smiled and waved her hands for the two to go on talking without her.

"Isabella and I are very much in love. But, from one American to another, can I ask you to keep our secret?"

"Of course, but what secret?"

"Well, you can't tell her mother about us. Don't tell anyone. Someday, very soon, we'll tell everyone. But she's not ready now."

"I don't understand."

He took a sip of his wine and continued. "I'm fluent in Spanish and French. I love languages. Two years ago I came to Spain on business and met Isabella. I found her adorable from the start. We met while in line to buy a tuna sandwich at a café. Man, was she ever fascinated with the United States! You know, like it was another planet. I found her curiosity so cute that we talked all night—in fact, until morning. We talked like this night after night. You've probably found how the Spaniards love their nights, too. They don't stop talking. Five nights felt like five years with Isabella."

They laughed, and Isabella joined in.

"So why the secret?"

"You know Rosario. She's . . . how do I put it? She's from the older school. It's like she almost misses Franco's control. She adores her children, her country and, might I say, the old Spain? That's the problem. I'm not from Spain. This mattered to her. She has no idea we're still seeing each other. She has no idea we're so in love and that those feelings are not going to die."

"Do you think she's worried Isabella will marry you and move to the States?" asked Vicki.

"Yes, but we haven't made that decision yet." He finished his wine and nodded to the waiter to pour another. "Maybe we can live in both places. I'm pretty close to my family back there, and you know how close their family is here. I don't know. I don't know what to do."

"Oh, Isabella." Vicki squeezed her Spanish sister's hand tightly, and Isabella reached over to kiss her on the cheek. "Where are you staying?" she asked Ron.

"I've got an apartment here in Madrid. I've also got one in New York, but I'm here every chance I get."

"And no one knows of your relationship?"

"Her friends do. They take her out with them all the time; then she catches a taxi to meet me. They all feel guilty for it, yet they all respect her parents so much. Telling them might only hurt their relationship."

Just then, Rafael came walking around the corner, and it was the first time Vicki ever saw him look at his wristwatch.

"*Rafael, aqui, estoy aqui,*" Vicki called him over to their table. "*Ahh, Victoria, Victoria.*"

"*¿Quien eres?*" Isabella asked the well-dressed Spaniard now standing at their table.

"*Es Rafael,*" answered Vicki, wanting to give a last name but not wanting to admit she didn't know his last name.

Rafael introduced himself to both Isabella and Ron, kissing them each, once on each cheek. He and Ron spoke in Spanish for several minutes as Vicki whispered into her Spanish sister's ear something about Rafael helping her with homework and showing her Madrid's hot spots and being her friend and picking her up on the corner and treating her wonderfully. Isabella laughed and told her to have him come to the apartment instead of the corner.

A few moments later, the waiter walked over, indicating to Rafael that more food was waiting, hot, at their table.

"Ron, my Spanish is pretty good now, but please, just in case, let Isabella know I've kept Rafael my secret until now. He hasn't yet told me his last name, or where exactly he lives, or a phone number, yet I like him more each time he picks me up on that stupid corner. I make him meet me there in case he is some crazy man," she added.

"Vicki, he appears to be quite normal. I wouldn't worry so much."

"That's what my heart tells me."

She stood up and put her arms around Rafael.

Ron took a moment to translate the conversation for Isabella, who then replied in Spanish, "Never ignore the heart. Nourish it, Victoria."

"Nourish the heart?"

"*Si, si.* Red wine, olive oil, romance, and listen very closely to it. The heart likes to be listened to."

Vicki laughed. "I will, Isabella. I'll wine and dine my heart, and, most importantly, I'll listen to it."

"Please don't tell our secret," added Isabella.

"What secret? What are you talking about?"

"Thank you," said Ron. "I love her so much."

As much as Vicki loved food, especially authentic Spanish cuisine, she neither tasted nor smelled anything the rest of the evening, as if all her senses drifted directly into her conversation with Rafael. They touched on the subjects that convert strangers to friends and then topics that turn friends into couples. He talked about growing up an only child since his mother couldn't have any other children. He told her he had reached a crossroads in life, for he had come to understand the difference between spirituality and religion. She told him she knew she loved God and that the Bible was His word. But that was about all she knew at this point in her life.

He whispered that he loved his work, yet loved life more. She admitted she tended to turn life into one big productivity checklist, but over the last several months her perspective had been changing. He told her he wanted to treat a wife like a queen, and that he had it in him to offer a wonderful life to someone willing to accept it. She told him she had so many things to do in life, and finding Mr. Right wouldn't happen for years yet. They discussed all of this and more, without mentioning their last names.

He dropped her off on the corner, telling her to consider his proposals. It was mid-November, and he had to leave for Italy on business. He wouldn't be returning to *España* until mid-December.

"You will love me then," he said.

"I'm not saying I don't love spending time with you," she said. "You will fall in love with me then," he stated.

"By then, it'll be time for me to leave your country," she added.

"You will not want to leave."

She could hear the American national anthem calling her back. Yes, she would want to leave, to return to her own country, her own home.

Thanksgiving, truly an American holiday, arrived and went without turkey, sweet potatoes and family, but with calamari and olives.

Thank you Lord, for answering my prayers. Thank you Lord for knowing every aspect of me down to the very number of hairs on my head. I hope you don't keep up with the number of hairs on my legs. Thank you for loving me unconditionally. Thank you for the plans you have for my life. It feels nice to know I do not have to plan my life completely on my own. You've got plans for me as well, and I can surrender my own agenda and relax a bit. Thank you for bringing me through difficult times and restless nights. Thank you!

She spent her next few weekends on bus trips to nearby Toledo and Salamanca, and a ten-hour train ride to Barcelona. There she found a cathedral with baroque ornamentation and gilt. Despite its elegant, untouchable exterior, its doors were unlocked, so she walked in and knelt in the very last pew. She recognized the music that was being sung, "Ave Maria," Grandma's favorite. It had been played at her funeral. Vicki tried to pray, but her mind quickly jogged up the aisle to the front row, just as Grandma always used to lead the entire red-faced, furious family directly to the first pew when they arrived late. Dressed in satin oriental slippers, the petite woman used to say that running into church was her only form of exercise, so she might as well make the distance all the way up to the front.

Vicki, still sitting in the back of the church, watched up front as Grandma dug through her purse for butterscotch candy. Vicki listened and waited for the loud whisper.

"I do not have a temper, so don't think that I do but I can't get this damn candy wrapper off." Grandma always said that, and sometimes she said it so loudly that Vicki feared the priest overheard the word "damn."

"Then I'll go to confession after mass and take care of it," Grandma would say. "Damn" and "hel"l were the only swear words Grandma used, so she confessed.

The smell of sandalwood drifted throughout the church and, like the waves hitting the beach, each time Vicki breathed deeply, another whiff of sandalwood assailed her.

She smiled, knowing that the woman she loved dearly had returned to her Maker, like the seashells she found while walking the beach, the ones too gorgeous and loved to be kept, the ones tossed back into the water where they came from. She lit a candle for Grandma and left the church.

As she walked, she found herself replaying Rafael's proposals in her mind, like shifting from one canvas to another, painting one, then the other. *A worldly education. Stay in my country a little longer. Fall in love with me and you will love your life.*

The canvases she painted in her mind would surely make Howard proud. They would probably compete with Picasso. But suddenly she felt disturbed. She loved Rafael as a friend and nothing more. On the other hand, nothing beats a relationship that begins as a friendship. They had never kissed, so perhaps a kiss would add red, or at least pink, paint to the painting in her mind. She told herself not to think about this man, or his proposals, any longer, but she couldn't help it. He stayed on her mind. As she saw new things in Spain, she could hear his slow, sophisticated Spanish explaining their significance to her in a passionate way. Yes, Rafael walked passionately through life, all the while carrying some sad secret. She would welcome any story, any secret that might come whispering through his lips, the lips she now craved to kiss.

In mid-December she turned twenty-two years old, and each person in her Spanish family kissed her *dos veces*, once on each cheek. Rosario made paella, and the entire family claimed it to be the best in Spain. She also baked a chocolate-glazed torte, and everyone drank *Rioja* wine. A few times Vicki caught Isabella deeply involved in a daydream stare, but they never spoke a word about either Ron or Rafael. Perhaps she felt that sharing it with others might further betray what her own parents didn't know. Vicki respected this.

After eating a piece of torte, Isabella handed her a box of dark chocolate, and together the women indulged in the moment, perhaps to satisfy the cravings they each had, one for Ron, the other for Rafael. Why did chocolate do this? It terrified Vicki that chocolate brought Rafael to mind. Didn't that mean something serious? Like love?

The women closed their eyes and savored each bite. They did this until the last round truffle disappeared. Isabella held her stomach, concerned with weight gain. Vicki did notice that Isabella had put on pounds in recent weeks. Overdosed and fatigued, they lay on the hardwood floor of the apartment holding their stomachs and laughing at first, and then crying from feelings of gluttony and abuse.

"*Mañana, mañana, mañana,*" said Vicki. "I will eat healthy tomorrow." Mañana came and Nacho invited her for a walk through the Rastro, Madrid's biggest flea market and a tradition thriving over five hundred years. They started at Plaza de Cascorro and walked downhill toward Rio Mananares, then walked shoulder to shoulder in crowds down Calle Ribera de Curtidores.

"Have you lost anything since you've been in Madrid?" he asked her.

"No, why?"

"Because you'd probably find it here for resale," he said as they stopped to look at an assortment of used-looking leather purses.

"Wise to wear one of these," declared Vicki as she pulled money out of the fanny pack securely fastened around her waist. She bought a bullfighting poster and a copy of a Valazquez painting, and wanted badly to buy some of the Franco-era furniture. Instead she bought her father a leather day planner at another table. She had already bought her mother blue-and-silver earrings from a day trip to Toledo, and her sister a Madrid T-shirt.

They wandered for hours down the streets that once were the center of the slaughterhouse and tanning industry. Nacho didn't care if he drew attention to himself as he sang, "God rest ye merry gentleman, I dunno the rest of the words."

Vicki nudged him, hoping he'd be quiet just a bit, and then stopped. It was his country, and he could do as he pleased. His voice echoed through the chilly street while a group of little boys tossed a couple of pennies at him.

"I'm just a man who loves to sing and play life key by key," he sang his own words to the holiday tune that reminded Vicki of a list, not exactly her typical Christmas shopping list, but something deeper.

As they walked and he sang her mind journeyed further from the materialistic lis, to a place she had never visited before, a place that might put the North Pole out of business. Instead of costly objects, her mother needed to know how much she loved her as a friend, not just a mom. Her father needed to know how much she loved him. Her sister needed to know that, no matter how far apart they might be living, she would always love her as a friend and a sister, and no distance could fade that love.

She looked around at the booths filled with Spaniards deep in price negotiations. She noticed the birds of the air and heard Spanish-sounding chirps. She smelled the aroma of bread from a nearby shop. How would she survive in America without true, authentic Spanish paella? She looked at her friend walking beside her. What would she do without seeing his beautiful face, full of expression, emotion and drama as he talked? He looked more alive now that he was reunited with the love of his life.

She felt comfortable and didn't want to say good-bye to the people and the city she had grown to love. Maybe she should stay just a bit longer.

"Nacho, remember when I told you I've never been to a symphony?"

"*Si, si.*"

"Well, I promise I'll go one of these days."

"Vicki, you have already been to a symphony."

"No, I haven't, really."

"*Si, si.* And you played a very important part."

"No, I would know if I've been or not. I hardly know anything about symphonies."

"You must know!" he shouted. "A person conducts countless symphonies in life!"

"Oh well, if that's the case, I've sat through emotionally provocative performances, yes?"

"No! You do not sit through the symphonies in your life. You are the conductor."

"And what does the conductor do?"

"The conductor sets the volume and the speed."

"Is that all?"

"The conductor interprets the music that the composer has written."

"Oh."

"You conduct countless symphonies in your life. It is up to you, the conductor, to interpret the music the composer has given you."

"Well, no wonder life can be exhausting."

"It doesn't have to be. Every symphony has four parts, four movements of music. Between those four movements, there is silence. It is up to you to do as you like in the moments of silence."

"You say we conduct countless symphonies. Well, how will I know when one symphony has ended?"

"Believe me. You will know!"

They left the Sunday flea market and walked to the Metro stop. "I guess it's time to say good-bye," said Vicki. "I'm leaving your country. I'm not going to see you anymore."

"You see me more. You see me when you close your eyes and remember me. Now go."

"*Hasta luego, Nacho.*"

"*Hasta luego, Vicki.*"

CHAPTER THIRTY

SCREAMING, CLAPPING PEOPLE NUDGED her from all directions, and she couldn't hear a single word Rafael kept shouting into her ear. As they sat in the stands on a sunny Sunday afternoon, waiting for the initial pageantry to start, she felt disgusted that people were waving flags and cheering for the onslaught of a bull, as if cheering a touchdown. Why hadn't reading Hemingway prepared her for this? It had, until she sat in the bleachers herself and now had to see things with her own eyes. She knew it was her first time and that her emotions were taking over. She knew she wasn't allowing the facts of bullfighting to penetrate her mind, and that she had allowed herself to revert to ignorance.

Here sat the only still body in the bleachers, and her face stuck out in the crowd, her nose red from fighting back tears—Rudolph the Red-nosed Reindeer amidst a group who cheered. She didn't want to ruin Rafael's time, but then again, she didn't want to hide her feelings either.

Rafael fanned her face with a folded brochure and explained that the *corrida de toros* wasn't a sport but a spectacle. He told her that his country respected it as art and asked her how many paintings, sculptures, music, dance, and literature revolve around football?

"*No mucho,*" she answered. Nonetheless, the poor bull. She told him that in ancient Egypt, Mesopotamia, and Crete, bulls were the objects of worship. Her ancient civilization professor once told her so. "Now look at them."

The black creatures stood in their little pens in the arena below. "They look naive and adorable," said Vicki.

"No! Fierce and untamed," shouted Rafael.

She asked him how they trained bulls to "charge."

He said they aren't *trained* to charge. He said *toros* are born with the instinct to attack anything that threatens their predominance.

She laughed when the Spaniard next to her said bulls don't know the cloth is red. They're color-blind.

As the bulls grumpily stood in their suffocating pens, she blew her nose, aware that such creatures, only five years old, would soon experience what Rafael called the ultimate test of their existence: their performance with the bullfighter. He said that bulls lived a spoiled, noble, enviable life, spared from slaughterhouses.

She disagreed, and like a rebel in an animal research lab, she sat in Madrid's Plaza de Toros, feeling compelled to run down the bleachers and let the five-year-old creatures loose. She felt foreign, and Rafael was a stranger with different values. She longed instead to be at an American football game.

Like the energy of a bull, rising and rising as it sits in the tiny pen waiting to defend itself, her own questions. about Rafael - who he was, why he never told her his last name, were also rising. She had to know. She felt sick from not knowing who he was. Yes, she loved his company. Yes, she had learned a lot of culture from him, and yes, she once craved to kiss him, but the chocolate took care of that, and now she demanded to know more! She too prepared to fight.

"*Rafael, tu estas un hombre muy mysterioso. ¿Quien estas?*" She tried to sound both serious and mad but knew her tone in Spanish always came out the same. That of an American with a Dutch accent, carefully choosing words with the right meaning, and hoping she made the right choice as she said them.

"*Victoria . . .*"

A loud trumpet sounded, interrupting him. She couldn't compete with the crowds as they sprung from their benches, jumping up and down. It was an opening parade of some sort. Men attired in sixteenth-century clothes entered the arena on horses. The three bullfighters, killers, *mata-dores*, celebrities, or whatever they're called, walked into the arena wearing colorful costumes and black hats.

Their objective was obvious, to kill a bull, she told Rafael.

"No!" he shouted, offended. He said the objective was to artistically and intricately maneuver the cape and *muleta*! And while doing so, to elegantly dance with the bull in all its animalistic *brutalidad*.

"Oh," she said.

Individual teams accompanied the three bullfighters, and Rafael explained to her that the team members handled all sorts of things, including using the cape and placing sticks in *los toros*. He said the team members once dreamed of becoming *matadores*, bullfighters, and it may have been their only ambition in life for quite some time. But they never made it past the novice stage, so they were just part of the teams now. Only *matadores* had the right and permission to kill full-grown *toros*, he added.

Some workers entered the scene and smoothed out the sand in the arena, and Vicki's mind paved over Rafael's proposals. She knew his offer to stay in Spain sounded good, and she found herself considering it, but first, she demanded once more that he tell her everything. She asked for his last name again and didn't know why she felt obsessed with the question when she herself never told him her own last name. She felt bothered, perhaps because he kept his secrets stuffed far down like toys stuck in the toes of a stocking. She couldn't wait any longer. Everyone else shared their stories, their fears, and their feelings. Why wouldn't he? She asked him why he wouldn't tell her. Then she said it.

"I will never see you again, Rafael," she told him in Spanish.

"No!" He yelled louder, as if she had triggered his temper. He warned her never to say such a thing again.

Everyone in the arena below stood in designated spots. The president of the *corrida* took out a white handkerchief and waved it, and a bull charged out of the tiny pen after its morning of rest.

"Rafael!" Vicki yelled.

His eyes followed the action in the arena below, but he answered. "I do have secrets."

Those words struck her. She felt fear, like the charging bull. But then she glanced in the arena below and decided that no one feared anything. She saw no fear in the bull, or the matador, as if dying meant nothing in the arena below. How could a young man stand face-to-face with a ready-to-charge bull yet show no fear? She herself, sitting safely on the bleachers next to a stranger in some ways and a friend in others, felt more fear than the matador waiting for the bull's charge. Crazy! Absolutely crazy! But her fear wasn't crazy. It felt real. Rafael knew she would soon leave his country, and he'd never see her again. So maybe he planned to kill her out of passion, like the scene in the arena. It must be passion in the arena below. Why else would these young men make this their life's ambition? Passion. It had to be. A passion planted long ago and shared by an entire country.

The initial stages continued, and the *torero* was experimenting with his cape and the bull. "His objective, Victoria, is to find out if the *toro* favors one of its horns over the other. Yes, the *torero* needs to get in touch with the animal's natural tendency. He needs to test the bull's eyesight and try to understand and learn whether it charges in a long, smooth manner or short and choppy," said Rafael in Spanish.

She glanced back and forth from the bullfight to the man next to her, watching his face for reassuring clues—something that would reassure her that the blood below meant nothing serious. She also watched the man about to battle the bull. His good posture and perfect walk proved that he felt no fear. She glanced around at the Spanish faces in the bleachers around her. They looked as if they loved life too much to fear death. She envied them.

The matador led the big black animal into the center of the ring. The *picadores* stabbed the bull. "In order for the bull to follow the cape smoothly, it needs to be slowed a bit. Its head must be lowered," explained Rafael. The picador pierced the animal with a few knives, correcting any defects in its charge. "Now, the bull won't hook to the right anymore, and it won't swing up its horns as often. *Tal cosas* could have killed the matador if not adjusted."

A trumpet sounded to signal the final act of the drama. The matador, with sword in hand, asked the president if he could kill the bull. The president gave permission, and the matador dedicated the animal's death to his mother!

The creature, now angrier than ever, jumped around, arching its shiny black back and neck and kicking up its hind legs.

Rafael watched below as he confessed. "*Soy triste*. I have been unhappy for many years, Victoria. My wife only wants my money. She does not want to talk to me. She does not care what I say or what I feel. We are not friends. We are strangers, and we always have been. Our marriage has confidentially been declared a mistake. She loves my possessions, not me. She doesn't laugh when I laugh, and she doesn't cry when I cry. Her face looks like stone."

Married!? He was married! His sudden truth stunned her. Instinctively she had known it. Thank goodness she had never given into her romantic impulses. He did not look at her. Instead, he continued watching the sight below. Maybe she hadn't heard him correctly. How could he make such a confession and act as if nothing had changed between them?

After positioning the bull exactly where he wanted it, the matador lifted his sword to shoulder level and waved the *muleta* slowly, to guide the dangerous horns past his right hip. His target: a three-inch-wide opening *entre* the shoulder blades.

"If he misses the target zone, he'll hit bone, and the fans will be outraged at him," said Rafael. The steel thing hit the target, but it wasn't well placed, and it didn't kill the bull.

"The matador must be scared to death."

"Death is not the enemy, Victoria. Fear of death is," stated Rafael.

She wanted to scream at him for having a wife. She couldn't believe it. She had known he had a secret, and she continued to meet with him. He was also a beautiful man both inside and out, and of course he should be married. This she should have expected. She couldn't get mad at him and his situation, nor could she get mad at this country for its custom. In fact, she couldn't take her eyes off the scene below, and the more she saw, the more she wanted to know . . . about the Spaniards, the country, and Rafael's sadness. "*Digame mas, mas.*" She told him to tell her more.

"When I pulled up to the curb to ask you for *direcciones*, I noticed *tres cosas*," said Rafael. "*Primer*, I noticed your expressive eyes as you listened when I talked." He pointed to her features as he spoke, staring at her. "*Segundo*, I noticed the several differing tones of your voice. *Tercer*, your smile."

The matador used a shorter sword, fitted with a crossbar close to the tip. As he pierced the base of the *toro*'s skull, Vicki looked around at the fans to see if they, too, were crying. No, they were clapping. Only Rafael had tears rolling down his cheeks.

Why could she not feel his sadness? She wanted to tend to Rafael but had a hard time taking her eyes off the arena below. It said so much about Spain, and the people as a whole. It revealed much about the people, perhaps more than any conversation could ever reveal. She wanted to go, again and again, to buy a season's pass. She wanted to stay in Spain longer.

The bull collapsed on the ground, and people, and Vicki, shouted louder as a team of mules dragged the dead animal out of the arena. Everyone waved handkerchiefs.

Rafael pinched her ear. "They are requesting that an ear be given to the matador," he said in Spanish.

"Well, not mine," she shouted back in the same language.

Rafael laughed. "No, not a human ear, the bull's ear. The matador gives the ear to the butchers in exchange for the bull's body." The matador ran around the arena once, as if the waving handkerchiefs meant more than applause. Another trumpet sounded, which meant time for the *segundo* bull to enter the sunny arena. The crowds cheered for *mas, mas*.

"*Victoria, estoy sufriendo*," whispered Rafael as he stood up and tugged on her sweater so she'd follow him. The fight wasn't over, but he led her down the bleachers and out to his car.

They drove into the country with a clear sky overhead. "Bullfighting—*hoy* isn't all that it once used to be, Victoria," said Rafael.

"Why not?"

"Now it shares the fame with soccer matches."

"It looked pretty significant to me," she said.

"*Tambien*, there have been changes in Spain's economy. Many ranches were sold. On the ranches in the past, owners could selectively breed *los toros*. Breeding the right sort of bull for a fight almost classified as an art, or a science, I don't know which. No, bulls of today don't always have the space for exercise and natural grazing on ranches."

"The bulls looked healthy," she said.

"They aren't as wild as they once were."

They pulled up to a brown acorn-style cottage, and Vicki was pleased to notice horses, not bulls or sheep, grazing behind a white picket fence. Several smaller cottages were up and down the hill.

Rafael got out of the car, telling her to stay put, and walked up to a building that looked like an office. When he went inside, she quickly rummaged through his glove compartment, in search of anything that might have his last name on it. But, like her own glove compartment, Rafael kept a tidy car with not a crumb of evidence.

He returned to the car and told her he had rented horses for a few *horas,* but she refused to take part in the adventure. She credited herself as too smart for that. In fact, she was borderline paranoid. She refused to be murdered somewhere in the country of Spain on her semester abroad. She also noticed her mind getting a bit dramatic, but she blamed it on television and movies. A simple horseback ride in the country on a gorgeous, calm day almost always led to murder in the movies.

"No. I don't want to ride horses at a time like this. You're married, and you should be riding horses with your wife." She knew she said it in English, and she felt a nervous feeling in the pit of her stomach, moths killing butterflies – they were taking over.

They sat together on the trunk of his Mercedes, which was parked inconspicuously under the shade of towering trees.

"Ay, Victoria." Rafael reached above him and pulled an oak leaf off a low-hanging branch. "I married young. Many years ago, I discovered that my wife had cheated on me, over and over again. I should have known. I loved her more than she loved me. I should have read her face. She looked like stone."

He made an awful stone face, freezing all his expressions. "No laughter, no tears, no yelling. Numb to life. I've never seen emotions come from her. She is made of makeup and designer clothes, my designer clothes, and nothing more."

"Well, you did choose her to be your wife, and now, you probably have a family with her—kids you are responsible for."

"No, Victoria. She refused to have children, telling me only after we were married that children demand too much attention. The truth is, she demands too much attention, and children would take that away from her."

"You wanted children?"

"*Si, si, claro que si.*" He extended his arms up and outward in a fashion like the trees around them. "But she went and had surgery without telling me. In Spain, do you realize how abnormal this entire thing is?"

"Rafael, this is abnormal for anywhere in the world. Have you discussed divorce?"

"*Si, si.* No, no. My country, under Franco, didn't allow divorce."

"But Franco is dead, Rafael."

"But fear is alive, Victoria."

"Then you too will die," said Vicki.

"I will not die!"

"No, but you are living a dead life."

"I am alive now that I know *Victoria de los Estados Unidos. Si,* I am alive again."

"*¿Quien estas, Rafael?*"

"No. My name is not important. I want you to know me, Rafael." He pounded on his heart.

"I can't know you if I don't know your past. I do not know you," said Vicki.

She got up and walked away, and he followed. "I practiced law, as many university students in *España* do. Then, I inherited money from my father. He owned banks throughout Spain, so I do not have to work, ever again. I am made of old money, but designing clothes is my passion in *vida,* my only passion, next to my new friendship with you, *mi preciosa.*"

She felt a smile for the first time since they had arrived at the ranch.

She tried to contain it, but couldn't. She didn't want to be a stone, numb to emotions, especially to a man so appreciative of details. Emotions happened like reflexes, yet Rafael cherished them after years of living without.

"Follow me," he said. "I have a surprise for you."

He popped the trunk of his car and took out a pile of black dresses and white cotton tops with sheer floral sleeves. "Try them on for me, *por favor.*"

"Where should I try them on?" she asked.

"*Aqui.* Here."

She laughed with the excitement of new clothes, yet felt horribly shy, embarrassed to model in front of a man who worked with European models on a daily basis. Her emotions ran in circles. She felt honored that he wanted to give her this wardrobe. She also felt insecure that perhaps it was a hint that her clothes were ugly. What if they didn't fit past her thighs? She would hug him anyway. No, she would hit him for being married. She felt in love, yet frightened. Were these the emotions he saw and liked on her face? Well, Rafael deserved credit himself. He was a man who provoked many emotions, and he stirred hers all at once.

"I designed them over the past few months with you, Victoria, in my mind."

She walked behind a tree trunk, wishing it were a thick banyon instead of an oak. He could see part of her. Her stomach? Her thighs? She didn't mind him seeing her stomach. She minded her thighs. She slid her top over her head then unsnapped her pants. As she struggled to pull them off, she knew the tree trunk no longer hid her behind. She tossed the pants on the ground and grabbed the black dress, hanging on Rafael's finger. She pulled it up, wondering if it might get stuck at the waist. No, of course not. Designed by a successful European fashion designer, it had to fit. Well, now she'd find out if he really designed it for her, with her in mind. Yes, it pulled up over her waist and up to her neck perfectly, as if painted onto her body. If there was such a thing, she would declare it her soul dress, a dress made just for her, a dress perfectly in tune with her body, her style, her emotions. If the dress had cost four hundred dollars in America, she'd open a new credit card to buy it. She'd grow old wearing this dress that he designed for her, sexy yet classic.

"I help you. I help you." He piled her long blond hair in a bun on her head and zipped the dress up to her neck. "*Si, si.* I made this for you, *Victoria*, for you."

She believed him now as she walked with a sway of her shoulders once around his Mercedes, spinning a couple times, then returned to where he sat on the car.

"*¿Te gusta?*" she asked.

"*¡Me encanta!*" She loved the dress, but knew she'd never have a place to wear it. She didn't live a soap opera life, nor did she attend the type of American parties that called for this sort of dress. She longed to be a part of a social world that wore these dresses. However, no matter how dressed up she might become, she wanted to remain full of emotions, full of life.

He grabbed her around the waist and pulled her close, kissing her for the first time on the lips. "*Te quiero,*" he whispered in her ear.

"No, no." She wiped her lips and backed away, not sure where this dress and its maker might take her.

"*Si, si. Te quiero,*" he said again, smiling.

She knew his words meant both love and want, and this she had to stop. Despite the fact that he had married a stone, he was still married to that stone. She wanted to kiss him, to hold his hand, to walk to places she had never seen with him, but she refused to do this with a married man. She felt pity for him, yet he had choices to make concerning his marriage, his situation.

"*Te quiero,*" he said, pulling her close again. Then he whispered something else in her ear, and she had to pause to interpret. Her heart pounded in a way she never felt before, a pounding that terrified her more than her worst panic attack ever could, a pounding that excited her more than her first innocent kiss years before, a pounding that sounded as foreign as the sound of Madrid's city streets back when she first arrived in this country. She had no idea her heart was capable of so many different rhythms, like rain, pounding, beating, pouring, dropping, and so on, depending on the season, the place and the other weather patterns occurring simultaneously.

"No!" shouted the woman from Holland, Michigan, a woman with values, with fears, with dreams of her own, a woman who picked a tulip, then felt guilty for months, guilty on a deeper level than penalties and fines, guilty for having taken something that didn't belong to her.

"*Si, si.*" He kissed her neck slowly this time, whispering, "*Mas, mas.*"

"No. I have to tell you something, Rafael." She pushed him away.

"*Si, si, digame,*" said the man from Spain, a native to a country with a rich history of passion and drama, a country drunk on romance. "*Te quiero.*"

"You cannot have me, Rafael. You cannot love me."

"*¿Por que? ¿Por que?*"

"You are married. You are not mine to take. I'm certainly not going to influence something so significant. I don't want to live with that burden."

"But I do not love her," he replied.

"Then be a man and do something about it."

"I will. I want to, but not now. Now I am with you."

"Well, don't think you can go on living in a miserable marriage while wining and dining me on the side. Forget it." She had said it all in Spanish, and gave credit to the Spanish soap opera she had watched so many times with Rosario.

"*Ahora, ahora, te quiero.*" He still wanted her.

She allowed him to kiss the back of her neck, and it sent chills down her spine, the kind that, in a romance novel, would sweep a woman off her feet and right into mad passionate love for endless hours, only to be left both spent and content. Grandma would be skipping ahead a few pages just to get to the steamy part of this letter. But this wasn't a romance novel. This was life, her life. She couldn't help it that she viewed marriage as sacred, as Rafael began to slowly unzip her dress, kissing further down her back. He then pulled it down off her waist. Her mind raced. This was her life, no one else's. Why would she let a few romantic moments in Spain screw up her entire life to come? Then again, it might add incredibly dramatic colors to her canvas, but what would it do to someone else's canvas?

She stepped back several feet. "No, Rafael. No," she said as she reached for her jeans on the ground. "Please wait for me in the car. I want to leave now."

On the corner of El Corte Inglés, he said there was nothing sacred about his marriage arrangement and, had he known back then that his wife would take a malicious turn in life, if he had seen through her insincerity, he never would have married her. He had tried every attempt imaginable at making the marriage work. He would never break a commitment without first trying everything to save it.

"No, *Rafael de España*, no," she told him, and got out of his car.

She didn't know what else to say and didn't want him to see her cry, so she put her sunglasses on, although the sun had gone down. She knew he wasn't about to smile, and she was glad because she couldn't stand to see those dimples one more time.

She also couldn't stand to see him without his smile, so she turned her back to him, kissed her two fingers, extended her arm back and started to wave, without turning to peek. She could see him in the reflection of the department store window, just as she had the first time they met. He didn't know she could see him as he wiped his eyes on his sleeve and made the sign of the cross. She started to walk away, but kept waving. She walked with a purpose. What purpose? She didn't know, just the sort of purpose that says this good-bye is forever. She heard his car drive away, and as badly as she wanted to turn to look one last time, she didn't. The backward good-bye wave would have to do, and she felt like a hummingbird that flies backward to move away from flowers whose nectar they've been sipping. Just like these small birds, her legs and feet felt too weak to walk, but she had to. She couldn't fly.

CHAPTER THIRTY-ONE

MAÑANA CAME ALL TOO soon. Sure, there'd be another tomorrow, but it would be a tomorrow in the United States, not Spain. Vicki wanted to stay anchored there a little longer, in the country that lusted for life and stayed up all night. She wasn't ready to pull up anchor, yet her life and school were calling her back.

Maybe someday she would return to Spain to operate a bed-and-breakfast in the mountains, live on a yacht in Barcelona, or rent a tiny studio apartment near her Spanish family and turn her letters to Grandma into a novel of some sort.

On her hands and knees and in a temper, Rosario scrubbed the wooden floors for hours, moving Vicki's heavy suitcases over so she could clean the floor under them. It took no words to understand her loss. She had allowed a stranger into her home, her kitchen, the most private and intimate aspect of her life, the part that now smelled of paprika and garlic-scented *chorizo*, slowly simmering on the stove, and now that stranger was leaving.

At quarter to nine, she kneeled down next to her *señora* to rest before her flight, and placed her hand on the woman's hands, blistered from cleaning. Rosario stopped, and for a moment the two sat in silence on the floor, listening to traffic and voices from the street below. They didn't need or attempt to talk. The woman handed Vicki a sheet of stationery. There was a quote scribbled in English, and Vicki knew Rosario had gone to great lengths to get this translated. It read:

> *What do you have to fear? Nothing. Whom do you have to fear? No one. Because whoever has joined forces with God obtains three great privileges: omnipotence without power, intoxication without wine, and life without death.* —St. Francis of Assisi

Isabella had left the apartment earlier in the evening because she had weekend social plans brewing in the streets below, and Vicki knew they were probably with Ron. Lorenzo went to mass but hugged Vicki tightly before he left.

Together the women dragged the luggage down the flights of stairs to the street below, and Rosario flagged down a taxi. She kissed Vicki on both cheeks, closed her eyes, and made the sign of the cross, and then blew a kiss as her American daughter climbed into the taxi and drove away.

The taxi headed down the narrow street, and Vicki didn't trust herself to turn around to see the *señora* standing alone on the curb with her dirty apron and strands of hair falling from her bun for fear she would burst into tears. She did, however, catch a glimpse of Lorenzo, standing in a bakery window eating a huge cream puff. She laughed at the man who claimed to be at mass.

Next, the taxi stopped in traffic at the El Corte Inglés corner. Cars were honking, and one man got out of his car to yell at someone in another car. She ignored the scene and instead watched a homeless woman, sitting on the pavement outside the department store. People were dropping coins into her bucket, but the old woman never smiled. Then a man dressed in black pants and a black turtleneck walked over to the woman and handed her what looked like a cup of something warm to drink, still steaming. He sat down next to her and opened the woman's hands, placing the mug between her palms, and held them for a moment.

Vicki tried unrolling the window of the cab, but it must have been on safety lock. She tried opening the door, but the cab started to move. She pounded on the windows. One more smile, one more wave. She had to tell them both how much she loved them. She wanted now to tell Rafael how she appreciated him, and that of all the Spaniards she had grown to know, she loved him the most. She wanted to thank this man for teaching her about the Spaniards from the inside out. She wanted to remove the excess sweaters that had crowded her suitcases and wrap them around Triste. She loved this country, and she loved its people. She loved Rafael. If she could only stay a little longer.

"Wait. Let me out. *Stop!*" She cried either out loud or to herself, she didn't know which.

The taxi driver stared in his rearview mirror and kept driving. She felt like an animal in a cage being taken away, somewhere. She was leaving the country she now loved, the country that taught her to live life and not fear death at a time in her life when she needed that particular lesson.

As she watched out the back window of the cab, the gray bundle and the black velvet next to it grew smaller and smaller, as did the Spanish city, located at the foot of the Guadarrama Mountains. She didn't want to leave and found herself already mourning this country, bordered by the Atlantic Ocean and the Mediterranean Sea. She didn't know which she loved more: the people or the place. The tears in her eyes clouded her vision, turning the scene behind her into a Salvador Dali surrealist painting.

At the airport, she had a good hour before her flight. Vicki felt an adult butterfly emerging in her stomach, pumping body fluid through its soft veins and expanding its wings.

Dear Grandma,

TIME, WEATHER AND DEATH—these three words transcend any culture and language. These three things are completely out of our control, yet everything is planned around them. Even if a fiesta is planned for mañana, TIME moves on at its own pace, turning that fiesta into nothing more than a memory. WEATHER behaves rudely, when it likes, pouring rain on the guests of the fiesta. DEATH, should it be told, shows up just before the fiesta. And for that person, who may have been living in a countdown of anticipation, the fiesta never comes. This is why people fear death. They cannot control it.

P.S. Please give Pooch a hug for me, Gram. I'm assuming dogs make it to Heaven? They must!

CHAPTER THIRTY-TWO

HER BREATHING AND CHEST pains still teased her every so often, even though she anchored herself securely in a familiar place—an old rental home with mutual friends in Saugatuck, not far from campus. It was the house she and Rebecca had picked out together and planned on sharing after they returned from Spain.

Vicki needed to study and to attend a class, but none of that mattered at the moment. *Mañana,* she told herself. She could always go to class and study tomorrow.

Today, she decided to place the important things at the top of her list. And this meant she had choices, several stages, just as a woman at the beach could choose to take her shoes off and safely walk along the shore with nothing more than her toes getting wet. She could further choose whether or not to take her clothes off and tread the chilly water waist-high. After that, she might shuffle her feet fearfully, paranoid of jellyfish or stingrays. Or, she could choose to dive under, getting her hair wet, forgetting about her makeup. Yes, a woman could choose to go only as far as the white, shallow waves washing gently against her, or she could ride the waves and risk being dashed on the mammoth spikes barricading the great ocean beyond.

Aware now of her choices, the degrees to which she could participate in daily life, Vicki refused to bury herself in the sand of all her daily lists of things to do. Granted, she would not ignore responsibility or productivity, but she would transform a tedious list of errands into a life-changing map simply by adding one magnificent thing a day, something that might bring significance to her day. She promised herself she would start the New Year facing the wind like a windmill, with sturdy arms embracing the winds and generating beautiful and unlimited energy. And as the wind died down she would rest, knowing with fresh faith that it would soon start up again.

Spain, Tarpon Key, and the Till Midnight café with Rebecca were moments she could never forget. They had introduced her to vessels, magnificent vessels, the likes of which she might never cross paths with again. In fact, her life might never be that exciting again, but it didn't matter. She no longer feared death. Her anxiety attacks returned every so often, but not concerning death. She knew at once that they had turned into a bad habit, started by her mind. Anything could trigger them. She only needed to break the mental habit now, and she would. She would conquer it at her own pace, not on a deadline.

She remembered what Nacho once said, "Go to the symphony." Well, she couldn't. She had no cash, nor a sufficient block of time, nor information about any symphony. So she bought Ludwig Van Beethoven's Symphony No. 9 in D minor, Opus 125, and played the cassette in her car as she drove to Holland and around campus. Her mind traveled farther than campus, farther than Tarpon Key, farther than Spain. How could it not? She was appreciating one of the highest artistic achievements of the human mind. As she listened to the sweeping majesty of Beethoven's greatest work, the campus changed before her eyes. It became more cultural, more beautiful. Just because she didn't have a lot of money or time or resources, didn't mean she couldn't add a few sparks to her now-ordinary life. Even in winter, she could find creative ways to feed on the nectar of flowers.

Suddenly, as she turned right onto College Avenue, Beethoven's stately music erupted. Startled by the unexpected sounds filling her car, she accidentally switched lanes, cutting someone off behind her. Horns honked, and she laughed, because it fit well with Beethoven's piece, a rebel bassoon player, a naughty spirit.

When the music came to its magnificent finale, there was enormous silence, and she knew instantly that the third movement of the symphony in her own life had come to an end, the symphony that started the night she first scribbled her dreams and goals on the white paper tablecloth. She parked her car, not minding the silence. She embraced it as she walked quietly and alone to Till Midnight and took a seat at a small, round table draped with a white paper tablecloth on the sidewalk in front of the café.

The tulips she and Rebecca had seen together last spring had disappeared, their season of stardom past. As surely as the seasons would come and go, new tulips would return to take their place in the same soil come early May. As she looked around, the day stood still. No candles were lit, and a closed sign hung on the restaurant door. Despite the chilly air and the light snow, the tables were already covered with paper tablecloths, sheltered by an awning and heat lamp above. She could see but not hear the staff as they scurried about inside, preparing to open in an hour.

Aware of the hours of studying to do, but more aware of the special things in life that come first and should always fit into any hectic schedule, she sat down at the same table where she and Rebecca had last planned their future together. She understood now that silence served a very important purpose. She closed her eyes and could hear the voices of the people she had encountered, their words and stories like building blocks of wisdom, just as the waves, casually over time, deposited the grains of sand that slowly formed the islands of the world.

She could hear valves, vibrating strings, and pipes all at once, an orchestra tuning up, and she knew the silence was coming to an end. She was ready to enter the fourth and final movement of her own personal symphony as she opened her eyes and noticed silver-frosted clouds draping the horizon. She picked up a red crayon from the table and, with the confidence of a conductor who had gained interpretations from scores of musicians, she began to write fast and furiously on the white paper tablecloth.

As if a bow was stretched over the strings of the violin, she heard Rebecca's voice, full of emotion, and wrote, "Live within the present."

She thought of Captain Porter Smith and their passionate battle with the tarpon, and she could almost hear the silvery fish breathing, like the breathier, throatier sound of the viola accompanying the violin. She wrote, "Find a domain and bring passion to your life."

She remembered Denver classifying her as a submarine and telling her it was okay to feel down. His voice was loud and clear like that of a trombone, and she was sitting directly in front of it, with its long u-shaped slide moving back and forth, poking her. She wrote, "Anchor long enough to repair and refuel but always work your way through dark waters."

She could picture Rebecca's mother writing her that letter, like someone fingering the valves on a trumpet, and scribbled, "Celebrate life."

She watched a waiter inside running from table to table, like fingers swiftly sliding over the strings of a triangular harp, and it reminded her of Ruth. She wrote, "Build your own fortress with walls made of boundaries."

She felt an emotionless chill thinking about John Bark and wrote, "Surrender your dreams to God."

She could hear Howard's voice, like the piccolo, the baby brother to the flute and sounding just an octave higher, with its shrill tone adding much color to a piece of music. She wrote, "Start fresh daily, adding beautiful colors to your plain white canvas."

She thought of Evelyn, her voice regal and resonant, yet evoking melancholy, and wrote, "See something new out your same old window."

She heard Connie's loud, boisterous laugh, like a rebel bassoon player and scribbled, "Add laughter to your life."

She could hear the motor of Simon's boat making its way through the water with a crisp, clear fluidity similar to the sound of a flute and wrote, "Discover an island where you can rediscover yourself."

She thought of Ben sitting on the dock, a tuba player adding much background depth. She wrote, "Hop, skip and jump toward goals, enjoying the process as much as the destination."

Her thoughts quieted for a moment, and she almost put her crayon down, but they must have been crying wolf, because suddenly she remembered what her parents had told her as she boarded the plane to Spain. Their voices, like clarinets, created a flowing melody as she wrote, "Abandon comfort zones and discover adventure."

Again, she thought the music might end, but voices travel far, perhaps farther than any voyager in history. She could hear Rosario's voice like a fiddle, the instrument all the other instruments tune to, all the way from Spain. She wrote, "Don't rush any part of life. Savor it like a delicious meal."

She could almost taste sangria as she thought of Lorenzo and his deep voice, one of three trombones, and wrote, "Indulge in fiestas but never lose your dignity."

She felt the chilliness of the seat she now sat on, and it reminded her of Triste, a violin going up one notch. She wrote, "Get on with your life. Live life!"

She remembered the flamenco dancer and the tambourines she danced to and, with a smile, wrote, "Dance through life."

Her heart pounded as loudly as any instrument when she thought of Isabella and Ron, and wrote, "Nourish the heart – red wine, olive oil, romance, and careful listening."

Drums sounded when she noticed a tray with red cloth napkins near the door and thought of the matador and wrote, "When death comes around, stare it in the eyes."

She closed her eyes and could hear Nacho's piano music and remembered the time he told her she was the conductor of countless symphonies in life and that it was up to her to interpret the music given to her by the composer. It was up to her to set the pace, the volume and to make an interpretation of that music. He had told her there were four parts of music in a symphony with silence between the parts. She opened her eyes and wrote, "Do as you like with your moments of silence."

Suddenly, everything went quiet again, and she listened desperately for Rafael's voice. She knew this time was more than just a pause. The music had definitely ended. She couldn't write anything as she thought of him. Their time together had been incomplete. She longed to know what she might have learned had she spent more time with him.

She put her crayon down and stared at the frozen flowerbed where last year's tulips had stood in perfect harmony waiting for the infamous tulip festival to begin. The cup-shaped, solitary flowers died each year, but every winter their bulbs divided under the snow-packed earth, and new ones bloomed in the spring.

She spoke as if someone sat across from her. "No, a believer in God and all that is spiritual, I will not fear death! Death will be the start of eternal life with God. For now, while I'm alive, death will serve as a reminder."

All at once, the music burst forth again, and she could almost hear the tulips, in perfect harmony, the red with the red and the pink with the pink, their petals opening in unison, as if synchronized to the movements of a conductor, and at the end of her new list, she added, "Remember the tulips. Just as their season of stardom comes and goes, you too will one day pass."

As death was added to that list, it put everything into perspective.

The music of the fourth and final movement ended. There would surely be other symphonies in her life, but this particular one she declared done. Of course, she would always hear the memory of its music in her mind, and now, in the immediate silence following that music, she valued her time and the very moment, and neatly folded the tablecloth with her new scribbles. She knew this list would bring her an immediate yet long-lasting sense of accomplishment, as well as joy, because everything she wrote could be started right away. It wasn't the type of list that could be defeated with excuses. And this list wouldn't cause stress. It had no deadlines and inflicted no pressures. Instead of consisting of a set of things she had to do in life, it was simply a way of doing things in life.

She rose from the table, unable to contain herself any longer, a woman sitting quietly through an entire symphony, bottling her desire to clap and scream and shout within herself like a bottle of champagne, and now ready to explode with excitement, she jumped away from the table and did an angel in the snow. A few passing cars honked. She took a handful of snow and tasted it. Still in angel position, she closed her eyes and felt the refreshing coldness of Michigan's wintry mantle.

When she opened her eyes again, the robust clouds overhead shimmered in shades of white she had never seen before, matching the snow beneath, and in the far distance, the horizon between sky and earth blurred where the grayish whites met. Thin tree branches wrapped in snow looked so perfect that she could swear a little elf from the North Pole had stayed up all night carefully and perfectly hand-painting each and every twig in a thick coating of opaque white.

She lay in the snow a good five minutes. Things she had never pondered before drifted through her mind. One could determine the life span of butterflies by capturing them and marking their wings with a square-tipped marking pen, then watching for them later. She didn't want to be captured. She didn't want to know the number of her days.

Dear Grandma,

Everybody will lose someone or something they love at some point in this life, as we know it. A loss can be a family business sold, a move from a hometown, distance from a big or little sister. It could mean the end of life-long friendships. Losses great and small come in various ways.

Some people will grieve; others will be grief-stricken. I recommend actively grieving, I mean going on a grief journey. Grieving is a long process. You have to rediscover the world about you.

Some will turn their grievances into fears and phobias. Others will turn their grievances into an appreciation for life, for the living moment itself, the present.

P.S. I look forward to seeing you again, Grandma. I hope you'll be there some day when I walk through that door to eternal life. I wonder what my symphony will sound like then!

CHAPTER THIRTY-THREE

DICTATED BY TIME ZONES, the New Year would arrive first in Spain. With forty-five minutes left before the year changed, Rafael knew his Spanish custom of tardiness might postpone a meeting or delay a luncheon or make Victoria stand desperately by herself on the corner. Alas, he knew that his tardiness would not, could not, prevent the New Year from coming. He wanted badly to take hold of the skinny little hands of the clock, to twist and pull them until they fell off, to put the worldwide celebration on hold until someone with tools could repair them and set the clock in motion again. No, though he could not control time, or the coming of the New Year, he could control his own decisions, and this—this he would do. He had to!

Sitting in the leather seat next to him, his wife shouted and cursed at him. "Drive faster!" she demanded. Instead, he thought of his latest line of clothing, the line that took Spain by surprise with its subtle Americana twist, the line he labeled, "Living Victoriously." The screech of his wife's voice interrupted his daydream once more.

They were late for the event of the century—wining, dining, and gossiping with Spain's best, Spain's royalty, and its most gorgeous and impressive people. As he drove slowly in the direction of the Palacio Real, he dreaded entering a New Year with no love, no children to call his own, no friend to share his emotions with. He couldn't stand thinking about spending another year with his wife and her materialism, rudeness, and self-serving selfishness.

They had driven to Palacio Real hundreds of times before, so he had no excuse to give his screaming wife as he made a wrong turn and drove an extra couple of blocks before stopping his car on the corner outside El Corte Inglés department store. For years, words like "*loco*" and "*estupido*" had left her mouth like balls at a batting cage, hitting him head-on. Now, they only rolled past him. He refused to look at her, but through the corner of his eyes he saw her throw her hands up in a tantrum as she belittled him with crude names. The combination of her perfume and hair spray smelled like a sweet Tento de Virano and sangria mixed together, and it made his head throb and his eyes water. He watched out the window as a woman walked by with two babies in a double stroller, and again he felt desperate to become a father. He mourned the fact that his wife never wanted to have babies. She had a right not to want them, but she had never told him this. In fact, she had once lied, saying she wanted children. She had said it simply to get him to marry her. Her self-centeredness burned his stomach. As the young mother turned the corner, he made a left turn, ignoring his wife's cursing, and drove to the palace. He knew he had changes to make in the New Year. He would make these changes. He would do so - *mañana! Mañana, mañana, mañana!*

The gray bundle stood in the long line at the corner shop that often served the homeless free soup. The city celebrated, getting ready to welcome the New Year. She reached into her pocket and felt the wrinkled paper the American woman had handed her. She smiled, thinking of the romantic young woman from another world, far away. The woman had reminded her of herself years ago, before she had allowed the aftermath of death to take over her life. She didn't know what she would do with the piece of paper that had Vicki's full name and phone number scribbled on it. She laughed at the naive girl's crazy offer. If she had understood her sophisticated textbook Spanish properly, this girl had invited her to visit America.

Si, si, she had invited her to visit with her family there. How *loco*! She would never leave *España*. Impossible dreams, but the romance of it all made Triste smile as she carefully folded the paper and tucked it in her pocket, then sipped her warm soup twenty minutes before midnight.

"Our Father in heaven," she prayed silently in Spanish, "hallowed be thy name."

Isabella told her mother she had important news to share. She had wanted to make the announcement days, weeks, even months *before* the clock struck its infamous twelve, making it last year's news. She wanted her mother's disappointment to belong to a year gone by, but instead, her mother would be returning to the kitchen at any moment, ready to hear the shocking news. It would hit her seconds before the arrival of the New Year and would probably haunt her for life.

Rosario's hands were shaking as she pulled the department store bags out from under her bed. She wiped the tears that were running down her cheeks. She remembered years ago, when Isabella was a child, she had told her that mothers had eyes on the backs of their heads. That is why she had known about Isabella sneaking *galletas*. In reality, it had been the crumbs on her mouth. Other times, it had been her father tattling on his cookie competitor. Tonight, Rosario would give her daughter the ultimate lesson in mother's intuition. She would walk into the kitchen, but instead of holding the empty cookie bag up, she would pull the baby clothes out of the bag.

"A mother knows things," she would tell her daughter. "A mother doesn't really have eyes on the back of her head, but she has something more. She has intuition, and you too will have it soon."

Rosario quickly tucked the clothes back into the bag. Her husband hugged her. He had used his entire holiday bonus from the post office so that his wife could buy these baby clothes for their daughter. They both knew that screaming and yelling wouldn't solve anything, nor would silence and shunning. They would accept their daughter's decision, and the man she chose, and they would look forward to the arrival of Isabella's baby. Together they walked into the kitchen to meet their daughter and to tell her they already knew and had known for quite some time, and together they would then celebrate the New Year.

Dense crowds filled Puerta del Sol as midnight approached. With each stroke of the clock, the Spaniards would swallow a grape, a tradition bringing good luck for the rest of the year. Nacho didn't need luck. He was reunited with the love of his life, his music. He would be performing with Madrid's symphony and had been practicing continuously until his friends from childhood urged him to take a break and welcome in the New Year in this popular square, the heart of Madrid.

Dressed in a red-and-black-checkered flannel nightgown, Evelyn peeked out the window of her trailer home near the beach. There wasn't a view of the Gulf of Mexico like she once had on the island; the view that one day frightened her and the next day inspired her to change her life. She never took swimming lessons in the literal sense, but instead, the water, which once reminded her how minute and insecure she felt in her overwhelmingly large world of abuse, began showing her something different. Maybe it was simply her perspective that had changed. As she stared out that window her last few days on the island, she saw opportunity and a larger life for herself, something she had never seen before.

God showed her something new out that window.

"Goodie. The moon is just about in its midnight position," she said out loud to the brown, stale plants sitting around in their pots. They had suffered and died in captivity and were now the framework of a spider's mansion.

"Lord, give me strength to make these changes," she said, looking around at the fist holes that provided rude peepholes into her bathroom. Cheerios added design to the coffee-stained fabric table booths.

Just outside, the man who had beaten her many times walked up the pathway and pounded on the door. "Open up. I know you're in there. I brought you some good stuff. Let's party like it's the millennium," he shouted.

She opened the door, hoping he wouldn't break it down again, but this time he knocked her down, laughing as she crashed into the table, bruising her knee.

"Don't lay another hand on me," she screamed.

"You know you deserve it."

She didn't say a thing because she knew this man was dangerous. Inside, she knew now that she did not deserve it, that no creation of God deserved this kind of treatment. As she picked herself up from the floor and stood up, she continued to pray, this time from the Lord's Prayer. "Your kingdom come, your will be done, on earth as it is in heaven," she whispered.

Then she picked up her Bible, tossed it in her bag, and said, "I'll go get us beer, and I'll be right back, babe."

She knew exactly where she was going. She had read about the woman's shelter a few weeks ago, and all she had to do was get to a pay phone and make the call. Yes, she deserved better than this. She had waited for years for the cards to tell her to leave this crazy man. They never did, so she stayed. Now, she had made the decision on her own, and with the strength of God she would enter a New Year and a new life, both at the same time. She would run and not look back, and this time she would make it on her own.

She would start small at first, setting the basic boundaries, laying a few bricks at a time. Soon she would set more limits, pouring concrete over the brick. Eventually, she would live within a fortress bigger, better, and more beautiful than anything she ever dreamt of as a little girl. Nothing would penetrate the walls of her fortress, the walls made of boundaries and limits.

"There's room for two more," Denver shouted as he waved people onto his houseboat. "Okay. I'll come back for the rest of you in a half hour."

"Happy New Year," shouted the voices in line. "Happy New Year, and thank you for helping us."

"But O the ship, the immortal ship! O ship aboard the ship!" Denver shouted out a famous quotation from Walt Whitman. "Ship of the body, ship of the soul, voyaging, voyaging, voyaging."

He left with his group of fifteen people down the Sacramento River. Television crews swarmed the area, but he refused interviews. He didn't want publicity. He simply wanted to carry out his plan. He wanted to make the most of his second chance, to spend every penny his brother had given him in the most meaningful manner. Each time he took a group of fifteen homeless people down the Sacramento River, he offered them hot cider, cheese and bread, fruit, and a pep talk.

"You're all vessels," he told them. "You're all vessels in need of repair, and believe me, you can repair yourself."

He had been doing this for months now, and cameras had been following him ever since. "I'm going to sing you all a song that I think you can relate to. It's called, 'Life is so sad, life is so sad.' Then, I'm gonna lend y'all some twigs, some twigs to start repairing yourselves again."

The homeless appeared to be interested in his message, and often times Denver had them join hands and close their eyes. "Give us today, our daily bread," he would often say, reciting the Lord's Prayer.

"And forgive us our debts as we also forgive our debtors," whispered Howard. A nurse entered his room and handed him a party favor, but he felt too weak to blow. He glanced at the clock on the white wall and counted down, as he did all night, not for the New Year, but for when his brother would be finished with the boat rides and would stop in to visit him. He knew he wouldn't see another year, and perhaps not another night. It didn't matter now. All that mattered to him was that his money had gone to a good cause and that Denver had repaired himself. He could rest in peace now.

The flowers didn't need a calendar telling them when to blossom. As Connie walked across the carefully laid stones leading to her garden, grape hyacinth spread itself like a royal velvet carpet, welcoming its queen. Purple wisteria sprayed her with its sweet perfume, and when she walked a few feet further, she stopped to hear the soft waterfall drips of a fountain where cardinals and bluebirds were bathing together. The birds took flight as she splashed her hands in the cold, clear water, then rinsed her face, refreshed.

She could smell fresh grass, the kind as safe as what she once could smell as a child, so she skipped forward and sat down Indian-style, surrounded by rows and rows of pink, yellow and red rosebuds, resting snugly as long as they liked, perhaps only minutes or hours away from blossoming, maybe tomorrow morning. There was no hurry. They were counting down for nothing. She sat there often, whenever she wanted, and sometimes it felt like hours before she continued on in the garden.

When she felt the warmth of the morning sun, she stood up and walked toward the flowering crabapple tree and sat on the white wooden chair made for one, just below the pink flowers, scented tissues for the taking. Often, she reached up, pulling some off, then wiped her tears. They were magical tears, the kind that made her rose petals unfurl.

When she felt ready, she walked toward the west end of her garden, glancing at her reflection in the pond. When she had first started coming to the garden, she didn't like what she saw. Now, beautiful green foliage, mosses, and grass pushed up from the pond like mini-skyscrapers, and baby ducks knew her voice and came waddling over to greet her. She would bend down to their level and hold her hands out to them and offer them breadcrumbs. She enjoyed nurturing them, and she enjoyed how much they loved her. Her reflection in the pond was always changing as the baby feet of the ducklings would speed it up. Sometimes, when the ducks weren't around, it was hauntingly clear and still.

Some days she could see so much work that needed to be done in the garden while other days she felt content with her progress. A garden is a lot of work, she would tell herself, but it brings much joy.

"Mommy, I want Cheerios," cried one of the baby ducklings. "I want Cheerios."

Connie opened her eyes. The sun was rising, and her children were waking. Her husband would want his coffee soon, and her babes needed diaper changes and breakfast. She would return to the garden tomorrow morning, as she did every day, same time, waking just one hour before the rest of her house and sitting with her eyes closed and her imagination wide open near the large window on the east side of her home, the side that welcomes the waking sun, the start of a new and glorious day and year. She had no real garden. It didn't matter. She created a place she could go to, a place in her mind.

At twenty minutes before midnight, Captain Porter Smith watched the moon overhead and the stars that dropped more magnificently than the ball in Times Square. He had recently made the local news for catch ing a one-hundred-and-thirty-pound tarpon near Sarasota, Florida, and in the New Year, he would catch an even bigger one. Apparently, the man he had taken fishing that night had published a novel and then had become a state senator and the father of quadruplets shortly thereafter. It must have been a very motivating battle.

As she carefully lifted the third snowball and set it atop the two larger mounds of packed snow, shortly before midnight, Vicki wore only the warmest wool mittens while playing outdoors with Michigan's wintry elements. She quickly opened the box full of her grandmother's belongings and reached inside for the straw beach hat that once served its purpose on Sanibel Island. It instantly brought character to her snow lady. She then added her grandmother's dark sunglasses and placed the purple scarf around its neck.

She reached deep into her own coat pocket and pulled out her list of New Year's resolutions. She liked the simplicity of this year's list: *build a snow lady; plant seeds; play hopscotch; cook with fresh garlic and basil; sit in the grass; make a baby laugh; and tell Mr. Right how much you love him and how badly you want to spend your life with him.*

And this she would do within the hour. She would show him this exact list, and he would read it himself. She hung her list on the branch, her snow lady's arm, then hurriedly headed over to start her car and scrape its windows.

She wrapped her scarf around her face to shield her skin from the winter wind as she hurried across the airport parking lot at ten minutes until midnight. What a place to celebrate the New Year, she thought as she ran up the elevators and to the terminal, rubbing her fingers together to warm away the numbness. She could hardly wait to see him. It didn't matter that their New Year's kiss would happen in the airport and that her teeth would be chattering from the cold. She had it all planned. She would toss her arms tightly around him and tell him how much she missed him, and then, back at the house, she would introduce him to her snow lady and show him her New Year's list. She didn't quite know what sort of arrangements she would need to make after that, nor did she care. She would graduate, and then do whatever was necessary, and he would wait for her. He always said he would wait for her to do the things she had to do.

As the plane landed at five minutes till midnight, crazy passengers passed around paper party hats and noisemakers. Ben didn't feel like celebrating. He felt so sure of his decision to take the one-year assignment in Brazil, helping to save the world's largest rain forest where every year an area the size of Belgium was being lost or badly damaged. At first, the opportunity hit him in the head like a cold water balloon. After all, he had declared his days of exotic travel a thing of the past. But then, more balloons kept coming his way. His passion for faraway places had simply been dormant. Man has a right to change his mind with time.

He knew that by taking the assignment he would not be able to see Vicki this summer, and that might alter their future together. He didn't know if it was the sort of place Vicki would like. She had mentioned that she wanted to travel and had seemed disappointed when he had once said he was done with traveling. Maybe she would go with him, and together they could build their home, their floating Amazon hut, whatever, or at least she might wait for him to return. He wanted her for a wife. He could hardly wait. He had gone over the proposal a million times in his mind and shared the idea with a woman sitting next to him on the plane.

"We'll get out of the car, and I'll mention that I haven't seen snow in years. Then, as I struggle to carry the luggage toward her place, I'll slip and crash in the snow."

"Don't lose the ring," replied the woman.

"Then, she'll run over to help me, and she'll probably be laughing. Instead of getting up, I'll get on my hands and knees."

"Will she be on the ground with you?"

"No, of course not. I hope not. She'll be standing next to this crazy snow person she keeps talking about."

"A what?"

"A snow man of some sort. She called me on my cell phone and said something about it reminding her of her grandmother. She gets a bit eccentric at times."

"I guess so. Will this snow creature intervene in any way?"

"Let's hope not."

CHAPTER THIRTY-FOUR

THE SUN ROSE AND SET some 365 times, over and over again. Fridays arrived, but Mondays crept quickly around the corner every time. Vicki reached the end of her journal, her letters to Grandma, and saw time flipping by like the pages of a book. She wanted to read life slowly, paying attention to the details. Sometimes she read the same sentence twice. She couldn't ask summer to take its time. There would be too much ice cream consumed. Winter arrived when it liked, and with it, she imagined shark's eyes, fighting conchs, and other seashells crawling around Sanibel sandbars at low tide, attacking each other for dinner, leaving the empty shells to wash onto shore. Fall had much to do in such little time. She would never be able to control the timing of the leaves turning orange or crisp, or falling to the ground, or the time it took people to rake them into piles and burn them before the snow. She could only control her own pace, and she wanted to walk through life, slowly, as a conductor who had once wanted the piece played only loudly but now interpreted it differently and decided when the volume should change.

Once in awhile her breathing troubles still haunted her, and she continued writing about the episodes, allowing her fears to be expressed through the writing. Often she prayed. Sometimes she would close her eyes and visualize herself on the dock of Tarpon Key or in the park outside the Prado Museum in Madrid. She no longer feared death. That fear and its ridiculous obsession belonged to her dark days, or, in Picasso's language, her "blue period" of madness. She painted with a rose palette now.

As her days grew busy from the demands of practicing psychology, she handled things well and simply remembered there was a time for everything. She cried at the thought of the cold, dead ground where the tulips once stood. She smiled when she thought of spring and the ducks arriving from the south. She closed her eyes and laughed at summer and the people lining up to buy ice cream. She went through the motions of the backward good-bye wave just thinking about fall and the ducks heading south again. Yes, there was a season for everything, and this God knew.

Her patients each had a unique story to tell, and she cherished listening to them. She had put much time into her thesis and had felt proud turning it in. Using Denver's analogy, she classified personality types and diagnostic states as vessels. Some ships anchored at a specific point for quite some time. Others just needed to refuel for a brief period. Her paper went more in depth than that and triggered significant debate and discussion in the psychology department. Now, in her practice, she specialized in anxiety disorders and in helping her patients through their dark days of life.

On February 14, at four o'clock in the morning, the phone rang, waking her. She had programmed her phone to only ring once, so almost instantly a voice came on the answering machine, a familiar voice from her past shouting, *"Victoria, Victoria!"*

As if riding on the wings of a butterfly, Vicki flew to the phone so quickly she could hardly catch her breath. *"Hola?"* she said as she held the receiver tightly to her face.

The man on the other end of the line said he couldn't refuse the wrinkled piece of paper that Triste had one day waved before him. He had tucked it away for quite some time; then, with the help of an interpreter, he had called the school and tracked her down. Her home phone number was unlisted so she knew he had gone to great investigative lengths to reach her.

They both had much to say, and several times they both talked at once, and then laughed. His voice came like an echo across an ocean, and she tried hard to picture his face, but the waves were too high. She had no photographs of him, only those in her mind. Still, they had faded with time. As he spoke of his life in recent years, she stared at the silk tulips standing proudly in a vase on her desk. The voice on the phone said he had spotted her standing tall on her first day of classes and that he had picked her, of all people, to ask for directions.

"You spoke funny Spanish," he said in a strange English accent, "but you stood tall and proud, like a flower."

"Rafael," she said, smiling. "You've been learning English. I'm proud of you."

"Tell me, Victoria, have you been changing with time?"

"Wiser and better, and you?"

They talked long enough to generate a phone bill that could have paid for an expensive four-course, or as Rafael would say, "five fork" dinner. Neither knew how to say good-bye, so Rafael finally took charge.

"*Te quiero Victoria de los Estados Unidos. Te quiero.*"

He hung up before she could get his phone number, and, once again, she had forgotten to get his last name.

Awake, she didn't care about time. She'd always have the next day's siesta to catch up.

Dear Grandma,

You'll never guess what time it is. It's four o'clock in the morning, and being awake at this hour reminds me of the sleepless nights I went through after Rebecca died. I don't know that I'll ever hear from Rafael again, just as I don't know that I'll ever make it back to Tarpon Key. I might not need an island as remote as that again.

Last night I had a nightmare. I was holding on for dear life to a raft I made myself out of a few logs and ropes. Of course it was dark out and the waves stood high. With my hands in the water, I paddled my way toward a little island but never made it there. Suddenly I saw Ben, as crazy as this sounds, bobbing up and down in the water. There were other men as well, men I once dated, and men I once left. I couldn't see their faces or remember their names, nor did I care about them. I only cared about Ben, and I cried my eyes out seeing him in the Sea of Forgetfulness. Perhaps I made a mistake? Perhaps he didn't belong there? I searched around in the water for Rafael and called out to him, but I couldn't find him. I don't believe he had been tossed in there just yet. Then my raft fell apart, and a big boat rescued me. Unfortunately, they were heading for the mainland and refused to take me to the island.

My life is comfortable now, like a warm breeze blanketing my skin. I once lived inside pink walls that smelled of waffle cones.

When the cone broke, I felt so cold. I wondered why anyone would ever want to leave a comfort zone. Now I find myself loosening the bedding at night so my toes can stick out. Yes, I feel confined when my toes can't breathe. Anyway, now I value the voyages we take from one comfort zone to the next.

P.S. Do you see my writing to you? Do you read these letters?

CHAPTER THIRTY-FIVE

VICKI HAD BEEN SWINGING in the white wicker chair on her porch for hours, listening to the water as it gently arrived on Sanibel's shore. Her hair, now gray and somewhat purple, lent her a look of wisdom, like a seasoned woman who had sailed through life, through choppy water, through calm water, through storms and through sunsets. She could close her eyes and let herself sit in silent contentment, a woman who had conducted countless symphonies in life and used the silences to hear the music. She read the very last letter she had ever written to her grandmother, over thirty years earlier.

Dear Grandma,

Sitting here at the Lighthouse Beach inspires me in a special way. I sit here all the time. I am thankful to be living here on Sanibel Island and to be raising my babies here. Sometimes I miss my psychology practice, but I'm glad I have never missed my babies' first steps or first words. I know I can return to work any time I choose, and I can work just a couple days a week if I like. There's so much I once wanted to do in life, and now I just want to savor life. Have I lost my ambition? No, I don't believe so.

This is the last letter I will write to you, so I'm writing to say good-bye. You see, Grandma, I've been coming here to the Lighthouse Beach to write for a long time now and, well, one day, when I began a typical letter to you, I suddenly realized you had better things to do up in Heaven, so instead, I addressed that particular letter to God. Sure, I could have started writing, 'Dear Diary,' but I didn't feel like locking my worries and dreams into a book. Diaries are too good at keeping secrets, whereas God, well, hopefully He shares some secrets with his angels, who then might want a project to work on.

Grandma, I haven't written to you since, and I'm only writing this time to explain why I stopped my letters to you. As I scribbled my dreams and goals to dear God, the results were powerful beyond belief. I felt such immense peace when I surrendered my life and all the things I wanted to do over to God and to His will. I am confident He reads what I write. I still write to God on a regular basis, often sitting at the Lighthouse Beach just as the sun wakes. Sometimes I scribble so fast and passionately that no person would ever be able to read my handwriting, but it doesn't matter. God doesn't check for grammar or penmanship.

So Grandma, this is why the letters to you have stopped. I love you and always will and I know I will see you again. This is why I must now live my life. I must enjoy my time.

P.S. Until we meet again!

She could hardly wait for her company to arrive as she closed the last letter to her grandmother, then closed her eyes. She allowed herself to look back for a moment, but only as long as it took for a soft wave to arrive on shore, carrying treasures from the Gulf of Mexico with it, yet leaving that body of water behind.

She opened her eyes and knew from the location of the sun that it would soon be time to plug in the string of miniature white Christmas-tree lights that decorated the porch and windows of her Sanibel bungalow. She wanted everything to be lit up and festive when they arrived.

She walked inside and down the hall, framed with pictures of her children, fully grown. Noah, her firstborn, was now in his late forties and living in Ann Arbor, Michigan, of all places. This, she was glad of. He lived far from her, yet close to the world she grew up in, her old Midwest comfort zone. It had provided her with a wonderful place to visit several times a year, ever since he had started and graduated from the University of Michigan.

They spent their winters on Sanibel Island, then always visited Noah in early May. Afterward, they would drive to Holland for the Tulip Time Festival, in which she proudly wore a Dutch costume and scrubbed the streets in the parade. Wearing the wooden shoes reminded her of who she was and where she had come from. It still didn't matter after all these years that her blood wasn't Dutch. She had decided years ago to participate, to become a part of this comfortable town. This she had done and continued to do every year, scrubbing those streets with pride and passion, always dumping a cold pail of water on her husband's head when he least expected it.

With disposable cameras full of tulips and windmills and yellow sand dunes, she and her husband would then leave for Europe, where they spent every summer and autumn. She especially savored her time there because her daughter, Emma, had met a man while in Europe, and together they had made a home there.

She always walked slowly down the hall framed with photographs, but she heard a bell go off in the kitchen—it had been about forty-five minutes so she knew the cake was done baking—and she bustled along because she didn't want this cake to be overdone. She inserted a toothpick into the center. It came out dry, so she quickly removed the three nine-inch round pans from the oven and let the vibrant red cake cool on the counter.

Then she walked over to the table and ran her hands over the white paper tablecloth and fidgeted with a bouquet of tropical flowers standing tall in their vase. She set two white candles in holders next to the flowers, then opened the drawer of a hutch and pulled out a box of crayons. She scattered the crayons across the center of the table and sat down.

She did this every time she had guests. She would tell them to scribble things that they could do that would make their life instantly better, small things, like resting five minutes a day on a park bench where they could sit and think. They liked the activity and often said it changed the course of their future simply by altering their daily activities. It put things into perspective.

She took a pound of cream cheese out of the refrigerator and began mixing it with three quarters of a pound of butter. She felt the tightness of her skirt around her waist and blamed it on all the olive bread she had enjoyed over the years. She never blamed it on the cake she was baking. She made this special cake once a year and never allowed herself any guilt. Sometimes a woman just needs instant gratification without guilt. As she slowly mixed in two pounds of confectioners' sugar, she glanced up at her wedding photo hanging on the wall in the hall, and her wedding dress to this day still amazed her. She knew she had bragged about that dress for years, but how could she not? Never had a gown been so perfectly designed to fit her body. Well, it wouldn't fit now after years of olive bread, but it certainly fit back then. The fabric had felt so personal, comfortable, as if painted on with a silk brush. It made her smile, knowing she had made the right decisions concerning her Mr. Right. Now, hindsight offered nothing more than pleasant memories of life gone by.

Once the icing in the bowl was smooth and well mixed, she added three cups of pecans then walked over to the crucifix hanging on a nearby wall and thanked God for the years she had lived, long past her naive fears of death. She knew that without the spirit of God in her life she would never have had the energy or courage to leave old comforts behind and enter new waters. "For thine is the kingdom and the power and the glory forever," she whispered.

Just then, she could hear the cane of her husband as he made his way into the room. He walked slowly now, slower than ever. The arthritis in his knees and elbows only allowed him short journeys from the bedroom to his favorite chair on the porch or to the kitchen for home-cooked paella. Vicki loved taking care of him because he had always taken care of her. Always. Their age difference only mattered physically and had only started to show in the last few years because he had always stayed active, passionately becoming involved in life and its activities. His mind was as sharp as when they first met, and this was what she loved most about him. Besides, she had known he was older when they met. She knew it when they fell in love, and she knew it when she chose him for her husband. Back then, she knew much about him, yet so very little.

"Dear, when will the Red Velvet Cake be ready?" he asked.

"When Noah, Emma, and the kids arrive, sweetie. You can have some then."

A mischievous glint lit up his eyes. "There's something I haven't told you in a long time," he said.

"Yes, what is it?"

He took her hand in his and kissed it. His words struck her like fingers gliding across the strings of a harp and they made the butterflies within her silently dance. "Just that - *Te quiero Victoria de los Estados Unidos, te quiero,*" he said quietly, and she realized his words were the symphony's rondo, the one delightful theme she had heard all along, over and over again.

She laughed. "I love you too, Rafael de España, and you just told me that an hour ago."

VICKI'S FINAL SCRIBBLES

ON THE WHITE PAPER TABLECLOTH

Live within the present.

Find a domain and bring passion to your life.

*Anchor long enough to repair and refuel and
make your way through dark waters.*

Celebrate life.

Build your own fortress with walls made of boundaries.

Surrender your dreams to God.

Start fresh daily, adding beautiful colors to your plain white canvas.

See something new out your same old window.

Add laughter to your life.

Discover an island where you can stop and think.
Think magnificent thoughts you have never had time to think and
notice magnificent details you have never noticed before.

Hop, skip, and jump toward goals,
enjoying the process as much as the destination.

Get to know yourself.

Abandon comfort zones and discover adventure.

Never rush any part of life. Savor it like a delicious meal.

Indulge in fiestas but never lose your dignity.

Get on with your life. Live life!

Dance through life.

Nourish the heart with red wine, olive oil,
romance, and careful listening.

When death comes around, stare it in the eyes.

Do as you like in the silent moments.

Remember the tulips.
Just as their season of stardom comes
and goes, you too will one day.

RED VELVET CAKE

The Bubble Room
15001 Captiva Road
Captiva Island, Florida

CAKE
3¾ cups self-rising flour
2¼ cups sugar
3 eggs
1½ teaspoons vanilla
1½ teaspoons vinegar
1½ teaspoons baking soda
1½ teaspoons cocoa
2¼ cups vegetable oil
1½ cups buttermilk
3 oz. red food coloring

ICING
1 pound cream cheese
¾ pound butter
2 pounds confectioners' sugar
3 cups pecans

DIRECTIONS
Preheat oven to 350 degrees.

Mix all ingredients together and pour into
three greased and floured 9" cake pans.
Bake for 45 minutes to one hour or until a toothpick
inserted into the center of the cake comes out dry.

For icing, mix cream cheese and butter until smooth.
Add sugar and mix. When smooth and well mixed, add pecans.

Yields one three-layer 9" cake

SANIBEL
SCRIBBLES

READER'S GUIDE

---

1. ISLANDS. Simon the dockmaster says everyone needs to discover an island. The island he refers to is symbolic. What does it represent? Do you believe everyone needs to discover an island of their own? What sorts of "islands" do you go to in your life?

2. VESSELS. When talking to Vicki, Denver says the staff house is a harbor full of vessels and then describes the other characters as vessels. Did you find these classifications illuminating or limiting? If you were to classify yourself, what sort of vessel would you be?

3. OUTLOOK. Vicki savors her view out a window at the staff house. What do you think the view out the window or the water represented to her?

4. TIME ALONE. Vicki tells Ben, "A tulip needs morning sun to open. And as much as that tulip needs morning sun, a woman needs time alone. She discovers immense power from within, power she never knew she had, once she spends a moment with herself." Do you agree? What sorts of things do women do when they're alone and without their friends or family? Do they discover this power?

Do you think women appreciate their own company and times in which they are alone? Why do you think women sometimes might feel uncomfortable being alone?

5. JOURNEYS. At one point Simon encourages Vicki not to "underestimate the journeys you've been on. They don't have to be geographical or physical journeys." What sorts of journeys do Vicki and some other characters go on? What sorts of journeys have you been on? Do you agree with Ruth who said, "Often these journeys make up the women that you are and the ones you are becoming"?

6. SIESTAS. In a letter to her grandmother, Vicki describes Spain's siestas. Do you think siestas would work in America? Would you want them?

7. SYMPHONIES AND SILENCE. The motifs of symphonies and silence appear in different parts of the novel. What do you think symphonies symbolize in different parts of the story? What is significant about the silences?

8. MAKING TIME. Vicki promised that when she returned to the United States she would carry a blanket in her car at all times, and stop and sit in parks whenever time allowed. Oops! Time would never allow such a thing, so she would have to make time instead. And she goes on thinking of all the things she would make time to do. What sorts of things do you wish you had more time for? What is the one thing you think you could make time for in your everyday life that you aren't currently doing? What would you scribble on a paper table cloth?

CHRISTINE LEMMON is author of three inspiring novels —
Sanibel Scribbles, Portion of the Sea, Sand in My Eyes, and the gift book
Whisper from the Ocean. She has worked as an on-air host for a
National Public Radio affiliate, business magazine editor,
and publicist for a non-fiction publishing house.

She lives with her husband and three children on
Sanibel Island, the setting of her three novels.
VISIT CHRISTINELEMMON.COM

ALSO BY CHRISTINE LEMMON

CHRISTINELEMMON.COM

SAND IN MY EYES

An Older Woman Growing
Flowers, A Younger Woman
Caught up in the Weeds, and
the Seasons of Life.

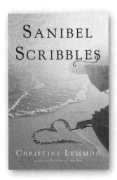

SANIBEL SCRIBBLES

A Story About a Woman's
Journey to an Island, and then
Spain, Facing Mortality and
Embracing Life.

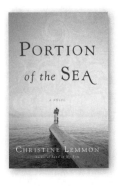

PORTION OF THE SEA

A Tale About the Treasures a
Woman has—Heart, Soul and
Mind—and the Struggle to
Keep Them Afloat.

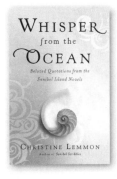

WHISPER FROM THE
OCEAN ~ GIFT BOOK

Treasured Quotations from
Christine Lemmon's first
three novels. Hardcover.